THE WIDOW'S PLIGHT

THE WIDOW'S PLIGHT

The Quilting Circle Series
Book One

By Mary Davis

MBI

The Widow's Plight
Published by Mountain Brook Ink
White Salmon, WA U.S.A.

The website addresses shown in this book are not intended in any way to be or imply an endorsement on the part of Mountain Brook Ink, nor do we vouch for their content.

This story is a work of fiction. All characters and events are the product of the author's imagination other than those stated in the author notes as based on historical characters. Any other resemblance to any person, living or dead, is coincidental.

The author is represented by and this book is published in association with the literary agency of WordServe Literary Group, Ltd., www.wordserveliterary.com

Scripture quotations are taken from the King James Version of the Bible. Public domain.

© 2018 Mary Davis
ISBN 9781-943959-38-9

The Team: Miralee Ferrell, Judy Vandiver, Nikki Wright, Cindy Jackson
Cover Design: Indie Cover Design, Lynnette Bonner Designer

Mountain Brook Ink is an inspirational publisher offering fiction you can believe in.

Printed in the United States of America

To my hubby, Chip. Thirty-three-plus
years and counting!

Acknowledgments

A special thanks to Miralee Ferrell for believing in my story, to Nikki Wright for marketing help, to Judy Vandiver for editing my manuscript, to Lynnette Bonner for a beautiful cover, and to Sarah Joy Freese and WordServe Literary Agency. I'm so thankful to work with all of you!

One

LILY LEXINGTON BREMMER WOULD NEVER LET anyone hurt her son again. She stared at the fading green and yellow bruises on her five-year-old son's neck and pictured the others on his small body. As he lay with his head in her lap, the train rocked back and forth, his arm wrapped around the little toy train engine she'd bought him at one of the stops. It was carved of wood and painted. He didn't play with it, merely held it in the crook of his arm.

She combed her fingers through his nearly black soft curls. Her poor son hadn't had toys to play with. But now things were different. The toy train would be the first of many.

The train they rode rattled along the track. The Pullman passenger car held nearly thirty people in the twenty seats. Most of the passengers hadn't taken notice of her or her son. People had come and gone, come and gone over the week-long trip. She was ready to leave this train for good, stretch her legs, breathe fresh air, and wash off the soot and dirt of the journey.

She had moved near the front of the car when a seat had opened up. She didn't know why, but she felt safer there. Closer to the door. Closer to an escape.

The well-groomed man across the aisle in a charcoal-gray business suit tossed glances her direction every few minutes. His attention heightened the nervousness of her already jittery insides. Was he interested in her? Or was he trying to puzzle out how a fair-skinned, blond-haired, blue-eyed woman could have a son with olive skin, dark hair, and rich brown eyes? No matter their contrasting appearances, he *was* her son.

The train's steam whistle blew long and loud. Then

the conductor strolled through the car. "Next stop Kamola."

Leaning down to where her narrow-brimmed straw hat rested against the wall under the window, she retrieved it and pulled out the two adorned hatpins. She secured the hat onto her head as the train rolled into the station and shuddered to a stop.

Lily had run almost as far from her past as she could physically get. Clear across the country.

Toby would be safe here. She rested her hand on a part of his little arm she knew didn't have any bruises and gently shook her son awake. "We're here. Time to wake up."

He blinked his brown eyes at her.

Why did he have to look so much like his father?

But now that they were starting over, she didn't have to call him by his father's name even if he was a junior. She would use the nickname Toby. No one to order her not to.

Toby wrestled around to a sitting position then leaned against her arm. His dejected expression pulled on her heartstrings. Maybe he was just tired. The past week had been hard for them both.

She shifted her son away from leaning against her, stood, and tugged on the hem of the gray striped jacket of her traveling suit. Reaching up to the polished wooden shelf overhead, she pulled down the larger of their two carpetbags, the one made of pink floral carpet, and set it on the green, plush bench next to her little boy. Then the smaller tan and black one. They didn't have a lot, but they had each other.

Standing in the aisle with her reticule hanging from one wrist, she grabbed a carpetbag in each hand. "Hold on to Mommy's sleeve."

"I too tired." Toby slumped over on the bench.

"Toby, please. I need you to walk. I have to carry our bags."

He lay lethargic and only blinked at her.

She tucked the smaller carpetbag under her arm so it partially rested on the one in her hand. She held out her free arm. "Okay. Stand up, and I'll carry you."

Toby slipped his thumb into his mouth but didn't move.

She wished he wouldn't do that but hated to tell him not to after all he'd been through in his short life, so she clenched her teeth in frustration. She couldn't do everything. She needed him to at least stand. "All right. If you won't move, I'll have to leave you on the train. Good-bye."

As she turned, Toby grabbed her sleeve. "Don't go."

She turned around, and Toby stood on the bench with his arms outstretched, his engine in one hand. She wrapped her free arm around him and settled him on her hip. He hugged her around her neck and put his head on her shoulder. His elbow and train pressed painfully into healing bruises on her back. She ignored the discomfort and kissed the top of his head.

Getting off the train without falling was her main concern. Though small and thin, carrying Toby as well as the carpetbags was all a bit cumbersome. She shuffled sideways in the aisle to the exit, looked at the steps, and hesitated, hoping she didn't miss any of them. She situated herself so she would descend with Toby first. But what if she tripped? She would land on her baby. With her hands full, she wouldn't have the benefit of holding onto the brass handrail.

She backed up and shifted around so the carpetbags descended first. They wouldn't be a soft landing, but she wouldn't injure her son. Before attempting the first step, she contemplated tossing the bags to the platform, but her mother's hand mirror might get broken.

The other disembarking passengers lined up behind her. One of them called out. "Can you hurry, ma'am?"

She couldn't do this safely and stepped out of the way. "Go ahead."

The first man, the one in the business suit, scowled at her as he passed and stepped off the train. He must be the one who'd asked her to hurry. Next came a couple of men who appeared to be cowboys, one with a saddle slung over his shoulder. Then an older man and woman. And several other people alighted from the coach. The last passenger, another man, stopped in front of her.

Even at her own height of five feet seven inches, this man towered over her. Dressed in a black canvas duster, and a black crease-topped hat, he also looked like a cowboy but less trail haggard. Was he going to scowl at her too?

He extended his hand.

At this simple courtesy, she flinched.

After pulling out the carpetbag wedged under her arm, he tucked it under his own above his smaller, brown carpetbag. "Let me get these."

"That's all right. I can manage."

His smile added to the kindness in his meadow green eyes. "I saw how you were managing. I wouldn't want you to fall and hurt yourself or your boy." He took her other bag and stepped off the train. After setting all three bags on the ground, he turned and held out his hand.

She stared at it. Dare she take it? Hands could be kind or cruel.

His hand inched higher. "I don't have a rattlesnake, ma'am."

Giving a wan smile, she shifted Toby on her hip and placed her hand in the cowboy's.

His fingers wrapped around hers. His hold was gentle yet firm enough to keep her steady.

After stepping down, she retrieved her hand. "Thank you."

"You're welcome." He tipped his hat then glanced around. "Is your husband onboard?"

"No, I'm a widow." Why had she told him that? Would it have been better to let him believe her husband would be along soon? He probably already figured out that she was alone. He had been in the passenger car for the past two days.

"You have family or friends meeting you here?"

No sense denying it. She shook her head. She was alone. Just her and Toby. Making a new start.

He took off his hat, showing a shock of light brown hair matted down, and held his hat to his chest. "I'm Edric Hammond, at your service." He waited.

If she planned to stay in this town, there was no point in not introducing herself. He and everyone else would learn her name soon enough. "I'm Lily B—Lily

Lexington." Now that she was a widow, she would use her maiden name again. "This is my son, Toby."

"Pleased to meet you both." He returned his hat to his head and picked up all three bags.

She waggled her free hand. "I can get those."

His gaze shifted from her to Toby. "You have your hands full. Where are you staying?"

"I don't want to inconvenience you."

"No inconvenience. Where to?"

Her only thought a week ago had been to flee. Leave as fast as she could before anyone stopped her. Where she would end up or what to do once there hadn't entered her thinking. "I-I don't know. I'm new in town. Is there a hotel close by?"

"The White Hotel is right across the street. Are you staying in town long?"

Why so many questions? "We plan to settle here."

"Then you'll want to stay at Aunt Henny's until you find a place. It will be cheaper by the week and more comfortable. And Aunt Henny will be glad for the female company."

So that was why he wanted to know. "I don't want to inconvenience your aunt."

"She's not my aunt. Well, she's more like everyone's aunt. Everyone calls her Aunt Henny. I'm not even sure if anyone in town is related to her. She runs a boarding house."

She liked that idea. "Is it far?"

"Right up the street." He eyed Toby. "Is he getting heavy? Do you want me to carry him?"

Toby tightened his grip around her neck.

She instinctively squeezed him in return. Let a stranger have him? "No. I'm fine."

"If you'd like to wait here, I can get a buggy."

"No, I'm fine." She didn't want to put him out or owe him anything, and walking would be nice after being cooped up on the train. "I can walk."

He nodded. "Right this way."

He sauntered around the side of the station, and his long strides carried him across the dusty street in no time.

Unable to match his pace, she took quick steps, kicking at the hem of her traveling suit skirt. She managed to mostly keep up. Not knowing his temperament, she would not risk angering him.

He stepped up onto the boardwalk, stopped, and turned to her with a frown.

Her own stride faltered. What had she done to upset him?

He dipped his head. "I'm sorry for leaving you behind. I forget most people can't keep up with my long legs. And I'm often in a hurry to get places."

So he wasn't mad at her. She stepped up onto the boardwalk. "If you have someplace to be, I can take our bags. Point the way. We'll manage."

"I'll not be rude twice in one meeting." His mouth pulled up into a smile then. "Besides, if Aunt Henny found out I abandoned a lady new to town, she would give me a tongue lashing like there was no tomorrow."

"I don't want to keep you from your business."

"This won't take long. I wouldn't want to raise Aunt Henny's ire. She is not a person I want upset at me." He winked.

Who was this Aunt Henny? Should Lily be afraid of her?

"Shall we?" He took one tentative stride.

She nodded and fell into step beside him.

"Where do you hail from?" he asked.

"Philadelphia."

He let out a long whistle. "You've come a long way and with no family or friends to meet you. What brings you to our fair town?"

I'm running away. But she couldn't tell him that. "After my husband passed, I wanted to move as far away as I could."

"Well, I do believe you succeeded."

Toby grew heavy in her arms. She shifted him. A week of train travel had taken its toll and made her worn out and weary. What little sleep she had managed to get had been poor. Hoping the boarding house wasn't far, she gazed up at the White Hotel as they passed under its awning. Maybe they should have stayed there. At least for one night.

The parts of town she could see told her this wasn't a large place, but neither was it a small prairie settlement. Several blocks wide and several blocks deep. Some three and four stories high brick buildings in amongst the wooden ones.

They stepped off the boardwalk, crossed an alley street, and back up onto the next boardwalk. They did this three more times before the businesses gave way to homes. A large white house stood a short distance ahead. She would like staying there.

But Mr. Hammond walked right on by. Then another and another.

How far was this place? Her idea of not far and Mr. Hammond's differed vastly. But then if she wasn't so exhausted, it might not seem far. Her arms screamed in pain from holding Toby. She wanted to set him down, but knew he was too tired to walk. And too afraid. She was almost too spent to walk herself. "Is it much farther?"

He pointed with her pink floral carpetbag. "That green house, right there."

A mint green, two-story house stood in a chaos of brightly colored flowers inside a white picket fence. A front porch that stretched across the front, welcoming. And a sign out front that read, *Aunt Henny's Boarding House, Home to the Weary Traveler.*

She was definitely a weary traveler.

A sigh escaped her.

Home.

It felt like home. Or at least a home. Warm and inviting. It had been a long time since she'd felt at home anywhere.

Mr. Hammond unlatched the gate and held it open for her.

She nodded her thanks as she stepped through the opening and walked up the red brick path to the door. The porch held four rocking chairs, two at each end. Each pair flanked a small table.

Mr. Hammond set the three bags down and knocked on the door.

It pulled open to reveal a middle-aged woman with pinched lips, squinty eyes, and her graying dark hair pulled up in a severe knot on top of her head. She eyed Mr. Hammond, blocking the doorway, not inviting them in. Nor did she appear as though she ever would.

This woman did not seem friendly at all. No wonder Mr. Hammond was afraid of her. The White Hotel was looking better all the time.

Mr. Hammond pulled his mouth into a congenial smile. "Mrs. Martin. How are you faring on this fine day?"

"Don't try to charm me, Edric Hammond. You think with an agreeable smile and dashing good looks you can get whatever you want. I know your kind. You can't fool me."

He removed his hat and held it to his chest. "I'm trying no such thing. I've brought a boarder for Aunt Henny."

Lily breathed a sigh of relief that this disagreeable woman was not Aunt Henny. She didn't think she could board with someone so unpleasant on a first meeting.

Mrs. Martin squinted at Lily. "Henny isn't taking on any boarders at this time. Show her to the hotel."

"All her rooms are taken?"

If she wouldn't have to walk and carry Toby, and if she weren't so tired, she would gladly return to the hotel. As it was, her arms ached to set Toby down, but he held her tightly around the neck, nearly choking her.

Mrs. Martin folded her arms across her ample bosom. "She has no boarders. I sent them away."

Mr. Hammond's smile disappeared and his eyebrows rose. "Mr. Lumbard and Mr. Tunstall? Why on earth would you do such a thing? Aunt Henny depends on boarders."

"Henny is in no condition to have boarders."

Mr. Hammond's eyebrows now pulled together in concern. "Condition? What's wrong with her?"

From somewhere inside, a woman's voice called out. "Who's there, Agnes?"

When Mrs. Martin turned to answer, Mr. Hammond took the opportunity to scoot past her and disappeared inside.

"Mr. Hammond!" Mrs. Martin followed him.

What should Lily do now? She could hear voices but not what they were saying. Stay? Or flee? The voices raised in argument. She should go. Could she pick up their carpetbags without releasing Toby? Maybe one of them but not both.

"Toby, sweetie, Mommy needs you to stand for one little moment." She leaned over and pulled Toby's legs off from around her waist.

His grip tightened around her neck.

"Please, Toby. Mommy needs to pick up our bags. Then I'll carry you."

As soon as she got his feet to touch the ground, he drew them up again and hung from her neck. His weight knocked her off balance, and she reached out to catch herself but found two strong hands around her. One on her wrist and the other around her waist.

She sucked in a breath.

Tobias!

Turning, she yanked away and saw Mr. Hammond's startled expression. Toby gripped her tighter, clamping his legs around her waist, and held her with the force of a bear. She tottered on the edge of the top step. If she dropped Toby, he would land fine and she might be able to catch herself. But Toby would never let go of her. She would fall and would have to hope she didn't break any bones when she landed at the bottom of the four steps.

Mr. Hammond's eyes enlarged with surprise, his arms outstretched. "Whoa, there." He grabbed both her upper arms on still tender bruises. For a moment, she thought he might tumble off the porch with them, but he yanked her toward him. She stopped safely against his chest with Toby in between them. Toby whimpered.

Mr. Hammond's green eyes stared at her. She stared too. He'd saved her from a nasty tumble. Both he and she breathed heavily from the episode.

He cleared his throat. "I'm sorry for startling you."

Startling her? More like terrifying her to her innermost depths. Not really him but the image of Tobias that Mr. Hammond's touch had evoked. She could feel a burst of tears welling up inside her. She could not cry here and now... in front of a stranger.

She clamped her teeth together, took a deep breath, and swallowed her emotions. "Yes, I was startled. I'm sorry for reacting so. I'm quite exhausted from traveling. I'm sure that's why."

Toby wiggled in her arms. Likely to get Mr. Hammond to let go of them.

Mr. Hammond took Toby's hint and stepped back but kept his hands on her upper arms. "Are you steady now?"

She nodded. "Yes, thank you."

He slowly released her arms, and when he seemed satisfied she wouldn't fall over again, he let his arms drop to his sides. "I thought you two were going to tumble headlong off the porch for sure."

"If not for your assistance, we would have." Now she owed him something for saving her and Toby. She hadn't wanted to be beholden to anyone.

"I'm glad I was able to avert a tragedy." His gaze searched her face. After an uncomfortable moment, he cleared his throat again. "Do you cook?"

Taken aback by his sudden subject change, she answered. "Yes." Then regretted it. Why would he be asking her such a question when they'd just met?

"Cleaning and housekeeping?"

Why was he asking her these questions? He wasn't interviewing her for a wife, was he? She wasn't *that* beholden to him.

Two

"MR. HAMMOND, I DON'T THINK—"

A voice from inside called, "Edric? What are you doing? Bring her inside."

Mr. Hammond held open the screen door. "Aunt Henny is anxious to meet you."

Lily wasn't sure she wanted to enter, but she adjusted Toby and stepped over the threshold.

Mr. Hammond picked up her two carpetbags and set them inside the front door. Then he walked a little deeper in the house and motioned to the left. "Mrs. Lexington, may I present Aunt Henny. This is Mrs. Lexington and her son, Toby."

Lily turned to see a middle-aged woman with her brown hair pulled over her shoulder in a braid, reclining on a settee. A stack of pillows propped up her casted right leg. On her lap sat a red and yellow quilt square.

She waved Lily over. "Come in, dear child. Sit. You must be exhausted."

Lily let her shoulders relax slightly at the woman's friendliness. "Thank you. But I'll stand." If she sat down, she would likely not get up again. And not knowing if she was going to be allowed to stay here, she didn't want to risk it.

"Poor thing. You must be simply too exhausted to even think straight." The woman called Aunt Henny shifted her gaze to Mr. Hammond. "Edric, take her bags up to the first room on the right." She looked at Lily again. "It has a nice view of the meadow and the mountains in the distance."

Mrs. Martin planted her hands on her hips. "Henny, you are in no condition to take on any boarders at present. Especially a boarder with a child."

"Agnes, I appreciate your concern for me, but I'll be

fine. I'm not an invalid."

Mrs. Martin let out a huff of air. "I'm only looking out for your well-being. I haven't the time to take care of you and your boarders."

"I appreciate all you've done for me, but I think the Lord has it covered now."

Mrs. Martin's gaze darted from Aunt Henny to Lily and back. "I'll stop by in the morning to check on you."

"I'd like that. See you tomorrow."

Mrs. Martin left.

Aunt Henny sighed. "She means well." The older woman gazed at Lily. "Please sit."

Lily hadn't realized that she had not only been staring like a person touched in the head, but she was leaning on the entry frame to the room. She straightened and was about to decline when Mr. Hammond appeared at her elbow and guided her to a chair. She sat without thinking.

Her body relaxed into the soft padding. She would never get up now. She shifted Toby sideways on her lap.

"Edric, would you fetch us all some water?"

Mr. Hammond left and returned shortly with three glasses resting in one upturned hand with a plate of cookies balanced on top. And a fourth glass in his other hand.

My, he has big hands. A shiver ran up Lily's spine.

He gave a glass of water to Aunt Henny first.

Aunt Henny took the water then flicked a hand in Lily's direction.

Mr. Hammond set the cookies and one water on the tea table and brought Lily a glass.

She thanked him and took a long drink of the cool liquid. She hadn't realized how thirsty she was.

Then he knelt and held out a half-full glass to Toby. "Are you thirsty?"

Toby nodded then hid his face in Lily's chest.

"Thank you. I'll give him some of mine."

"He's awfully shy."

He had his father to thank for that. "He's tired from the trip."

Lily felt a bit refreshed already. Maybe she hadn't

been so much exhausted as she was thirsty. She held the glass out to Toby. Instead of taking it, he put his mouth on the rim and pushed the edge down. He had reverted to being helpless. The trip and all the new people must be overwhelming him. She tipped the glass while Toby slurped a drink.

Mr. Hammond knelt in front of Toby again, holding out a molasses cookie. "Would you like one?"

Toby nodded but didn't reach for the treat. He looked up at Lily.

She nodded. "You may have it."

Toby glanced at the treat and then at her again.

She knew what he wanted. He wanted her to get it for him. He was afraid to reach out toward the man... a stranger. She didn't like her son acting helpless. If he was going to grow into a self-sufficient man, he needed to do for himself. He wasn't an infant. "If you want the cookie, you will have to take it yourself."

Toby pushed out his bottom lip then looked at the cookie.

Mr. Hammond waited patiently while Toby stared at the treat. Finally, Toby lifted the hand without the train and inched it toward the molasses cookie, testing whether or not he would get slapped or the treat would be pulled out of his reach. He retracted his hand three times before he touched the cookie with one finger. When no reprimand or blow came, he took it between two fingers.

Mr. Hammond's smile broadened as he let go.

"Say thank you." She hoped her son wasn't too frightened.

He whispered something that could have been thank you, but it was hard to tell. Then he turned his face into her.

"You're welcome. That's an awfully nice engine you have there."

Toby curled his arm tighter around the train and held it closer.

Mr. Hammond reached for the plate and held it out to her. "Cookie?"

"Thank you." She took one and bit it, enjoying the

sweetness.

Replacing the plate on the table, he took one and sat in a wooden rocking chair by the unlit fireplace.

Toby just held his cookie, still not sure if he would really be allowed to eat it. How often had his father given him a treat or toy, only to have it slapped out of his hand and crushed under his father's boot. Toby needed to learn that not every man behaved as badly as his father had.

"So," Aunt Henny said, "Edric tells me you'll be staying a while with me."

The poor woman was injured. Mrs. Martin was right that Aunt Henny couldn't take on boarders. "I don't want to impose. You are obviously in no condition to have us here. We can go to the hotel."

"Nonsense. Edric tells me you cook and clean."

He dipped his head in a sheepish manner. "That's why I was asking you about housekeeping."

So he wasn't scouting out a wife. He was probably married anyway, being strong and handsome as he was. He carried himself like a man who took command wherever he went. And that frightened her a little, but strangely there was comfort there too. He had been kind to her. But then so had Tobias... in the beginning.

"If you will do a little cooking and cleaning for me, you and your boy can stay here at no charge. You would need to gather the eggs and tend the garden. You'd be earning your keep. It would help me as well as Agnes. She's been running herself ragged these last three days, taking care of her family and looking in on me. What do you say?"

"I would be more than happy to do what I can to help." Then Lily remembered what Mr. Hammond said about this woman needing the income from boarders. "Would you like Mr. Hammond to tell your boarders to return?"

"You don't need to do that," Aunt Henny said. "You'll have plenty to keep you busy taking care of me and your boy."

"It won't be that much more work to cook for a few more rather than three. I'm sure you depend on the income you receive. Since we won't be generating any by staying here, we can at least help you retain what you formerly had."

Mr. Hammond spoke up then. "I had a feeling bringing you here was what God intended."

God? How long had it been since she had thought about God? Hadn't He abandoned her a long time ago? And after what she had done, He wasn't likely to be looking out for her ever again.

Aunt Henny clapped her hands. "Then it's settled. But if you find having the extra boarders here is too much work, let me know. I can survive without boarders for a couple of months."

"I will." Such a blessing to have a roof over her head and work to do that allowed her to keep Toby with her. What little money she had wouldn't last long if she had to pay for her lodging. "Do you mind if I ask what happened to you?"

"Stepped in a gopher hole. Doc says I'm going to be laid up for some time."

Toby, still holding onto his cookie, rose up, put his mouth to her ear, and spoke so soft she could barely hear him. "I gotta go potty."

Mercy. She better be quick. Toby often waited until it was almost too late. As she stood with Toby in her arms, she tried taking his cookie and spoke. "Where can I find the necessary?"

"No. My cookie."

"Edric, would you show her the way?" Aunt Henny motioned toward the back of the house.

"You can't take it with you. It will be here when you return." Lily pulled the cookie and it broke.

Toby fisted his hand with the remainder of the crumbled cookie.

She set the broken pieces on the edge of the plate.

Mr. Hammond walked through the house and across the kitchen and held open the screen door for her. Then he pointed. "Right out there."

She nodded her thank you and rushed to the small building. She set Toby on the floor, but as she fumbled with the buttons on his trousers, a dark, wet spot grew on the front of them. Too late. She sighed and leaned against the wall in the confined space. At least he had held it long enough to not wet her as well.

"I didn't make it. I sorry, Mommy."

"I know, sweetie." She knelt. "Let's get these wet things off you." She untied and removed his brogans, pulled off his wet socks, then his trousers, and underclothes. "Wait here while I get you dry clothes."

Toby threw his arms around her neck. "Don't leave me."

She hugged him close. "I won't." She hated her baby being so afraid. In time, their new life would change that. "Let's take off your jacket and tie it around your waist."

Once his coat was in place, she rolled up his wet socks and underclothes in his trousers and handed Toby his brogans. "You need to carry these."

Toby wrapped one thin arm around them and held them to his chest, keeping tight hold of his train.

She scooped him up in one arm and grabbed his wet things with her other hand.

As she approached the back porch, the screen door swung open, and Mr. Hammond stood next to it. He'd been waiting for her? Since he was not Tobias, it was likely a simple kindness and not a trap.

She dropped Toby's wet things on the porch step and entered. "Thank you."

As she passed by Mr. Hammond, Toby hid his face in her shoulder and tightened his grip around her neck.

She whispered to him, "It's all right." She entered the parlor. "I need to get him fresh clothes. Which room did you say would be ours?"

Aunt Henny smiled in an understanding way. "The first door on the right. Edric, did you take her bags up?"

"Not yet." He stepped past her and picked up the carpetbags. "Right this way."

"I can get those."

"You have your hands full." He pointed up the stairs with the smaller bag. "After you."

She climbed the stairs and her earlier fatigue hit her in the legs. She wished Toby would walk but knew better than to try, especially with Mr. Hammond so close.

As she was about to reach for the doorknob, Mr. Hammond extended his hand. "Let me get that."

More out of fear from her late husband's rage than of following proper etiquette, she sidestepped, allowing him to open the door.

He did and stepped aside for her to enter first.

Her insides turned, but then she remembered he wasn't Tobias and Aunt Henny was right downstairs.

The room glowed with the afternoon sun radiating in. A cheerful place with a pink patchwork quilt on the double bed. Tears pricked her eyes at the welcoming sight. She and Toby would be safe. She wanted to crawl under the quilt and sleep.

Mr. Hammond crossed to the bed and set the carpetbags down. Then he left without a word and shut the door.

Toby finally lifted his head from her shoulder. "He didn't hit me or nuthin'."

"Of course not." Unlike a week ago.

"But I wet myself."

She set him on the floor and knelt in front of him. "I took you far, far away so no one would ever hurt you again. You're safe here. We both are."

He blinked at her. No emotions registered on his sweet little face.

Did he believe her? She wished he would smile. It had been so very long since he had. Maybe in time, he would feel safe and smile for her.

A soft knock sounded on the door.

She started. Who could that be?

She stood and opened the door slowly.

Mr. Hammond held a basin with a pitcher of water in it. "Aunt Henny asked me to bring these up. The water is warm." His boots thumped on the floor as he stepped inside then placed the basin and pitcher in the hole in the washstand. He took two towels from over his shoulder and hung them on the side of the stand.

"Thank you."

With a quick nod, he left.

For such a large man, he didn't seem threatening. He seemed meek and mild. Could he even be pushed to anger? Of course he could. He was a man after all.

She washed up Toby and put dry clothes on him but left his brogans off. "Shall we go downstairs?"

Toby shook his head.

She didn't want to fight with him. "All right. You stay up here. I'll be downstairs."

"Don't leave me." Toby tucked his train under his arm and grabbed her hand.

"I need to go back down." Etiquette dictated she must. "You can come with me."

Toby shook his head so his whole body twisted back and forth and swung her arm with him.

She knew he wouldn't want to stay up here alone. She needed to entice him. "Your cookie is downstairs."

Toby released her hand, grabbed his train, and held his arms up to her. His one hand was still fisted around the bit of cookie he had.

Her muscles almost cried out at the thought of carrying him. "You can hold my hand on the way down and sit on my lap when we get there."

"Nooooo." He wrapped his slender arms around her legs.

She pulled him free and knelt in front of him again. "I'm too tired to carry you, so if you want your cookie, you will have to walk." She stood and held out her hand to him.

He shook his head.

"Very well. I'll be up later." She turned away from him and opened the door.

Toby latched onto her hand and leaned into her side. The train once more under his arm.

Once downstairs, she sat. "Go get your cookie. It's on the edge of the plate."

He looked from his cookie pieces then over to Mr. Hammond across the room. He must have determined that the large stranger was far too close to risk it and scrambled up onto her lap. Then he opened his hand with the mashed part of the cookie in it and shoved the crumbs into his mouth. Maybe he was afraid that, too, would be taken from him.

Toby needed to learn that not everyone was out to

hurt him. He had reached for a cookie once without consequence. As much as she wanted to simply hand him the treat herself, she knew this was an opportunity for him to experience something new. Something strange. Something good, for them both.

Mr. Hammond stood, took a fresh cookie from the plate, and held it out to her boy. If Toby wasn't going to get one for himself, he would at least have to take it from Mr. Hammond.

Toby reached out his hand but stopped just short of touching the cookie and looked up at this man offering him kindness.

Mr. Hammond nodded and smiled. A kind smile.

Toby grabbed the treat and clutched it to his chest.

"What do you say?"

The two words were fast and soft.

"You're welcome." Mr. Hammond stood to his full height that had to be well over six feet. "I should be getting home."

"Naturally," Aunt Henny said. "I'm sure you are anxious to see Estella and Nancy. Give them a hug for me."

Three

OF COURSE. HE WAS MARRIED WITH a wife waiting for him and a daughter. No wonder he'd been so patient with Toby.

Mr. Hammond scooped up his crease-top hat from where he'd put it on the arm of the settee. "I'll bring some milk by in the morning for the boy."

"You don't have to do that." She didn't want him troubling himself with her anymore.

Aunt Henny spoke as Lily finished. "That would be lovely. Maybe I'll churn a little into butter."

"I'll see you ladies in the morning." He donned his hat and left.

Aunt Henny waved her hand toward the plate. "For all his manners, he never offered me a cookie." She winked at Lily.

Did she think he had been showing Lily undue attention? He had a family, and it hadn't been Lily he had been kind to but Toby. Which made sense since he was a husband and father. And likely a lot better father than her husband had been.

Lily stood, holding onto Toby, and handed the plate to Aunt Henny.

"Thank you."

She sat again, and Toby turned in her lap to face out for the first time. He raised the cookie in his hand to his mouth and bit off a piece. Needless to say, he felt more at ease with Mr. Hammond gone. Her poor boy. This town was the place for him to learn to feel safe.

For both of them.

"Mrs...? I don't know your last name."

"I'm just Aunt Henny to everyone."

"But we're barely acquaintances. It wouldn't be proper."

"You're not back East, dear. We don't stand on formalities here. And I certainly won't tell you my last name if you are thinking for one minute of using it. It's Aunt Henny or plain Henny. Whichever you prefer. Most folks in town probably don't even know my last name."

She had never called a woman older than her by her first name. Her mother had taught her that it was impolite. But to this woman, she would be rude not to use her first name. Especially after she had insisted. "Very well... Aunt Henny." Though strange, she liked the sound of it. It made her feel like she had family again.

Aunt Henny smiled. "I think we are going to get on quite well."

Meow. Meow.

Aunt Henny turned toward the kitchen. "That's my cat, Miss Tibbins. Toby, would you go to the back door and let her in?"

Toby looked at Lily. She nodded her permission but then was surprised when he scooted off her lap and ran toward the cat's cries.

"He's a shy one, isn't he?"

Thanks to his father. "He's been through a lot. It will take him time to adjust to a new place."

"If there is anyplace worth adjusting to, it's Kamola."

Toby's voice came from the kitchen. "Come on, kitty. Come inside. Kitty?" He appeared in the doorway. "She won't come in."

"She doesn't know you yet," Aunt Henny said. "Hold the door open and stand very still."

Toby scampered away, and the screen door creaked then silence. Soon he said, "She comed in!" The screen door slammed shut.

Came, Lily mentally corrected him.

A long-haired calico ran into the room and stopped to stare at Lily. Toby followed close behind. Miss Tibbins darted under the rocking chair.

Toby stopped in the middle of the room and patted his thighs. "Come, kitty. Come."

She smiled at her son trying to get a cat to come. "Cats don't come like dogs do."

"Sit on the floor very still," Aunt Henny said, "and

she might come up to you."

Toby slumped down into a cross-legged sitting position and stared at the cat. Miss Tibbins sat as well and stared back at him from under the rocking chair. After a minute, Toby shifted around to lie on his stomach and propped his chin on his hands. Miss Tibbins lay down as well. This was going to be a battle of patience. Lily knew that a cat possessed such perseverance, but did Toby?

"Lily, tell me about yourself. Edric said you came from Philadelphia. You're a long way from home. What brings you all the way out here?"

Fear. She had nothing in Philadelphia anymore. "After my husband passed away, I couldn't bear to stay." More like she dared not stay.

"How long have you been widowed?"

A week. Should she say? What would Aunt Henny think of her for leaving so soon after her husband's death? "Not long."

"Didn't you have any family to help you through this difficult time?"

"No. My husband and Toby were the only family I had. Now it's just Toby and me." And she was glad they were free of him at last.

"Not to worry. I'll be your family now. Your Aunt Henny."

She liked the sound of that. "Thank you. I can't tell you what your kindness means to me. To have a job where I can keep Toby with me, is more than I could have hoped for."

"He's a sweet boy. And Edric was sure taken with him."

"Mr. Hammond was very kind to him."

"And to you."

"Me?" He was married. "He could see I was a bit bewildered, took pity on me, and was polite. I appreciate him directing me here."

"Polite?" The woman gave a half smile as though she wasn't convinced.

He had. His actions could be construed no other way. But Aunt Henny didn't seem to believe her.

Edric strolled the three blocks over to his street. He couldn't stop picturing Lily Lexington—or rather Mrs. Lexington—or would it be more proper to think of her as Widow Lexington? He would have to ask Pa which was the most proper. For now, he would think of her as Lily, and he conjured up the image of her tenderly holding her son. He was a lucky boy to have such a loving mother.

He turned onto his street. The strong, young trees lining both sides swayed in the breeze. Almost as though they were waving to him, welcoming him home. He could see Estella and Nancy playing at the side of the house. He hoped they didn't see him until he got inside the yard. They were his darlings. Estella and Nancy giggled as they played at an overturned crate.

He reached inside the white picket gate and silently lifted the latch. They hadn't seen him yet. He stepped inside. But as he closed the gate, it gave him away with slight creak.

Seven-year-old Estella's head jerked up, and she saw him first. She stood in her old, blue play dress, mud caked on her hands, then ran toward him. "Papa!"

Five-year-old Nancy, in her red play dress jumped up and charged behind her sister. Mud flew off her flailing hands.

He set his carpetbag on the ground and lowered to one knee with outstretched arms, bracing himself.

Estella crashed into one side of him and threw her muddy arms around his neck. "You're home." She kissed his cheek. "I missed you."

Nancy finally caught up and hugged his other side and kissed him. "I miss you too." Nancy put her muddy hands on each of his cheeks. "I made a mud cake wiff grass."

"I can see. Have you been having fun?"

"Yes!" his girls said in unison.

Nancy let go of him, and he knew he had mud on his

face, but he didn't care. He was home with his girls.

Enid never would have let them play in the mud. They were expected to be clean and proper at all times. Estella had a dried smudge of mud across one cheek and all over her hands. Nancy, on the other hand, looked like she'd bathed in the mud. Her cheeks, chin, nose, neck, and the length of both arms had dried and fresh mud on them as well as her dress.

He scooped them up and stood with one in each arm. He kissed Estella on the cheek. "I love you." He kissed Nancy on the cheek. "And I love you."

His pa strode out with a white apron tied around his waist. "Supper's almost ready."

Pa studied the girls. "What have you got here? Two big lumps of mud?"

Both giggled, but Estella spoke for them as she usually did. "No, Granpapa. It's Estella and Nancy."

Pa squinted. "Couldn't be." He leaned in closer to Estella. "But this one does sound a lot like my little Estella." He turned to Nancy. "And this one giggles just like my little Nancy."

Both girls giggled more.

Pa tousled their hair. "You two get cleaned up for supper."

Edric didn't want to let his little ones go but bent and set them on the ground. "Go wash up." The girls ran off, and he called after them. "Make sure you get all the mud off."

Pa picked up Edric's carpetbag. "I'll get this. Come inside."

"I can carry that." He reached for the bag.

"You've had long days of travel. I'm not too old to carry a little ol' carpetbag." Pa headed for the house. "Train arrived an hour ago. It's not more than a ten-minute walk from the station. You run into trouble?"

"No." Edric opened the screen door and held it for Pa to enter. "A passenger needed lodging. I walked her to Aunt Henny's."

"And stayed a spell, apparently." Pa set the bag next to the sofa on his way to the kitchen. "I'm surprised Agnes let you in."

Edric took off his black duster and slung it over the back of the sofa then followed Pa into the kitchen. "She didn't exactly *let* me in. I kind of snuck past her."

"You're a better man than me then." Pa opened the oven, and using a towel, pulled out a pan of cornbread. "I've been trying to make a polite visit for two days to see how Henny's doing."

"She's doing well. Supper sure smells good."

"Chili and cornbread." Pa pressed his finger on the top of the bread then returned it to the oven. "You know Agnes kicked out all the boarders. Did you take the passenger to the hotel?"

Edric shook his head. "She's going to help Aunt Henny out for her room and board. Aunt Henny was happy to have her there."

"That will be good for Henny to have someone looking after her both day and night." Pa took the lid off a cast-iron pot on the stove and stirred the contents.

Edric leaned against the doorframe. "What's the proper way to address a widow woman?"

"You mean like Widow Baker on Tumble Weed Lane?"

"Would it be all right to call her Mrs. Baker?"

Pa lifted the spoonful of the spicy bean stew to his face and breathed in deeply through his nose. "Sure."

"Is it ever appropriate to use a widow's first name?"

"Not unless she invites you to." Pa returned the lid to the pot. "What's this all about?"

"Nothing. Just wondering."

Pa gave him a sideways glance of disbelief before resuming his cooking duties.

Edric listened to his girls laughing outside as he watched Pa move about the kitchen. "What are we doing here, Pa?"

Pa leaned against the counter, wiping his hands on a towel. "Fixin' to have supper. But I suspect you know that and are trying to get at something else. What's on your mind?"

Edric leaned against the doorframe. "Am I doing wrong by the girls to not find them a new mama?"

"You and I have done quite well these past two

years."

"True." Pa had stepped in and taken over cooking and looking after the girls while Edric worked. He didn't know what he would have done without Pa's help. "But don't they need a mother's love?"

"We love them plenty."

"But a woman's love is different. More tender."

"Love is love. And we got more love for those two girls than any woman could ever have. When Enid passed, you swore you wouldn't have another woman in their lives. What brought on this sudden change of heart? This widow woman you can't figure out?"

He *couldn't* figure her out. There was something mysterious and hidden about her.

"Is that why you have that smile? Because of her?"

"Smile? What smile? I'm just happy to be home and see my girls."

Pa waved a wooden spoon in his direction. "No. You smile at Estella and Nancy one way, big and broad like a little kid yourself. This is different. It's contemplative and distant."

He still remembered the feel of her in his arms when he'd saved her from tumbling off the porch, and the way his heart had raced with her there. "You should have seen her with her son. The way she held him, cradled him, protected him. The way she cared for him. She is nothing like Enid." His late wife rarely hugged or held their girls.

"We should hope there aren't many like her."

"Her son didn't make it to the outhouse in time and wet himself. She didn't yell at him or tell him he was bad. The look in her eyes said she felt sorry for him. Then she let him have a cookie. Before supper. I watched her for nearly two days on the train. She never spoke one cross word to the boy."

"It's one thing for a parent to love their own flesh and blood that way, but to love another woman's children is very different. If you feel the need to take a wife again, fine, but you think hard about how it will affect our girls. They're happy now." Pa opened his mouth to continue but stopped when Estella and Nancy charged through the kitchen door.

Estella held out her hands and turned them over and over. "All clean."

Nancy held out her hands and turned them over as well. "All clean." She had missed a smear of mud on her neck. He thought about getting a rag and cleaning it off, but he didn't want to be like his late wife, always finding fault with the way they did everything. Nothing was good enough for her. She would have been livid if any of them came to the table with such an obvious infraction of cleanliness. And because of that, he let the dirt go. His girls needed to be happy and free. A little dirt never hurt anyone. Their hands were clean, and that was good enough.

And they were happy. How could he have entertained the thought they might need a mama? He would not subject them to a woman's harsh words.

Estella and Nancy climbed up onto their chairs at the table while Pa spooned chili into bowls. Edric went to the basin by the back door and washed his hands and the mud from his face Nancy had gotten on it then sat in his chair.

Pa put a plate of cut up cornbread on the table and sat. "Whose turn to say grace?"

"Since I've been gone, it must be mine," Edric said.

Estella put a small hand on his arm. "Oh, Papa, may I say grace? Please."

"Of course."

Estella put one small hand in his and one in Pa's and lowered her head. Then she looked up to make sure Nancy had bowed her head. "Dear Jesus, thank You for the good smelling chili Granpapa made. Granpapa's a good cooker. And I mostly thank You for bringing Papa home safely. Granpapa said he would be fine, and we prayed and prayed he would be fine, and he comed home. Make it so he never has to go business tripping again. Amen."

Edric whispered his amen and raised his head. Pa was right. His girls didn't need a new mama. When a child asks to say grace and puts her heart into every word, they were doing something right. He squeezed

Estella's hand. "That was lovely, darling."

Nancy bobbed up and down. "Me too. I want to pray."

His girls were still desperate for approval. Even after two years. He squeezed Nancy's hand. "You can say grace tomorrow night." Then he looked across the table at Pa. "We are doing all right, aren't we?"

Pa nodded in return.

He took a piece of cornbread and crumbled it on the top of his chili. Did Lily and her son like chili? He could picture her coaxing him into trying it. Her son looked to be about the same age as Nancy. Maybe they would become friends and play together. He would like that. Then he would see Lily often.

He mentally shook his head. If he and Pa were doing fine raising the girls, why couldn't he stop thinking of Lily? Maybe if he thought of her as Widow Lexington. No, she was too young and beautiful to be a widow. Mrs. Lexington. No, that was worse. That attached her to another man. Lily it was.

But he would *definitely* stop thinking about her.

Four

LILY WOKE SLOWLY. FIRST AWARE SHE existed. Then the bed beneath her. Then the small body next to her. Toby. Warm and soft. He was still dry, so she'd better get him up quickly to keep it that way.

She opened her eyes and blinked. The vision of the room in their new home reminded her that she and Toby were safe. For the first time, they were safe.

She rose and lifted Toby out of the bed. "Time to get up."

Toby stood, but his eyes remained closed and his arms hung limp at his sides.

She walked him across the room.

He opened his eyes long enough to use the chamber pot. Then shuffled over and sagged against her. Looking out the window, she could tell that dawn had come and gone a long time ago. Had Aunt Henny needed her?

She dressed in a pale blue shirtwaist and a blue and gray plaid skirt. By the time she had clothes on Toby as well, he was fully awake.

She took his hand and went out their bedroom door then stopped short, inhaling deeply.

Bacon?

Or ham?

Mercy. Had Aunt Henny cooked? Lily was supposed to be helping the older woman and cooking for her. Not the other way around.

She hurried down the stairs and into the kitchen. "I'm so sorry. I oversl—" She stopped short once again. Sitting at the rough kitchen worktable were Aunt Henny, with her leg propped up on a chair, and Mr. Hammond. Both held cups of coffee, and an empty breakfast plate sat in front of each of them.

The injured woman shouldn't be cooking.

Mr. Hammond stood. "Good morning."

Toby scooted around behind her skirt.

She wasn't sure what to make of the scene. "I-I-I..." She glanced between the two and tried to recover her senses. What should she say? "Good morning." She nodded to Mr. Hammond first, as he had been the one to address her, then looked at Aunt Henny. "You shouldn't have cooked. You should have woken me."

"I didn't. Edric made breakfast." Aunt Henny held up her cup toward Mr. Hammond. "And you were so tired after your long trip. You needed a little extra sleep."

Mr. Hammond gripped the cast iron skillet on the stove. "We saved some for the two of you. It's still warm."

She stared at Mr. Hammond as he dished up two plates of scrambled eggs and bacon. He cooked? Was it any good? Good or not, she would eat it and be grateful. It had been very kind of him to cook for Aunt Henny.

He set the two plates on the table. "Please, have a seat."

How she must look standing there, staring like a dullard.

Toby remained hidden behind her as she moved to the table. He wasn't likely to sit in a chair on his own with Mr. Hammond present, so she pulled him with her and onto her lap as she sat. Toby buried his face in her shirtwaist.

Mr. Hammond slid the second plate over to her as well. He had evidently assumed Toby would sit in the fourth chair but, gratefully, didn't make a fuss about him on her lap. He poured a glass of milk and set it on the table near Toby. "It's goat's milk. I hope he likes it."

"Thank you. It will be fine." As she turned Toby around to face the table, his stomach growled. Hers answered.

She put Toby's fork in his hand then took up her own. He would have to feed himself or go hungry. She refused to treat him like a baby. Toby laid his hand and fork in his lap. When he became hungry enough, he would eat. Or when Mr. Hammond departed.

She stabbed a chunk of blackened scrambled eggs. She hoped it was edible and put it in her mouth. Tasty.

He had cooked the eggs in the fresh bacon grease, which caused them to be black, not from overcooking. They were a little dry from sitting on the stove warming, but she could tell that fresh, they would have been moist. Interesting that a man could cook a decent meal. Though eggs weren't terribly difficult. What did his wife think of him being able to cook? Did she take advantage of his talent?

Mr. Hammond brought her a cup of coffee and warmed up Aunt Henny's and his own before sitting again.

Though Toby still sat with his fork in his lap and hadn't touched a bite, Lily ate every last morsel. "Thank you, Mr. Hammond. That was quite good." She turned to Aunt Henny, whom she realized hadn't said much. "I promise to be up earlier tomorrow and cook breakfast."

Aunt Henny patted Lily's hand. "Don't worry about it. I'm surprised you're up already. I expected you to sleep until noon. There will be plenty for you to do."

"If you'll tell me where paper and pencil are, you can dictate a list of the chores you need me to do."

Mr. Hammond stood. "I can see you are in good hands. I should head out."

Aunt Henny held up her hand. "Edric, would you do me a favor?"

"Of course."

"Would you show Lily the way to Waldon's Mercantile?" Aunt Henny turned to Lily. "Tell Franny— she'll be behind the counter—that our quilting circle is on for tomorrow. She'll get the word out to the other ladies."

"Are you sure you should go? I wouldn't want you to get further injured." She also wasn't sure she could get the disabled woman out and about town.

"I won't be going out. The quilting circle meets here once a week. I don't see any reason we can't meet with you here to help me get ready for the ladies."

"I would be glad to."

Aunt Henny waved her hand toward the pantry shelves. "Third shelf down on the left is a pencil and the list I started before this happened to me."

Lily tried to stand with Toby clinging to her, but Mr. Hammond motioned her to sit. "I'll get it." He retrieved the items and handed them to her.

Lily read the short list and held the pencil over the paper.

Aunt Henny shifted her casted leg. "I want to make a chocolate cake." When both Lily and Mr. Hammond gave Aunt Henny hard looks, she continued. "When I say I, I mean Lily will make the cake." She named several items for Lily to get. "Tell Franny you're working for me and to put it on my account."

Mr. Hammond stood, waiting patiently. "I'll also tell Miss Waldon that Lil—Mrs. Lexington is in your employ so she doesn't have any trouble. I'll stop by the hotel afterwards to inform Mr. Lumbard and Mr. Tunstall of their good fortune in getting to return sooner than expected."

"Thank you, Edric. You are a dear." Aunt Henny turned to Lily. "The shopping basket is in the bottom of the pantry."

Lily scooted Toby off her lap. "We are going for a walk. Run upstairs and get your coat and Mommy's shawl."

Aunt Henny waved her hand about. "The child hasn't eaten a thing. Leave him here."

"I don't want to burden you."

"We'll be fine. Let him stay and eat. He can keep me company."

Lily wasn't sure Toby would stay without her. It would be easier to leave him here. She stood and sat Toby in the chair. "You stay here with Aunt Henny. I'm going to take a walk with Mr. Hammond." She pointed to Mr. Hammond, knowing the big man being along might keep Toby from objecting.

Toby stared at her. He neither agreed nor disagreed. She hoped he wouldn't make a fuss when she tried to leave.

"Toby," Aunt Henny said, "maybe you can find Miss Tibbins and play with her. I'll show you her favorite toy."

Surprisingly, Toby turned to Aunt Henny. He didn't smile, but his slight change in expression told Lily he wanted to play with the cat.

Lily touched her son's shoulder to regain his attention. "You have to eat first, before you can play with the cat."

Toby lifted his fork off his lap and stabbed a bit of eggs. Then he glanced up at Mr. Hammond.

Mr. Hammond tipped his head toward Toby. "It was nice seeing you again, Toby." Then he turned to Lily. "I'll wait for you by the front door." He grabbed the shopping basket then faced Aunt Henny. "Let me know if there is anything I or my family can do to help you."

"I will. Thank you for the milk and making breakfast."

"I was glad to do it." He walked out of the kitchen.

"You be a good boy for Aunt Henny."

Toby nodded as he put the first bite of eggs into his mouth.

Lily passed Mr. Hammond before heading up the stairs. "I'll only be a moment."

"No rush."

She hurried anyway, grabbed a white crocheted shawl from her room, pinned on her hat, and was at the front door in no time.

Mr. Hammond held the door open for her with one hand and put on his black creased-top hat with the other.

His wife was a fortunate woman. He could cook—at least eggs, but that was nothing to sneeze at—and he had the manners of a gentleman, even if he looked like a cowboy and towered over her. His size scared her, but his gentle manner calmed her. He had tried hard to befriend Toby yesterday, and today, but not pushed. He seemed to be waiting for Toby to get used to him.

She wondered what he did for work that allowed him a lazy morning. Perhaps a rancher?

Outside stood a saddled, black mare. Mr. Hammond held the gate open for her, hooked the handle of the empty basket over the saddle horn, took hold of his horse's reins, and started the conversation with his first step. "Do your parents still live back East in Philadelphia?"

"They both passed away when I was seventeen." Maybe if they had lived, she wouldn't have rushed into marriage with Tobias Bremmer. He'd taken advantage of her youth and vulnerability.

"I'm so sorry."

"Thank you." It had been a long time since someone had cared enough to ask after her parents and express their sympathies. "And your parents? Do they live around here?"

"Pa lives with us. Ma passed two years ago."

"My condolences."

He gave a nod, and they walked in silence for a bit, until he spoke again. "If you have no relatives or friends here, what made you choose Kamola to settle in?"

Every time she thought about settling someplace else in the new Washington State, Kamola kept coming to mind. It was almost as though the town was calling to her. "It seemed like a nice place to live."

"It is a nice place. Peaceful for the most part." He almost seemed nervous talking to her. What could this big, strong man have to fear from her?

But fear or not, she would rather he stopped asking questions of her. It would be best if no one got to know her really well. "Tell me more about Kamola."

He turned on a street she hadn't been on yesterday while walking from the train. "It's a cow town mostly. Cattle ranches all around the town. But we have a teacher's college, Washington State Normal School. They recently completed the first building, Ballard Hall. It's named after the principal, Benjamin Ballard. Aunt Henny's two boarders, Mr. Lumbard and Mr. Tunstall, both work there." He continued to tell her about some of the town's other residents.

Soon enough, they came to Waldon's Mercantile. Mr. Hammond looped his horse's reins around the hitching post, removed the basket from his saddle horn, and held the door open for her. He then guided her over to the counter and tipped his hat to the young woman behind the counter. "Miss Waldon, this is Mrs. Lexington. She's new in town and is working for Aunt Henny. Aunt Henny sent her to pick up a few things."

Miss Waldon held out her hand and shook Lily's. "Call me Franny. I'm pleased to meet you. I'm sure Aunt Henny appreciates your help while she's laid up."

Mr. Hammond tipped his hat. "You're in good hands. I best be off." He turned and left.

Lily watched him dip his head slightly to a woman entering, then he swung up onto his black horse and rode off down the street.

"He's not in the market for a wife. Too bad."

Lily never thought he was. He was married, after all. And she was not looking for a husband. One husband in a lifetime was quite enough, thank you. But perhaps Franny was looking.

Lily shook her head. How embarrassing to be caught staring. She shifted the empty basket. Hopefully, she could shift Franny's attention as easily. "Aunt Henny told me to let you know that she would like the quilting circle to come over tomorrow."

"Mercy. She's not up for that already, is she?"

The same thing Lily had thought. "She won't be doing anything. I'll do all the work for her. I think maybe she's lonesome for company not being able to get out."

"The poor dear. I'll let the other ladies know."

Just as Aunt Henny said she would.

Then Franny called out. "Trudy."

The woman, who had entered when Mr. Hammond had left, came over. She appeared to be in her middle thirties. "Hello, Franny. I didn't want to disturb you while you were with another customer."

"Trudy, this is Mrs. Lexington. She's new in town and is working for Aunt Henny."

Trudy's face brightened. "How's Aunt Henny?"

"She's well."

Franny jumped back in. "Aunt Henny wants to have the quilting circle over tomorrow."

Trudy's eye widened. "Is that wise?"

"Mrs. Lexington is going to take care of everything, so Aunt Henny doesn't have to lift a finger."

"Please call me Lily."

"How rude of me." Trudy held out her hand. "Lily, I'm very pleased to meet you. We have all been worried over

Aunt Henny's injury. I planned to come by this afternoon for a short visit, but maybe I'll wait until tomorrow. I'll bring a stew for lunch."

"And I'll bring a pie." Franny motioned a hand in Lily's direction. "We don't want you to have to do everything. The ladies will be so pleased."

So it was settled. Tomorrow, Aunt Henny's boarding house would be full of ladies. And she suddenly missed Toby. She wasn't used to having him out of her sight for very long. She pulled out the list.

Leaning on her crutches, Henny watched Toby scoping out the backyard.

The boy stayed close while he searched for Miss Tibbins. He clomped up the back-porch steps and spoke to her through the screen. "She not *any*where."

Henny pushed open the screen. "She's probably out hunting. Why don't you come inside? You must be tired from your search."

"What if she's lost?"

"She's not. She'll return when she wants to."

"But I want to play wiff her."

"We can't make her come."

He hung his head and waddled inside. He followed her into the parlor.

She lowered herself onto the settee. "Toby, would you put my crutches against that chair?" Fifty was too young to be acting like an invalid, but it was good for the boy to feel useful. And good for his mother to as well.

Toby puckered his mouth in concentration and wrapped his arms around the crutches that were taller than him. They wobbled a bit, but he got them set aside.

"Very good. You're a strong boy."

"The milk made me strong."

She smiled at him. His untucked shirt from when he went to the privy gave her an idea. "Toby, would you lift your shirt for me." She wanted to confirm or dismiss her suspicions.

He grabbed the hem and pulled it up, covering his face.

Henny nearly gasped at the array of yellowed bruises across his stomach and chest but schooled herself to keep from unsettling the boy. More bruises covered his back and arms. But the most alarming were the ones around his neck. Someone had choked this poor boy.

Edric stepped out of the White Hotel. Mr. Lumbard and Mr. Tunstall were quite happy with the news that they could return to their rooms at the boarding house. He swung up onto his horse and headed toward Waldon's Mercantile. Why, he wasn't sure.

But then he saw Lily—or rather Mrs. Lexington—with her shopping basket. Was it heavy? Should he help her with it? That might make it appear as though he had been waiting for her and was interested in her, which he wasn't. He and Pa were doing fine with the girls. They didn't need a mama, and he didn't need a wife.

She shifted the basket to her other hand.

Maybe he should have brought the buggy. Why hadn't he thought of that when he left the house this morning? It would have been much more pleasant for her to ride than to walk. Then he could claim he was heading in the direction of Aunt Henny's and offer her a ride.

No, no, no. That would look as though there might be something between them. That he was interested. And he wasn't. He didn't need half the tongues in town to start wagging with presumptions and rumors. No, that would be no good at all.

He kept picturing her holding her son on the train, at Aunt Henny's yesterday, and then again this morning. She hadn't scolded her son for not eating. Nor had she threatened him with going hungry until supper if he didn't eat. She left it up to him to eat or not and made no fuss about it. She seemed to be so patient with him, and he, in return, loved his mama a great deal.

And her eyes. Blue as a deep pool of water. He hadn't noticed her eyes yesterday. Was it because she had on that blue shirt today? Or because yesterday he couldn't take his eyes off her arms? Arms that held her son in a loving embrace.

She seemed like the kind of gentle person who could have compassion for someone else's children and love them. Or was that wishful hoping?

He shook his head. What was he thinking? He was behaving like a smitten schoolboy. He and Pa were doing just fine.

Just fine.

So he watched her retreating form sway down the street like leaves dancing in the breeze.

And sighed.

Five

LILY SHIFTED THE SHOPPING BASKET FROM one arm to the other. It hadn't seemed this heavy when she'd started out. Aunt Henny's mint green house came into sight, so she wouldn't have any trouble making it home.

Home.

That sounded strange and yet so right. She would have to get used to home being a safe place again. And Aunt Henny did almost feel like family with her warm welcome, and how she offered to take care of Toby. Lily hadn't had any reservations about that. But she was anxious to see her baby. She had seldom let him out of her sight.

And there he was, sitting on the front porch, waiting for her, singing. He rarely sang. And only for her. So who was he singing for now? Anticipation of her return? The cat?

He looked up and saw her. She waved. He jumped to his feet. "Mommy! Mommy's back!" Then he yanked open the screen door and ran inside.

Wasn't he going to come greet her? Hadn't he missed her? Hastening her steps, she hoped nothing was wrong.

Toby burst out the door and ran to the gate. He reached it at the same time she did and opened it for her. "You comed back!"

She smiled. "Of course I did. Did you miss me?"

"Lots and lots." He lifted his hands toward the basket. "I'm big to help you."

"It's heavy." She knew it was too heavy for him.

"Aunt Henny told me to."

She lowered the basket and held it by the handle. "Why don't we both carry it?"

Toby fell into step beside her and wrapped his small hand around the basket's handle as well.

It warmed her heart to hear him calling the older woman aunt. She shook her head. The word meant nothing to Toby. He'd never had an aunt so didn't know what one was. To him, it was simply her first name.

"Did you have a nice time with Aunt Henny?"

He nodded with large movements. His dark hair flopped about. He stumbled then caught himself by pulling on the basket.

Lily had to struggle to not lose her own balance.

Toby straightened. "I eated all my eggs. Cleaned my plate good."

"Did you have fun playing with Miss Tibbins?"

He shook his head. "She goed outside and not comed home. We called and called. Aunt Henny sayed we can't make her come. We just has to wait."

"That's too bad. She'll probably return later, and you can play with her then." She took the steps slowly so Toby could keep up with her. "Would you open the door?"

Toby released the basket and opened the screen. He was learning to be a gentleman already.

Lily bent at the knees in a slight curtsy. "Thank you."

Toby let the screen slam behind them.

Lily flinched. He still had a few manners to learn.

He ran into the parlor. "Aunt Henny, she's back."

"I could hear," the older woman said.

Lily shifted her grip on the laden basket and entered the parlor. "Toby, what have you been told about slamming doors?"

He lowered his head. "Sorry."

"Would you please go try it again?"

He gave a heavy sigh and marched to the front door.

Lily took the opportunity to address Aunt Henny. "Forgive him for letting the door slam."

Aunt Henny smiled from where she reclined on the settee. "He's still young. He'll learn."

The screen squeaked ever so lightly and tapped shut.

Toby trotted to her side, grabbed the handle of the basket, and pulled toward the kitchen.

Lily moved with him but spoke to Aunt Henny. "I'll put these things away then bring you a cup of tea."

"That will be lovely."

As Lily directed Toby where to put some of the things from the basket, she pulled down a cup and brewed tea.

"I'm going outside to look for Miss Tibbins." Toby opened the back screen door.

"Stay where I can see you." Lily crossed to the door. "Don't go any farther than that big tree or the necessary. And don't go in the garden."

"Okey-dokey." Toby closed the screen painfully slow to keep it from slamming, then spun around and jumped from the porch to the ground, skipping all three steps. "Miss Tibbins! Here, kitty, kitty, kitty."

She smiled at his carefree attitude. As long as he was hollering for the cat, she wouldn't have any trouble knowing where he was. He seemed to be settling in quickly.

She found a wooden serving tray hanging on the wall and took it down. Then she prepared a cup of tea and put it on the tray with the sugar bowl and the cream pitcher with some of the goat's milk Mr. Hammond had brought.

Aunt Henny set her red and yellow nine-patch quilt block aside.

"I didn't know if you like cream and sugar in your tea." Lily held the tray near the older woman.

"Both." Aunt Henny scooped in two full teaspoons of sugar and a splash of milk, then took her cup by the saucer, stirring with the spoon. "Thank you. You can leave the tray on the table."

Lily set the tray on the tea table then unbuttoned one of her shirtwaist cuffs.

"Aren't you going to join me?"

Lily folded up the sleeve several times until it nearly reached her elbow. "I thought I'd start on the kitchen. I want to clean it before I start cooking. Franny seemed quite excited about the quilting circle meeting tomorrow. A woman named Trudy was there. They're going to bring food." She unbuttoned her other cuff. "Will you have the ladies in here?"

"If the weather holds, we'll sit in the front yard. Otherwise, we will be..." Aunt Henny paused and stared for a moment before continuing, "...in this room."

Lily looked down to see what had captivated the woman. She too stared at the green and yellow fading bruises that covered her forearms along with a nasty burn scar. How could she have been so absentminded? Her hands shook. Tobias would beat her for her carelessness.

No. Tobias wasn't here. He couldn't hurt her or Toby ever again.

She clasped her hands behind her. "I should get to work."

Grateful that Aunt Henny didn't try to stop her, she turned, shifting her arms in front of her, and walked into the kitchen.

Aunt Henny had noticed the old bruises. The older woman either thought they were from normal daily living or knew exactly how Lily had gotten them. Either way, she had chosen to be polite and not mention them. Or she didn't want to think about how Lily had sustained such injuries and pretended the bruises weren't there, as so many others had usually done. People considered it none of their business what a husband did to his wife and children. A husband could do anything he wanted, and the prevailing thought was that the wife probably did something to deserve it. At least among the men.

She covered her face with her hands and cried silent tears.

Edric stopped at Aunt Henny's gate and took a deep breath. What was he doing here?

He'd been making his way around town and ended up here. Opening the gate, he stepped through, then closed it behind him, but didn't move.

He shouldn't be here.

What excuse could he give?

Trying to think of one, he strode up to the door and knocked.

"Come in," Aunt Henny called.

Taking a deep breath, he entered and took off his hat. He stepped into the parlor, giving the room a sweeping glance. Where was Lily—or rather Mrs. Lexington—no, Widow Lexington? "How are you faring, Aunt Henny?"

"Well." The older woman sat on the settee with her leg propped up. "Have a seat." She motioned toward a chair with the sewing in her hand.

He listened for activity in the kitchen as he lowered himself onto the chair. But heard nothing. Shouldn't the boy be running around somewhere? They hadn't left, had they? They'd only recently arrived in town.

"She's out back."

Edric snapped his attention to the injured woman. "What? Who? She?"

Aunt Henny smiled. "Lily is in the backyard with her son."

He gave a distracted nod. So that was why he couldn't sense her in the house. "Pa and I are doing just fine."

"I know."

"I don't need a wife, and the girls don't need a mother."

"I never said you did or they did. Even so, there is nothing wrong with you being attracted to her. She's a widow. You're a widower. She's beautiful. If you weren't attracted to her, I would be concerned."

He pulled his eyebrows down hard. "I'm not looking for a wife. Now or ever. I'm perfectly content with my girls."

"I'm sure you were... until a beautiful widow with her young son got off the train in our little town. You can't help but be drawn to her. You've always been drawn to the vulnerable and helpless. It's who you are. And she's pretty, and kind, and a good mother, and a hard worker... and available."

Aunt Henny knew him too well. Defender of the weak and innocent. But that didn't mean he had to think of her as anything more than the newest resident of Kamola.

Aunt Henny went on. "By the end of today, half the town will know she's arrived and planning to stay. Franny will see to that. Men will start swarming a beautiful, available lady like her."

Some of the men in the area were real cads. She wouldn't be interested in any of them. But there were a good many decent fellows looking for a wife, especially one as pretty as Lily. And none too picky about one with a son in tow. He didn't want to picture her with any of them. "So she's working out for you?"

"Yes, but that's not why you came by."

He didn't know why he had come and cleared his throat. "Mr. Tunstall and Mr. Lumbard are both quite happy to be able to return. They both said they would be here for supper." There. That was a plausible excuse. Not that he had needed to tell her that.

"Thank you. Lily has already made up their beds, and I'll let her know to expect them for supper."

Edric fidgeted in the chair. He had probably stayed as long as he dared without it seeming suspicious. Disappointed he hadn't seen Lily, he stood, turning his hat in his hand.

"Before you leave, would you take a quick peek out back and make sure Lily and Toby are fine?"

He felt an immediate, unbidden smile but forced his mouth not to show it. "Of course." He walked to the kitchen screen door.

Toby stood at one end of a white sheet hanging on the clothesline. Lily tiptoed around the other end and snuck up on the boy. He squealed and ran. She gave chase.

Enid never played with Estella and Nancy that way. Never played with them at all. The girls had to remain clean and reserved at all times.

Lily was a good mother. The kind of mother all children should have.

"I need you to do me a favor."

Edric startled at Aunt Henny by his side, leaning on her crutches. He hadn't heard her come up on him. "Anything. What do you need?"

"Keep a lookout for any strangers in town."

Edric mentally sighed. Was this her way of telling him to keep an eye on Lily? What was the older woman up to? Why did she see fit to push him toward Lily?

She looked up at him, and he could see real concern in her gray-blue eyes.

His gut tightened. "What's wrong? Who should I be looking for?"

Aunt Henny pointed out the door. "You saw the bruises on the boy's legs yesterday, when he came in from the privy, didn't you?"

The boy'd had greenish-yellow bruises up and down his calves and shins.

"He's a boy. Boys play rough. Run around and fall a lot. I don't think a few bruises are anything to worry about."

Aunt Henny's face held a sad expression. "He has more bruises on his arms and back. And on his neck—"

"Neck?"

"Yes. The most recent, a week or so old."

Edric frowned. The boy had been severely maltreated? He studied the pair in the yard, now lying on the grass, resting from their game. "Not Lily." She had been kind and held the boy protectively.

"Lily?"

A slip of the tongue. He needed to get past it. "She loves her son. You saw the way she cradled him in her arms."

"At first, I wondered if it could be her, but she also has bruises on her arms. I think she might have one on her neck as well right below her collar. She has a scar in her hairline and another old nubbly one on her forearm."

"From what?"

"Probably a serious burn."

The burn could easily be explained from cooking. And the scar above her forehead could be from childhood. But an uneasy feeling coiled in the pit of his stomach.

Aunt Henny shifted on her crutches. "They have both seen some bad times."

He clenched his fists at the thought of someone harming the pair, both in the past and in the future. He wouldn't let that happen. "You think whoever hurt them might be coming after them? But who?"

"Who is the most likely?"

He thought a moment. "Her husband?"

"Most likely and the reason she's not wearing widow's weeds."

"But he's dead. She said so."

"All I know is those two are running from something. Or someone. If that person comes to town looking for them, I want you to know about it first. And I want to be second."

"I'll check every person who arrives in town. If anyone asks about her, I'll know about it." He hated the thought of someone hurting that helpless little boy or Lily.

"Don't let on to Lily that you know anything. I'm sure she would rather people not know about her background."

He stared at the happy pair. "I won't say a thing. And you let me know if anything comes up. If she talks about anyone, has any unexpected visitors, or seems frightened or something."

"You know I will."

"I should get going before she wonders why I'm here."

Aunt Henny gave him an innocent look and blinked several times. "You only came by to let us know that Mr. Tunstall and Mr. Lumbard will be returning this evening, right? Because it would have been such a shock for them to show up... when I had told you to inform them they could return."

A smile pulled at one side of his mouth. Why did he even bother trying to fool this woman? He jammed on his hat. "I'll bring by more goat's milk in the morning."

Lily lifted a spoon to her lips, blew on the beef stew she'd made, and took a sip. She let the flavor sit in her mouth a moment before swallowing. She couldn't think of anything else it needed. She heard male voices in the other room.

Toby scurried into the kitchen and hid behind the open door.

She looked at her terrified son. "Toby?"

He shook his head.

She set down the spoon and left the kitchen.

Two gentlemen stood in the parlor with Aunt Henny. Two vastly different men. One in his mid-to-late twenties with dark wavy hair slicked back, startlingly similar to Tobias's features. The other man was much older with white hair and a well-trimmed matching beard.

Lily waited to be introduced.

After a few pleasantries about Aunt Henny's well-being, the older man turned to her, as though he'd sensed her presence. Aunt Henny motioned to her to come into the room.

Lily stepped forward, and Aunt Henny made the introductions. The older man was Mr. Lumbard, and the younger, Mr. Tunstall, both taught at the teacher's college.

Lily returned their greetings. "Your rooms are ready, and supper will be served shortly."

Mr. Lumbard took her hand and bowed over it. "I am so very pleased you have come to us. Supper smells divine."

Mr. Tunstall pulled the older man away. "Don't mind him. He flirts with all the young ladies."

At supper, Toby refused to sit in a chair but cowered beside hers, taking an occasional peek at the two men. She wished her son would simply sit and eat, but knew if she made a fuss, it would only draw unwanted attention to him. There would be plenty of time for Toby to get used to the men.

Six

LILY COATED ONE LAYER OF THE chocolate cake with frosting and placed the second layer on top. Toby swiped a drip of frosting off the outside of the bowl with his finger and popped it into his mouth.

Mr. Tunstall and Mr. Lumbard had eaten breakfast early and left, joking about it being safer to escape for the day before any of the ladies arrived. Something about not wanting to be caught in traps.

The wind had picked up during the night and continued to blow. Though the day was still warm, the ladies would quilt indoors.

When a firm knock sounded on the front door, Toby scurried into the corner. He would need to learn that no one was going to hurt him here.

She wiped her hands on a towel and went to the door.

Mr. Hammond removed his hat and held up a corked quart bottle. "I brought milk for your boy."

"Thank you." She took the bottle of still warm milk and stepped aside for him to enter. Mr. Hammond certainly had a thoughtful and kind nature.

Mr. Hammond held his hat at his side. "I presume Aunt Henny hasn't changed her mind about entertaining the quilting circle today with your help."

"The ladies are bringing food and making a full day of it."

Aunt Henny called from the parlor. "Edric, don't just stand in the entry, come all the way in."

Edric stepped into the room and greeted Aunt Henny. "I brought milk for the boy." He glanced around the room.

Lily was sure he was looking for Toby. She turned toward the kitchen where Toby's dark, curly head peeked around the edge of the doorway. "Toby, come say good morning."

Fear swirling in his wide, brown eyes, Toby stared at the big man but did as he was told. He sidled up next to her and grabbed a wad of her skirt. "Good morning," he said so quietly, Lily could barely hear him.

She was about to tell him to speak up, when Mr. Hammond crouched in front of him. "Good morning, Toby. Are you being good for your mama?"

Toby nodded into the folds of her skirt.

Lily held out the quart of milk to her son. "Mr. Hammond brought you milk. What do you say?"

Toby glanced up at her but quickly returned his gaze to Mr. Hammond lest the man grab him or strike him. "Thank you."

"You're welcome. A growing boy like you needs milk to keep you strong and healthy."

Lily handed the bottle to Toby. "Take this into the kitchen and put it on the table."

Toby turned and started to run but tripped, sprawling on the carpet. The bottle slid across the floor.

Mr. Hammond lunged and scooped up the bottle. The cork held.

Toby scuttled across the floor on his bottom, wiggled between chair legs, and hid under the dining table. "Sorry, sorry, sorry. I didn't mean to. I sorry."

Lily didn't get more than two steps toward her son when Mr. Hammond held the milk up to her from where he knelt. "Let me, please."

She took the bottle. "But..."

"I'm the one who scared him."

It took all her strength not to crawl under the table with her frightened boy. Instead, she nodded.

Mr. Hammond crawled over and sat on the floor. "It's all right, Toby. No harm was done."

"I sorry. I sorry."

Lily also sat on the floor near the table just behind Mr. Hammond so Toby could see her. Her poor baby was shaking. She hoped he didn't wet his pants. She couldn't smell anything yet. That was good.

"I know you are. It was an accident. I'm sorry I

frightened you."

Toby stared at the big man.

Tobias certainly had never said he was sorry.

To anyone.

Edric's heart ached for the trembling boy. What had been done to one so young that he would be this frightened? He hunched his shoulders to look as small as possible to not scare the boy further. "Toby, you can come out. No one is going to hurt you."

The boy glanced to his mother and back.

If Edric could show the boy that nothing bad would happen when the past clearly told him it would, he could feel safe. He reached up to the top of the table and took down the bottle of milk Lily had placed there. "See. No milk spilled. Come on out."

Toby glanced to his mother again, and Edric could see out of the corner of his eye that she nodded.

At least she trusted him. To a degree.

Edric set the milk aside. "It's all right. I'm not going to hurt you. I promise." When the boy didn't move, Edric pushed two chairs away from the table. "Come on out."

Toby looked at the opening as though considering it but didn't move.

Edric scooted forward a little at a time.

Toby's eyes grew bigger with each movement, but he didn't dart away.

Soon, Edric had his large frame hunched all the way under the table. He looked around. "This is nice under here. I can see why you like it. It's like a fort." He saw Toby take a deep breath. Had the boy been holding his breath?

After a moment, Edric held out his hand, palm up. "Let's get out from under here."

Toby stared at the offer of peace, raised his small, sweaty hand, and placed it tentatively in the much bigger one.

Edric scooted backwards, and Toby moved apprehensively with him. Once out from under the table, Edric remained sitting while Toby pushed to his feet. The boy would be less nervous if he stood a little taller than Edric. He took the bottle and held it out to Toby. "You want to put this in the kitchen for your mama?"

Toby clutched the bottle to his chest and backed up all the way into the kitchen, always keeping his gaze on Edric. When the boy reached the kitchen table, he set the milk on it carefully.

Edric smiled. "Very good. You didn't spill a drop."

Toby's mouth pulled slightly. Not into an actual smile, but something that could be one day.

Edric stood and helped Lily up from the floor.

Tears pooled in her eyes. Were they from fear? From heartache at seeing her boy so terrified?

Her thank-you came out in a hoarse whisper.

No. He believed her tears were actually of gratitude.

She moved past him to the kitchen.

Aunt Henny, who had watched in silence, held out her hand to him.

Stepping closer, Edric took it.

The older woman squeezed his hand. "You are a good, good man, Edric Hammond. And an excellent father. I didn't think you would succeed in drawing him out."

Edric hadn't thought so either. He leaned in and spoke softly. "I will keep my eye out for strangers. If anyone dare lay a hand on that boy or his mother, they will be sorry." He straightened and snatched his hat from the floor. "I should be going."

Lily returned to the parlor, tears dried. "I'll see you to the door."

He gave her a nod and looked over her shoulder into the kitchen where Toby stood in the doorway. "I'll see you later, Toby. Enjoy the milk." He followed Lily.

She held the door for him. "Thank you."

He wanted to fold her in his arms. Assure her he wouldn't let anyone harm her or Toby ever again. But the first was inappropriate, and the second would only serve to acknowledge a painful past and embarrass her. So he gave a nod. "You're welcome." He pushed open the screen and stepped out. "Have a good day with the quilting ladies."

Lily watched Mr. Hammond tug his hat on as he walked down the steps. The wind pulled at the bushes and trees, leaves fluttering wildly. Why couldn't she have met a man like Mr. Hammond when she was young and vulnerable?

He'd been so patient with Toby. Her eyes again watered at his kindness.

He held the gate open for Franny Waldon who carried a pie in her hands. Her skirt flapped against her legs. Franny spoke to him for a moment before continuing up the walk. Lily watched Mr. Hammond stroll down the street, then she pushed open the screen door for Franny and took the pie.

"Thank you. I came early to help. And to have a little time with Aunt Henny before the others arrive. How is she?"

Aunt Henny called from the other room. "I'm fine, Franny. Come on in."

Lily left the friends to catch up and put the pie on the dining table. Then she moved a straight-backed chair into the parlor.

Franny jumped to her feet from a padded chair. "Let me help you."

Lily waved her off. "I can manage. You enjoy your visit."

Soon ten women were crowded in the parlor, each with a basket or cloth bag with her quilting work in it. All chattering. All knew each other well. And the dining table sat loaded with food.

Lily was not a part of this group. She was nothing more than the servant. Sighing, she slipped back into the kitchen. Toby stood in the middle of the room like a soldier waiting for orders, holding his toy train.

"Toby, Aunt Henny has guests over, so you need to stay out of the way. You can help me here in the kitchen."

Toby nodded.

Such a good boy.

Lily's thoughts returned to the handsome Mr. Hammond. Could Aunt Henny have been correct in assessing that he was indeed attracted to her? Dare she long for a man's affections? Should she discourage his attention no matter how benign? He was a married man after all. She really couldn't afford to have a man, or anyone, inquiring about her past. But Mr. Hammond offered a kindness she desperately missed. And he'd been so patient with Toby. Toby could use a father like him.

Aunt Henny called from the other room. "Lily?"

"Toby, you stay here. I'll be right back."

Toby nodded.

She smoothed her hands down her white apron and went into the parlor. "Yes, ma'am."

A couple of the ladies giggled.

At her?

It didn't matter. She would serve Aunt Henny well so the older woman would have no issues with her ability to perform her duties.

Aunt Henny had on a gentle smile. "I can see most of the food laid out on the table. Is everything in order in the kitchen?"

"Yes, ma'am."

Did she hear giggles again?

Aunt Henny motioned toward a straight-backed chair closest to the settee she lay on. "I've saved a chair next to me for you."

"Ma'am?"

Again the giggles.

Two or more of these ladies were definitely laughing at her. Why? She resisted the urge to look around the circle to find out who.

"I don't expect you to stay shut away in the kitchen all day. You'll join us. It's the best way to get to know the ladies."

Lily shifted her gaze between Aunt Henny and the empty chair. She'd never imagined she'd be included. Did she want to be part of this group? A group that wanted to get to know her? She glanced around the room at the expectant faces.

The woman closest to Lily squeezed her hand. "You must join us. We want to know all about you."

Lily bristled at that. She didn't want anyone getting to know her. That could be dangerous. She turned her gaze to Aunt Henny. "I have Toby to look after. He's in the kitchen."

A woman who looked to be in her forties with graying hair spoke up. "He can play outside with my four youngest children. Neva and Betsy have children outside as well."

"I don't know. He's young. He doesn't know his way around. He could get lost." She mentally shook her head. She was making excuses. But she couldn't join these ladies who would pry into her past.

The same woman spoke. "My June is thirteen. She looks after the younger ones."

"Including my wee one," another woman said. "Liam is only ten months old."

Lily's gaze darted around the circle of smiling ladies. "I don't have any sewing supplies."

Every woman moved at once as though planned. They bent and stooped, digging into their bags and baskets.

"I have some scraps for you." A woman held up a yellow striped swatch.

"I have a green plaid."

"I have a pretty black and pink calico."

"This beige will offset the black nicely."

And on it went around the room until every lady held up pieces of fabric for her. Even Agnes Martin held a blue calico and looked eager for Lily to join the group.

These women were welcoming her. A stranger.

Aunt Henny looked triumphant. "I have needles and plenty of thread."

The longing to be included pulled at her. But they would want to know about her. She couldn't let them.

The woman with the four children stood. "I'll go with you and introduce Toby to the other children."

Lily mutely let herself be led away through the kitchen. She could think of no other excuses to get out of joining the group.

The woman knelt beside Toby who stood, looking out through the screen door at the children playing. "Would you like to play with them?"

Wide-eyed, Toby stared at the woman and nodded. The woman held out her hand, and Toby took it. Then Toby looked back at Lily for permission.

Lily couldn't deny her son friends. "Don't go any farther than the backyard."

Toby smiled and went outside.

Lily waited by the screen door.

The oldest girl held Liam on her hip while dancing around with two other children. There were eight children in all. Toby made nine. Another boy a little older than Toby grabbed his hand and led him over to the large maple tree.

The woman returned to the house. "He'll be fine. I'm Dorthea."

Lily gave a shy smile. "I'm Lily."

"We all know who you are. This town isn't big enough to keep secrets in."

Lily's insides tightened. Secrets were precisely what she needed to keep. "I really should stay in the kitchen and make sure everything is in order."

Dorthea hooked her hand around Lily's elbow. "Everything is fine in here. The ladies don't expect you to wait on them."

"But Aunt Henny hired me. I need to do my job. Not sit around."

"There is nothing to do in here until we eat. Now, about Aunt Henny. She would never tell you in front of the others, but she doesn't like being called ma'am. It makes her feel old. Some of the younger ladies have never heard her called ma'am, and that's why they giggled." Dorthea pulled her into the next room.

Lily's stomach bunched.

Dorthea addressed the group. "Ladies, as you all

know, this is Lily Lexington." Then Dorthea went around the room introducing everyone. Marguerite and her two adult daughters, Isabelle and Adelaide. Adelaide, the younger, looked like her still beautiful mother. Isabelle looked nothing like the two. Lily had met Franny and Agnes. Betsy Jones, Liam's mother, and Neva Whittier smiled their greetings. And Trudy, who she'd met yesterday, looked to be in her thirties. "We don't expect you to remember everyone's name right off."

Lily sat on the edge of the chair, unsure. The ladies passed the swatches of cloth around the circle. The colors piling on her lap blurred. She settled into her chair. What had she done to deserve such kindness?

Aunt Henny spoke. "Now you will need to decide what pattern you want to make them into."

She knew the perfect one. "Sunshine and Shadow." Her mother had talked about making a quilt in that pattern to mirror life. The good and the bad. The light and the dark. Lily's own life had gone from the sun shining down on her to the cold dark shadows. But in this town, she hoped to return to the warmth of the sun. A new beginning for both her and Toby.

"That will be a wonderful quilt," Aunt Henny said. "My sewing basket is right beside you on the floor. Dig around for what you need."

Lily began by separating the scraps she'd been gifted into darks and lights.

"Lily?"

Lily looked up at the woman across the circle who'd addressed her. Trudy, from the mercantile.

Franny who sat next to Lily spoke up. "That's Trudy. If we all use our names when we speak, Lily can learn them faster."

Trudy pursed her lips slightly. "I met her yesterday, but I was going to reintroduce myself."

"I'm sorry, Trude." Franny turned to Lily. "I tend to open my mouth first and think about what I said later."

Agnes spoke up. "Do you even think later, my dear?"

Franny made a face at Agnes. "At least I'm not bitter."

Agnes huffed.

"Now, ladies," Aunt Henny said. "I'll have none of that in my home."

Franny lowered her head. "I'm sorry. I really am trying to tame my tongue."

Aunt Henny gave a slight nod. "Thank you. Now, Trudy, you were going to ask Lily something."

"I'm Trudy MacVay. I'm not married—"

Franny leaned toward Lily and whispered, "She's a spinster. She's sensitive about it, so don't ask her if she's married or has children."

Never marrying was hard for some women. Lily wished she'd never married. But then she wouldn't have Toby. She would live through it all again to have her son.

Trudy continued, apparently unaware of Franny's comment. "–and I live with my father and grandmother. I was born and raised in Kamola. That's a little about me. I wanted—well I'm sure we all want to know a bit about you."

The women around the circle nodded.

Lily would take her cue from Trudy on what to say. "I was born and raised in Philadelphia. My parents passed away six years ago when I was seventeen."

The youngest lady in the group gasped. "Whatever did you do? I couldn't imagine losing my parents."

"That's Adelaide," Franny murmured in her ear.

"I married and had Toby."

"How did your husband die?" Adelaide asked.

Die? Yes. Tobias was dead. She tried not to think about him. But now she pictured Tobias with his big hands around Toby's neck. Though Toby had made choking sounds, he hadn't fought his father. He knew better. His sweet little face, bright red as life receded from his eyes.

Her hands shook. Her breaths came in short gasps. Her vision blurred.

Lily shot to her feet, barely aware of the fabrics from her lap scattering onto the floor. "I need to check on Toby." She hurried from the room. She pushed through the screen door and searched for Toby.

He sat with the other children, staring at the oldest girl who had the baby on her lap. She appeared to be telling a story. Toby looked up at her, smiled, and waved.

Lily waved back. He was safe.

He was safe.

She relaxed her shoulders and slowed her breathing.

He was safe.

Watching her son, Lily slumped down onto the back steps and leaned her head against the support post.

He was safe.

Seven

EDRIC STOOD ON THE TRAIN STATION platform, leaning against the clapboard building. The iron horse chugged to a stop, billowing smoke.

He studied the departing passengers. Many he knew waved or greeted him. A handful he didn't know. A red-haired man with his wife and young son weren't a threat. Same for the old woman with a pair of younger women.

But the dandy with the blond curls and expensive suit could be. Maybe he was only stretching his legs before continuing on with the train. After a moment, the dandy grabbed a brown carpetbag and headed off the end of the platform.

Edric jumped off the opposite end and rounded the building as the dandy crossed the street.

After waiting for a freight wagon, traces jingling, Edric crossed too.

The dandy entered the White Hotel.

He waited outside until the man went upstairs. He strode in and greeted the clerk, a young man with spectacles. "Howdy, Grant. That man who registered a moment ago, what's his name?"

The clerk turned the book.

Edric read the name, Joseph Franklin from Washington D.C. "Did he say how long he'd be staying or what his business is?"

"He's waiting on tomorrow's stage. Heading south."

Edric tipped his hat. "Thanks." He left. Mr. Franklin wasn't likely a threat either.

If he actually left town.

Lily had sat for a long while on the back steps, watching Toby play. Then she stayed in the kitchen, fussing over the lunch preparations and making coffee.

She could hear the ladies' voices from the other room, but purposely did not focus on them. She didn't want to find out they were talking about her. Or wondering why she had run out. Or speculating about the stability of her mind. Or that they didn't even notice she was gone.

A gentle touch on her shoulder caused her to jump, and she spun around.

The young woman, close to her own age, smiled. "I'm sorry for startling you."

"I didn't hear you come in. Can I get you something?"

The young woman shook her head. "I'm Isabelle, Adelaide's sister. I wanted to apologize for her inconsideration. She's young and thinks only of herself sometimes. She should have realized you were still in mourning from your husband's passing."

Yes, mourning was a handy excuse she could use for a good many things. Even if it wasn't true.

Isabelle continued. "Even then, it's rude to ask someone directly like that on so personal a matter. I do hope you'll rejoin us."

"Maybe later. We shall be eating soon."

Isabelle smiled. "Lovely. What can I do to help you with lunch? Then we can call the others to eat."

At first, Lily wasn't sure she wanted Isabelle in the kitchen with her. Would the other woman presume it would give her permission to pry? But Isabelle turned out to be quite pleasant, talking about the town and its people. She seemed to want to educate Lily about life in Kamola.

After lunch, Lily rejoined the circle of ladies.

They smiled and bid her pleasantries, but no one asked any personal questions beyond if she liked Kamola and did she think she would stay.

Lily cut two pieces of fabric then wove the needle in and out of the cloth.

Isabelle spoke. "Did you see Sheriff Rix today?"

Lily held her breath. The sheriff was the one person

in town Lily would make sure she avoided at all costs.

"He was looking fine." Franny sighed.

Dorthea spoke. "I dare say that the two of you are too young for him. Trudy would be more to his liking and closer to his age."

Lily looked down at the sewing in her lap. The prying questions of the quilting ladies would be hard enough to avoid.

But the sheriff?

Her chest tightened, and her stomach rolled. She bit the inside of her cheek, wanting to flee but couldn't a second time. What would these ladies think? Her hands fumbled with the needle and fabrics, unable to make a decent stitch.

She closed her eyes and took a deep breath. Just focus on sewing, not the conversation. She couldn't change what happened in the past. A good future for Toby was all that mattered.

Edric stood outside Aunt Henny's gate. He had left his office early so he could stop by and check on Aunt Henny without Pa wondering why he was late.

The buggies and wagons the ladies had come in were all gone. It would be safe. He didn't want to be looked at like a side of beef.

He pushed through the gate and up the walk, then climbed the steps and raised his hand to knock. He paused. Through the screen at this angle, he had a view of the kitchen doorway. Wayne Tunstall leaned across that doorway, and Lily was a step or two on the inside, talking to him.

Edric's insides twisted. It had begun. The eligible men in town would be swarming Lily in no time. He had seen her first. That was a stupid thought. Like it gave him some sort of rights to her.

Pa's voice echoed in his head. *The girls don't need a mama. We are doing just fine.*

They were doing fine. He was fine. And his girls were happy. But...

Nothing wrong with you being interested in her. You are both widowed. Aunt Henny's voice this time.

Movement drew his attention. A few feet on the other side of the screen, Toby stood, staring up at him.

Edric squatted. "Good afternoon, Toby. Did you enjoy the milk?"

The boy nodded.

"Why don't you come out and sit with me?" Edric moved away from the door and sat on the top step, turning so he could see the door.

After a moment, Toby walked up to the screen and stared at him. Then he touched his nose to the wire mesh.

"Come on out." Edric patted the step.

Toby opened the screen a few inches and scooted halfway out. One leg and one arm still inside.

That was probably the most Edric could hope for right now. "I saw you in the yard playing with the other children today. Did you have fun?"

Toby nodded again.

For some reason, Edric was drawn to this boy. He wanted to help him. Help him not be so afraid. He reasoned it was because of his own young daughters. Besides, no child should be this afraid. Or maybe it was something more. "I have two little girls. Nancy is about your age. Maybe I'll bring them over for you to play with. Would you like that?"

Toby bit his bottom lip and nodded.

"How does tomorrow sound?"

The little boy's head continued to bob.

"After lunch?"

Toby shook his head this time. "Affer breffuss."

After breakfast? "I'll see if we can arrange that." This was encouraging. Maybe the boy was getting used to him.

Toby's gaze shot across the yard, and his eyes widened.

Edric turned to see Job Lumbard pushing through the gate and heard the screen door bang behind him. He glanced around. Toby was gone.

Edric stood and held out his hand. "Good afternoon, Job."

"Edric." The older man shook his hand. "I see you were talking to the boy."

"Trying to."

"I didn't mean to frighten him."

Edric swung his gaze to the door where Toby had been. "He'll come around."

"I don't know how someone so young can have that much fear coiled up inside him."

"He'll learn Kamola is a good place." Edric followed Job inside. He saw Toby sitting at the top of the stairs.

The boy watched with big, brown eyes.

Wayne still stood in the kitchen doorway.

Job set his satchel at the bottom of the stairs and entered the parlor. He went to Aunt Henny, and taking her hand, he kissed the back of it. "Henny, you are as lovely as ever."

"Thank you, Mr. Lumbard. I see you dragged in a stray." Aunt Henny winked at Edric.

He smiled. "It's good to see you too."

Job smiled too. "He was talking to the boy on the porch."

Aunt Henny raised her eyebrows. "Talking?"

Edric nodded. "Mostly he bobbed his head. But he did say two words to me."

"Really? That is progress."

Wayne walked over and shook Edric's hand. "Job and I are in your debt for finding Mrs. Lexington so we could return home. She's a wonderful cook and pleasant to look at to boot."

Edric bristled at the last statement. She was only recently widowed. But who was he to say whom she could and couldn't be interested in? He needed to make sure that when she was ready to start looking for a husband, he was in the running. He just wouldn't tell Pa what he was up to. At least not yet.

"Have a seat," Aunt Henny said.

Wayne and Job excused themselves to their rooms until supper.

Edric sat. "Toby would like me to bring the girls over tomorrow morning to play. If that's all right with you."

"That would be splendid. Bring Saul and stay for lunch."

"Pa would like that." This had been easier than he'd expected. He hoped Lily didn't mind. "He tried to visit you, but Mrs. Martin wouldn't let him in."

Toby darted through the room and into the kitchen, shooting a look at Edric as he passed. He must have bolted down the stairs when Wayne and Job went up.

Aunt Henny picked up the conversation as though Toby hadn't run by. "I was quite tired and in a great deal of pain those first few days. I appreciate Agnes looking out for me. I do hope Saul wasn't put out."

"I don't think so. He merely wanted to see that you were all right."

"Mr. Hammond," Lily said.

Edric shot to his feet, not having heard her enter the room. His hat tumbled to the floor. He scooped it up. "Good afternoon."

"Good afternoon. Are you staying for supper? I can set another place."

"No, thank you. Pa and my girls will have a fit if I'm not home to eat with them."

"Very well."

"But Aunt Henny has agreed to let my girls come over tomorrow to play with Toby."

"Girls?"

"My daughters, Estella and Nancy. Estella is seven and Nancy is Toby's age."

She stared at him a moment as though he'd said something strange. Did she not want her son to play with his daughters? Then she said, "Will your wife be coming as well?"

Enid? "My wife passed away two years ago."

"Oh. I thought..."

So that was what the strange look had been for. She thought he was married. "So it's all right for me to bring my girls over tomorrow to play?"

The tightness around her eyes and mouth loosened. Her face brightened. "Toby would like that."

"Good. We'll see you in the morning." He looked toward the kitchen, where Toby was peeking around the corner. Edric waggled his hat at the boy. "See you tomorrow."

Toby nodded.

"I'll walk you to the door," Lily said.

Edric stared at her a moment like a schoolboy, then remembered he should move in the right direction.

"Thank you for thinking of Toby," she said. "It will be good for him to have other children to play with. He sure enjoyed himself today."

"That's what he said."

Her blue eyes widened. "He spoke to you?"

"More or less. I asked him if he had fun, and he nodded. But he did speak actual words to me. I asked him if he'd like me to bring my girls over after lunch. And he said, 'After breakfast.'"

"I'm surprised."

Edric had been also. "I'll see you in the morning."

"I'm looking forward to meeting your daughters."

He looked forward to it too. He wanted his girls to meet her and Toby. He was eager to see how they would get along. But he mostly looked forward to spending time with Lily, to see if what he was feeling was real. Would it develop into genuine affections? Or when he was around her more and got to know her, would he find out she wasn't as wonderful as he imagined? Or that she wouldn't treat his girls with the same kindness she did Toby? That was what Pa believed. And the sooner he knew it, the better. Then he could return to life as normal. Just himself, his daughters, and Pa.

They were all doing just fine.

When he opened the gate to his yard, Estella and Nancy came flying out the front door and into his arms. He scooped them up.

Why was he even considering that Lily needed to treat his girls as she did Toby? They were happy with him and Pa. They didn't need a mother. He would not stir up their lives by bringing another woman into the household.

He went inside the house and into kitchen.

Pa stood at the stove, frying chicken. He pointed the spatula at the girls. "Go wash up."

Edric set his daughters down, and they ran out.

He tried to sound casual. "Aunt Henny has invited us over for a visit in the morning."

"I've been wanting to see how she was doing."

"I told her that. We're invited to stay for lunch. The girls can play with Toby."

Pa straightened and turned. "Wait a minute. This is about that widow woman, isn't it?"

Pa was smart... and protective of his granddaughters.

Edric cleared his throat. "Well, I would appreciate your take on her. I value your opinion."

"I can tell you right now my take. No woman will be good enough for our girls." Pa clamped a hand on Edric's shoulder. "Son, the girls are happy. Why do you want to upset things?"

"I guess I can't shake the idea that Estella and Nancy might need a mama." Why, all of a sudden, he thought his daughters needed a mother, he couldn't say.

"I don't wonder. They had a mama and don't need another one. You hardly know this woman. You just met her. Ask yourself why she traveled all this way by herself. Why didn't she stay put with people she knew? She could have a terrible past. Our girls don't need any more trouble in their lives. They've had enough for one lifetime."

Edric knew Pa wanted to say more. He wanted to say words against Edric's late wife. He had a whole pile of things he could say against Enid, every one of them accurate. Every little thing Enid did that tore this family apart and hurt the girls.

Enid had refused to let Edric's ma and pa visit or spend any time with the girls. She'd said that his folks were spoiling the girls and causing them to be ill-mannered. Ma and Pa only got glances of Estella and Nancy at church on Sundays. It broke Edric's heart to see his daughters unhappy and his folks cut off. He didn't know what to do. But his duty had been to his wife and children.

Enid hadn't always been so strict. She had been kind and loving until Estella was born. Then she became possessive and fearful. No one could give her advice on how to take care of the new baby. She thought everyone was trying to take Estella away from her. Then as Estella grew and Nancy came along, she was obsessed with the girls behaving properly at all times. She felt people would judge her an unfit mother if the girls were dirty or misbehaved in any way.

After Enid's death, plenty of eligible women in town had shown interest in him directly or by flirting. But none of them pulled at his heart the way Lily and her son did. Maybe because they were vulnerable? Or because Lily had a son and was proving to be a good mother? Or because she didn't seem so overtly interested in him and wasn't trying to catch him?

Or maybe because he'd suddenly found he might be lonely?

He had Pa and the girls, but a wife filled a different kind of place inside a man's heart. He'd liked being a husband. And for the first time since Enid's death, he wanted to be a husband again. Lily had reawakened that long buried need.

But Pa was right about one thing. The girls didn't need a mama. So, if he were to marry again, it would have to be either after the girls were older, or someone who could love them as her own. Either way, he would have to make sure any woman he was interested in knew that his daughters were his responsibility to raise. She would not have a say.

Then why get married? Was he being selfish?

Lord? Should I put this whole nonsense out of my head? Or is this yearning from You? Are You trying to tell me it is time to move on? Do the girls need a woman in their lives?

"You'll get to meet her tomorrow. If you sense anything's amiss with her. I won't pursue this any further. I respect your judgment."

"But will you respect my answer?"

Lily felt almost giddy as she readied Toby for bed. She couldn't stop thinking about Mr. Hammond returning tomorrow. And he wasn't married. She shouldn't be happy about that. He probably loved his late wife dearly. She should be thinking about Toby making friends. But she was selfish.

She pulled the covers up to Toby's chin. "Do you like Mr. Hammond?"

Toby wiggled his mouth back and forth, then shrugged.

Well, he didn't say no.

"Are you excited to have other children over tomorrow?"

He nodded. "I like playing with the kids today."

"You had fun, didn't you?"

"Lots and lots."

Toby hadn't had friends back in Philadelphia. His father hadn't allowed him to.

"You will have lots of friends here. Now go to sleep."

He closed his eyes.

Toby could afford to have friends, but could she? Dare she dream of a normal life without daily fear?

She couldn't quite imagine it.

Eight

EDRIC STOPPED ESTELLA AND NANCY OUTSIDE Aunt Henny's gate. "Let me see how you look."

His girls stood next to each other for inspection. They were clean and neat even with faded stains on their play dresses. He'd tried to get the stains out a number of times, but they proved permanent. "Maybe I should have dressed them in something else."

Pa shifted the crate with various fruits and vegetables in it and nodded toward the gate. "You girls run on up to the door and wait for us there."

The girls skipped away, Estella swinging the flour sack of blocks they'd brought.

Pa turned to him. "You're acting like Enid. The girls came to play. Not to be scrutinized. Any other clothes wouldn't allow them to get dirty. You worried this widow won't like Estella and Nancy because of how they're dressed? If this woman is making you so nervous, then she's not right for you or our girls." Pa stepped through the gate and joined his daughters on the porch.

Edric took a deep breath. Pa was right. If Lily didn't like his girls the way they were, then he shouldn't even be considering her. He jogged to catch up.

Estella tilted her head to look up at him. "Do I look pretty, Papa?"

Edric's heart sank. Estella had obviously picked up on his nervousness, and she was questioning her appearance. He squatted to look into her questioning face. "You look beautiful. Just like a princess."

Estella smiled.

Nancy pressed in. "Me too, Papa?"

"You too." He wrapped his arms around the girls' thighs and picked them up. "My two princesses." If Lily had any trouble with the way his daughters looked, then he would not think about her for one minute more.

Pa smiled at him and knocked.

After a moment, the door swung open. Toby glanced at him holding his girls. He shifted his gaze to Pa then darted away.

"Toby?" Aunt Henny said from within.

Edric stepped inside, and Pa followed.

Lily appeared, wiping her hands on a towel. "Please excuse my son. He's still learning manners."

Edric's heart picked up its beat at the sight of her. "He's young. Mrs. Lexington, this is my father, Saul Hammond."

Lily curtsied to Pa. "Pleased to meet you."

Pa nodded. "Nice to meet you as well."

"And these are my daughters, Estella and Nancy." He looked at each one in turn.

Lily made a curtsy. "Pleased to meet you, ladies."

Estella reached out her hand and touched Lily's pale hair. "You look like an angel."

"Thank you. You look like a princess." Lily turned to Nancy. "You must be a princess as well." She shifted to the side. "Aunt Henny's waiting in the parlor."

Edric set Estella and Nancy down.

Upon entering, Pa put the crate of produce down and went straight over to the settee. "Henny, how are you?"

"I'm good, Saul. It's good to see you. Have a seat."

Pa took the seat closest to Aunt Henny.

Lily disappeared into the kitchen and returned a moment later. "Toby must have gone upstairs."

Aunt Henny shook her head and pointed behind the settee.

Lily walked over to the end of the settee and held out her hand. "Come on, Toby. Company is here. They came to meet you."

Edric sat in a chair so he wouldn't look so big to the boy. Estella and Nancy stood next to him. Edric saw the small hand reach up from behind the settee and grab Lily's.

Toby stepped out and huddled tight against Lily's skirt.

"Toby, you know Mr. Hammond," Lily said. "This is

his papa. He is also Mr. Hammond. These are Mr. Hammond's two girls, Estella and Nancy. Say hello."

As the boy said hello, he turned his face into Lily's skirt and his greeting came out muffled.

His girls curtsied, and Estella said, "Pleased to meet you."

Nancy echoed.

The boy turned his head enough to look at the girls out of one eye. Then his gaze flickered to Pa, and he scuttled back behind the settee.

Lily opened her mouth, likely to call her son back out.

Waving her hand, Aunt Henny mouthed, "Let him be."

Nancy crawled across the floor and wiggled under the settee from the front. Soon she was whispering to Toby, and he whispered back.

Estella turned to Edric with questioning on her upturned face. She had been old enough to remember her mother's scolding reproach of such behavior.

"You can go."

If Lily thought his girls' behavior was abominable, then she was not the woman he'd thought she was.

Scurrying around the near end of the settee, Estella joined the whispering pair already in residence there.

"Why don't we go out on the porch?" Aunt Henny said.

Pa stood. "We brought lemons to make lemonade."

Lily's face brightened. "How wonderful. I can make it while you men get Aunt Henny situated on the porch."

Edric handed her the sack of lemons, and she disappeared into the kitchen. Then he followed like a shadow behind Pa helping Aunt Henny.

Once the older pair was settled, Edric said, "I'll go help Mrs. Lexington." He went inside and through the house to the kitchen. He could hear the children talking behind the settee.

Lily stood at the table with the lemons in a bowl, an empty pitcher, and a large knife.

"May I help?"

Startled, Lily dropped the knife on the floor and

jumped back to save her foot from being impaled. "I'm sorry."

"No problem." He retrieved the knife. He could see her breathing was heavy from the start. "I'm sorry for frightening you."

She stared at the knife in his hand. "I'm the one who is sorry."

Her tone sounded a bit like Toby's terrified one when he said he was sorry for dropping the milk.

He laid the knife on the table. "I am here to do your bidding."

She stared at him for a moment, a look of disbelief in her eyes.

"Honestly. I can halve the lemons or juice them."

She placed the juicer in front of him. "Thank you."

Lily struggled to steady her breathing. This man was not out to hurt her. She picked up the knife, shifted down the table to make room for him, and felt better about her holding the knife instead of him. She mentally traced the scar at her hairline.

Mr. Hammond made fast work of the lemons she cut, keeping up with her. In no time, the pitcher had enough lemon juice for the lemonade.

She mixed in cold well water and sugar.

Mr. Hammond poured three small glasses for the children while Lily put the pitcher and four taller glasses on a tray. He carried the tray out to the porch, where Aunt Henny and the elder Mr. Hammond sat in the two rocking chairs at one end. Lily and Mr. Hammond sat at the other end in matching chairs.

The children came out for their refreshment. Toby perched on the steps with Estella on one side of him and Nancy on the other. Mr. Hammond's girls seemed to like Toby, and he them. It warmed Lily's heart to see her son making friends.

Suddenly, Toby screamed and ran to her. He stood

on the side of her farthest away from Mr. Hammond.

Estella raced over to Mr. Hammond. "Papa, a snake! Catch it! Catch it!" The girl was obviously excited and not at all scared.

Lily doubted Toby had seen a snake before.

Mr. Hammond rose and went to where Nancy hopped up and down. "I think it's gone. It went home."

Pointing, Estella shrieked. "There it is, Papa!"

After a short chase, Mr. Hammond came up with a foot-long snake.

Estella stroked it as though it was fine silk fabric and giggled. Nancy followed suit and giggled as well.

The older girl turned to Toby. "Come pet the snake. He's nice."

Her son looked up at her.

Lily smiled uncertainly and nodded for him to go.

"It's just a little garter snake," Mr. Hammond said. "It won't hurt anyone."

Nancy plodded up the steps and grabbed Toby's hand. "He's soft. Come on." The little girl pulled Toby toward the snake.

He kept hold of Lily and pulled her along, off the porch, and into the yard where Mr. Hammond crouched.

The squirmy thing had an orange stripe down the center of its back and black and pale yellow along its sides. Its tongue flicked in and out.

Lily didn't mind if Toby petted the snake, but she had no intention of touching the thing and held back.

Nancy stroked the reptile stretched between her papa's hands. "Pet him. He's nice."

Toby looked up at her.

Estella stroked and stroked the striped back.

Toby pushed Lily closer. "You do it."

He wanted her to touch it?

"I don't want to pet it. But you can." Lily couldn't tell if he was afraid of the snake or the big man who held it.

"You."

Lily caught Mr. Hammond's gaze. He nodded.

She took a deep breath.

The snake's body wriggled a little, and it's flat head turned so that she could see the side of it. It looked as though the snake was smiling at her.

If a five-year-old little girl could pet it, certainly Lily could too. She took another deep breath and stretched out her hand.

Her heart sped up, and her breathing came in gulps. She wanted to pull back, but she knew Toby wanted her to touch the reptile first to know it was all right. If she felt it was safe enough for her small son to touch, certainly she could. She focused on keeping her hand from shaking.

The scaly body was cold and soft.

She forced herself to draw her hand back slowly and not jerk it away. "Your turn."

Stretching out his small hand, Toby petted the snake. A smile tugged at his mouth just enough to see the initial impression of his dimples.

It had been some time since she'd seen them. It did her heart good and was well worth the cost of touching a snake.

"Can I hold it, Papa?" Estella asked.

Mr. Hammond directed his daughter where to take hold of the reptile.

She grabbed it right behind the head. The snake wrapped its tail around her thin arm, and she giggled. "It tickles. You want to hold it, Nancy?"

Nancy shook her head.

Toby shook his too.

Mr. Hammond smiled. "It's time to let the snake go."

"But I want to keep him."

"You can't keep him. He needs to go home. He probably has a family."

"Can we see them, Papa?" Nancy hopped from foot to foot. "Can we?"

"Not today." He turned back to his oldest daughter. "Put him in the grass by this bush."

Nancy tugged on his sleeve. "What if he can't find his way home?"

"He can. He's a smart snake."

Estella crouched and opened her hand. The snake wriggled away. All three children gave chase until the snake disappeared under the porch.

Mr. Hammond offered his elbow to Lily.

She took a deep breath then hooked her hand around his arm.

He led her up the steps and to her chair. "That was brave of you." He sat back down.

"It was just a bitty snake." That had terrified her. Her insides still quivered.

Nancy ran up the steps and pulled open the screen door.

"Play outside, Nancy," Mr. Hammond said.

She spun to him. "Essie told me to get the sack of blocks." Then she disappeared into the house. She returned a moment later and dumped out the bag. The wooden pieces clattered to the porch. Estella and Toby joined her.

She held a wooden block out to Toby. "This is puzzles. It has pictures on it." She rotated her wrist back and forth in short jerks to show the sides. "You have to find all the ones that match and put the picture together."

Toby took the block, but Lily could tell he didn't really know what to do with it. Lily wanted to help him, but thought she should wait and see what he did.

Estella said, "Let's do the horse first."

Both girls started turning the cubes over in an array of blue sky, green grass, and brown hair. The girls quickly moved the twenty-five blocks around to form a horse standing in a field. A hole gaped in the middle.

Estella turned to Toby. "Put your block in."

Toby turned his piece over and over, looking at each side. Lily was about to help him when Nancy turned the block in his hand. "That way. Put it in." She pointed to the empty space.

Toby slid the block in place in the right direction.

Lily sighed in relief.

Nancy said to Toby, "Do you want to do the kittens or the sheep next?"

"Kittens."

After lunch, Edric held an empty pail. Estella and Nancy were supposed to be picking blackberries and filling the bucket in his hand. Instead, their berries went into Lily and Toby's basket.

Nancy plucked another half-ripe berry. She hadn't understood the difference between ripe and not quite ripe. She held the half-green berry out to Lily. "Is this a good one?"

Lily smiled. "It's wonderful. Put it in the basket."

It warmed his heart that she didn't scold or correct little Nancy. She could separate out the bitter ones before making the cobbler.

"Oh, no," Estella moaned. A large berry squished between her fingers, the juice running down her hand.

Instinctively, Edric lurched to protect his daughter from a scolding remark, how she hadn't been careful and to not get any on her dress.

"Oh my." Lily squatted next to his girl. "Do you know what this means?"

Estella shook her head.

Lily shrugged. "You have to eat it." When Estella hesitated, Lily plucked a berry, squished it, and popped it into her mouth, licking her fingers.

Estella put hers in her mouth and smiled.

"Mine won't squish," Nancy whined.

Lily took the green one and handed her a fat, black one.

Nancy grabbed it in her fist. Juice squeezed out between her fingers. Then she ate it off her palm.

"I don't want a squishy one," Toby said.

Lily held out a plump one. "Open your mouth." Toby did, and she popped it in.

After that, more blackberries went into mouths than the basket. Estella and Nancy's hands were stained with the juice.

What a fit Enid would have had. No, Enid wouldn't have let the girls go picking in the first place. Because it was unladylike, and they could get dirty. And dirty they got, with new stains on their play dresses. But they were laughing and having a good time.

If he was going to get cobbler, it was up to him to pick enough berries.

Later, as Edric and Pa walked home with Estella and Nancy skipping ahead, Edric turned to Pa. "What did you think of her?"

Pa didn't speak for several moments, then he sighed. "She touched a snake."

By Pa's tone, Edric couldn't tell if that was a negative comment or not. Enid certainly never would have gotten anywhere near a snake, let alone touch one.

"Your ma never touched a snake."

Edric mentally groaned. Pa hadn't liked Lily. "Ma didn't want to. Lily did it for her son."

"Your ma never would have touched a snake for you. She would have told you that snakes were nothing to play with."

In fact, Ma *had* told him that.

"Widow Lexington is a hard woman to dislike."

Edric's shoulders slumped. Then he straightened. Hard to *dis*like? He turned to Pa.

Pa smiled. "I see why she has captured your attention. She loves her son more than I thought a person could."

"She does."

"And she treated our girls kinder than some people treat their own kin."

"So you liked her."

Pa sighed. "Yes, I did. But that doesn't mean I think you should invite her into our lives. The girls are happy."

Edric smiled to himself. Pa had liked Lily. He knew Lily was different. "Did you see the way our girls were desperate for a woman's attention?" Estella and Nancy adored Lily.

"She's hiding something. She left all she knew to come

to an unknown town and live among strangers. Why? And until you know exactly what she's hiding and why she came here, don't risk breaking Estella's and Nancy's hearts."

Edric knew what she was hiding. Abuse. Why she had come? Probably needed a fresh start. He couldn't fault her for either of those.

Nine

SUNDAY MORNING, EDRIC DROVE HIS WAGON up to the white picket fence in front of Aunt Henny's. He set the brake and jumped out. "You girls stay in the wagon."

Estella and Nancy nodded.

Pa jumped down as well.

Lily answered the door. She wore the blue shirt and skirt from the other day. Her golden hair hung down to her waist in a messy braid. They would have a wait until she pinned her hair up. Though he enjoyed seeing it down. He hadn't realized how long it was.

Lily walked to the parlor doors. "Aunt Henny is ready."

Edric followed. "We'll help her into the wagon while you finish getting ready."

"I'm not going this morning. Toby was up sick during the night."

Disappointment swirled inside Edric. With a closer inspection, he noticed dark shadows under her eyes. She must have had a rough night.

Aunt Henny gave her a nod. "You go rest."

Mr. Tunstall came down the stairs. He spoke to Edric. "Do you need any help?"

Edric turned to the younger man. "Pa and I can get Aunt Henny into the buggy. But you are welcome to ride with us."

"I'd appreciate that."

Lily's voice sounded a little slow and tired. "Is Mr. Lumbard going with you as well?"

Mr. Tunstall cleared his throat. "He's under the weather this morning."

"I do hope he doesn't have what Toby has."

Mr. Tunstall glanced at Edric then back. "What ails Mr. Lumbard is nothing he caught. You needn't worry yourself over him. I'll check on him after church."

Edric knew that Mr. Lumbard suffered from an overindulgence of the spirits. He generally kept it in moderation during the week. But more often than not, on a Friday or Saturday night or both, he drank himself into a stupor. He wouldn't likely crawl out of his room until Monday morning.

Lily locked her door and slipped back into bed with Toby. He was finally sleeping peacefully.

She had been both relieved and disappointed about not going to church this morning. It had been years since she had attended. Tobias hadn't allowed her to go. And after what she had done, the Lord might strike her down if she set foot inside His house.

The following days fell into a pattern of Mr. Hammond bringing by milk each morning. Lily found she looked forward to Mr. Hammond's brief visits. Today was no different for her, but it was for Toby. He sat out on the front porch with his elbows propped on his knees and his chin in his hands. Waiting.

Hard to believe.

He had asked if the big man was bringing milk today.

Leaving her son at his post as lookout, Lily returned to the kitchen. She too wanted to sit and wait for Mr. Hammond but knew that would be improper.

Soon the screen door slammed, and Toby ran into the kitchen. "He's here! He's here!"

The excitement in her son's voice warmed her. "Don't make him stand on the porch, let him in."

Toby shook his head but didn't look scared. He had made a lot of progress in a week. Though she could tell he was excited about Mr. Hammond's visit, he wasn't ready to let "the big man" know. He couldn't quite believe a man, any man, wouldn't hurt him.

She wiped her hands on a towel and hurried to the door. Hopefully, Mr. Hammond had let himself in.

But he hadn't, because he was just opening the gate. Toby must have run inside at first sight of him.

The back of her skirt moved, and she turned to look. Toby was right at her hip. He looked expectantly as Mr. Hammond approached. He climbed the steps and Lily pushed open the screen door. Toby scooted around behind her. He wanted to be there yet was still afraid.

Mr. Hammond crouched and held out a bottle. "Here's your milk."

Toby reached from behind her and took the milk. He hugged the bottle to his chest and walked in long, slow strides to the kitchen.

Mr. Hammond smiled. "Good job."

Toby turned, and his lips quivered as though he might smile.

Lily stepped aside. "Won't you come in?"

Mr. Hammond stood. "I can't, but I would like to talk to you out here for a moment."

Not knowing what this could be about, she stepped outside. Her stomach tightened.

"My girls have been begging me to invite you and Toby over for supper."

Her insides relaxed. "We would like that."

"Tonight?"

"I'll have to check with Aunt Henny."

Through the open window, Aunt Henny said, "Go."

Mr. Hammond chuckled. "You are invited too, Aunt Henny."

"Lovely," the older woman called back.

"I'll bring my buggy by around six."

Aunt Henny made arrangements with Mr. Tunstall and Mr. Lumbard to supper at the White Hotel restaurant.

Lily smiled all day in anticipation of supper. She and Toby picked blackberries. Poor Mr. Hammond had wanted cobbler, but at the end of their harvesting the other day, they had only a cup and a half between the five of them. Today, she would bring him cobbler.

Toby helped her by pouring in the sugar and telling her what part of the bowl hadn't been stirred enough.

The cobbler came out of the oven, smelling sweet and

delicious. A knock sounded on the front door.

"He's here," Toby squealed.

"Why don't you go let him in?"

Her son pushed her toward the entry. Evidently, he still wasn't brave enough.

"I'm going." She untied her apron and shucked it off. She opened the door with Toby at her side.

Mr. Hammond removed his hat. "Howdy. You all about ready?"

She stepped back. "Yes, Aunt Henny's waiting in the parlor. I just need to get my shawl and something from the kitchen."

"Would it be the delectable smell that's making my mouth water?"

"It would. Toby, help Mr. Hammond with Aunt Henny." Lily headed for the kitchen.

Lily could hear Mr. Hammond and Aunt Henny coaxing Toby. She peeked out to see her son watching from the safety of the corner of the dining table. At least he'd stayed in proximity to the man.

The ride was short. The elder Mr. Hammond helped Aunt Henny down, and the girls clamored for Toby. Lily put her hands on Mr. Hammond's shoulders when he took her by the waist and lifted her down. He stared at her a moment before releasing her. Her cheeks warmed.

From the floor of the buggy, he took the crate with the cobbler wrapped in cloth. "You still aren't going to tell me what you made?"

"You will have to wait until after supper."

He had tried so hard to pick enough berries but gave in every time one of his girls wanted one. Hadn't even hesitated. He obviously loved his daughters very much. After supper, she had a treat for him.

The interior of the house had a woman's touch, with ruffled curtains, milk glass oil lamps, and doilies adorning any flat surface. Not so different from Aunt Henny's with Queen Anne style furnishings. But there was one masculine item, a large, leather chair. It didn't match anything else in the room. It stood in defiance to the femininity surrounding it.

Lily had barely stepped through the doorway when

Estella and Nancy each grabbed one of her hands. Estella smiled up at her. "Come see our room."

Nancy nodded. "Come see our room."

Toby grabbed onto the back of Lily's skirt, and Mr. Hammond chuckled as the girls pulled her upstairs.

Lily stepped into a room with heavy brocade drapes of hunter green. Even though they hung open, they seemed to stifle the light from the windows. The two beds also had the dark green on them. But there were refreshing splashes of pink and yellow that were at odds with the bed and window coverings.

Each girl brought her a china doll in a plain brown dress, telling her how their papa had gotten them for them before their mama died.

Nancy cradled her doll. "This is Dolly. Mama sayed we couldn't play with them and we had to be extra careful because they could break. But Papa lets us play with them." Nancy's doll had a missing hand, a crack across the face where she'd been glued back together, and the dress was a bit worn.

Lily turned to Estella. "What's your doll's name?"

"Rose. Because she has rosy cheeks." Estella gently set her doll on her bed against the pillow.

The girls showed her everything in the room from their toys and books to their clothes and shoes. They had everything little girls needed, and yet they gazed up at her as though she were an important person to be adored. She wasn't.

They were such sweet girls, desperate for attention. But she had seen how both of the Mr. Hammonds had doted on them, so it wasn't lack of attention. They must miss their mama.

She knelt and wrapped her arms around the two girls and squeezed them. "You have a lovely room."

Toby came over and leaned against her.

When the foursome went to leave the room, Mr. Hammond stood in the hallway, leaning against the wall, watching. He seemed pleased.

"Your girls have been showing me everything in their room."

Nancy held one of her hands and Estella the other.

Toby stood behind her.

Mr. Hammond's mouth shifted up in a satisfied smile. "I can see that."

His smile made her feel lighter somehow. Like all the troubles of her past were melted away, which she knew they weren't. His expression held a depth Lily couldn't comprehend. As though he were saying so much more than simply being happy but held a secret. She wasn't sure if that was good or not. It pleased her, but at the same time, it made her feel uneasy.

This man bemused her. Tangled her up inside. Or was it her own warring emotions that confounded her?

In the kitchen after supper, Edric dished up servings of blackberry cobbler while Pa poured coffee. Lily had set the dessert on the back of the stove to keep warm. Edric had to press his lips together to keep from drooling.

Five of them hadn't been able to pick enough berries. How had she? Probably because there weren't as many mouths to eat them. He was well pleased with her success. It had been a long time since he'd had cobbler of any kind.

He peeked out the doorway into the living area and sucked in a breath.

Lily sat in his oversized, cowhide chair. Squeezed on her lap were all three children. She had her arms around his daughter, holding a storybook out in front of Toby in the middle, reading. Toby twisted his head around to look at his mama and smiled. His cheeks dimpled deeply. So that was what he looked like when he smiled. He was a cute little fellow.

Nancy petted Lily's golden hair. Estella tentatively touched Lily's hair as well. He imagined it soft and silky.

Lily didn't look irritated at all at his girls pawing at her. She kept reading. In the pauses between sentences, she smiled at one girl or the other.

If he didn't know better, he would mistake his

daughters as hers. Enid certainly wouldn't have let the girls mess up her hair, and they were her own flesh and blood. She also never read to them or hugged. Or gave them much attention except to scold them.

Edric motioned to Pa. "Come look."

Pa stepped over and stared, silent for a long while. "I certainly hope she is all she appears to be. I don't want our girls' hearts broken." Pa could finally see what Edric saw.

He couldn't envision Lily ever hurting anyone, let alone two little girls who adored her.

His heart warmed to see Lily with the children. All of them happy.

Later, after he'd seen Aunt Henny, Lily, and Toby home, he carried his girls up to bed and tucked the bedcovers in around them. He caressed Estella's cheek. "I love you."

Estella said, "I love you too, Papa."

He touched Nancy's face. "I love you."

"I love you more than I do."

Edric smiled at Nancy's way of saying she loved someone more than she could express. He was a blessed man.

"Papa," Estella said. "Is Toby's mama going to be our new mama?"

His first response was to say yes, but he had no way of knowing. And he didn't want to get his daughters' hopes up with his wishful dreaming. "I don't know. Did you like her?"

Estella sighed. "Ever so much."

He turned to Nancy. "Did you like her?"

"More than I do."

He was pleased and surprised at Nancy's response, but not too surprised. She was obviously quite taken with Lily. As he was.

Then Nancy whispered soft as a breeze, "Papa?"

Edric leaned over his youngest. "What is it?"

"I think she's an angel."

Lily did look like an angel.

Nancy's eyes widened. "Will she have to go back to heaven with Mama and Granmama?"

"No, darling. She's not that kind of angel."

Satisfied, Nancy smiled and snuggled deeper into her pillow, evidently happy with that answer.

He kissed Nancy on the forehead then Estella. "Sweet dreams."

Ten

THE FOLLOWING WEEK, LILY ONCE AGAIN accepted Edric's
offer to walk her to the mercantile. This was the fourth
time he'd done so. Each offer after that first, he'd said he
could take her in his buggy and give her a ride home, but
she declined, enjoying the walk. Though she appreciated
his offer to escort her home, she would hate to take up
more of his day.

She had started thinking of him as Edric, but still
addressed him properly as Mr. Hammond. He had been
proper as well, but she expected it wouldn't be long
before he invited her to use his first name. Would she do
likewise and invite him to use hers?

Today turned out to be a little different from the
others when he'd escorted her. As she prepared to leave,
Toby motioned to her. She knelt.

He whispered in her ear. "I go?" Then he eyed Edric.

There was no need for him to go, but she couldn't
turn him down. He was telling her he was brave enough
to walk near Edric.

"Of course." She stood. "Toby would like to go."

Edric smiled at her son. "I'm glad you're coming."

Toby's eyes lighted as though he wanted to smile but
didn't. Instead, he chewed on his bottom lip.

He stayed on the side of her opposite Edric and held
her hand. He peeked around her at the big man. Edric
smiled at him but kept talking. Soon Toby was hopping,
which pulled on Lily's arm, but she didn't stop him.

At the mercantile, Edric said good day and led his
black horse off across the street. Toby waved at the
man's back. Though Edric hadn't seen it, Lily had. She
would tell him about it the next time she saw him.

Lily opened the door for Toby, and they entered. The
store teemed with people this morning, most of whom

Lily had never seen before. The bustle of people tightened her insides. But why? She had met many of Kamola's residents and had become comfortable with them. Was it because she didn't know these people and any one of them could be like Tobias Bremmer?

She grabbed Toby's hand and moved to an empty corner of the store. Closing her eyes, she took several deep breaths. No one here was going to hurt her. She was safe. Toby was safe. With another deep breath, she opened her eyes.

Toby stared up at her with a worried expression. He'd obviously sensed her distress, which had been silly and based on nothing at all.

She squeezed his hand. "I'm fine."

He didn't look convinced with his bottom lip poking out. He popped his thumb into his mouth and leaned into her side.

Her poor baby. Kneeling, she hugged him and offered a bright smile. "Do you want to hold the basket for me?"

He straightened and nodded.

She held out the basket, knowing he would have to stop sucking his thumb. And he did, clutching the basket with both hands.

A good many of the shoppers paid and cleared out of the store. There were still a couple of people when Lily approached the counter.

Franny smiled. "Good morning." She took the items out of Lily's basket and tallied them on a slip of paper. The whole time her smile seemed to grow. Something had Franny in a good mood.

Lily couldn't help but smile in return. "You look like a debutante with a new dress."

"Me?"

"You've been smiling the whole time you've been tallying my order."

"I'm smiling for you."

"Me?"

Franny nodded. "You and Edric Hammond."

Lily's cheeks warmed.

Franny went on. "We were wondering if Sheriff Rix would ever take interest in another woman."

Lily's stomach tightened at the mention of the sheriff and mentally shook her head. Franny had changed subjects awfully fast. "What?"

"Don't play innocent."

Franny had totally confused her. "I don't..." Nausea seeped up inside her. It had to be something she ate.

Franny put her hand on Lily's. "I didn't mean to upset you. I know it's probably too soon for you to be courting. You haven't been widowed that long. He's a very nice man. You could do a lot worse than Sheriff Rix. There are plenty of women who would love to be the next Mrs. Hammond."

Sheriff Rix? Edric?

She took several shallow breaths.

Edric? The sheriff?

It couldn't be. No. She must have heard wrong.

Her chest tightened. She struggled to draw in breath.

"Lily, you look terrible. Are you all right?"

No. She was not all right. With shaking hands, she replaced her items into the basket one at a time. She snatched up a spool of thread with one hand and a bottle of witch hazel with the other. The spool caught on the edge of the basket and tumbled to the floor.

"Let me get that." Franny scooped it up and put it into the basket. "Are you—"

"Put all this on Aunt Henny's bill. Thank you. Good day." Grabbing the basket, she motioned Toby toward the door. She didn't want to engage in any more conversation. She needed to get out of there. Needed to run.

Stepping outside, she drew in the deepest breath her lungs would allow. It was still insufficient.

Toby stepped to the edge of the boardwalk and pointed. "Sheriff."

Lily jerked her head up and looked across the street. Her head felt light and dizzy. She reached out a hand and leaned on the building.

Edric stood in front of the sheriff's office two buildings down. He smiled and tipped his hat. The sun glinted off the tin star on his shirt.

Lily grabbed her son's hand and hurried down the

boardwalk. How could she have not seen the sheriff's office across the street before? How could she have been so ignorant? Why hadn't she asked him or Aunt Henny what he did? Had she chosen to be blind to it? Of all the men in this town, why did she have to meet him first thing? How could she have allowed herself to become attracted to the sheriff of all people? Why hadn't she seen his star before? Had he been hiding it from her?

"Mommy?"

Lily turned to her son. He was running to keep up with her quick stride. She hadn't realized she was walking so fast. She slowed to a strolling pace. It wouldn't be prudent to draw attention to herself. "I'm sorry."

Toby held up his arms. "Carry me."

He could feel her distress and wanted to be comforted in her arms.

She stopped and took a deep breath, closing off her emotions. Hide them deep inside. She had learned well under Tobias how to push away her feelings. With another calming breath, she was in control once again. She crouched. "I can't carry you and the basket. You're a big boy and can walk, can't you?"

"I want to be carried."

"I know you do. How about if we sing a song?"

He nodded and chose Skip to My Lou.

Walking again, Toby swung her arm with his as he sang, the distress forgotten. She had to remember to control herself better for her son's sake.

When he reached the verse about painting a red wagon blue, he broke off to ask, "Can I have a red wagon now that it is just us and Him is gone?" He often referred to his father as "Him."

"Of course."

"Do I have to paint it blue?"

"No. You can paint it any color you want."

"I want red." He returned to singing that verse, more loudly than before.

Lily returned to securing her emotions.

Edric stared down the street after Lily and Toby, torn by what he should do. Her behavior had been strange, how she hurried off like that. He wanted to go after her to make sure she and the boy were all right.

But the incoming train's whistle blew, and he had a job to attend to. He would stop by Aunt Henny's on his way home to check on Lily.

With one deputy already patrolling town and another one coming on duty this afternoon, he left his office and strode to the train station, arriving as the passengers were disembarking. He watched a man of average height and build with medium-brown hair sticking out from under his hat and a set of saddlebags hung over his shoulder, but no distinguishing features.

The man left the platform.

Edric was about to follow him when another average-sized man with brown hair exited the coach. Much like the first man.

The second man waited for something to be unloaded from the baggage compartment. While he waited, a third man of the same general description joined the other passengers waiting for luggage. He too had saddlebags. But this man had a pockmarked face that rendered him hard to look at.

Edric would keep an eye on all three of these average, brown-haired men.

The second man picked up a leather traveling bag, and Pockmarked picked up a studded saddle and heaved it over his shoulder by the horn.

He followed these two as they left the platform. Pockmarked headed for the saloon while the other man headed for the hotel. The first man was nowhere in sight. Edric would locate him later.

The man at the saloon wouldn't likely be going anywhere soon, so Edric headed to the hotel. He entered after the man with the traveling bag went up the stairs.

Behind the counter, Grant nodded a greeting and

spun the register book around to face Edric. "Howdy, Sheriff."

"Howdy, Grant."

The clerk pointed. "His name's Hal Jenson, from Virginia. He's looking for his brother who came out west years ago."

Could be true. But Edric would keep an eye on him. "Grant, you're making my job too easy."

"I reckon you're on the lookout for someone. We don't want any trouble at the hotel. If I suspect anyone of shady dealings, I'll let you know."

Edric rapped his knuckles on the counter. "I'd appreciate that." He headed for the saloon.

Pushing through the swinging doors, he saw Pockmarked right away in the back corner. Edric sidled up to the bar.

The barkeep joined him, wiping down the mahogany surface. "I know better than to ask if you want a whiskey, but I do have sarsaparilla."

"No, thanks, Nelson." Edric watched Pockmarked in the mirror behind the bar.

"I know you, Rix. You only come in here if you have a reason."

Rix was a nickname he'd been given several years back when he'd hired on as sheriff. The town counsel had thought it sounded more sheriff-like than Sheriff Edric.

He angled his head toward the mirror. "What's your take on the cowboy in the corner with the saddle?"

Nelson looked that direction. "The one with the unfortunate face? He's looking for work. I gave him the name of a few ranchers who might be hiring."

"Think he's on the up and up?"

"He not the one who concerns me. It's the fellow by the stairs who's likely to be trouble."

Edric shifted his gaze in the mirror but couldn't see the area by the stairs from this angle, so he turned around.

He saw the first man off the train, the one who had disappeared before he could follow him. The man's expression held hostility. He grabbed one of the saloon girls' wrist and pulled her toward him. Though startled, she giggled.

"You expecting trouble from someone?"

"Not sure." None of these men had done a thing suspicious except arrive in town by themselves. Was he following false trails?

Nelson poured a sarsaparilla. "If you intend to hang around here, you'll look less obvious if you're holding a glass."

Edric gripped the sweet drink. "Thanks. I think I'll stay for a bit."

The first man landed in Edric's jail before the hour was up for roughing up one of Nelson's girls.

While Edric had been dealing with the unruly man, Pockmarked had left, presumably to a surrounding ranch. Edric would look into where he ended up and what kind of worker he was.

Henny stroked Miss Tibbins's soft fur. The cat lay curled on her lap.

Toby sat on the floor working the block puzzle. He seemed determined to get as proficient as Edric's girls, but he didn't appear to have the same knack for it.

Lily came in to retrieve her teacup.

The girl looked positively pale. Not that she ever had much color. Her blond hair and blue eyes were such a contrast to Toby's dark hair and brown eyes.

Henny touched Lily's hand. "You don't look well. Maybe you should rest."

"I'm fine." Lily smiled, but Henny could tell it was forced. Lily glanced out the window. Her smile fell. "I do have a headache. I think I'll rest a bit." Lily dashed off up the stairs.

Henny looked out the window and saw Edric coming up her walk. She glanced toward the stairs. "Hmm."

Edric climbed the stairs and knocked.

Toby's eyes rounded, and his gaze darted between

Henny and the entry. Evidently perplexed.

"Would you open the door for Mr. Hammond?"

Toby hesitated before going to open the door, then he darted into the kitchen.

Henny did hate not being able to get around. "Come in, Edric."

She heard the faint creak of the screen, then Edric stepped into the parlor.

He glanced around the room and settled his gaze on Toby peeking out from the kitchen. "Where's Mrs. Lexington?"

"She has a headache and went to rest."

"Has she had a headache all day?"

"She only mentioned it a moment ago. But she has looked pale since this morning."

"I thought something might be wrong. She dashed off after the mercantile."

Something was wrong all right, but Henny suspected it was more than a headache. The young woman had a fear from her past chasing her and seemed afraid of her own shadow at times. Though she worked hard, Henny would guess she hadn't always been a maid and cook.

"Three men got off the train today that I'm keeping an eye on. One's already in jail."

"Oh, dear. Do you think he might come after Lily and her son?"

"My guess is no. He just seems like the angry sort who causes trouble wherever he goes. But I'm going to watch him and the other two while they're in town."

Henny sure appreciated Edric looking out for Lily and the boy. She felt trouble in her bones.

Trouble coming for the pair.

Eleven

LILY'S HANDS SHOOK AS SHE PULLED the thread through her quilt block. She had cut all the fabrics and sewn nearly half the needed blocks for her sunshine and shadows quilt. The other ladies around the circle chattered about this and that. Lily wasn't listening. It took all her concentration to keep the needle going in and out, and *not* run from the room.

Where was Toby? Was he still safe? She didn't like him being out of her sight.

Someone touched Lily's arm. She jumped, letting out a small screech.

"I'm sorry," said Trudy. "I didn't mean to scare you."

Lily's breathing came in short gasps. "I'm sorry. I was thinking about other things."

"Isabelle asked if you would like some of her pink calico."

Lily glanced across the circle at Isabelle holding out a sizable piece of fabric. Lily stood. As she did, she lifted her block from her lap. Her skirt front came with it.

Adelaide, Isabelle's younger sister, giggled.

"I have lost count of the number of times I have done that," Aunt Henny said.

Lily's face heated. She obviously hadn't been paying as close attention to the task at hand as she had thought she was. She gripped her skirt in her free hand and yanked the two apart, breaking the thread. She took the offered fabric with her thanks and put it on her chair with the ruined block then walked out.

Once through the kitchen, she stepped onto the back porch.

Toby ran around the yard with the other children.

She sucked air in, finally able to take a full breath.

He was safe.

For now.

But for how long?

Should they move to another town? But it too would have a sheriff. Or at least concerned people who might want to know about her past. She would be more careful next time.

Or could she go someplace without people? But then how would she provide for Toby? It would hurt Aunt Henny's feelings if she just left. It would hurt her own feelings too. She liked Aunt Henny a lot, and Kamola too. She'd felt at home here from the start. Maybe for the first time since her parents had died.

Lily felt coldness on her cheek and touched it. Tears glistened on her fingertips.

What was wrong with her? She never had this much trouble before. She had to gain control of her emotions. If she didn't, she and Toby would never be safe.

The screen door creaked behind her. She heard Aunt Henny's crutches thump the wood boards.

"Don't worry about sewing the block to your skirt. I think we've all done that. Except for maybe Agnes and Marguerite."

When Lily turned, Aunt Henny sucked in a breath. "It's not worth crying over." She wiped Lily's cheek with gentle fingers.

"It's not the quilt block. Sometimes I simply need to lay my eyes on him."

"I understand. He's a good boy."

"A very good boy." It would break her heart if something bad happened to him.

"If you ever want to talk about anything, I will listen."

"Thank you." But Lily knew she wouldn't be talking to Aunt Henny or anyone else about all that troubled her.

She was alone.

Edric couldn't understand Lily's strange behavior. Last

week, when she'd come out of Waldon's Mercantile, she hadn't smiled or waved back when he'd tipped his hat to her. She'd hurried off as though a demon chased her, and he hadn't seen her since. She seemed to be avoiding him. Or was he overly suspicious due to his job?

Today, he would talk to her one way or another and put his fears to rest, even if it meant he was late for supper, and Pa questioned him. He knocked on Aunt Henny's door.

To his disappointment, Toby came. The boy stepped back. His way of invitation.

Edric opened the screen and entered. If Lily wasn't in the kitchen or somewhere else to be found, he would stay until she appeared, and he could talk to her.

Toby ran in and stood near Aunt Henny, who sat reclined on the settee as usual. Her cat lay curled on her lap.

He couldn't hear any noise from the kitchen. "Is Mrs. Lexington cooking?"

"I heard the back screen. She must have run out to the privy."

Run from him was more like it. "Toby, can you go find your mama?"

Toby nodded and dashed out of the room.

Edric turned to Aunt Henny. "She's avoiding me. Do you know why?"

"She's not avoiding you. I think timing has been bad of late. When you leave, she asks if you were here and is sorry she missed you."

"She's been conveniently absent whenever I stop by, both morning and afternoon." He could understand missing her on one or two occasions, but a whole week, twice a day? "If I've done something, I want to fix it."

"I'm sure you haven't done anything."

Aunt Henny was wrong. He had done something to upset Lily. But what?

"I don't think she's been feeling well the past several days." Aunt Henny paused as though she wasn't sure if she should say any more, but she continued. "I've been wondering if she might... be with child."

That hit Edric all wrong. "What? How can that be?"

"She hasn't been widowed that long."

He wasn't sure how he felt about her possibly being pregnant. Protective for sure. But he didn't like the idea of her carrying the baby of a man who had hurt her and Toby. She shouldn't have to deal with that. He didn't want to deal with that.

"Have any more strangers come to town?"

Edric focused back on Aunt Henny. "Every day." It was a challenge to keep up with them all. He hadn't realized how many people arrived each day. "On most trains. And the stages. People in wagons and on horseback. But no one I have found overly suspicious."

"Keep a lookout."

"I will." He would make sure Lily and her son were safe. As long as they were in his town, he wouldn't let anyone harm them.

Edric waited for Lily to return until even Aunt Henny kept glancing at the kitchen doorway with suspicion. "She's not coming back in until I leave."

"Be patient with her. You are an imposing man. She is newly widowed."

"I realize her loss is recent." And if she were pregnant, that would only compound things. "I haven't done anything to pressure her. Something changed last week. I want to know what."

"And you won't stop until you do?"

He needed to know. He stood.

"You're leaving? I'm sure she'll be right in."

Toby poked his head around the kitchen doorway for the third time.

Edric suspected the boy was checking to see if he were still there and reporting to his mama. He pointed his hat at Toby. "I'll see you tomorrow." He turned to Aunt Henny. "She won't be back in. She's avoiding me."

"I'll talk to her."

He gave a nod and left. He was the one who needed to talk to her. Rounding the house, he waited at the corner.

Toby ran from the outhouse and in through the kitchen door.

A minute or so later, Lily exited the outhouse. She

smoothed her hands down her green plaid skirt, straightened her shoulders, and strode toward the house.

Hiding in the outhouse was a good way to insure he would not come looking for her.

When she had almost reached the porch steps, he cleared his throat. "You're avoiding me."

She faltered in her stride and turned, losing her balance. Her arms flew out, and she righted herself, staring at him.

He stepped away from the corner of the house. "I just want to know why you're avoiding me."

"I—" Her gaze darted back and forth. "It's not... I'm sorry."

He trod across the dry grass to the porch. "What did I do last week to upset you?"

She looked downright terrified of him.

"It's not you. I'm just..."

He knew what she wanted to say. "You are too recently widowed. You are not ready to begin thinking about courting." And she could be pregnant. "Last week, you suddenly realized that my visits might be construed as courting." And most men wouldn't be interested in a woman carrying another man's child. He wasn't most men. He felt more protective of her because of it.

She took a deep breath as though contemplating his words, and her expression changed slightly from fearful to demure. "It's barely been a month since my husband's death."

"I would never push you into courting or presume you've finished grieving for your husband."

Lily struggled not to burst out laughing. Grieve Tobias? She was relieved to be free of him. But the excuse of mourning her late husband had kept the quilting ladies from asking prying questions.

Edric continued, "I want to be your friend... for now. But I won't lie to you. When you are done with your mourning period, I hope you will look favorably upon me."

Look favorably upon him? That was the problem. He was quite favorable. He'd managed to get Toby to start trusting him a little. But with him being sheriff, she needed to stay far away from him. "I don't see your sheriff's star."

He glanced down at where she'd seen it last week. "I leave it at the office. I put it on in the morning when I arrive and take it off before I go home."

She tilted her head. So that was why she had never seen him wearing it. He hadn't been hiding it. "Why don't you wear it all the time so people always know you're the sheriff?"

"During the day, I'm the sheriff. The rest of the time I'm just a papa. And I have deputies. They'll come get me if I'm needed."

Just a papa. How sweet. He was a very good papa. His girls were fortunate.

He shifted his feet. "Can we still be friends?"

She was being foolish. Wherever she went, there would be a sheriff. She couldn't avoid all people. And wouldn't it be better to live in a town with a sheriff who was kind and trying to befriend her son, rather than one with a mean sheriff? A sheriff who might look into her past and use it for his gain?

"Friends."

Edric smiled. "I promise to mind my manners and not step over the lines of propriety."

Had Tobias Bremmer been half as considerate, he would have given her time to mourn her parents. Then she might have seen him for the cruel man he was and never married him. She'd believed his lies that she needed him to take care of her.

Was Edric also showing her only the side of himself he knew she wanted to see? Capable of taking care of her and Toby. She pictured him with his girls and knew he was the kind person he portrayed himself as. He was a good father and a good man.

But would that stop a sheriff from digging into her past?

Having two girls would make him more likely to want to find out all he could about her.

But if they remained only friends, he would have no need to.

Twelve

TWO DAYS LATER, EDRIC KNEW SOMETHING was wrong the moment he stepped over the threshold of his house. There was no aroma in the air of supper cooking. Pa always had supper going, if not done by the time he got home. And his girls were nowhere to be seen or heard.

Terribly wrong.

He rushed into the next room, fearing he might find Pa on the floor near the stove. The kitchen stood empty. He pushed through the kitchen door leading outside. The yard was empty too. "Pa!" Had something happened to one of the girls, and Pa'd had to leave the house with them? He ran back inside. "Pa!" He heard excited voices on the stairs.

His daughters' voices. And Pa's. They all sounded happy.

He raced to the foot of the stairs to see the trio descending. "What's wrong?"

Pa furrowed his brows. "Nothing's wrong. What makes you think something's wrong?"

"Supper's not going, and I couldn't hear anyone in the house."

Estella reached the bottom first and held the skirt of her dress out on both sides. "Do I look pretty, Papa?"

Nancy held her skirt out as well. "Me too?"

"Both of you are lovely." Edric gazed up at Pa, looking for an explanation.

"Henny invited us to supper."

"What? And you said we'd go?" He'd promised Lily not to push her. She could misinterpret this as him inserting himself into her life. He'd planned to stay clear of her for a while, so she would know he was a man of his word. How could he do that if he was sitting at the same supper table with her? "Girls, go wait on the porch for Granpapa and me to hitch up the wagon."

The girls skipped out the front, while he and Pa headed out the back.

Edric turned to Pa. "I wish you would have consulted me first."

"I thought you'd be happy to spend time with the Widow Lexington."

He would.

He didn't suppose he could get out of this. This would have to be fine. He would try to use this unfortunate opportunity to prove to her that he could be around her and simply be her friend. She had nothing to fear from him.

But as soon as he walked in Aunt Henny's and saw the anguish on her face and her hunched shoulders, he realized the depth of her concern. What he didn't fully understand was why so much anxiety over it? He would never hurt her or Toby.

He dipped his head to her from where she stood in the kitchen. Then he sat with his back to the doorway and talked with Wayne Tunstall and Job Lumbard.

Not too long after arriving, Edric watched as Aunt Henny fussed over where everyone was to sit at the table. The first arrangement had Toby and Lily seated to Aunt Henny's right with Edric beside Lily. He wouldn't have minded if not for his promise. But his girls protested, each wanting to sit next to Toby. Aunt Henny tried her best to seat Edric next to Lily.

In the end, Aunt Henny took her usual place at the head of the table with Pa on one side of the table with their little girls, and Edric at the opposite end from Aunt Henny. Lily sat couched between Aunt Henny and the boarders with Toby on her lap. All the commotion of figuring the seating arrangements had been too much for the boy, and he clung to his mama.

This vantage point was better than sitting next to Lily. He could steal glances at her when she wasn't paying attention, since he had to look down the table in that direction anyway. Though he didn't particularly care for Wayne to be seated next her.

Aunt Henny turned to Pa. "Will you say grace?"

Everyone closed their eyes and bowed their heads, except Job Lumbard. Lily was slow in lowering her head, but she did.

After grace, the serving dishes went around the table. Edric stole glances at Lily. She had yet to attend church since arriving in town, and she'd seemed reluctant to bow her head for the blessing. His insides tightened uneasily. Did she have a relationship with the Lord? He had assumed so but had never asked. And had no evidence that she did, other than her gentle nature and kindness. But that was no proof.

Lily thanked Mr. Tunstall each time he held a serving dish for her to spoon out of.

He whispered, "My pleasure," before passing each one on.

She smiled and glanced up to see Edric frowning at Mr. Tunstall. Edric turned away when Nancy pulled on his sleeve. True to his word, Edric hadn't sought her out this evening. He appeared to be avoiding her, which suited her fine. She certainly didn't need a sheriff taking such an interest.

Any more than he already had.

She struggled to dish up food, cut Toby's, and try to eat, all with her son firmly planted on her lap. When she had learned that Edric and his family were invited to supper, she had offered to have her and Toby eat in the kitchen. Aunt Henny would hear none of it.

The conversation turned to religion.

Lily did not want to talk about God. She shifted her son to the other side of her lap to partially block her from most of the table guests. She did her best to appear as though she were not paying attention to the conversation, but she heard every word. And cowered inside.

Toby wiggled and squirmed to get back to the other side of her lap then glared at Mr. Tunstall seated next to them.

She would focus on her son. Pretend she needed to feed him. Something she normally tried not to do. Stabbing a piece of chicken with his fork, she held it in front of his mouth. He pulled it off with his teeth then laid his head against her while he chewed. She took a bite of her own food. Just having it on her tongue made her feel like gagging. She struggled against the impulse and swallowed hard, hoping her stomach wouldn't rebel.

"If you'll excuse me." Mr. Lumbard pushed back from the table. "I've had about as much religion as I can stomach for one meal."

She knew exactly how he felt.

"Mrs. Lexington, everything was delicious." He marched through the kitchen and out the back door.

Oh, she wished she could excuse herself as well, but she supposed that would be a little too obvious, and everyone would want to know why.

The elder Mr. Hammond stared across the table at her and pinned her with his gaze. "What do you think, Mrs. Lexington? Is God kind and just in all His actions? Or is He cruel and uncaring?"

Lily sucked in a breath. Though she knew the right answer, she didn't feel it anymore and didn't want to talk about God.

What had God ever done for her? Growing up, she had faithfully gone to church. Loved God. Believed all His promises. Then He took her parents and ignored the abuse her husband dished out on a regular basis. And where had God been when her son was nearly killed? He had been absent. He had been neither kind nor just. He had left her to fend for herself and Toby. He didn't care.

She wanted to flee. Should she answer how she truly felt or give the answer everyone expected?

Edric spoke up. "Even when God is kind and just, it can appear as though He is cruel and uncaring. 'For my thoughts are not your thoughts, neither are your ways my ways, saith the LORD. For as the heavens are higher than the earth, so are my ways higher than your ways, and my thoughts than your thoughts.' We can't see everything as God can. He does know best. If that were not true, why believe at all?"

Lily had looked up as Edric spoke, his voice becoming more resolute with each word. She had thought he'd been scolding her, but he was staring at his father.

The elder Mr. Hammond gave a slight nod and took a swig of coffee.

"Lily, dear." Aunt Henny inclined her head. "I think we might be ready for dessert."

Lily eagerly excused herself, carrying Toby on her hip and their two stacked plates in her other hand.

Later, Edric watched as Nancy folded herself into a heap on Aunt Henny's floor. He shook his head. Should he make her get up? Or let her be?

She whimpered like a lost kitten.

Estella stepped between him and his view of his youngest daughter. "I'm being good, Papa." Her wide eyes begged for approval.

He pulled Estella in and hugged her. "Yes, you are being good." The girls sensed the tension between him and Pa. They had always been sensitive to tension between him and Enid, which rose frequently in the last year before she passed. They fussed and cried more. He shifted his gaze to Aunt Henny. "I think we should be going. The girls are tired." He held a hand out to Nancy. "Come here, darling."

Nancy looked up with her bottom lip jutting out and came to him.

He hugged her too. Gripping his daughters firmly, he stood. "Thank you for everything." Then he called to the kitchen. "Mrs. Lexington, supper was delicious. Thank you."

Mother and son came to the doorway. Lily said, "You're welcome. I'm glad you liked it."

Edric smiled at Toby. "I'll see you in the morning."

Toby nodded.

It pleased Edric that Toby responded to him even after all the upheaval this evening.

Pa held the door open for Edric, and the four of them stepped out into the cool night air.

"Would you like me to carry one of them?" Pa asked.

"I've got them."

Estella clung to him with her head on his shoulder, while Nancy continued to whimper.

Halfway home, Pa spoke in a low voice. "I'm sorry."

Edric didn't reply. He hadn't been this irate with Pa since he was twelve and his dog had been bitten by a rabid raccoon. Pa had tried to explain to him the necessity of putting Baxter down before he got sick and suffered in pain. Edric had run off and hadn't spoken to Pa for over a week.

When they arrived home, Pa said, "Why don't you girls go up and get ready for bed? We'll be up in a minute to tuck you in."

Both girls' grips tightened.

"I'll take them." Edric marched up the stairs to the girls' room. As he dropped them on the near bed, the springs creaked.

Shaken out of their sour moods, they both giggled as they bounced.

Edric smiled as well. "That's my girls." He helped them get ready for bed and tucked them in. Then he went downstairs where Pa waited for him.

Pa stood from the settee. "Can we talk about this?"

"The barn." Edric strode out. The girls didn't need to overhear them and get upset again.

Once in the barn, Edric waited for Pa to start.

Pa took a deep breath. "I'm sorry."

"How could you put her on the spot like that?"

"She hasn't been to church since she arrived in town. I thought you'd want to know how she stands with the Almighty."

"I do. But not like that. She's a shy person. Did you have to do it in front of everyone? I told you what she's been through."

"She's hiding something. I don't want our girls to get hurt by her."

"I would never let anyone harm them. You know that."

"Love can be blind and do foolish things."

Edric glared at Pa for insinuating he would do something foolish that would harm his daughters.

Pa looked contrite. "I promise never to do anything like that again. I'm sorry."

"I'm not the one you need to apologize to."

"You're right. I will." When Edric didn't respond, Pa continued. "Would you like me to go back over tonight? Or can it wait until tomorrow?"

"Tomorrow's fine." Lily was likely putting Toby to bed anyway. "How do we stop living in fear like this, that someone will hurt our girls again?"

Pa shook his head. "I don't know. I guess my love for my granddaughters makes *me* a bit foolish now and then."

Aunt Henny continued to stare out the window long after her guests had bade her good night. This evening hadn't gone exactly as planned. Toby had been frightened. Mr. Lumbard had left in a huff and not returned yet, missing the wonderful apple pie Lily had made.

Lily had been put on the spot. Aunt Henny hadn't known the poor girl's face could become any paler than it naturally was. Then she had hidden in the kitchen the remainder of the evening.

And the tension between Saul and Edric had been almost insufferable. Which caused Estella and Nancy to act up, ending with Nancy lying on the floor in a whimpering heap.

The only one who seemed to have been unaffected by the evening's events was Mr. Tunstall. Not that he had been oblivious to what was going on, he just didn't have a personal stake in any of it. He'd tried his best to help with smoothing things over, but the damage had been done.

Lily shuffled around in the kitchen, finishing up her work. When it was completed, she and Toby came into the parlor. "If you don't need anything, we'll go up to bed."

"There is one thing. Have a seat."

A concerned expression settled on the girl's face as she sat. "Yes."

"I am sorry so many of us frightened Toby. I should have let you decide where the two of you would sit."

"That's all right." Lily shifted forward to stand.

"Please stay."

Lily settled back.

Aunt Henny hesitated before speaking. "I noticed you were quite uncomfortable when Saul asked you about God. And you have managed to avoid going to church since arriving. I thought it had to do with your son being afraid of all the strangers who would be there. But after tonight, I think it may be more."

The girl paled again.

"It's all right." Aunt Henny tried to get Lily to look at her, but the girl seemed too afraid. "When I first saw you, the Lord told me to look after you. If you don't believe in God, I'm not going to throw you out."

After a moment, Lily spoke. "I do believe in God. We don't... I just..." She took a deep, slow breath. "My husband wouldn't allow us to attend church."

"Your husband wasn't a kind man, was he?"

Lily's eyes widened.

"I saw the bruises when you first arrived."

The girl rubbed her arms. Whether it was from the memories of the injuries or a self-conscious action, Henny couldn't tell. "Give the Lord a chance to heal your wounds, both outside and those you're holding inside."

Though the girl didn't look convinced, she did nod before heading upstairs.

Lily lay on the bed with Toby snuggled beneath the quilt.

She gently smoothed the side of his hair until he'd fallen asleep. Carefully scooting off the mattress, she got up and readied herself for bed.

The elder Mr. Hammond's words ricocheted in her head. *Is God kind and just or cruel and uncaring?*

Edric had said that though God was kind, it could sometimes seem as though He were uncaring.

She went to the clothes cupboard and took out her pink floral carpetbag, setting it on the nearby chair. Taking several deep breaths, she opened it. Her father's leather-bound family Bible lay in the bottom. She had unpacked everything save for this one item. Holding her breath, she took hold of the black book and pulled it out. She took it over to the bureau where she'd left a lit candle.

Dare she open it?

She stared at the well-worn cover a long while. Finally, she tucked the book back into the carpetbag and returned it to the cupboard.

Where it was safe.

Thirteen

As Lily moved about the kitchen, cleaning up after breakfast, Aunt Henny called from the next room. "Lily, would you pack a lunch for two?"

Lily wiped her hands and stood in the kitchen doorway. "Of course. What would you like in it?"

"Bread. Cheese. Some of those cinnamon cookies you made."

"Old time cinnamon jumbos?"

After she had packed the lunch in a basket, she set it on the table. "Are you going somewhere?"

"Sarah Combs lives far out of town. She's long in the tooth. I haven't had a chance to check on her since I broke my leg. I need to know she's doing all right."

"Should I rent a buggy from the livery?"

"No, Edric's coming with his wagon. He's so kindhearted. Don't you think so?"

"Yes, he's very nice." But that didn't mean it was wise to foster an interest in him.

Lunch for two. That meant Lily would have a little time to herself alone with Toby.

Edric arrived, and Toby opened the door for him.

He held his hat in his hands. "You ready to go?" he said to Aunt Henny.

"I don't think I could make the trip. Take Lily."

Edric stared. "What? But—? If you aren't up to it, I can take you tomorrow."

"I would feel better if I knew today that she's well."

Lily found herself staring too. This was why Aunt Henny wanted a lunch for two.

Edric sputtered then said, "I can go by myself."

Aunt Henny shook her head. "You know how she feels about men. She'll be more comfortable with a woman there. She'll like Lily."

He swung his gaze to Lily. His mouth hung agape. "Maybe Toby wants to come?"

"No, leave the boy with me. He can fetch me anything I need. He's such a good little boy."

Edric turned back to Aunt Henny and frowned. But he loaded the lunch and the food Aunt Henny wanted delivered to Sarah. He offered Lily a hand up into the buckboard but nothing more. He climbed aboard and snapped the reins. The horse lurched into motion, jerking the wagon forward.

On the trip, Edric didn't say anything and continued to scowl.

Had she done something to upset him? Should she ask him about it? Tobias never liked her to question him. So maybe she would keep quiet. But if she questioned him, she could find out what kind of man he was.

Her heart sped up, and her hands sweated as she dug up her courage to ask. She opened her mouth, closed it, opened it again. It was none of her business why he was in a foul mood. She stared straight ahead.

After a bit, she glanced over. His scowl had deepened.

Without giving herself a chance to think, she spoke. "You're frowning. Are you mad at me? Did I do something wrong?" Her breathing came in short gulps. "Oh, never mind. I shouldn't have asked. None of my business. Please pretend I didn't say anything." Her heart really raced now, threatening to burst out of her chest, pounding so hard it hurt. She braced herself for a blow.

Edric heaved out a breath. "I didn't realize my displeasure had spilled out all over my face."

"I shouldn't have asked. I'm sorry. Ignore me."

He glanced at her, his features no longer hard. "I could never ignore you."

She wished he would. "I'm sorry for bringing it up." She just wanted him to forget about it. To pretend nothing was wrong.

He sighed. "I don't like being manipulated."

What? How dare he accuse her? She felt her own surge of displeasure. "You think I've *manipulated* you in some way?"

"No. Not you." He snapped the reins on the slowing horse's back. "Aunt Henny. She led me to believe I would be doing something for her. That I'd be taking *her* someplace. I promised you I wouldn't step over the lines of propriety. I keep my promises. Then Aunt Henny invited us to supper. But she didn't ask me, she asked Pa, and he accepted, and he told the girls before I knew anything about it. She must have suspected I would turn her down. Then this little trip. She manipulated me." He turned to her. "Manipulated *us*."

Lily breathed easier. So he wasn't mad at her. "I know this wasn't your idea." She recalled the look of horror on his face when Aunt Henny had sprung her on him. And how he'd tried to get out of it. Tobias had charmed and manipulated her into marrying him. Then he had changed. "Well, we can't do anything about it now. But we don't have to let it spoil the day."

He glanced at her. "You aren't mad?"

"It's not your fault." A giggle escaped her lips.

"What's funny in all this?"

"Your face."

He turned toward her again. "My face is funny?"

"The expression on your face when Aunt Henny sprung the change of plans on you. You were so shocked, your mouth hung open. And you tried so hard to get out of going or postponing the trip." It felt good to laugh for a change. It had been a long, long time.

A smile pulled at his lips. "You had quite an expression too."

"I'm sure I did."

"At least you didn't let your mouth hang open."

Well, she was grateful for that. Her mother had taught her better than to let her mouth hang agape, ever. And if Tobias had caught her doing such a thing, there would have been no words that could have calmed his fury.

Halfway out to Sarah Combs's place, Edric stopped the wagon in a grove of trees near a stream. They ate the lunch Lily had packed.

Edric sat near the stream breaking twigs and tossing them into the water while the horse drank.

Lily came and sat near him.

He glanced over at her. "I'm trying to be good. But you make it difficult."

"I make what difficult?"

"Keeping my distance from you."

She hadn't meant to cause him distress. "Do you want me to leave?"

"No." He tossed another stick into the water.

"How am I making it difficult? It was Aunt Henny who threw us together today."

"I don't know. It's everything about you. You're nice and... um kind. You treat people well. You... um... love your son so much. The way you hold him and comfort him." He heaved a sigh. "You show me what a woman and mother should be."

"And that's bad."

"It makes you hard to resist. My feelings for you are strong. The more I'm around you, the more I *want* to be around you. I've never met anyone like you. You are so good with the children. Toby *and* mine." He tossed the last of his stick into the water. "If I invite you to call me Edric, will you?"

To do that would put their friendship on new ground. She had long since started thinking of him as Edric. Keeping their relationship formal would be for the best. But she said, "I would like that... Edric. And please call me Lily." She was drawn to him as well.

His mouth broke into a wide smile. "I'd like that, Lily."

Even though he sounded a bit uncertain about using it, she liked the way her name sounded on his lips. No. She mustn't. Just friends. She couldn't allow herself anything more.

Edric took a deep breath. "My wife would manipulate me."

She didn't know what to say to that. She knew how helpless it felt when you realized someone was manipulating you. By then it was too late to get out of it.

"People tried to warn me when I was courting her. But I was young and foolish enough to think they were simply jealous of my good fortune. They didn't understand that I wanted to do all those things for her, wanted to turn my life upside down to please her." He picked up another, thicker stick and twirled it between his fingers. "After we were married, and the girls were born, she resented anytime I left the house, saying I didn't love her. Wouldn't let me do anything that wasn't for her."

He scratched in the dirt with the stick. "She wouldn't even let my parents see the girls. She was afraid everyone was trying to turn the girls against her. Even me."

"I'm so sorry." Lily had heard of women who changed after giving birth. Some who even harmed their baby without realizing it.

"That's why Pa was asking you about God the other night. He wants to make sure you won't hurt our girls."

"He came by and apologized." Should she say something about God? She didn't want to. But he had been so open with her, she felt she owed him as much in return. "I didn't love my husband."

With his eyebrows raised, he tilted his head toward her but didn't question her. Was he surprised by her statement? Or surprised she would speak of such a thing?

"I was seventeen when my parents died." She took a deep breath. "I was devastated. I didn't know what to do. Tobias swooped in and handled all the arrangements. He dealt with all the callers and financial people. But there were a few things he couldn't do because he was a family friend and not a relative. He said he would marry me to help me deal with everything else. If we were married, he could make decisions for me, and I wouldn't have to be bothered or upset by them. I believed him." She swallowed hard.

Snap!

She jumped. The thick stick in Edric's hands was now in two pieces. The white-knuckled grip he had on them tightened her insides.

"He took advantage of you when you were in a vulnerable state. That's worse than being manipulated. I had a choice. I chose to take care of my wife... for better or for worse. You had no choice."

She had vowed for better or for worse as well. Not that she remembered anything about her wedding or the vows. Tobias had plied her with sherry each evening before taking her up to bed. At least in the beginning.

This errand had turned into a sober event. She didn't like it. They still had the rest of the drive out to Sarah Combs's and the long ride back. This mood would be insufferable.

Edric stood and held out a hand to her. "We should probably be on our way."

She took his offered help and stood as well. "Thank you."

He should have left her to stand on her own, because now he didn't want to release her hand. He slowly let go. "You're welcome." Had she noticed he held her hand a little longer than necessary? But not so long it was inappropriate.

At the wagon, he took her hand and put his other on her elbow to assist her up. Her foot slipped, and she fell backward. He gripped her corseted waist to stop her fall. His heart sped up. He quickly hoisted her up and let go.

She settled onto the seat. "Thank you."

"Uh-hmm." He rounded the wagon. That brief moment of holding her caused feelings to race through him. He climbed aboard. He couldn't allow his feelings to get out of control.

Taking a slow breath to tamp down his racing emotions, he coaxed the horse into motion.

He noticed she hadn't said anything about her husband's abuse, but the brute had been worse than he'd imagined. When he had snapped the stick and scared her, pain stabbed his heart. He wanted to take her into his arms and comfort her.

He had brought up God to see if she would talk about Him. Instead, she had talked of her brutal husband instead. What was he to expect when he'd just spoken of his wife?

If she wasn't right with God—wouldn't even talk about God or go to church—he had no business thinking or wishing to be more than friends with her. His heart ached at the hope lost.

He hated to see her so down. He hated that he had spoiled the afternoon. What could he do to change that? "My girls are quite taken with you. They still talk about you touching that snake. And Nancy mentions you in her prayers every night."

"That's very sweet of her to think of me."

He had brought up God again in a roundabout way with prayer. He hadn't intended to. And Lily hadn't really dodged it but edged around it to the safety of Nancy.

Why was it so important she talk about God? Because God mattered. Knowing Lily didn't ever love her husband, meant her mourning period was for public decorum. He would likely be able to start courting her sooner than normally required. But if she didn't have a relationship with God Almighty, courting would be out of the question.

That thought caused the anguish already in his chest to wrench painfully.

Then he sat up straighter. He would just have to show her the way to God. Come right out with it.

The wagon rounded a bend, and Sarah Combs's place came into view. He would speak to Lily another time. Pray and see what the Lord would have him say.

Fourteen

ON THURSDAY, WHEN AGNES CAME TO visit with Aunt Henny, Lily set out to take a walk. Toby had declined to go with her, finding Miss Tibbins far more entertaining.

Thick, gray clouds hung heavy overhead. They hung inside her as well. Pressing and threatening to consume her. How long would it be before someone from her past came looking for her?

She walked and walked, enjoying the unusually cool, late summer day. Soon, she found herself standing outside the small country church, staring up at it.

But not too close.

It wasn't like the imposing stone churches back East. No spires reaching for the sky. No stained-glass windows with blood red patches. No prying eyes judging everything she did. At least not today. The people would be here on Sunday to judge the members of the community, present or not.

Today, it was nothing more than a clapboard building with a single bell in a quaint steeple. This building didn't look threatening at all. She took a step closer then glanced up to the sky. Would she be struck down? No lightning streaked across the looming clouds.

She had managed to avoid attending church so far. But how much longer could she? Tobias had kept her from going to church before. He always had an excuse why they couldn't attend. Then the blows began, intermittently at first, then more and more often. Slaps turned to closed fist blows, and the bruises became obvious. Her husband became adept at hurting her without the marks showing. She couldn't face the people she had known all her life. Couldn't hold her head up.

Tobias kept tight control of where she went and whom she saw. Both got fewer and fewer. Her friends, even the ones who knew what Tobias was doing, stopped trying to visit her. Until all she had left was her little boy.

Once upon a time, she had looked to God for her comfort and strength–before her parents were taken from her. And now, she felt Him gently calling to her soul to return to Him. She had tried to ignore His presence, but the elder Mr. Hammond had asked about God, then Aunt Henny brought Him up, and Edric did as well. She had avoided each encounter, protecting herself from hurt and shame.

A dove fluttered up and perched on the open ledge of the steeple. It tilted its white head to her, cooing softly, as if to say, "Come in. You are always welcome."

Not her. Not after what she had done.

"*Coo. Coo.*"

She shook her head.

Thunder cracked overhead, and the clouds opened up, releasing their bounty in a cascade.

She ran up the church steps and huddled under the door's awning to get out of the downpour. It wasn't much protection. Another crack shook the air, and the wind blew toward her, bringing the rain with it. She would get soaked. Instinctively, she reached for the knob, though it would probably be locked.

The knob turned.

Her insides fluttered.

A gust of wind pushed her over the threshold. She gasped and closed the door behind her, shaking off the rain. "Hello?"

No one answered her call.

The interior was dim with the dark clouds looming in the sky. Rows of simple wooden pews flanked each side of the center aisle. No padding. No ornamentation. Nothing lavish at all in the church. Was this truly a church?

The plain wooden cross behind the lectern drew her forward. This wasn't an extravagant cross like she was used to in the grand churches she grew up in. This was more like the roughhewn cross that her Lord had been crucified on. Dying for her.

In that moment, the weight of all she had done and

endured broke her. She fell to her knees at its base. "Forgive me, Jesus. My sins are many and great."

Her tears flowed. "I should have sought comfort in Your arms instead of Tobias Bremmer's. I should have trusted You to take care of me and not been fooled by Tobias's promises. I should have sought Your guidance on whether or not to marry him."

Though lighter, her heart still sat heavy in her chest, like a burning coal. And she knew why.

She pictured the day of her greatest sin.

Tobias had come home in a terrible mood. He'd lost another large sum of money. Her father's money.

Lily hurried to the entry to greet her husband. He always wanted to see her as soon as he walked through the door.

He slammed the door and raked his hand through his hair, holding on to a fistful for a moment. He unbuttoned his coat and yanked at his tidy cravat. His immaculate grooming was undone in a matter of moments. "My brother is going to regret the day he ever crossed me." His dark hair a disarrayed mess. Tobias grabbed her by the arms. "He's not welcome in my house. Ever! Do you understand?"

It wasn't his house. It had been her parents'. His flushed face and the fierce light in his eyes terrified her. She could sometimes calm him when his rage was directed at her for something she might or might not have done. But there was no cajoling him out of his wrath at another person. If she tried, it would only anger him more. All she could do was nod.

He kissed her roughly. His tight grip caused pain to shoot through her arms, and she winced.

He pushed her up against the wall. "Something wrong?"

"You're hurting my arms."

"What do you want from me? Don't I take care of you?" His fingers dug deeper into her flesh.

Her eyes watered at the pain. "I don't want anything. You take care of me. You're a good husband."

His grip loosened.

Though relieved, she couldn't relax. His anger could

flare with no provocation. Maybe if she could pacify him long enough, she could talk him out of his mood. She patted one of his hands on her upper arms. "You must be tired after a long day. Let's go into the parlor."

He released one arm and put his hand low on her throat and tightened his grip there. "You're my wife, and I'll do as I please with you." He knew precisely where to squeeze so her collars would cover the marks.

It was best not to fight him. She gasped and choked for air.

A small, scared voice spoke behind them. "Don't hurt Mommy."

Lily turned her head to see her son. "Go to your room," she rasped out.

Tobias also turned.

With one look from his father, a dark spot grew on the front of Toby's trousers.

Tobias cursed. "He can't be my son. He's too stupid." He squeezed her throat tighter. "Whose is he?"

Spots danced before her eyes. She tried to say "yours" but no sound could be forced out around his hand on her throat.

He threw her aside.

She hit her head on the wall on the way down.

"Get over here, you worthless excuse for a son."

Lily shook her head and turned toward the pair.

With both hands, Tobias grabbed Toby by the neck and lifted him, feet dangling a couple of inches off the floor.

She scrambled to get up and clawed at Tobias's hands to free her son.

Tobias held fast.

She wasn't strong enough to free her son. She ducked under Tobias's arm and wedged herself between the two, pressing all her weight down on one arm.

Finally, Tobias released Toby with that hand, causing Toby to lower to the floor. He grabbed her hair and yanked her out of his way, sending her backward to the floor. "I'll deal with you in a moment. This shouldn't take long."

Toby's gaze met hers. The life was leaving his eyes.

He seemed to be telling her good-bye.

"Nooooo!" She sprang to her feet and charged at Tobias, ramming all her weight into him.

The only evidence of her attempt was a small sidestep by Tobias and his menacing laugh.

"No, Tobias! Please!" She frantically looked around then grabbed the brass bowl of red apples off the entry table and swung it at his head. The fruit tumbled to the floor.

He stood for a moment, stunned. His arms drooped limply to his sides. Then he collapsed into the marble entry table, knocking it over as he went down.

Toby was free.

Dropping the bowl with a clunk, Lily scrambled over to her boy. He sucked in a huge gulp of air and opened his eyes.

She wrapped her arms around him and shielded him with her body before glancing back to see when Tobias would strike.

He lay sprawled on the floor.

She waited for him to move and get up, coming after her with a vengeance. After several minutes, she set Toby aside and stood. Slowly, she inched toward Tobias, expecting him to grab her. A shiny, red apple lay next to his head on the wood floor.

Not an apple.

Blood!

Where was it coming from? Not from the side of his head she'd struck him on. She saw a smear of blood on the edge of the toppled table and gasped. Tobias must have banged his head on the table too. Either way, she had caused it.

After that, she had packed a few clothes in carpetbags, grabbed what little money and jewelry she could, and left with Toby. They caught the first train possible. She hadn't cared the direction.

The numbness of the events had carried her through the next few days as they traveled. Then she'd stuffed her feelings aside. She had to think only of caring for Toby. Now it was a month and a half later, and the image of Tobias lying lifeless still haunted her.

She didn't deserve to look up but reached out to touch the base of the wooden cross in this small country church. "I didn't mean to kill him. I only wanted to stop him. Wanted to protect my son." She had believed Tobias had meant to kill Toby that day. She sobbed at the base of the cross. "Forgive me. Forgive me."

A warm peace flowed through her.

God had forgiven her.

She raised her head, letting her gaze travel up the cross.

For you I have died.

The Christ had sacrificed Himself for even this sin.

She whispered, "Thank You. Thank You. Thank You."

Stunned by forgiveness, her soul welled with inexpressible gratitude until the words of a hymn crossed her lips. "Amazing Grace..." With tears rolling down her cheeks, she sang all the verses. Then three other hymns.

At long last, she was free of her sin. Free! At least in God's eyes. Man was another matter altogether.

She dried her cheeks and stood. The plain, unornamented pews now seemed welcoming. She could see herself sitting in one on Sunday.

She had spent enough time. She needed to get back to Toby and so walked out of the church. The sun shone through the still falling rain. A bright rainbow arched across the sky. God's promise. The rainbow reflected on the dark clouds in a second arch. Double the promise. She stretched out her arms and tilted her head back, letting the rain cleanse her too.

"Lily."

The sun seemed warm rather than its usual burning, the air fresher, and her soul lighter.

"Lily!"

She suddenly realized someone was speaking to her. She lowered her head and blinked her eyes open.

Edric sat upon his horse a few feet from her. He jumped down. "Are you all right?"

For the first time in six years. "I'm fine. Thank you."

"Why are you standing out here in the rain? You

could get sick."

"It's not cold. Not really."

He took off his coat and wrapped it around her. "Let me take you home. I can sit you on my horse."

The warmth of his coat nestled around her, and she slipped her arms into the sleeves. "That's not necessary. I would like to walk."

He studied her face, rain dripping off his hat. "I'll walk with you. If that's all right?"

Surprised at the pleasure his company brought, she replied, "That would be nice. Thank you."

That evening, she pulled out Father's Bible and opened to the twenty-third Psalm and read it. Though she'd memorized it as a child, she now let her eyes linger on the words, and the promises washed over her. She focused on the third verse and repeated it aloud. "'He restoreth my soul.'"

She had walked through the valley of the shadow of death, and God had restored her soul.

Like the Sunshine and Shadow quilt she was stitching, God had taken her out of the shadows of cruelty and placed her in the sunshine of loving people like Aunt Henny and the ladies of the quilting circle.

On Sunday morning, Edric stared in awe as Lily walked out to the buggy with Toby. Estella and Nancy scooted over to make room for her to sit between them with Toby on her lap. Aunt Henny found enough room to fit with Lily and the children in the back. That left Edric, Pa, and Mr. Tunstall in the front. It was a little crowded, but the trip would be short.

Mr. Tunstall sat in a pew with fellow professors. The rest of them took up a whole pew, sitting as though they were a family all mixed together.

Edric flanked one end of the pew with Pa and Aunt Henny at the other. Lily sat in the middle with the children around her. Despite the fact he wasn't sitting next to Lily, he could still steal glimpses of her.

Lily going to church this morning changed everything. Even though she held the hymnal open, her eyes were closed. She was no heathen. Her serene expression as she sang every word showed an unmistakable love for God. A love for God he hadn't had the opportunity to see before.

Now there was nothing standing in his way of courting her.

Except propriety.

And his promise.

He would still wait a while before asking her.

He stole another glimpse. But hopefully soon.

Fifteen

THE FOLLOWING MONDAY MORNING WHEN EDRIC stopped by to drop off the milk, Toby trotted to the door. It was good for her boy to get used to other people. Lily watched from the kitchen, even though her son had grown brave enough to go by himself and didn't need her to monitor him. She thrilled at getting a glimpse of Edric.

She was a fool. He was still the sheriff. And she had committed a crime. A serious crime. Though God had forgiven her, she couldn't allow a sheriff—even one as kind as Edric—to get close enough to discover her secret. She had to think of her son and not herself.

Toby took the milk and walked slowly back into the kitchen. She waited for Edric to tip his hat to her and leave as he usually did. But he didn't. Why was he still here? Standing on the other side of the screen, he motioned for her to come to the door. Though he wasn't scowling like the other day, he still didn't look happy.

Her insides pulled taut. What could he want? "Toby, you stay here in the kitchen."

"But—"

"Do as you're told. Stay here. Do you understand?"

Toby pushed out his bottom lip and nodded.

She smoothed her skirt, drying her damp palms, and headed for the door. With each step, the dread inside coiled tighter and tighter until she could hardly breathe.

Edric's solemn expression didn't soften.

She stayed on the inside of the screen door. "Good morning." She had to squeeze the words out around her tightening throat.

Edric stepped back. "Can we talk outside?"

She wanted to say no, that she had a lot to get done for Aunt Henny. But she didn't. She held back on her excuses, able to give him a few minutes. She pushed the screen open and stepped out, letting the door close behind her. The thump as it shut made her jump.

Edric didn't seem to notice. Instead, he looked past her.

She glanced over her shoulder and saw Toby standing in the kitchen doorway.

"Let's go over here." He walked off the porch and directed her around to the side of the house. He took off his hat and turned it round and round in his hands.

Her breathing came in short catches. She stood with her back to the house.

With a pained expression, Edric raked a hand through his hair. "I am sorry to have to do this to you."

Oh no! He knew! Her knees weakened. She leaned against the house. Would he put her in jail?

He continued. "I couldn't stop it. It was like watching a flash flood coming straight at me. I couldn't stop it. I was helpless." He slumped his shoulders, defeat etched in every bit of his stance.

Her head went light. What would become of Toby? Toby. She had to pull herself together. She drew in a deep breath and pushed away from the house. She would make herself an opportunity, grab Toby, and run.

Where no one would find them.

Edric continued. "One, I might have been able to handle. But not both. Before I knew what had happened, I had agreed."

Oh dear. Was someone coming to get her right now? Or was Edric going to haul her off to jail this minute? Was that why he wanted to talk to her outside, away from Toby?

Her throat felt as though she had swallowed dirty rags. Her words came out tight and rough. "Agreed to what?" She held her breath.

Looking disheartened, he said, "A picnic."

She continued to hold her breath while she tried to make sense of his words. Slowly, the air seeped from her lungs. "What?"

"It was like a military assault. They surrounded me. First Estella said a picnic would be nice. Then Nancy chimed in with how much fun we would have. How we could go to our favorite meadow."

This large man—the sheriff no less—was upset over a picnic? With his daughters?

"Once they got me to agree, they said you and Toby were coming with us." He slumped his shoulders in defeat.

No. Going on a picnic with the sheriff and his daughters was not a good idea. She had to keep her distance. She already cared too much.

Edric heaved a big sigh. "As I said before, I don't like to be manipulated. And I didn't want you to think that I was manipulating you. Using my daughters, no less. I promised we'd just be friends, but I couldn't say no to them."

The poor man. He loved his girls too much to deny them. But a picnic was out of the question.

"I told them they could come over this evening to invite you and Toby. So I thought if I warned you first, you could have a reason why you and Toby can't go. That way you won't be caught off guard, as I was. I am so sorry."

In a peculiar way, this was very sweet of him.

"Thank you for informing me. I will be ready for them."

"Thank you for not being angry." He mashed his hat back on and strode away.

Watching him walk off, successful in his mission to warn her, she found she *wanted* to go on the picnic. But she knew she mustn't.

She returned inside the house.

As she walked through the parlor, Aunt Henny lifted her head. "Is everything all right?"

"Yes. Fine, thank you." She continued on to the kitchen before Aunt Henny could make any further inquiries.

Toby stared at her with a questioning expression.

She picked him up and hugged him, grateful they didn't have to leave town.

At least not yet.

But she should make plans in case they needed to make a hasty departure.

Edric took a deep breath before opening Aunt Henny's gate.

Estella squeezed his hand. "Don't worry, Papa. They will say yes and come on our picnic."

But he knew differently. He stopped and knelt in front of his daughters. "I don't want you to get your hopes up too much. They may not be able to come. If Toby's mama says no, I don't want either of you to argue with her."

Nancy put her soft little hands on his cheeks. "Don't worry, Papa. They will come. I prayed it." She released him and skipped up to the porch. Estella followed.

Lord, don't let them be too disappointed.

He quickly caught up. "Remember, stay on the porch. Let Mrs. Lexington come out here." That would hopefully keep Aunt Henny from gerrymandering the situation. He saw Lily coming to the door before he knocked.

She stepped out onto the porch. "Isn't this a pleasant surprise?"

His daughters curtsied, and Estella spoke her practiced words for the pair. "We cordially invite you and your son on a picnic on Wednesday."

"My, what a lovely invitation. This Wednesday?"

His girls nodded, their lopsided ponytails bobbing. Even after two years, try as he might, he still hadn't gotten the hang of getting them the same level on both sides. And Pa had no better luck.

Lily pulled her mouth to one side. "Well, I'm not sure. Let me think."

Edric was grateful Lily was being so polite, pretending to think and not turning his girls down too quickly or harshly.

"I'm not sure Wednesday is going to—"

Toby grabbed her hand, and she looked down at him. "Can we go, Mommy?"

Lily took in a deep breath, presumably to strengthen

her resolve. "I don't—"

"Pleeeeeease," Toby said.

Nancy joined in. "Pleeeease."

Then Estella. "Pleeeease."

Edric put a hand on each of his girls' shoulders. "What did I tell you?"

His girls quieted, but their eyes still pleaded. More potent than any words. And they both chewed on their bottom lips.

Lily looked from imploring face to imploring face.

He waited for her to say no so he could support her and keep his girls from begging any further.

She knelt to be eye to eye with her son.

The boy looked so hopeful and didn't seem to be concerned with Edric's presence at all. "I wanna go real bad. I never beed on a picnic before."

Prepared, Edric waited.

"It should be fun." Lily wrapped an arm around Toby and turned to the girls. "We would love to go. Thank you for your kind invitation."

Toby's face broke into a huge dimpled smile.

Edric opened his mouth then stopped. She was going? Pleasantly surprised, he smiled. Before he could stop them, his girls flung themselves at Lily where she knelt with Toby.

Though she swung her arms around them too, she couldn't keep her balance.

"Girls!" Mortified, he reached out to help but was too late.

The four toppled to the porch floor.

Edric lifted Estella off then Nancy.

Lily lay there, laughing. She wasn't upset at all. He had to smile. He held out his hand to her.

Surprisingly, she took it. Hers small and delicate compared to his large, callused one. He pulled her up.

When she stopped laughing, she said, "Thank you."

"Why don't you kids go play for a bit?" he said.

The kids ran off around the side of the house.

Lily looked down at her hand still in his.

He released her but wouldn't say sorry for holding her hand. "I thought you wouldn't go." He saw hesitation in her expression before she spoke.

"Could you say no to those three faces?"

He chuckled. "I couldn't even say no to my two. I guess you didn't stand a chance against such opponents. I thought maybe you were stronger than me."

"I guess not." She gave a mischievous grin. "I've never been good with military assaults either."

He was pleased they would all be going on a picnic. But he couldn't let her know just how pleased. "If you would like, I can come up with an excuse for us to back out."

"And disappoint the three of them? They would only strike again."

His heart soared.

Sixteen

ON WEDNESDAY, EDRIC LOADED THE BUCKBOARD with a picnic lunch, a quilt, and his darlings. "Are you sure you won't come, Pa?"

Pa shook his head. "What do you want me along for? I'll check on Henny later. You go and have a good time."

What did he want Pa along for? So it might not feel so much like he was courting Lily.

Nancy stood in the bed of the wagon and held her arms out.

Pa went over and took her hands. "Sit down, little one. You don't want to fall out."

"I will. And I will bring a flower from the meadow for you."

Estella stood as well. "I'll bring you a flower too."

Pa chuckled. "All right. Now sit down."

The girls did.

Edric climbed up onto the seat, almost giddy. He couldn't wait to see Lily.

When Edric pulled the wagon up in front of Aunt Henny's, he saw Toby sitting on the porch. The boy jumped up and yelled through the screen. "They're here! They're here!" He hopped up and down on the porch. "Hurry!"

Edric set the brake and jumped down. "Stay in the wagon, girls." He was glad to see the boy was excited over his arrival. Or at least his girls' arrival.

Like a spring breeze, Lily glided out of the house in a pink striped dress, and his breath caught. He couldn't let his feelings for Lily get out of control. Or at least couldn't let them show. He had to remain friends until she was ready for more.

She held out a basket.

He took it. "But we brought lunch. We did the

inviting."

Her mouth curved up softly. "Dessert."

His mouth watered. "I can't wait." He set her basket next to the one already in the back of the wagon. Then he held his hands out, palms up, to Toby. "May I lift you in?"

Toby looked at his mama.

Lily nodded.

Though Toby seemed unsure and went rigid, he let Edric lift him in. Progress.

Edric made his voice soft and undemanding. "Now go sit up there by Estella and Nancy."

The girls wiggled apart, and Toby sat between them.

Edric walked Lily around to the front. "May I help you in as well?"

She held out her hand.

A rush went through him as he helped her step up. When she grabbed the railing with both hands, he gripped her corseted waist and assisted her the rest of the way in. By her intake of breath, he had surprised her. But he didn't want her to fall. It was the best way to steady her and see her up safely.

He took several deep breaths to slow his racing heart as he rounded the buckboard. He climbed onto the seat beside Lily, released the brake, and snapped the reins.

Guiding the horse toward a dip in the road, he hoped the jostling would bump Lily up next to him. A few more ruts and holes should do the trick. If he was very fortunate, she might even grab hold of his arm for balance.

Manipulation?

He drew in a slow breath and steered the horse to the smoothest parts of the road he could find.

When they reached the meadow, Edric helped Lily down first, then the children. Even Toby.

Estella walked next to Lily, carrying the quilt. "This is our special picnic quilt. Granmama made it."

Lily touched the yellow and blue pieced coverlet. "It's very pretty." She helped Estella spread it out in the shade under a solitary oak tree centered in the meadow.

Lunch consisted of hard-boiled eggs, cheese,

biscuits, fresh carrots, small tomatoes, and goat's milk.

Halfway through lunch, Estella gasped. "Nancy, one of your ponytails is falling out!"

Edric had known that one was suspect when he'd tied the ribbon in it this morning. But what bothered him was Estella's overreaction. It was a mirror of his late wife. He was about to tell Nancy she could take them both out as she was known to do from time to time, but Lily spoke first.

"I can fix that." She reached for Nancy's hair and pulled out the dingy white ribbon.

He really should get the girls some new ribbons.

Estella spoke in a low whisper. "Do you know how to braid hair?"

"Why yes I do."

Nancy whipped her head around, pulling her hair from Lily's grip.

Edric stifled a laugh.

With wide, pleading eyes, Nancy asked, "Would you braid my ponytail? You don't even have to do the other one."

"I would be happy to. But don't you think it would look better if I did both?"

Nancy nodded her head enthusiastically.

Estella stared and said in a small voice, "Me too?"

"Of course." Lily combed her fingers through the loose side of Nancy's hair. "You'll have to sit still."

Stunned to see Nancy sit motionless, he stared in awe. She was always moving or wiggling. Even in her sleep. The reason Estella wouldn't share a bed with her.

Edric watched Lily divide the hair into three sections. If he studied her motions closely enough, maybe *he* could braid his daughters' hair.

After a few quick flips of the sections, Edric gave up on following the process. Maybe he could get her to teach him.

When Lily had half of Nancy's hair braided down to nearly the tips, she wound the ribbon around it and pulled it tight. Then she looped the end of the braid up and tied it under the top of the braid just over his daughter's ear. "How do you like that?"

Nancy fingered the braid and pulled it away from her head so she could see it. "It's prettiful. Do the other one." She hopped around so the other side of her head faced Lily.

Lily went to work.

Edric felt useless with his girls clamoring for Lily's attention. He'd been right that his girls needed a mama in their lives. And Lily seemed to be the perfect choice. He glanced at Toby who was staring at him. "You going to get your hair braided too?"

Toby shook his head, his dark hair flopping back and forth. He certainly didn't look a thing like his fair-haired mother.

With Lily focused on his girls, Edric wished there was something he could do for Toby in return. He looked around. A smooth, flat, black rock the size of a silver dollar caught his attention. He picked it up and brushed off the dirt with his thumb. "You like rocks, Toby?" Edric had liked rocks when he was Toby's age.

Toby shrugged but stared at the rock.

Edric held it out to the boy. "This is for you. You can keep it in your pocket."

Toby opened his small hand.

Edric dropped the stone into the boy's palm.

Toby curled his skinny little fingers around it.

"What do you say, Toby?" Lily said.

Edric hadn't realized she was aware of his exchange with her son.

The boy's dark gaze latched onto Edric. "Thank you."

"You're welcome." It wasn't much. Picking up a rock wasn't a skill like braiding, but he had done something.

Lily made short work of Nancy's other ponytail and both of Estella's. Both girls swung their heads back and forth, making their braid loops swing. Estella and Nancy stood in front of Edric. "Do we look pretty, Papa?" Estella asked.

Edric blinked the moisture from his eyes and wrapped his arms around them. "You are pretty no matter how your hair is." He glanced over at Lily. "Thank you."

"I enjoyed it," Lily said. "Who's ready for dessert?"

"Me!" all three children said at once.

"We have apple pie and cinnamon cookies."

Edric swallowed, remembering the tasty treats. "Are those the same kind of cookies you took out to Sarah Combs's place?"

She nodded.

"Then I'll take both."

"Papa." Estella tilted her head. "You can only pick one."

Nancy giggled. "Papa's silly."

Lily smiled. "How about if everyone has both?"

The children cheered.

Lily served up the desserts, giving everyone a little of each.

Edric simply stared at her. She was so good with the children. All of them. His heart swelled with warm emotions for her. He reined them in. He couldn't let his heart go running wild.

After dessert, Nancy stood and grabbed Lily's hand. "We have to pick flowers for Granpapa."

Estella grabbed her other hand.

Lily laughed as the girls pulled her up. She turned to Edric. "Are you coming?"

He wouldn't be as fortunate to hold her hand, so he patted his belly and lounged back on the quilt. "I ate too much to move."

Lily turned to her son. "Toby?"

Toby reclined in the same manner as Edric.

Lily's smile was endearing. "We'll return in a few minutes."

Edric watched Lily and his girls tromp through the meadow picking all sorts of flowers. He couldn't believe Toby had chosen to stay with him. He'd be sure not to make any sudden moves to scare the boy.

Toby straightened and stared hard at his mama retreating from him. His breath came in short gasps. Being separated from her seemed to be a little too much for him.

"I think you better go with the girls. They may need your help."

Toby stood and swung his gaze around to him as

though asking permission.

"Go on."

Toby took off after the others and quickly caught up. This was a great place to watch Lily with the children as well as being able to keep an eye out for bears or cougars that might wander into the meadow.

All three children picked flowers and loaded Lily's arms with a plethora of color. She sat in the grass focused intently on the flora.

What was she doing?

Soon he saw.

She lifted a crown of flowers onto each of his girls' heads. And a green one onto Toby's.

Enid never would have let the girls put anything as dirty as meadow flowers in their hair. His girls were happy. His vision blurred.

Later, the four joined hands in a circle and spun around and around, laughing. Lily treated his girls with great kindness. He had watched her closely every time she was around his girls for any sign that she could be cruel to them. She encouraged and helped them to do things well. Lily would be a good mother to any child. A good mother to his girls.

He stared beyond the foursome and held his breath. Had he heard something? Or felt it? He sat up and placed a hand on either side on the ground and closed his eyes. Was the slight vibration simply the rhythm of the earth, or something more? Something more menacing?

The vibration grew. He stood and scanned the horizon.

North.

Then east.

He could hear it. But from which direction? It didn't matter. They needed to make haste.

He ran for Lily and the children. They had stopped their frolicking and stood, looking around. They sensed it too.

Lily questioned him with a look. "What is it?"

He scooped up Toby and threw him into Lily's arms. "Run for the tree." The lone huge oak in the middle of the meadow might be too far. But they had to try. He hoped she didn't argue with him or question him. There might not be time.

Thankfully, she didn't hesitate but ran for the tree.

Estella and Nancy stared up at him, waiting for instructions. Estella said, "Should we run too?"

"No." He leaned over and wrapped an arm around each of them, picking them up. He ran as well. Energy surged through him. His long legs caught him up to Lily, and he passed her. When he reached the tree, he set Nancy down and lifted Estella into the tree. "Climb up to that branch and hold on."

Estella didn't question him and scurried up to where he'd told her. Then he hoisted Nancy up. "You sit on that branch just below your sister."

Nancy did as she was told. Her brown eyes, large and round.

Lily stopped at the tree, panting. "What is it?"

He turned his gaze to the northern rise as the first cattle in a much larger herd charged over the hill. Need he say it? "Stampede." He grabbed Toby, hoping the frightened boy wouldn't fight him. The boy had been afraid from the first day but had warmed to him. Would he revert to his old ways? Toby had a death grip around Lily's neck. Edric needed to get the boy up in the tree and out of harm's way.

Lily reached behind her head and untangled Toby's arms. "It's okay."

Edric heaved the boy up into the tree. "Sit on that branch and hug the tree."

Toby reached his arms toward Lily.

Alarm laced Lily's words. "Do as he says."

Though Toby's bottom lip quivered, he hugged the tree.

Lily stood only two feet from the tree, but it was two feet too far. The stampede was nearly upon them.

Seventeen

As a bull raced straight toward them, Edric grabbed Lily's arm. Yanking her out of harm's way, he thrust her against the trunk.

Lily gasped. "I can't climb the tree."

Not in her delicate condition. He was sorry he'd been forced to make her run. He prayed the baby was safe. He shielded her body with his right as the stampeding cattle barreled past the tree. He gripped two lower limbs above her head.

Even on the outer edge of the stampede, dust boiled up around them.

He coughed and then gazed up into the branches. "You kids hold on tight."

Estella and Nancy hugged the trunk as though it were a game. Silent tears rolled down Toby's cheeks. As long as the boy didn't let go. He had to hold on.

Edric wouldn't take his eyes off the boy. "Hold on tight." He had to yell to make sure they could hear him. "Everyone who holds on very tight will get to pick out a piece of candy at the store."

"I want a peppermint stick," Estella called loud enough to be heard over the thundering hooves.

Nancy echoing her sister was drowned out by the bawls and bellows of the frightened herd.

Toby stopped crying and stared, blinking several times.

Edric coughed again. Fortunately, the children were above the thick of the dust. "What kind of candy do you want, Toby?"

The boy shrugged.

"Do you like peppermint sticks too?"

Toby lifted one shoulder.

Lily coughed.

A cow coming around the tree bumped into Edric's

side. Pain shot through his hip and down his leg. He tightened his grip on the lower branches to keep his balance. He refused to let his discomfort register on his face. "Chocolate?"

Toby lifted the same shoulder as before.

"A gumdrop?"

Toby's eyes widened, and he nodded.

"A gumdrop it is." Another cow bumped into him on the other side, pushing him a step out from the protection of the tree. He jerked his leg behind the trunk as another cow cut around the tree and hit him. The energy surging through him strengthened him.

He braced himself better and focused on Toby. "You can have a gumdrop if you hold on tight."

The boy tightened his hold around the tree trunk.

"You're doing a fine job. Keep it up." He wanted to close his eyes against the stinging dirt but needed to keep watch on everyone. He blinked the grit around in his eyes. In a lull between clumps of cattle, he called, "Everyone who doesn't let go gets a candy. Hold on tight." He needed to keep reminding them so no one lost their grip.

Lily's arms wrapped around him, and she coughed against his chest.

He liked the feel of her so close, wanted to get lost in her embrace, but he couldn't allow it. Momentarily, he shifted his gaze away from the children but was still alert to the slightest movement from them. "Don't hold on to me. Stay tucked in close to the tree."

She looked up at him, confused, but removed her arms from him.

He lowered his head so his mouth was near her ear so she could hear him. "If I get knocked over, I don't want you getting pulled away as well." He got bumped again and jerked sideways but kept his footing.

Her eyes widened in understanding. She pulled her hands and elbows in close to her body. "You hold on tight too."

"I will." He couldn't worry about her right now. He looked up at the children and yelled over the cacophony, "Are you holding tight?"

All three nodded.

"That's good. Keep holding on." He coughed again. The dust was so thick he couldn't see where the stampede ended. Couldn't hardly see ten feet.

Toby yelled down. "We get candy?"

"Yes. As long as you don't let go." Edric's heart raced faster at the thought of any of them getting hurt. Or worse. His eyes watered at the thought—or rather the dust. "Any kind of candy you want."

Toby hugged the tree tighter, pressing his face into the bark.

If candy was what it would take to keep the children safe, Edric would buy them a barrel full. He had lost count of the number of times each of his sides had gotten hit by the stampeding herd. The pain now part of him.

Eventually, the rush of cows slowed. Soon, only a few stragglers were left, bringing up the rear and plodding at a trot.

Edric took a deep breath and coughed. He relaxed his grip on the branches. Everyone was fine. He leaned his head against the tree trunk next to Lily's. Everyone was fine. No one had gotten hurt. Except for himself. But a few bruises were nothing compared to what could have happened. His mouth tasted of dirt. He wanted to spit the grit out but didn't want to be vulgar in front of a lady. Especially a lady he fancied.

The sound of galloping hooves met his ears and then a man's voice. "Is everyone all right?"

Edric turned to see a cowboy. It was Poke. "We're fine."

"Oh. Sheriff."

Edric stepped away from Lily. "What happened?"

"Rattler. Spooked a horse and sent the herd running. We got them turning, and I think they will go around the town."

"Good."

Poke looked in the direction of the cattle. "I should go."

Edric nodded.

Poke galloped off.

Edric turned to Lily. She looked neither distraught nor calm. She could go either way. He hoped she held together.

Lily stared at the receding herd. She'd never witnessed or experienced a stampede. It had been over before she really knew what was happening. Much like the swing of Tobias's brutal hand. Terrifying and swift. Something one endured and hoped to survive.

Edric lifted Toby down. "You were so brave."

"I holded on. I get candy?"

"You sure do. Any kind you want." He put Toby in Lily's waiting arms.

She clutched her son tight.

Edric helped his girls down.

Toby wiggled out of her arms. The children skipped around the tree, chattering about the stampede and how they had all been brave. They seemed unaffected.

Edric smiled at the children frolicking.

Lily noticed a rip in her dress sleeve. That hadn't been there this morning. When had that happened? Then she remembered the tug on her arm one way when Edric had jerked her the other way and behind the safety of the tree. And she pictured the horn of the first bull piercing her sleeve. Her hands began to shake, and she struggled to draw in air. But not because of the lingering dust. "We could have all been killed, couldn't we?" She hadn't realized how close she'd come to death.

He turned his smile on her. "But we weren't." His words were even and measured. "We're all fine. No one even got hurt."

"But we could have." Toby could have been killed. Or she could have left Toby an orphan. Her whole body trembled, and her breathing came in gasps. "We could have all died. Trampled." The thought weakened her.

His smile faltered. He grasped her upper arms, and his voice turned firm. "Hold yourself together. Don't fall apart in front of the children. They need to see you strong."

His grip and tone flashed an image of Tobias in her mind. Panic swept through her. If she didn't pull herself together, he would hit her, now or later. She sucked in a breath.

No. This wasn't Tobias. But would Edric strike her if she didn't do as he bid? She didn't think so. He was thinking of the children's welfare, not of himself. Tobias had only thought of how her or Toby's behavior reflected on him. If it was good, he could be quite kind. If not... She shuddered.

She'd had plenty of practice schooling her emotions.

Pretending near death didn't bother her, she took a deep breath and straightened her shoulders. She pulled out of his grip. "I'm fine now. Thank you." Her words sounded flat. She walked over to the children and took Toby's hand, bracing herself for Tobias's attack from behind.

"Mommy, did you see how brave I was?"

"You were very brave." More so than herself.

Nancy grabbed her other hand. "I was brave too."

Lily crouched. "Very brave."

Estella stood in front of her. "Me too."

"You too." Lily wrapped her arms around all three and hugged them. "I'm so proud of all of you." She wanted to hold them all and never let them go.

Edric studied her, probably to make sure she wouldn't start crying. "The horse ran off with the buckboard, so we'll have to walk back to town."

Nancy took his hand. "Oh, Papa, is the horsey all right? He didn't get hurt, did he?"

"I'm sure the horse is fine. He would have run with the herd. He's probably waiting for us back home."

Estella pointed. "Look, Papa, our quilt. Can I get it?"

The yellow and blue coverlet they had sat on for their picnic lay in a heap a few yards across the meadow. It had gotten moved along by the herd.

"Certainly," Edric said. "But it might be ruined." The baskets were mere splinters and the pie tin mangled.

The children ran ahead with Estella in the lead.

"Are you going to be all right?" Edric asked.

Lily nodded.

He walked beside her but didn't touch her or even offer his arm to her. True to his word to not cross any sort of lines of propriety, but she could feel him studying her.

"I'm fine."

"Are you sure?"

"Positive. I had a momentary lapse. I assure you, I'm perfectly fine. I will not start weeping in front of the children."

Tobias never liked to see her crying or upset, even when he hit her. She had put her fear from the stampede aside. She would think of this event as only something she once read in a book. Her hands had even stopped shaking. She had succeeded at not feeling what she felt.

Estella held up the dirty quilt. "It's not too ruined. We can fix it."

Edric poked three fingers through a tear. "I don't know. It's pretty ripped up."

"Please, Papa. We can't go on more picnics without our picnic quilt. Please."

Lily held out her hand. "May I see?" She examined it. "It will take a bit of work and patching, but I can fix it."

Estella gazed up at her. "Oh, thank you."

Edric took the quilt. "I'll carry it." He slung it over his shoulder.

It wasn't long before Toby came to her with his arms raised. She picked him up so he faced her with each of his legs on either side of her.

"Do you want me to carry him?" Edric asked.

She was about to tell him she could manage, when Nancy held her arms up to him.

"Carry me, Papa."

Lily shrugged. "I've got him."

"Me too," Estella said.

Lily didn't know how he would manage to carry them both. They would likely have to take turns.

But with practiced ease, Edric swung Estella up onto his shoulders. She giggled as she went through the air.

"Hold on tight like you did in the tree," he said to

Estella as he bent at the knees. Estella locked her arms around his forehead. He lifted Nancy as though she were no heavier than the picnic quilt and settled her on one hip.

By the time the edge of town came into view in the distance, Lily's sore and aching feet burned. She wished she was already there and could sit.

Edric bounced along with both his girls clinging to him. How did he do it? She felt like collapsing. Could she make it?

He turned to her. "You're limping."

She had thought she was hiding it. "I'm fine." But she wasn't. Not really.

"You've probably worked a blister on one or both of your feet. Let's rest under these trees." He set Nancy down near a clump of saplings. She looked half asleep. Then he lifted Estella down. He spread out the dirty, torn quilt in the shade.

Lily hobbled over.

Edric gripped Toby, who had fallen asleep against her. The movement woke Toby, and his eyes flew open. He screamed in panic and flailed to keep hold of her.

She squeezed him. "It's okay."

Edric released Toby, who peered over his shoulder at the big man and calmed. No doubt he'd feared it had been his father grabbing him.

Lily took Edric's offered hand and lowered herself to the ground with Toby still clinging to her.

"It's still a mile or so to town. I'm going to continue and bring back a wagon."

Nancy held up her arms. "Take me with you."

"I need you to stay here. I'll be quick."

Nancy nodded and leaned against Lily.

Lily wanted to protest, to say she could make it the rest of the way. But in truth, she didn't know if she could walk one more step, let alone the mile or so to the edge of town. Then she would still have to get from this side of town to Aunt Henny's. It was best to stay put and wait for the wagon.

She wanted to take her boots off her aching feet, but knew if she did, she would never get them back on.

Better to wait until she got home.

Watching Edric stride away, she felt a palpable fear coiling around inside her. What if he didn't return? What if a bandit happened upon them? What if a poisonous snake slithered up to them? What if a bear came along?

She had to be strong for the children. Taking a deep breath to control her errant fears, she closed her eyes and prayed.

Eighteen

EDRIC HATED LEAVING LILY AND THE children there under the red alder trees, but he knew none of them would make it back to town. They were exhausted and thirsty. He could move faster alone. And faster he did. Though parched, he jogged. He didn't want to leave them unaccompanied any longer than necessary.

The first house he came to at the edge of town, he stopped and pumped water, drinking handful after handful.

Mrs. Gifford came out, drying her hands on a towel. "Mercy, Sheriff, I was wondering who was drinking at my pump. What happened to you?"

He splashed cool water on his face. "My horse and wagon got spooked by a stampede and ran off. I had to leave my family down the road. Do you have a horse and wagon I can borrow?"

"Harvey has our wagon. Is your family all right?"

"They're resting under some trees." He repositioned his hat. "Thank you for the water."

"I hope everything works out."

"It will." Refreshed, he strode off for the livery another half mile down the road.

Once there, he waved to Amos. "I need to borrow a horse and wagon."

"Sure thing, Sheriff. I only have the small buckboard."

"That'll do."

Amos called into the darkness of the livery. "Beanpole, hitch up the buckboard. And be quick about it. Sheriff Rix needs it."

Amos's gangly son of fourteen appeared. "Should I hitch Cinnamon or Turk?"

"Cinnamon. Turk's been cranky today."

Bean turned to Edric. "Howdy, Sheriff Rix."

"Howdy, Bean."

"I'll have that wagon ready for you in a trice." The boy ran off back into the shadows.

"What happened to your wagon?" Amos asked.

"Stampede spooked the horse."

"I heard about that. They got the herd turned before it reached town. But it sent a cloud of dust through here so thick so as a man could hardly breathe. You weren't caught in the middle of it, were you?"

Edric nodded. "We took safety at the big oak in the valley. No one got hurt. But they were all too tired to walk the rest of the way. Do you have a canteen I can bring water in?"

Amos picked up a ceramic jug. "I'll fill this while the wagon's being hitched."

Soon, Edric climbed aboard the buckboard with a full jug of water. "Thanks. I'll return this." He snapped the reins, and the wagon lurched forward.

Once on the edge of town, he goaded Cinnamon into a canter. As he approached the foursome in the shade, his chest welled with pride. His girls were nestled against Lily whose head was leaning against a tree. Toby lay huddled in her lap. All sound asleep. He breathed easier knowing his family was safe. They weren't all his... at least not yet.

He set the brake and jumped down then gazed at them. He could just stand here and stare at the peaceful faces. Somehow his girls had managed to hold on to their flower head-wreaths. Taking the jug from the wagon, he knelt. He hated to disturb their slumber. He wanted to caress Lily's cheek rather than wake her. Pushing the thought away, he patted her on the arm instead.

She pulled in a long breath and opened her eyes. "You're back."

He nodded. "I brought water."

She jostled the children. "Wake up."

They wiggled and stretched. Nancy and Estella jumped up and hugged him. Estella said, "Nancy was scared, but I wasn't."

Nancy petted his shoulder. "I missed you."

"I missed you all too. I brought water." He directed the children to cup their hands, and he poured water from the heavy jug into them. Each drank three or more handfuls. The gallon jug was more than half empty before everyone's thirst was satisfied. They all seemed to have forgotten the harrowing experience with the stampede. That was best.

He helped Lily onto the wagon seat and the children into the back.

This felt good and right to have Lily next to him. Like they were all part of one family.

He pulled up to Waldon's Mercantile, set the brake, and jumped to the ground. He helped Lily out then the children. "Do you all know what kind of candy you want?"

Estella pointed. "Nancy wants a peppermint stick like me, and Toby wants a gumdrop."

"I want a gumdrop too." Nancy batted her eyelashes at him.

Some poor fellow was going to be at her mercy when she got older. For now, he was the poor sap who couldn't say no to her. To either of his daughters.

"You can each have a peppermint stick *and* a gumdrop."

Cheers rose from the trio, and they ran inside the mercantile.

He held the door for Lily. "What kind of candy are you going to choose?"

She smiled. "I don't need candy."

"A deal was a deal. Everyone gets candy."

"You said everyone who held on tight got candy. As you recall, you told me *not* to hold on." She walked away.

He had been greatly disappointed to have to tell her not to hold on to him. Was she flirting with him? He followed her. "You can still pick a candy."

Estella reached into one candy jar and pulled out three peppermint sticks. She handed one to Nancy and one to Toby. Then she retrieved three pink gumdrops and passed those around.

Nancy jumped up and down. "What do you want, Papa?"

Estella huffed. "He always gets butterscotches."

"What about Granpapa?"

"He likes horehounds." Estella knew what everyone liked.

Franny Waldon came over with a sheet of brown paper. "For your candies."

While he paid, Lily stood out on the boardwalk with the children who sucked on their peppermint sticks. When he exited, he held out a piece of black licorice to Lily. When her eyes widened in delight, he knew he had chosen correctly.

She took the offered confection. "Thank you."

He drove them all to Aunt Henny's house.

Lily sighed at the sight of her home. The children ran to the door, energized from the nap, the water, and the sugar. She gathered the quilt into her arms.

Edric lifted her down. "You don't have to repair that."

"I promised your girls I would."

He seemed pleased.

Inside, Lily helped all three wash their sticky hands. Then Estella, Nancy, and Toby crowded around Aunt Henny to relay the story. Toby watched and nodded as the girls chattered.

Edric said, "You children stay in here. We need to go talk."

What did he need to talk about?

"How are your feet? Can you walk?"

"Much better after resting. I can walk now. How far are you taking me?"

"Beyond the chicken coop."

"All the way out there? Why?"

"Trust me."

She did, but that didn't stop her from being curious at his strange request.

Once the chicken coop stood between them and the house, he stopped her beside a sprawling black cottonwood tree.

He took a deep breath and looked at her. "All right. It's safe here."

She looked around. "Safe from what?"

"For you to cry."

She blinked at him. "I'm not going to cry. I'm fine." And she was fine.

"I saw you after the stampede. You were going to start crying."

"Yes. But I'm fine now." She'd successfully stamped out her feelings.

"You are not fine. I made you hide your fear for the sake of the children. But you need to let it out."

It was sweet of him to be concerned for her. "Truly, I'm fine." She held out her hands. "See, no shaking." He didn't understand her ability to stuff her emotions away where no one could see them and hurt her.

"You're really all right with what happened?"

She nodded. Like it'd happened to someone else. But a small twinge tightened her stomach.

"You aren't bothered by nearly being trampled by several hundred head of cattle?"

She remembered how the earth had trembled under her feet, nearly knocking her to the ground.

"I figured the thought of your son being in danger would have shaken you more."

Toby. She wouldn't have been able to save him by herself. She wouldn't have known what to do. She pictured his small body under all those hooves. Her hands began to shake.

"You're the strongest woman I know. Next to Aunt Henny."

Toby could have fallen out of the tree and been killed. Her sweet little boy could be dead. She sucked air in, gasping for breath.

"Lily?"

Her whole body shook.

Edric touched her arm. "Are you all right?"

She collapsed against him in wracking sobs.

He wrapped his arms around her and whispered soothing words. "It's all right. Cry it out."

He didn't tell her she was being foolish. He didn't admonish her or order her to stop. Or hit her. He told her to cry. And cry she did. He held out a handkerchief to her. She took it and wiped her nose.

As her weeping subsided, she realized he was gently rocking her back and forth. She took in shuddering breaths and sniffled.

"You're all right now. Everyone is safe." He pressed his cheek into her hair. Then he pressed his lips against her head.

That one simple, tender act crumbled the last of her defenses. She warmed all over at his gentleness.

He kissed her temple.

She reveled in his touch and tilted her head back.

His lips moved down her cheek and to her mouth, gently caressing her lips.

She kissed him back.

His kiss became more ardent. More consuming.

She didn't want him to let her go.

As though in response to her thought, his arms tightened around her, holding her safely in their embrace.

"Mommy!" Toby wailed from somewhere beyond.

Was it real? Or just in her imagination?

"Mommy!"

She jerked away and looked around, breathing heavily. "I have to go."

Edric took a deep breath. "I know. Go to him."

She swiped at the last remnant of tears on her cheeks and hurried away from the strength of Edric toward her frightened son.

Edric tucked his girls into bed. They had told the story of the stampede no less than five times—each—to Pa before Edric could get them settled. They had each plucked off one flower from their flower wreaths and gave it to Pa to fulfill their promise. Neither of them willing to give up their crown completely. He headed downstairs.

"They won't likely sleep a wink tonight." Pa trailed after him.

"They napped on the walk back and while they waited for me to return with a wagon. They'll be cranky for you tomorrow."

"We'll be fine. You were quite the hero in their eyes today."

"The candy didn't hurt." Edric rubbed his sore neck.

"You all right? You're walking like an old woman who forgot her cane."

The jostling he took today was catching up to him. And he knew he had bruises the size of Pa's flapjacks. "I'm fine. I'm going to check on the livestock."

Pa arched his eyebrows. "I already did that."

"I just need some fresh air."

"Do you want company?"

"No." He strode out, past the garden, and headed for their small barn.

Normally, he would have welcomed Pa's company, but not tonight. The night air was cooling off. He took several deep breaths to stave off the stampede inside him that threatened to trample his repose.

He made a quick check on all the animals. The horses were fine. The horse and wagon *had* found their way home. The chickens were roosting in the rafters, and the milking goat was settled in for the night. He sat on a small barrel then stood up. He leaned against a support post then pushed away. He sat on a hay bale then got to his feet. The barn seemed stifling and cramped.

He strode out and walked in the direction away from town, breathing deeply as he went.

The memory of the rushing cattle niggled his insides. If it had been only him and his girls, he would have climbed up the tree with them. He'd known Lily wouldn't be able to climb, so he'd stayed where he could better protect her. His girls could have died today. He didn't know what he'd do without them.

He tried to swallow the sudden lump in his throat without success. His legs lost what strength they had, and he fell to his knees. As tears welled, he fisted them away. He'd forced Lily to remain strong for the children, and he'd remained strong for both the children and her. Now he shook. The wind blown out of him.

It was his duty to stay strong for everyone else. For Estella and Nancy. For Pa. For the town and its people. And now for Lily and her son.

The thought of any one of them being trampled ripped him to his bones. As shredded as the picnic quilt.

He tilted his face heavenward. *Thank You for sparing our lives.*

He knelt there for a long time in gratitude.

And he knew he wanted to make Lily his wife. He had feared as much for her safety as for his daughters. He'd fallen in love with her. He wanted to make her part of their family. His girls adored her.

Pa still had his reservations, but Edric was sure Pa'd come around. He would see that Lily was nothing more than a widow trying to make a new start.

Then the cold hard truth hit him like a charging bull. He'd kissed her.

Not some little chaste peck on the cheek. A desirous kiss filled with his pent-up longings.

He'd promised her he wouldn't step over that line of impropriety. He'd taken advantage of her vulnerability. She had been upset about the stampede. He'd been upset too. She probably thought him a cad for forcing her to relive the harrowing event so he could take advantage of her.

But that wasn't why he had done any of it. He knew she needed to cry and get her fears out. If she kept them locked up inside, they would make her sick.

Then the kiss just happened. Holding her in his arms had felt so right. She belonged there. He'd been struggling not to let his fears spill all over the place and had forgotten to keep his attraction for her in check.

Now she would never trust his word again.

Nineteen

WHEN THE MORNING KNOCK SOUNDED on the door, Lily's heart thrilled, dancing in her chest. She couldn't wait to see Edric again. The memory of his kisses yesterday had wrapped her in a warm embrace all night and continued this morning. Wiping her hands on a towel, she headed for the door. She hoped she looked all right.

Toby raced ahead of her.

From her place on the settee, Aunt Henny smiled at Lily. But it was an odd sort of smile, not the older woman's usual, and accompanied by a knowing glint in her eyes. Did she somehow know Edric had kissed her? That things had changed between them.

Lily returned her attention to the door when she heard Edric's deep voice, but it sounded strange.

Toby backed away from the entrance, his eyes wide.

Arriving at his side, she understood why. Not Edric, but the elder Mr. Hammond, Saul, stood on the porch. Her stomach bunched in disappointment. Where was Edric?

Saul held up a quart bottle. "I brought the milk."

Why hadn't Edric? He had every single morning since her arrival. Without fail. She pushed open the screen. "Thank you. Come in."

He stepped inside. "I would like to visit with Henny if she's up to it."

"She would like that." Lily turned to retreat to the kitchen but stopped when Saul spoke again.

"Edric would like for you to come by his office some time today."

She swiveled back. "His *office*?" Her insides tightened painfully.

"He would like to speak with you in private."

Her nerves tingled from head to toe, like a million

needles pricking her. She cleared her throat. "He's not coming here?"

He shook his head. "He wanted you to know it was important."

She swallowed hard, picturing Edric's office... the *sheriff's* office. She had purposefully avoided it. Now, she couldn't. Why hadn't he come to talk to her here? Why his office? Was this to be more than a social talk? Had he looked into her past? She didn't want to go but knew she must. "I'm sure Aunt Henny will let me go later this morning. And I can pick up anything she needs at the mercantile."

As she walked back to the kitchen, each step became harder as though she were slogging through deep snow. She shivered, feeling cold as well. Ever so cold.

The sheriff's office.

Nausea rolled through her midsection.

She would deny it. Deny it all to protect her son.

Edric sat behind his desk, staring at a blank piece of paper. Pen poised. When would she get here? She hadn't come right away as he'd hoped. She did have duties to Aunt Henny to fulfill first. But would she come this morning sometime? Or not until the afternoon? Should he go ride around town quick to make sure there wasn't any trouble brewing anywhere? But what if Lily arrived while he was out? His deputy Montana was out prowling the town. He would inform Edric if he was needed.

Though he had wanted to see her first thing this morning, he had decided not to have this conversation at Aunt Henny's. He didn't want her to feel he was invading and trying to pressure her. She wouldn't feel a need to hide in the outhouse. She could simply leave if she so chose.

The chair creaked as he shifted his weight. Every muscle in his body ached from yesterday's incident. His sides were bruised from his knees to his ribs, and he was stiff all over. But it was worth every pain to keep his family safe.

He went back to not composing his letter to the governor. The ink had dried on his pen tip. He set it aside.

When Lily stepped through his open door a few minutes later, he shot to his feet, sending his chair scraping against the floor. He wanted to gather her up in his arms and kiss her but resisted the urge. That was the trouble in the first place. Overstepping the boundaries she had laid out. He hoped his actions hadn't damaged their budding relationship.

Lovely in her blue dress. The color ignited her eyes. "Good morning. You asked me to come."

"Yes." But at the moment, he just wanted to stare at her, taking in everything about her. Enjoy the moment. And her presence.

Her gaze darted around the dim interior and settled uncomfortably on the two cells.

He mentally kicked himself. This had been a terrible place to have asked her to meet him. Dreary and adversarial. But she had come, and he would confess his misdeed and hope she forgave him without reservation.

He stayed behind his desk. "Please have a seat."

"I'll stand."

That couldn't be good. She looked tense and was as pale as a black cottonwood tree in bloom.

He had hoped his actions hadn't bothered her this much. "I must apologize for yesterday."

Her eyebrows dipped. "Yesterday? For what? Saving our lives?"

"No. I was so relieved no one got hurt." Except himself. But she didn't need to know that. She didn't need any more worries or concerns in her condition. "Later... when I... kissed you. I shouldn't have done that. I promised you that I would wait for you to be ready. I overstepped my place."

Her stiff shoulders lowered, and her whole stance seemed to relax. Spots of pink highlighted her cheeks. "That's all right. I really didn't mind."

He stared at her a moment. She hadn't? Had he

heard right? Or heard what he wanted to hear? He came around his desk. "You didn't?"

She shook her head, and a gentle smile tugged at her rosy lips.

Encouraged, he ventured to ask, "Does... that mean you might be ready to court soon? I'm not trying to push you. I simply want to know where I stand."

She gave him a shy look and nodded. "Real soon. And you stand very well in my eyes."

He couldn't believe she was ready to court in addition to not being angry at him for kissing her. His heartbeat sped up. He caressed her cheek with the backs of his fingers. When she didn't pull away, he leaned in ever so slowly and kissed her. A soft, gentle kiss.

Why had he asked to only court her? Why hadn't he proposed? Courting meant he needed to wait a proper amount of time before proposing. Yes, it was fast, but this wasn't the first romance for either of them. They had both been married before, and he knew what he wanted.

Lily.

He slipped his arms around her, pulling her closer.

Her whole body stiffened in his embrace.

He jerked away. What had he done?

She looked frightened and helpless like a trapped animal.

"What did I do? I'm sorry."

Pale again, she stepped toward the doorway, her breathing shallow and fast. "Nothing. It's not you. I have to go." She stumbled at the threshold, and he reached out to steady her, but she waved him off, breathless. "I'm sorry." She scurried away.

What had just happened? He could think of nothing he did to frighten her. He went to the door and watched her hurry down the street toward Aunt Henny's. She appeared to be running away from him. But why? Should he go after her? Or give her time to collect herself?

Lily took quick, long strides, her skirt tangling around her ankles. Her breathing came in heavy gasps. She had to get out of there. She had to run. But she couldn't. Ladies did not run. So she walked as fast as she dared, her hands shaking. Down off one boardwalk and up onto the next. She clutched her hands together to still them.

Soon, Aunt Henny's house came into view. She opened the gate and walked toward the front porch but stopped. She couldn't go inside. She wasn't ready yet. Wasn't ready for Aunt Henny to ask what was wrong. To face Toby. She had to get control of herself.

She strode around the side of the house and leaned against the part of it between the corner and the back porch. She put one hand on her stomach, forced her shoulders to relax, and let her head fall forward.

A deep breath in.

A slow breath out.

It hadn't been Tobias trapping her.

In.

Out.

She was safe.

In.

Out.

She could feel herself calming.

In.

Out.

From inside, Toby's voice drifted out through the open back door.

She closed her eyes and let the terror continue to seep out of her.

Tobias wasn't here. He would never hurt either of them again.

She was safe.

Toby was safe.

In.

Out.

Slow and even.

"Are you all right?" A deep voice sounded beside her.

She sucked in a breath and jerked away. It was only Edric. She was safe. But she felt so vulnerable. She nodded. "I—I'm fine."

"You don't seem fine." Concern etched his strong, handsome face.

"Really, I am." She had been silly to react so. She wished she could control her wayward emotions. She used to be able to contain her fear. Keep it from ruling her actions. Hide it from Tobias and everyone. Her survival, and Toby's, had depended on it. What was wrong with her?

"What happened? I didn't mean to scare you."

She didn't want to have this discussion with him. She didn't want to have it with anyone. She wanted to forget her past ever happened. She only had the present and the future.

Edric studied her.

She couldn't tell if he was trying to figure out what her problem was, or if he was trying to figure out what to say. Either way, she should say something. *Tell* him something. She hadn't expected to care about any man the way she did him. She must tell him something or push him away for good.

She drew in a deep breath to steel herself. "I apologize for running off like that. It was rude."

"No need. I simply want to know what I did to frighten you so I don't do it again."

"It wasn't you." Tobias was to blame. She took a deep breath to still her quivering insides and clasped her trembling hands together. "When I told you I wasn't in love with my husband when we married, that was only part of it. I was quite young and..." How to word it so he wouldn't ask too many questions? Preferably no questions. Enough so he would understand not to. She wanted to be honest with him. But not too honest.

Edric waited with a look of encouragement.

"My husband wasn't always gentle in his touch." More like never gentle. "When you put your arms around me, I had the old feeling of being trapped. Waiting to be hurt again."

He raised and lowered his head in understanding. "I never meant to frighten you. But I put my arms around you yesterday, and you didn't react."

That was right. He had. And she hadn't. "I guess I

was too upset from the stampede. It blocked everything else out." She didn't know what else to say.

"Thank you for telling me." He studied her a while. "Will you still allow me to court you?"

Now it was her turn to study him. "You still want to?"

"My feelings for you haven't changed. I won't put my arms around you. I won't even kiss you if you don't want me to."

"It's not that I don't want you to, I just can't help remembering..." Remembering what she desperately longed to forget. And reacting to it. Reacting to a man who would never hurt her again.

"Are you willing to get used to it? To me? Holding you?"

She yearned for someone to treat her with kindness. "Yes." Tears blurred her vision. She blinked them away. She did want to get used to him holding her.

His mouth pulled up on the corners. He put a hand on her arm and slid it down to her hand. He squeezed it with both of his. "May I kiss you?"

She was glad he wasn't mad at her for running away from him. From her memories. She nodded.

Edric leaned toward her.

She anticipated the warmth of his lips on hers.

"Mommy!"

Edric jerked away as Toby ran down the back-porch steps and over to her. Edric smiled at her boy and stretched out his hand to ruffle her son's dark curls.

Toby ducked away, grabbed her hand, and pulled her to the porch steps. "Don't hurt Mommy!"

Lily knelt in front of Toby. "Mr. Hammond wasn't hurting me." Distress and pride vied for dominance inside her. Distress that her little boy was still so fearful Edric would hurt her. And pride that her little boy felt *safe* enough to have the courage to speak so boldly. Last time he had championed for her, he'd nearly been choked to death for his troubles. She shifted her gaze to Edric. He looked stricken.

Edric crouched where he was a few feet away. "Toby, I promise you that I will never hurt your mommy. Do you believe me?"

Her son stared wide-eyed.

Lily took both of Toby's hands. "It's all right, Sweetie. He's not going to hurt me. Or you."

Edric spoke. "Toby, I'll tell you what—I promise not to hurt your mommy if you promise not to hurt your mommy."

She knew that Edric understood Toby would never hurt her. She believed Edric was trying to get her son to see he cared for her as much as he did.

Toby nodded.

Edric held out his hand. "Then we should shake on it."

Toby's eyes widened even more, and he looked to her.

She nodded then stood, taking his hand, and walked him over to Edric.

Toby slowly lifted his hand.

She could tell her son was unsure. But she was sure. And once Toby saw that Edric wouldn't hurt him, he would be more and more comfortable around him. They both would.

Edric took Toby's small hand in his large one and pumped it up and down. "A man's word is never to be broken." Then he lifted his other hand slowly and ruffled Toby's hair. Toby didn't shy away.

Edric stood. "I need to get back to my office. May I stop by on my way home this evening?"

"I'd like that." She was grateful that the situation with the kiss, which could have come between them and kept them apart, had been settled so quickly. If Edric hadn't come after her, it would have festered and made her sick with worry. He seemed to understand her fear and didn't take it personally. She was fortunate to have him in their lives.

He tipped his hat. "We'll finish what we started here later."

What they started?

He winked.

And she understood. The interrupted kiss. Her cheeks warmed at his meaning. She looked forward to it.

He strode away.

Scooping up Toby, she walked around to the front of the house and watched Edric strolling down the street.

Edric swung his gaze back to her.

She raised her hand. "Wave to him, Toby." It surprised her when Toby did. He had warmed up to Edric. She wouldn't consider courting a man her son was afraid of and couldn't get used to. Her little boy had come a long way since they had arrived in town two months ago. So had she.

Edric waved back.

She realized that she loved him. And, oddly, that didn't scare her. But a different kind of fear rippled through her. Could she really have happiness?

Twenty

THE FOLLOWING MONDAY, LILY GLANCED OUT the front window as the elder Mr. Hammond and the two girls pulled up in a black buggy. Edric rode his black horse. He swung down. Everyone, including Estella's and Nancy's china dolls, tramped into the house while Aunt Henny finished getting ready.

Saul Hammond was taking Aunt Henny to the doctor to have her cast removed. Aunt Henny couldn't wait to get rid of the *deadweight* as she liked to call it. It would be interesting to see what the older woman was like when she was more mobile. Lily expected that she would be quite active even being in her fifties.

Edric pulled Lily aside. "Since we are courting now, I'd like to take you to supper. I thought it would be good if we spent some time just the two of us. The White Hotel has a nice dining room."

"I'd like that."

"Tonight?"

"Yes."

"Come on, girls," Saul Hammond said. "Aunt Henny's ready to go."

From where Nancy lay on the floor with Estella and Toby, she rolled onto her back. "I don't want to go. I want to play with Toby. Please, Granpapa?"

Lily piped up. "I don't mind if they stay."

Saul knitted his eyebrows together.

Edric smiled. "Splendid. The girls will like that."

"Yeah!" all three children cheered.

But Lily could tell that Edric's father wasn't keen on the idea. He didn't seem to like or trust her. But why? "Mr. Hammond, why don't you and Aunt Henny take lunch someplace? Aunt Henny has hardly been out of the house since my arrival."

Aunt Henny brightened. "You are a dear child. I would love to be out of the house for a few hours."

The three adults left.

Nancy lay on her stomach, helping Toby with the block puzzle. Estella cradled her pristine doll.

Lily sat on the floor with the children. She held out her hand to Estella. "Your doll is very beautiful."

"Her name is Rose, cuz she has rosy cheeks." Estella primped her doll's plain brown dress.

Lily already knew that from her visit to their house. "She's very pretty."

Nancy held out her doll with the crack across her face. "My dolly's name is Dolly. She's broked. I wasn't careful. Papa fixted her. She's missing a hand too." Nancy held up the arm with the white china hand broken off.

"She is still very pretty."

"She has an ugly dress." Nancy's doll wore the same plain brown dress as Estella's but was a little worse for the wear. It was dirty—dirt that even showed on the drab brown—one sleeve was torn halfway out of the armhole, and the hem was coming down. No lace trim, no ruffles, no gathers, or embellishments of any kind. Whoever made this dress either didn't see a need for a doll to have a pretty dress or didn't have the skills to do any more than something very basic.

"Do your dolls have other dresses?"

Both girls shook their heads.

"Would you like them to have another dress?"

"Papa and Granpapa can't sew a lick." Nancy waved her hand across her front.

Lily pictured Edric's large hands holding a tiny needle then shook her head. But if his girls pleaded with him, she knew he would certainly try. And maybe he even had in secret. "Wait here."

She returned with a yard of yellow fabric the color of wild primroses. She'd bought it to put a border around her sunshine and shadow quilt top, but it might be put to better use making doll dresses. She lowered herself to the floor. "How would you like a dress for each of your dolls out of this?"

"Yes," Estella said then looked down. "If you want to."

Nancy jumped up and down. "It's prettiful." Then the little girl petted Lily's hair. "It's the same color." She laid her head on Lily's shoulder.

Toby scooted over and crawled onto her lap. "And me?"

Her son wanted attention too.

"What about a neckerchief for you?"

Satisfied, Toby nodded and went back over to the block puzzle. He wasn't interested in the dolls or fabric but didn't want to be left out. Maybe she would buy some special red yard goods for his neckerchief.

"Take your dolls and lay them gently on the table." Lily took the fabric over as well. "I'll need to use one of the dolls' dresses as a pattern."

Nancy shoved her doll in front of Lily. "Use mine! Use mine!"

Lily glanced at Estella who nodded her approval. Estella was obviously very careful with her doll, no dirt, no tears, not even a wrinkle.

Lily carefully removed the battered dress. The doll had no under clothes and lay naked on the table. The dolls had porcelain heads with shiny-black painted hair, white forearms with hands—or rather one hand—and black boot-shaped feet. The rest of their bodies were cloth. She would quickly cut the pieces she needed and redress Dolly again. There was enough fabric to make the skirts of the dresses much fuller than the ones they had. She would do her best to make them as pretty as possible. Remembering her dolls from childhood, her favorite dresses were the ones with the most frills and fuss to them. She didn't have enough fabric to put ruffles on two dresses, but maybe some box pleats for fullness and pin-tucks for a little detail.

She cut the two skirt pieces with enough length for the hem and pin-tucks. Fortunately, a doll's skirt didn't need a mudguard on the bottom as ladies' ones did. Some lace to embellish the dresses would be nice, but the plain yellow would have to do. It was all she had. They would have voluminous skirts and very puffed sleeves. A dress she would have loved to have had for her dolls.

After cutting the sleeves and bodice pieces, she stitched darts in the fronts and backs, sewed the shoulder and side seems, then tried the bodices on each of the dolls for a fitting. They fit well. She set them aside, threaded a needle with brown thread, and set to repairing Nancy's brown doll dress.

All the while, the two girls watched her every move, soaking in every detail.

Estella spoke in such a soft, shy voice Lily couldn't quite hear. The girl seemed afraid to speak up or say what she wanted.

Lily wondered why. Edric didn't seem like the type to discourage her. "I'm sorry. I couldn't hear what you said. Could you speak louder?"

Estella shook her head. "Never mind."

Lily crouched down and put her hands on Estella's shoulders. "Please repeat your question. I really want to know."

The girl's eyes revealed the war inside her. Ask again or remain silent? Why was she so reluctant?

Estella sucked in a bolstering breath. "I asked if you would teach me to sew, but you don't have to."

These poor girls missed having a woman in their lives. No one to teach them to sew and cook.

Lily hooked an arm around Estella's waist and pulled her to her side. "I would love to teach you to sew." She turned to Nancy. "Would you like to learn as well?"

Nancy shook her head and pointed her thumb at her chest. "I'm going to be a sheriff like Papa."

Lily believed the precocious girl could. Society's mindset would need to change for people to accept her as sheriff. But if anyone could change people's minds, it would be Nancy.

Nancy skittered off, laid on the floor next to Toby, and pointed to blocks for him to put into place. Lily settled on the settee with Estella and the two doll skirt pieces. She threaded a needle and showed Estella how and where to sew the back seam.

Estella poked the needle into the fabric and removed

it.

After doing this several times, making no progress, Lily covered Estella's hands gently. "The only way to learn is to do. Pull the stitch through."

Fear flickered in the girl's eyes, but she nodded. Lily removed her hand and sensed the girl holding her breath. Estella inched the needle through the fabric and pulled, little by little. Lily resisted the urge to pull the stitch faster.

Estella jerked her gaze up to Lily's. Fear and worry fought for dominance. "Did I do it right?"

Lily nodded. "Very good! Now, do more stitches just like that one." Who had discouraged this little girl that she was fearful and had to perform perfectly? Certainly not Edric. He'd caught a snake for the girls and laughed when they had squished blackberries. Their grandfather? But he hadn't nitpicked the girls either.

Estella was meticulous and slow but made her way down the seam. At the end, Lily showed her how to knot it and cut the thread. The seam wasn't prefect, but for a seven-year-old, it was excellent. She was going to be a stickler for perfection and would outshine all the ladies in the quilting circle in no time.

"Very, very good. You are going to make a fine seamstress. Enough with the sewing for now. Who wants a molasses cookie?"

All three children clamored approval.

She poured them each a small glass of goat's milk and gave them a cookie. After they finished, Lily took the children outside where they hunted for rocks, sticks, and bugs. Fortunately, they didn't spot any snakes.

Nancy petted Lily's hand. "Will you be our mama for the fancy tea?"

Estella latched onto her other hand. "Oh, yes. Please."

"A fancy tea?"

"It is a mother and daughter tea," Estella said in careful practiced diction. "It's at Mrs. Kesner's house. She's the richest lady in town."

Lily wasn't their mother. "I'm sure they would let your father take you." It wasn't her place to attend with them.

Estella said, "Papa looks silly holding a little tea cup in his big hand."

Nancy giggled. "And sillier in a dress."

Both girls collapsed onto the ground in a fit of laughter.

By the time Saul and Aunt Henny returned, Lily and the children were in the front yard with joined hands, singing Ring-a-ring-a-roses. They all fell to the grass in giggles as the buggy came to a stop.

Estella and Nancy ran to the gate as Saul opened it for Aunt Henny. "Granpapa!"

With Aunt Henny's leg free from the cast, she hobbled with a cane.

Lily took the older woman's arm to help her up the walk. "How is your leg?"

"Doc says it's healed up fine."

"Did you have a nice time?"

"I did. I can't tell you how good it was to be out and about. I stopped by Agnes's. I went to the mercantile and talked to Franny. Trudy was there. And I bought more than I needed. Making up for all those weeks I couldn't go at all." Aunt Henny looked back to Saul who carried a sack of flour.

Lily saw Aunt Henny to a chair on the porch and went to the wagon. The children wanted to help. Lily handed a paper-wrapped parcel to Estella. It felt like yard goods. She handed a two-pound sack of coffee to Toby. She was about to hand something small to Nancy when the girl spoke up.

"I want the sugar." Nancy hopped up and down with excitement.

It was a five-pound bag. Lily wasn't sure the little girl could handle it, but she seemed so excited.

Lily held her arms out in front of her with her elbows slightly bent. "Hold your arms like this."

Nancy mimicked her.

Lily slowly lowered the sack into the girl's curled arms, testing to see if she was strong enough.

Nancy grunted, arched her back some, then headed up the walk.

When Lily looked up, Saul stood on the walk, staring at her. She couldn't read his expression. He turned to Nancy as she passed him, giving her a smile and encouraging words. Lily studied Saul watching his granddaughter all the way through the door. No, she didn't believe Saul would discourage his granddaughters. She turned back to the buggy to carry a load in herself. She lifted a crate with several items in it. Though heavy, she knew she could carry it.

Saul took the crate from her. "I'll get that."

"I can carry something."

"This is the last of Henny's things. The rest is ours." He walked away.

Didn't he trust her to carry anything? Evidently not. For reasons she couldn't put her finger on, Edric's father didn't like her. Even though he'd come with a gracious apology, he eyed her warily. Did he know her secret?

No. If he did, he would have told Edric. And Edric would have to put her in jail. She took a deep breath and headed inside. Aunt Henny had slipped inside as well.

Though Saul was setting the crate in the kitchen, his granddaughters were pulling on his sleeves.

"Come look. Come look."

He followed the girls back to the dining room.

"Miss Lily is making dresses for Dolly and Rose," Nancy said.

Estella held up the skirt for her doll. "And she's teaching me to sew."

Saul looked from the dress pieces to Lily. She gave him a small smile. His face pulled into a sour expression.

Didn't he like her helping his granddaughters? What was it going to take to make Saul Hammond soften toward her?

"It's time to go now," Saul said. "Aunt Henny needs to rest after her long day." The three hustled out the door.

Lily noticed the picnic quilt over a chair. She scooped it up and followed them outside. "Don't forget this." She handed it up to Saul.

The muscle in his jaw worked back and forth.

"I finished repairing it."

Estella clutched it. "Oh, thank you. It's like new." She leaned out of the buggy and hugged Lily. "I knew it could be fixed. Papa will be so happy."

Lily wished Saul could at least be a little happy. "I was glad to repair it."

Looking straight ahead, Saul spoke in a rough, husky voice. "Thank you." He snapped the reins. The buggy lurched forward.

Were those tears in the older man's eyes? Staring at the retreating buggy, Lily didn't know what to think, so she went inside.

Aunt Henny came limping down the hall with a white petticoat in her hand. "I have just the thing for those doll dresses." She flopped the petticoat onto the table near the dress pieces.

Lily fingered the fabric. "Silk?"

The top of the garment had been cut away.

"I used part of this years ago. But I think this lace around the bottom will be perfect."

The five rows could gussy up those dresses nicely.

"Are you sure you want to use this? It wouldn't take too much to make it a functioning petticoat again. Just a gusset at the top."

"I have more than enough petticoats. I think this one will be put to better use for those little girls' dolls."

"If I don't use more than two or three rows of the lace for the dresses, I can make each of the dolls a petticoat, bloomers, and chemise."

After removing three rows of lace, she used the dress pieces she'd made to cut out pieces for the underclothes. She had to stop to prepare supper for Aunt Henny, Toby, Mr. Lumbard, and Mr. Tunstall then readied herself for supper with Edric.

This was how she'd imagined courting to be. Giddy. And flutters in her stomach. She never had that with Tobias.

Twenty-One

EDRIC HELD HIS ELBOW OUT TO Lily in Aunt Henny's entry. "Shall we go?" He could hardly breathe. At long last, she was his sweetheart. Unbelievable.

Lily was about to take his offered escort when Toby ran over and wrapped his arms around her skirt. "Don't leave me."

Lily crouched down. "Remember we talked about me going out and you staying here with Aunt Henny?"

He clutched her around the neck and twisted to glance up at Edric. "Don't go."

"I'll return in a little while."

This would not end well. Toby would likely collapse into a fit, leaving Lily distracted and worried all night. Edric crouched as well. "Would you like to come with us?"

"You don't have to do that," Lily said.

"It's all right. He needs to know I'm not stealing you from him. It will help him get used to me." The gratitude in Lily's eyes told him he'd made the right decision. And he wanted to kiss her right there but knew that would upset Toby. If he wanted Lily, he'd have to pass muster with the boy first. He held out his hand to the boy. "If you want to come with us, you'll have to hold your mama's hand and mine."

Toby stared at Edric's large hand.

Edric curled all his fingers closed except the smallest one. Toby wrapped his hand around it cautiously.

Edric smiled then stood, helping Lily up as well.

In the White Hotel dining room, Lily sat across from him with Toby on her lap as a shield. Or was he a barricade? Edric knew Toby had purposely put himself between them. He could sit on his own chair but chose to be on her lap. Was Lily glad for the barrier as well? He couldn't tell. She had tried to get Toby to stay at the boarding house. Edric had been the one to insist on him coming. Now, he wished he hadn't. He remembered now that he'd wanted to spend time alone with Lily.

He would have to make the best of the evening and remember for the next time. "Estella and Nancy said you are making new dresses for Rose and Dolly?"

Lily's eyes widened in what looked like alarm.

"Their dolls."

"I'm sorry. I didn't ask if that was all right. Nancy called her doll's dress ugly, and one thing led to another. I won't make them if you don't want me to."

"It's fine. They are quite excited."

The panic on her face faded.

"They don't complain about their dolls' clothes, but I've known they would like something different for them for a while. I'm not so handy with a needle."

Lily smiled at that. "So they said."

He could have asked any number of single ladies in town who would have been more than happy to have an eligible man in their debt. But there was only one woman he wanted to be in debt to. "Estella was also very happy with the quilt repair."

Her concerned expression slid back in place. "I hope I didn't step over the line."

"How could you think that?"

She opened her mouth but closed it and looked away.

What had she been about to say? "What?"

"Nothing."

"Please tell me."

Still reluctant, she kept her gaze diverted.

"Did my girls say something inappropriate?"

She gave him a quick glance. "Oh, not either of them." Then she looked away again.

When she didn't continue, he said, "Who then? Tell me." He heard and felt that sheriff's demanding edge to his voice. He thought about taking it back until he saw Lily yielding to his demand.

"Your father..."

"Did he say something to upset you?" When was Pa

going to accept her?

"No, he didn't say anything wrong, but he looked upset. He frowned at the doll dresses and then again when I gave Estella the quilt. He said a quick "thank you" then couldn't leave fast enough."

He would have to sit down with Pa and convince him that Lily wasn't out to hurt anyone and wasn't harboring some dark secret that would harm their girls. He was sure he could convince Pa to come around and that Lily meant no disrespect by mending the quilt. She had done it for Estella. But since Ma had made the quilt, maybe he didn't like a stranger stitching on it. Edric knew Pa still missed Ma. He did as well.

"I'll talk to Pa." Edric reached across the table and covered her hand with his. "I can't believe he was actually upset that you fixed the quilt or are making clothes for the dolls. I'm sure it's a misunderstanding." Thankfully, his words seem to comfort her.

Toby's hand inched toward his and Lily's hands. What was the boy going to do? Add his hand to theirs? His little fingers wrapped around her wrist and pulled her hand away from Edric's. Lily seemed to let him. Toby obviously didn't like Edric to touch his mama. Maybe afraid Edric would hurt her like his papa had done. Toby eyed him. Edric pretended not to be bothered.

Supper went well, but Toby was a constant reminder that Edric wouldn't be able to hold Lily's hand or kiss her. Toby fell asleep on her lap on the ride back to Aunt Henny's. He offered to carry the boy inside, but she was right that the boy would be frightened if he woke.

At the foot of the stairs, she said, "I'll put him to bed and be right back down."

She hadn't dismissed him. For that, he was grateful. And she would *be right back down.*

"Was it a good evening, Edric?"

He turned to Aunt Henny on the settee. "Could have been better. But I need to take it slow with the boy."

Aunt Henny pushed to her feet. "Most men wouldn't have allowed Toby to accompany him out with his sweetheart."

He liked her calling Lily his sweetheart. "If I hope to

have any kind of future with her, Toby needs to learn to trust me."

She walked toward him. "He's not the only one."

Now he worried. "You think Lily doesn't trust me?"

"No. But she needs to see she can trust her son with you. That you know that she can't be separated from him."

"She's been separated from him before. Left him in your care."

"You missed my meaning. Lily comes with a child. You can't have one without the other."

"I know that. I wouldn't dream of taking her away from him. I wouldn't want my daughters taken from me. We both come with children."

"And I believe Lily won't need much time at all to be secure in that fact. I'm turning in. See you in the morning."

Soon, Lily returned down the stairs. "I'm so sorry about Toby tagging along."

"If I'm going to court his mama, he needs to get comfortable with me being around." Edric motioned to the settee. "Will you sit with me?"

Lily glanced around. "Where did Aunt Henny go?"

"She retired to her room." It had been kind of Aunt Henny to give them a little privacy. He took Lily's hand and guided her to the settee.

She sat, and he settled in next to her, stretching his arm around behind her.

"Thank you for a lovely evening."

"The pleasure was mine." After a pause, he asked, "What can I do to help Toby not be afraid of me?"

"He's not afraid of you. Not anymore."

"Lily, the boy won't let me be alone with you."

"He's testing the waters, so to speak."

He waited for her to continue.

"If he were truly afraid of you, he wouldn't have come. He would have hidden under the table or in the kitchen and let me leave with you. He is showing his bravery and trust in you by coming."

"And when he pulled your hand from mine?"

"He needed to see how you would react."

"To see if I would get angry at him?"

She nodded.

So that was why Lily had allowed him to do that. "Did I pass?"

"Splendidly."

"So if I wanted to take him fishing, just he and I, would he go?" He wanted to build a rapport with the boy.

"It might be premature for that."

"Maybe we could all go fishing some time next week. I know a great spot. My girls love to fish."

"I think that would be nice, but I'll watch."

"I can teach you."

She shuddered. "No, thank you."

He would have plenty of time to teach her to fish. This outing would be for Toby to get to know him better and trust him. And maybe even like him. "Is it premature for this?" He scooped up her hand in his.

She lowered her head as though suddenly shy.

With a finger under her chin, he lifted her face and gazed into her intense blue eyes. Her blond lashes framed them like sparkling stars. Yes, the night and stars. He leaned toward her but didn't want to startle her so said, "I'm going to..."

"I know." Her voice came out breathy in anticipation, and she closed her eyes.

He'd been wanting to do this since the other day when he'd almost kissed her. He leaned closer. He could feel her breath on his face.

"Mommy."

Lily jerked around toward Toby with his face pressed between two of the stair railing rungs. "You're supposed to be in bed. Go on. I'll be there in a little while."

"Can't." Toby scooted down two steps and put his face between the rungs again.

Edric leaned back. Another test? Was Toby never going to give him a chance to kiss his mother? Edric had been patient. More than patient. Maybe it was too soon for Toby. Or Lily.

She was always so patient and gentle with the boy. That was what had attracted him to her. But there were times when a parent needed to be firm with a child.

Needed to make the child do as the parent wished even if the child didn't like it. But when was the last time he'd remained firm with his girls and not given in to their wishes? He hadn't. He understood Lily's dilemma all too well.

It was time to go. As he stood, he lifted Lily's hand and kissed it. "Good night."

"You're leaving?"

He glanced at Toby. "I think it best."

"I can tuck him in bed. It will only take a minute."

Edric doubted the boy would stay as long as he was there. "I'll see you in the morning." He strode into the entry and looked Toby in the eyes. "I'll see you in the morning too." He walked out. What kind of future could he have with Lily if Toby objected to him ever being alone with her? And, if Pa never trusted her?

He drove the buggy home, put the horse in his stall, and found Pa staring into the fire in the sitting room.

"Did you have any trouble with the girls?"

"They were like the wind rushing down the canyon. All excited about new dresses for their dolls."

Nice of Pa to bring up the topic he needed to talk to him about. "Do you have a problem with Lily making dresses for the girls' dolls?"

Pa shook his head.

Something was wrong. "What happened with Lily today? She says you rushed off when she gave Estella the quilt."

Pa retrieved the quilt in question. "Do you see this?"

Edric squinted but wasn't sure what Pa was referring to. "See what?"

"My point. Her stitches are so small you can't hardly tell where all the rips were. I counted twenty-three tears of varying sizes. One of them was nearly seven inches long. Went clean through the front and back. Your ma would be right pleased. She always meant to do some repairs on this old thing."

Edric didn't understand. He looked up and saw tears glisten in Pa's eyes.

Pa nodded. "Real pleased. She would have liked her."

So, Pa was happy about the quilt. His rush to leave

when Lily gave them the quilt was to hide his emotions. "And you?"

"She's teaching Estella to sew and is taking the girls to that fancy tea at Mrs. Kesner's next week."

He hadn't been looking forward to trying to take the girls and being the only man there. Having all those ladies staring at him. And, the single ones baiting their hooks to reel him in.

After a moment, Pa clasped his hand onto Edric's shoulder. "Don't let her get away." He swallowed hard. "I best check on the animals." And he walked off.

No need to tell Pa he'd already done that. Let Pa collect himself on his own. So now, the only one standing in the way of him and Lily was Toby.

Lily sat in the circle of women, feeling comfortable in their presence. She had removed three rows of lace from the petticoat and cut the rest of the garment up into the pieces for the dolls' underclothes. Since her sunshine and shadow quilt top was all pieced together, she had decided to sew on the dresses for Edric's girls today.

She had been apprehensive about making the dresses until this morning when Edric told her his father had been quite touched by her work repairing the quilt. She had tried to get Aunt Henny to make the under garments, but she insisted that Lily make them all. But Lily would make sure the girls knew that Aunt Henny had donated the fabric for the underclothes and the lace.

Isabelle picked up one of the doll sleeves. "What are you making?"

"Dresses for Estella's and Nancy's dolls." Lily held up a bodice with one sleeve attached.

Isabelle's mother, Marguerite, inclined her head. "I see you're doing all you can to ingratiate yourself to our sheriff."

"I'm making these for Estella and Nancy." Edric had nothing to do with this. She merely wanted his girls to have a second dress for their dolls. She had always loved changing her dolls' clothes.

"What better way to win the heart of our fair sheriff than to win the hearts of his daughters."

"That's not what I'm doing." She glanced around the circle. Did everyone think she was manipulating Edric? No one would meet her gaze.

No one but Aunt Henny. "I think it's very Christian of you to do this while expecting nothing in return."

Several women nodded, and others vocalized their agreement.

Then everyone went back to their own work in silence and slowly resumed conversations around the circle.

Lily took a deep breath. She didn't care what any of these ladies thought. Estella and Nancy deserved these dresses, and she would finish them as quickly as possible.

Lily decided she would not run to the door when Edric dropped off the milk on Saturday. So on Sunday, she wasn't surprised when Edric kept his distance. He seemed wary of getting too close to her with Toby around.

When he dropped them off at Aunt Henny's after church, she asked, "May your girls come in? I have something for them."

Edric nodded his consent, and everyone traipsed inside.

Lily ushered the girls to the table where the dresses and under garments were laid out, along with Toby's neckerchief. She showed the girls which set belonged to who. "This one is the one you did some sewing on, Estella. You don't mind that I finished it, do you?"

She shook her head and wrapped her arms around Lily. "Thank you so much."

Nancy turned on Edric and planted her hands on her

hips. "I told you we needed to bring Dolly and Rose."

Edric's smile widened as he pulled his hands from behind his back with the dolls.

The girls squealed and ran to claim their dolls and immediately got to the business of changing their dolls' clothes. Lily wrapped the kerchief around Toby's neck.

Edric sidled up next to her and slipped his hand around hers. "Thank you."

She was glad to have him holding her hand. "You're welcome." So maybe she was motivated a little by Edric.

Twenty-Two

ON MONDAY, LILY WALKED INTO EDRIC'S office with a lunch basket. "I've come to make up for supper the other night."

A deputy stepped over to the covered basket. "I'm starved."

Edric knocked the man's hat off from behind. "Don't you need to go check on things around town?"

The man scooped up his hat and scuttled out.

"I'm sure there's enough for him."

"I'll not miss my one opportunity to have you to myself."

Her cheeks warmed. She had been thinking the same thing. Toby had wanted to come, but she'd persuaded him to stay with Aunt Henny so she and Edric could have a little time together.

He grasped her hand tentatively and laced his fingers with hers. "I wasn't sure you were really ready to be courted after Toby usurping our supper plans last week. But you coming today tells me you are. I thought maybe I was pushing you too soon. Thank you."

She thought about retrieving her hand but glanced at their hands instead. "Aren't you hungry?"

"You don't need both to get the food out, do you?" He brought her hand to his lips.

She tingled all over. This was how she'd imagined courting would be before her parents died and Tobias took over her life.

Turning her focus on the basket, she pulled out food... with one hand.

Edric did let go while they ate.

Later, Lily packed up the lunch basket. "I should let you get back to work."

"You don't have to rush off." He caressed her cheek.

In his longing gaze, her breath was swept away, and

with it, her regrets of the past. *All* her regrets. She wanted to pretend the past six years had never happened and to stay in this one moment.

"I'm going to kiss you."

Ever since that second kiss when she'd run away, he had told her each time he was about to kiss her. He obviously didn't want to frighten her again. And, he never did more than put his hands on her waist.

"You don't always have to warn me. I can see the intent in your eyes."

"You can, can you?" His mouth pulled up on the corners. "What are they saying now?"

"The same thing." Only more earnestly.

As he leaned closer, she closed the gap between them. His lips were soft and gentle. Ardent and encouraging. She wrapped her arms around him to let him know that it was all right for him to do the same.

Even then, he was still tentative in his hold.

When he pulled back, he touched her hair. "I never want you to feel trapped."

"Thank you." She released him. "Now, I really should let you get back to work."

He let his hand slide down her arm as she stepped back. Then he gripped her hand. "I wasn't sure when to tell you this. I hope now isn't the wrong time."

Her stomach flipped. "What is it?"

He sat on the corner of his desk and pulled her to him, resting his hands on her hips. "I know we have only been courting for a short bit, but... I love you."

Her breath caught. She was sure she loved him too but wasn't ready to say it yet. "Oh, Edric."

He put his fingers on her lips. "Shh. I don't expect you to feel the same so soon. But I thought it only fair to let you know how much you mean to me."

This was what she had been missing over the past six years. She felt as though she were returning to life. She felt like her old self before her parents died, before she had turned away from God. She felt wrapped in God's love once again. And wrapped in the love of Aunt Henny and Edric. The shadows of the past were clearing to the sunshine. Freed.

She kissed his fingertips before pulling them away from her lips. Then she kissed his mouth. "I'm still a little confused." She wasn't sure it was safe to settle down. That her past would stay behind her. She could still feel those shadows lingering in the distance.

"I'm sure you are. I'm not asking for anything from you."

"I appreciate that. Thank you." She stepped away, happy and giddy inside. She picked up the lunch basket and ducked out the door.

Edric remained seated on the corner of his desk, a crooked smile on his alluring lips.

"Get back to work." She smiled, turned, and crossed the street, stepping up onto the boardwalk on the other side.

She bounced as she went. He loved her! And she him. She never knew it felt like this. Happy and free. She should have told him. Should she go back? No. She would surprise him the next time she saw him. No. She would go back now. No. Wait—

"You are a hard lady to track down, Mrs. Bremmer."

Her step faltered, and her blood ran cold at the familiar voice behind her. Her breathing stopped. She dared not move, lest it make him real.

Maybe she had imagined the terrifying voice from her past.

A past best left buried.

Stepping through his office doorway, Edric stood by the post as Lily turned slowly to the dark-haired dandy in a bowler hat. The man hitched his hip on the railing. Lily took a step back. Even from this distance, he could see she had paled at the sight of the stranger. Did Edric need to intervene? The man had done nothing wrong... yet. He appeared to have only spoken to Lily.

The man spoke again.

Edric wished he could hear what was being said.

Lily shook her head.

Edric raised his foot to head across the street and confront the man when Lily spun around and hurried away. She looked more frightened than the times she'd run away from him.

He would have to have a talk with this man. Find out his intensions.

The man laughed as Lily retreated. His cheek creased in a dimple.

A dimple just like Toby's.

Edric froze in midstride, half on and half off the boardwalk. Breathless, as though he'd been punched in the gut.

The man turned and saw him, tipped his bowler hat, and strode off.

Edric watched until the man entered the saloon. Then he turned and went back into his office. He laced his fingers behind his head and paced. Who was that man? He didn't dare confront him right now. He might strike the stranger without cause.

Lily? Should he talk to her? If she was too afraid to tell him who the man was, he didn't want to take his frustration out on her. And she had looked terrified.

If he was the one who had hurt Lily and Toby, Edric might just kill him.

He drew in a deep breath and unlocked his hands from behind his head. He couldn't talk to Lily right now. And, he couldn't face the stranger. But he had to do something.

Lord, what should I do?

He needed to know who this man was. He strode across the street and over to the White Hotel.

Grant was slipping pieces of paper into a couple of the key slots behind the front desk.

"Grant."

The young man turned around. "Sheriff Rix. You haven't been in for a while."

He'd obviously become too complacent and sloppy. "You got any new guests?"

"Every day. I thought maybe you had given up on looking for whoever it was you was looking for. Or found the man."

"Been busy." Busy courting Lily. "Anyone I should know about?"

"I had an Elliott Marshall who checked in two days ago, but he checked out this morning. A Douglas Shift checked in earlier today. He was alone."

"Does he have dark hair? Bowler? Look like a dandy from back East?"

Grant shook his head. "He has real light hair." His eyes widened. "But that does sound like another guest we have." Grant ran his finger up the register page. "Here he is, T. Bremmer."

The name meant nothing to Edric.

"He checked in five days ago."

Five days? This man had been in town *five* days?

"That man from a few weeks back checked in again too. Hal Jenson. The man who was hunting for his brother. Mr. Bremmer and Mr. Jenson seemed to know each other."

So, Hal hadn't been searching for his brother. He'd been hired by this T. Bremmer to find Lily. And apparently, Lily knew him. "Did Mr. Bremmer say what his business in town was?"

"He was real evasive. Flashed his oily smile and said it was a family matter."

A family matter? That involved Lily? And a man who looked enough like Toby to be related? This was not good.

"Is he the man you've been on the lookout for?"

"Could be. Let me know if you overhear anything between Mr. Bremmer and Mr. Jenson."

"Come to think of it, he was acting real strange that first night he was in town."

"How so?"

"Well, they both came down to supper but stopped at the doorway. Then Mr. Jenson left, and Mr. Bremmer set himself down in that chair over there." Grant pointed across the lobby. "And set to reading the paper."

Edric stepped back to put himself between the chair and the doorway then looked into the dining room. The table he'd sat at with Lily was in plain view. "Thursday night?"

"Yup."

So, Mr. Bremmer had been watching Lily and him, and likely not reading the paper at all. Concealing himself behind it.

"Thanks." Edric stepped out onto the boardwalk.

Could Mr. Bremmer be Toby's father? Maybe he had been watching Toby. Lily had said her husband was dead. But, maybe the boy's father hadn't been Lily's husband. That would mean that Toby wasn't really her son. Maybe it was this man who had been abusing the two of them. And Lily took the boy to protect him. That would put Lily in a heap of trouble.

And danger.

Edric would have to run the man out of town. He pushed through the swinging doors of the saloon.

Nelson nodded a greeting, but Edric scanned the room. Mr. Bremmer sat at a table, playing cards with the man he assumed to be Mr. Jenson.

Edric strode over, pulled his coat back so his sheriff's star showed as well as his gun. "I think the two of you have out stayed your welcome."

Mr. Bremmer tossed his cards onto the table and slowly lifted his gaze. "We haven't done anything wrong, Sheriff."

"Let's keep it that way. There's a train leaving late this afternoon. I suggest the two of you be on it."

"When my business in town is concluded, I'll be happy to leave."

"What business is that?"

"That's between me and a certain lady."

"What business do you have with Mrs. Lexington?"

"Lexington?" Mr. Bremmer smiled. Toby's smile. But with a sinister bent.

Edric opened and closed his fists at his sides.

"Mrs. *Lexington* has something that belongs to me. When it's returned to me, I'll be on my way."

He would never let Toby be turned over to this man. He didn't care what the relationship between the two was. The problem being, he had no cause to throw this man in his jail. He needed to run these two out of town before either of them hurt Lily or Toby. Or tried to leave with them.

"I'll be watching the both of you."

"Looking forward to it."

Edric turned to leave. When Mr. Bremmer called to him, he stopped at the swinging doors.

"Sheriff, tell that sweetheart of yours that I will be talking to her again. Real soon."

This man knew he was courting Lily? Yes, he'd seen them at supper. Edric strode back over and leaned across the table, poking his finger into the man's chest. "You stay away from Mrs. Lexington."

The man's mouth pulled up on one side. "I'm not acquainted with any *Mrs. Lexington.* But I will be seeing your sweetheart. "

Edric wanted to punch that smirk right off his face, dimples and all. He strode out before he gave in to the urge.

Lily opened the front door. Aunt Henny called to her. She didn't reply but went straight upstairs.

Lily tossed their two carpetbags onto the bed. How had he found her? She and Toby had to leave. She had made a plan. Pulling the clothes from the dresser, she shoved them into the carpetbags.

Toby came in. "Mommy?"

She ran across the room, scooped him up in her arms, and locked the door.

He whimpered and gazed at the half-packed bags. "What are you doing? Are we going away again?"

She crawled up onto the bed and sat against the headboard, cradling Toby. "Yes, baby." How could she have been so foolish to think she could stay in one place and be happy?

Toby popped his thumb into his mouth.

Lily wished she could do something as simple to make her feel better. She would wait until after dark to slip out of the house.

Twenty-Three

EDRIC SAT ON HIS HORSE, STARING at the boardinghouse. He'd waited until his anger with Mr. Bremmer had subsided before coming. Lily owed him nothing. Let alone an explanation of who Mr. Bremmer was to her. She didn't know he'd seen the man. He could pretend he hadn't and knew nothing of him. Pretend the pleasure of a perfect lunch alone with her had continued indefinitely and carried him through the day. But it hadn't. And he couldn't.

He didn't want to know if this man was Toby's father. Or if he was Lily's husband.

But he *had* to know.

He couldn't go on not knowing.

What if Mr. Bremmer was both husband and father?

Lily would be ripped from his tenuous grasp.

And Toby?

A new pain of loss rippled through him. Loss as much for Lily as for a son. He hadn't even realized how much he'd been looking forward to having a son, until the boy was slipping away from him.

Now, he wished he hadn't had those impatient thoughts about Toby coming between him and Lily. The small threat Toby posed was minor compared to this man.

But maybe Bremmer was no one. Maybe he only happened to look like Toby. Maybe he'd said something rude to Lily and that was what had frightened her. Maybe she didn't even know the man. After all, Bremmer had said he didn't know any Mrs. Lexington.

But his gut told him all those maybes were wrong. This man had come out of the shadows of Lily's past.

And Bremmer changed everything. His presence had a bearing on Edric's future with Lily.

Now he wished he hadn't seen Bremmer talking to Lily. He wished he didn't know. He wished...

He turned his horse and headed for home.

As the sun moved lower in the sky, a knock came on Lily's door. She held Toby tighter. He didn't make a sound. Neither of them dared to breathe.

"Mrs. Lexington?" Mr. Tunstall called through the door.

She didn't answer. She couldn't answer. Fear kept her frozen like a statue. She had to keep Toby safe. If she moved, all her secrets would shatter around her, then she and Toby would be left exposed to danger.

He knocked and called again.

She shook her head to keep herself from crying out, holding in the agony rising in her throat. *Go away!*

His footsteps receded down the stairs.

She dared to take a breath.

No doubt Aunt Henny had sent him up. She must be fretting over Lily's rude behavior in ignoring her.

Lily didn't have the strength to ruminate on the older woman's concerns and needed to figure out a way to deal with her problem. She had to stay focused on protecting Toby.

A few moments after Mr. Tunstall had left, Toby whispered, "I'm hungry."

"I know, but we can't go downstairs. I'll get you something later. I promise."

He slid his thumb back into his mouth and rested against her chest. Her good little boy.

She kept her arms firmly around him to keep herself from shaking.

Edric paced in the barn. He had not spoken to Lily yet.

He had to think this through. He had posted one of his deputies at the hotel to keep an eye on Bremmer and his cohort.

Pa came in. "What has your union suit in a wad?"

Stopping, Edric stared. He didn't want to admit Pa had been right about Lily. She had a secret. And from the looks of her unwelcomed visitor, it was a big one. "Did the girls wake up? Are they all right?"

Pa held up his hand. "They're fine. Sleeping like logs. But something's not right with you."

He didn't want to say it. He still wanted to pretend this afternoon hadn't taken place. Tried to talk himself into thinking it was all a misunderstanding on his part. He had misinterpreted Lily's actions. And hadn't really seen the reflection of Toby in the man's face. "Someone's come to town looking for Lily."

Pa drew in a slow breath. "Are our girls going to get hurt?"

"Not if I can help it."

"What does this person want with her?"

"I'm not sure. Possibly the boy."

"Take the boy away from his mother?" Pa shook his head.

If she was his mother. "I won't let him."

"Does he have any claim to the boy?"

If the resemblance was any indication, he did. "I don't know." Had he been a fool to ignore the vast physical differences between mother and son?

"Is he the one who hurt her and the boy?"

"I don't know." He couldn't let himself think that Bremmer was the one to hurt Lily, or he might end up in his own jail for killing the man.

"Who did she say the man was?"

"I haven't talked to her."

"Afraid he has a legitimate claim?"

Exactly his fear. "I don't want to lose her. Or Toby." His insides tightened at the thought.

"I think she needs our help."

This was a switch for Pa. A month ago, he would have led Bremmer right to Lily and told him to take her away. "I don't know what to do."

"You can't let your fear of learning the truth stop you from doing what's right."

"What do you mean?"

"Your heart wants to protect itself from finding out you might not be able to have her. That this man might be her family and take her away from you. Your sworn duty as sheriff is to protect her. Protect her even if your heart gets broken in the process." Pa gripped his shoulder. "But you can't ignore this and hope it will go away or be forgotten like a child's tantrums."

Pa spoke what Edric knew to be true. He would sleep on it and pray. Not make any hasty decisions.

Put off until tomorrow the shattering of his dreams.

When the house had been still for some time, Lily finished packing the carpetbags as silently as possible. She gazed at her sleeping son on the bed. His life would always be like this, fraught with trouble, moving all the time, and fear, until he had grown into a man and could protect himself. She had been foolish to think she could settle in one place. Foolish to make friends. Foolish to fall in love. Tears pooled in her eyes. She blinked them away.

She rubbed Toby's arm. "Wake up, sweetie."

Toby rolled onto his back.

"If you're really quiet, I can take you downstairs to get something to eat."

Toby nodded.

"But you have to walk."

He nodded again.

She put her finger to her lips as she unlocked and opened the door. But she needn't worry. Toby knew how to be quiet for his own preservation.

They tiptoed down to the kitchen. She snatched two apples, two hardboiled eggs, and half a loaf of bread. She stuffed them into the larger carpetbag.

Toby moaned. "Gotta go pee."

Oh dear. She didn't have time to change him if he wet himself. "Hold it for just a minute." She clutched the carpetbags with one arm and opened the back door.

He grabbed the front of his pants and gritted his teeth.

She seized his hand and hurried out the door. Why hadn't she had him use the chamber pot in their room? Because then she would have to empty and clean it before she left.

Halfway between the porch and the outhouse, she heard, "You never disappoint, Lily."

She froze in place, pulling Toby close to her side. The voice from her past coiled around her. She didn't turn to him.

He chuckled. "So predictable." He stepped around in front of her.

"Timothy." Tobias's brother looked so much like him. She stepped back, heard something behind her, and spun around. A man she didn't know stood a couple of feet away.

"Don't even think of running," Timothy said.

She turned back to him. What was he going to do? Then she could smell that Toby had wet himself. She stiffened as her past drew closer.

"Did you know that Tobias and I literally flipped a coin to see which one of us would get to marry you?"

"What?"

He shrugged. "I lost. I think Tobias cheated. I would have treated you better than he did. Tobias always was a mean ol' cuss, but he was a charmer too. He could talk a mule out of its stubbornness."

"When my parents died and he started helping me, he'd planned from the start to marry me?" She'd assumed it was a side thought, an imposition, something that had to be done so he could help her through her crisis. Make decisions for her. Take care of everything. He'd told her numerous times how she was an inconvenience to him. That the only thing she was good for was bedding.

"Sweetheart, he planned so much more than that. Long before your parents died. He wanted your father's money."

"But how would he know they were going to die?"

"Let's just say their accident wasn't... quite so accidental."

She gasped. Tobias had played a part in their deaths? But it made sense. His comments about all his work and planning. He'd wished there had been another option than to marry her. How none of this was easy for him. He had never wanted a wife and certainly not a worthless child. How many times had he caused her to miscarry? Toby had defied him from the start.

Timothy chuckled. "He was right. You were too innocent to ever suspect him of anything."

Her eyes welled. Her poor parents. With one arm holding the carpetbags and the other holding Toby to her side, she didn't have a hand to wipe her eyes. So she blinked hard to clear her vision and tears rolled down her cheeks. "What do you want?"

"You have something that belongs to me."

She pressed Toby even tighter to her side. Toby clung to her leg, not making a sound. He *was* Tobias's heir. Whomever controlled Toby, controlled whatever was left of Tobias's assets. "I won't let you take my son."

Timothy stepped forward, his face now only a few inches from hers.

Though she refused to cower, her insides tumbled around like a rockslide.

"I don't want the boy, but it's good to know where your priorities lie. If you don't want any harm to come to him, you'll do exactly what I say."

She heard a rifle cock behind her. Was that Timothy's cohort?

But then Aunt Henny spoke in a low, threatening voice. "Leave her be."

Timothy shifted his gaze off Lily and raised his hands. He gave a jerk of his head, and Lily heard the man behind her move away. "We don't mean no harm, ma'am."

While still looking in Aunt Henny's direction, he whispered to her, "I'm staying at the White Hotel. I best receive a visit from you tomorrow if you know what's good for the boy. And don't be telling the old lady or your sheriff friend about me."

Timothy lifted his hat to Aunt Henny. "We'll be on our way, ma'am."

Lily stood stock still, barely daring to breathe, while Timothy walked away.

When Timothy and his friend had left, Aunt Henny stepped forward. "They're gone. You can come inside now."

Lily didn't want to go in. She didn't want to face Aunt Henny. It couldn't have escaped the older woman's notice that Lily had been trying to leave. Should she simply walk away? No, Timothy would follow her.

She heard soft footsteps approaching from behind.

Mr. Tunstall came up beside her. He took the carpetbag from under her arm and peeled the other one from her stiff grasp. "You're safe. Don't worry about a thing." He put his free arm around her shoulders to turn her around then guided her toward the porch.

Lily couldn't look at Aunt Henny so kept her gaze down.

Mr. Tunstall released her in the kitchen and carried her carpetbags upstairs.

Aunt Henny set the butt of the rifle on the floor. "Go clean up your son. We'll talk in the morning."

Lily's legs moved without her telling them to, taking their orders from Aunt Henny. When she got up to her room, her carpetbags were on the floor by the bed. Mr. Tunstall was nowhere in sight.

She gave her son a hard-boiled egg to eat while she cleaned him up

As she put him into bed, he said, "Is Uncle Timothy going to hurt us?"

She hoped not. "No, sweetie."

"Is *Him* coming to hurt us?"

"No. Your father will never hurt either of us again. Now go to sleep. You're safe."

If she thought they could escape, she would leave again right now, but Timothy or his friend would likely still be waiting for her. And this time, Timothy might not be so nice, and Aunt Henny wouldn't be there to rescue her. If she didn't show up at the hotel tomorrow, he would hurt Toby. She had no doubt of that.

Trapped. No choice but to find out what Timothy wanted and figure out what to do then.

The room she'd once thought of as cheerful was now a prison.

Twenty-Four

FROM WHERE SHE SAT ON THE settee, Henny watched Edric stride up the walk and called to him when he reached the door. "Come on in." Her leg hadn't gained its strength back yet.

The screen door creaked, and a moment later, Edric appeared in the parlor, glancing toward the kitchen. "I brought Toby's milk."

"They are both still in bed." At least she hoped so.

After last night's escape attempt, Henny had slept on the settee. Not very comfortable, but she had wanted to make sure the men didn't return, and Lily didn't try to leave again.

"Are they all right?"

She wasn't sure. "Sit down."

He sat, concern etched on his strong face.

"Two men came in the night."

Edric shoved to his feet. "What? What happened?"

She motioned for him to sit. When he did, she continued. "They stopped Lily and Toby on their way out to the privy." She would leave out the part about Lily having their bags packed and looked as though she were running away.

"Are they all right?"

"They're fine. A little shaken. I scared the men off with my rifle." Good thing the men didn't test her. She hadn't had time to load the gun. But Edric didn't need to know that either.

"Who were they?"

"I didn't recognize either of them."

"Did one of them have dark hair and resemble Toby? Did the other one look average with brown hair?"

"They could have been. I couldn't see them real well. Do you know them?"

"T. Bremmer and Hal Jenson. Do either one of those names mean anything to you?"

Henny shook her head. "You?"

"Mr. Jenson came to town a few weeks ago under the guise of searching for his brother. He left, and I didn't think any more about him. Mr. Bremmer arrived in town six days ago. He's friends with Mr. Jenson. Mr. Bremmer stopped Lily yesterday. She seemed scared and hurried off."

That was why Lily had gone directly upstairs when she came home yesterday afternoon and then hadn't left her room.

"You say one of them favors the boy?"

He nodded. "T. Bremmer."

"That can't be good."

"Nope."

"Have you talked to her about them?"

He shook his head. "I wanted to find out who they were first."

"Lily went straight up to her room when she came home yesterday. She didn't come out until she went to the privy in the night and those men showed up." It was a good thing Henny was having a restless night and heard her going out the back door.

"That man scared her, and I want to know why."

"Well, let her sleep. I'm sure she didn't get much of it."

"I'll come by later to see if she is up." He set the milk in the kitchen and left.

Without pause, Edric headed for the telegraph office. "I need to send a telegram to Philadelphia." He scratched the pencil on the pad of paper: *Inquiring about T. Bremmer and Hal Jenson.*

He handed his message to Mort. "Let me know as soon as you receive an answer."

From there, he headed to his office and pinned on

his star. He wanted to be official when he confronted Mr. Bremmer and Mr. Jenson. He strode over to the White Hotel.

His deputy Cord sat in a chair in the lobby, feet stretched out, hat low over his eyes, a cup of coffee cradled in his lap. Cord spoke before Edric reached him. "Howdy, Sheriff Rix."

"What happened here?"

Cord pulled his feet in and shoved back his hat. "Not a thing. Been quiet and peaceful all night. Mr. Jenson went up to his room around seven and Mr. Bremmer about eight. Neither have come down."

But they had been at Aunt Henny's. He was sure it had been them. "Which rooms do they occupy?"

"Corner rooms, front and back at the end of the hall. What's wrong?"

"They were out last night."

"They didn't come by me. I swear I didn't fall asleep all night. Sammy came over and relieved me a couple of times for an hour or so. He said he didn't see hide nor hair of them either."

Edric rubbed his hand across his mouth and chin. "They must have climbed out one of their windows. Likely, not more than one of them is up there now."

As though summoned, Mr. Bremmer descended the stairs.

Edric met the man at the foot. "You were at the boarding house last night."

Mr. Bremmer put on an innocent face. "I've been in my room all night, Sheriff. Just ask your deputy."

Edric wasn't buying it. The man had known a deputy was stationed here and made it look as though he were in his room. Edric knew better. "Stay away from Mrs. Lexington and Aunt Henny's Boarding House. I want you and your friend on the next train out of town."

"You can't force me to leave. I've done nothing wrong."

This man wouldn't be intimidated, and technically, he *hadn't* done anything wrong. Yet.

Edric wished he would so he could put him in jail where he couldn't hurt or scare Lily. "I'll be keeping an eye on you."

Mr. Bremmer glanced over at Cord. "Yes, I see the way you keep an eye on me. Would you like to join me for breakfast? Then you will know exactly where I am."

The thought of sitting at a table with this sorry excuse for a man turned his stomach. "Stay away from Mrs. Lexington."

Mr. Bremmer tipped his hat and chuckled. "Still don't know a Mrs. Lexington, Sherriff." He strolled off into the hotel dining room.

Cord came up next to Edric. "I don't like that man."

"Me neither. Go home and get some sleep."

When Lily woke, the angle of the sun told her that it was nearly noon. She hurriedly readied herself and Toby then went downstairs. Upon her entrance into the parlor, Edric stood, and she stopped short.

She shifted her gaze to Aunt Henny. "I'm sorry for oversleeping." She dashed into the kitchen and leaned on the worktable. Toby clung to her skirt. What should she do now? She hadn't expected Edric to be here. Did he know anything? What had Aunt Henny told him?

"Lily?"

She straightened at Edric's voice and put one hand on Toby's shoulder. Tears threatened to burst out of her. She schooled her emotions, swallowed down her tears, and turned to him in a calm manner. "Would you like a glass of water or something to eat? I smell coffee on the stove."

He stared at her a moment. "No. I want to know what's wrong. I saw Mr. Bremmer talk to you yesterday. Who is he to you?"

Her husband. But Edric meant Timothy. Her brother-in-law's words assaulted her thoughts. *Don't tell the old woman or your sheriff friend about me.* It was best that way. "He's no one."

Edric moved toward her. "He scared you. I could see

that from clear across the street."

She stepped back. He'd seen him yesterday. "Just leave him be."

"He came *here* last night."

Aunt Henny had told him at least that. She probably also told him that she had been packed to leave. "He's no one."

"He is someone. Tell me, and I can help you."

He couldn't help her. No one could. "I don't want to talk about him."

"Is he the one who hurt you and Toby?"

She shook her head. At least not yet.

He held out a hand and stepped forward again. "Lily."

She reached for the back door. "If Toby doesn't get to the necessary... Excuse us." She darted outside and hurried to the privy. She latched the door and leaned against it.

Once inside, Toby said, "I don't have to go potty."

Indeed not. He had used the chamber pot upstairs.

She touched his hair. "I know, sweetie." Then she crouched down. "Can you do something for me?" He nodded. "It's important that you go inside by yourself."

He tossed his little arms around her neck. "I want you to come."

"Mommy really needs you to go in by yourself. I have something that must be done. No one is going to hurt you in there. Can you be a big boy and do that for me?"

He pulled in his bottom lip and nodded.

She opened the door and watched Toby shuffle toward the house. He looked over his slender shoulder several times, and she had to shoo him on.

Once he reached the porch and slipped inside, she darted out of the privy and around the side of the house. She hurried down the street so Edric and Aunt Henny wouldn't see her.

Outside the White Hotel, she stopped to catch her breath. After a moment, she straightened, smoothed her hands down her skirt, and strode inside.

The clerk behind the reception desk wore glasses. "May I help you, miss?"

Her hands shook. She clasped them together. "I would like to speak with one of your guests, Mr. Bremmer."

He studied her a moment. "He's not here. He ate breakfast earlier and left."

What should she do now? If he wasn't here, how would she find him? She would have to wait for him to return. She looked around the lobby. She didn't want to sit out here where every person coming and going would see her. She glanced toward the dining room. "May I wait in there until he returns?"

"Of course."

There were a handful of patrons at tables. She chose a table by the wall and sat, facing the entrance.

If she could placate one brother, she could the other as well. Just tell him what he wanted to hear.

She didn't have to wait long.

Soon Timothy loomed in the doorway. He spoke to the man next to him who nodded and leaned on the doorframe. As Timothy walked over to her, he smiled—a smile so like Tobias's—endearing and disarming.

And dangerous.

A shiver ran up her spine. She clenched her sweaty hands on her lap.

He came to the table and sat. "Hello, Lily. I'm sorry, I should say Mrs. Bremmer. But I hear you are going by your maiden name. Wasn't Mrs. Lexington your mother?"

Lily glanced around, hoping no one heard him.

"Would you prefer we go someplace more private? Say my room?"

She glared at him. "What do you want?"

"You have something that belonged to my brother."

"I didn't take anything of Tobias's." Except his son. And she would never turn him over to Timothy. Besides, he said he wasn't interested in Toby.

"You took something. I searched the house. It wasn't there. If you're thinking you can use it against me, you'll fail."

"I didn't take anything." This was useless. He was accusing her of something she didn't do. What was he really after? She pushed to a stand.

Timothy remained seated but seized her wrist. "Sit."

She twisted her arm to free herself.

Timothy's grip tightened to the point of pain. "I know what you've done, Lily."

She pictured Tobias lying lifeless on the entry floor.

"You would hate for anything to happen to your boy. And what if the good sheriff found out what you've done?"

She sank back onto the chair.

"That's a good girl." He released her arm. "No more attempts to run off."

Tears welled in Lily's eyes. "I swear I didn't take anything from the house except our clothes." A little money and jewelry, but nothing expensive. He couldn't have come all this way for that.

"You must have taken something else."

"What are you looking for?"

"Several things. A ledger for one. There are papers missing as well."

"I didn't take anything like that. Nothing of Tobias's." She hadn't wanted anything of his.

"But you did take something. What!"

"Only my father's Bible and my mother's hand mirror, brush, and comb set."

"The Bible. Tobias could have hidden something in there."

"Not a ledger." She would have noticed that.

"No. But he could have tucked in a piece of paper telling where he hid it."

"Why would he do that?"

"Because he knew I would never think to look there. You find that piece of paper and anything else he might have hidden in that Bible and bring it to me."

She stood.

He grabbed her arm again. "Don't even think of running off, or I *will* take your boy."

Her insides wrenched. She jerked herself free. The other man blocked the doorway. She turned to her brother-in-law.

"Hurry back." Timothy gave a nod to the man who then stepped aside.

Lily hastened away and rushed out the door. She stopped short at the sight of Edric leaning on the hitching rail facing the plate-glass window of the dining room. She looked in and could clearly see the table she had been seated at.

His voice was low and gentle. "Let me help you."

She bit her bottom lip. If it were only that easy. If she only had herself to consider, she would gladly let Edric deal with Timothy. But Timothy might hurt Toby. And, if angry enough, he might strike out against Edric's family. His little girls. She couldn't allow that. "You can't." She took a step to walk away, but when Edric put his hand on her arm, she stopped. That light touch did more to keep her in place than any hold Tobias ever had on her.

"I won't let him hurt you."

She knew he wouldn't. But Edric was not an option for protection at this point.

"Don't you trust me?"

"I do trust you." That was the problem. She trusted him to do his duty as sheriff and put her in jail for what she had done. Trusted him to protect his daughters at all costs. "Please let me handle this." She scurried away. She could hear his footsteps behind her.

Edric followed Lily all the way to Aunt Henny's. He didn't know what to say to her. He had motioned to his deputy Montana to keep an eye on the two men. If she wouldn't tell him anything about the man, how could he help her?

She went into the boarding house and straight up to her room without even checking on Toby.

Toby sat on the floor with Estella and Nancy's block puzzle set. The boy stared up at him, unsure.

Edric crouched near him. "Toby, the men last night who came. Did you know either of them?"

Toby nodded.

"The dark-haired one?"

Toby nodded again.

"Who is he?"

Toby's eyes widened, and he scooted back on the carpet. He seemed more afraid of the man who wasn't there than the one who was.

It was no use. The boy was too frightened. Frightened of the man. Just like Lily. Edric stood and stepped aside. "Why don't you go see how your mama is?"

Toby ran from the room and up the stairs.

Aunt Henny shifted on the settee. "You didn't find out who they are?"

Edric shook his head. "And Lily won't tell me anything. I sent a telegram to Philadelphia inquiring about them. As we suspected, she went to meet him." He had nearly jumped through the window when Mr. Bremmer put a hand on her. Twice! "Toby's the spitting image of Mr. Bremmer."

Aunt Henny sucked in a breath. "You don't think he's the boy's father, do you?"

"I don't know what else to think. He looks more like Toby than Lily does."

"Children often favor one parent over the other."

That was true. His own two girls looked vastly different. Estella was the spitting image of her mama, where Nancy favored him. "I can't help but think she might have taken Toby."

"No. Toby adores her."

"She might have seen that Toby was being mistreated and took him away to protect him." That was the kind of thing he believed Lily would do for a child. Even one who wasn't hers.

"And if she's not his mother?"

"She can't keep him."

"You wouldn't turn him over to that man?"

No. But the law was the law. "I don't know what to do. Unless Lily tells me what's going on, I may have no choice but to take him from her."

Twenty-Five

LILY DROPPED HER FATHER'S BIBLE ONTO the bed and flipped open the cover. She fanned the pages from front to back. There were only a few scattered newspaper clippings.

The door opened, and Toby stood on the threshold. She ran to him and hugged him. She wouldn't let Timothy or anyone else hurt him. She closed and locked the door.

Back at the bed, she held the Bible by the covers to make all the clippings fall out and anything else that might be there.

"What are you doing?" Toby said.

"Mommy's looking for something." She sorted through the clippings, but there weren't any other papers. Nothing that Tobias might have written or put in the Bible.

She carefully unfolded each clipping. They were all old. Wedding announcements, obituaries, and the like. One was the announcement of her birth. All dating back to before her parents had died.

She sucked in a breath. Her parents. They would still be alive if it weren't for Tobias.

And Timothy. He might not have actually done anything to harm them, but he'd likely been in on the plan.

She shuffled through the papers again. Where was it? She thumbed through the Bible again. *Lord, where is it? There has to be something here.*

She pulled at the endpapers glued to the inside back and front covers to see if something was hidden under them. Nothing. They were stuck solid. She tossed the Bible aside, slumped to the floor next to the bed, and put her face in her hands. What was she going to do?

Toby sidled up next to her and patted her shoulder. She wrapped her arms around her little boy, pulled him onto her lap, and held on tight. She couldn't let anything happen to him.

But what to do? If Timothy was only half as brutal as his brother, he would harm Toby without a second thought to get what he wanted.

She fisted her hands. She didn't have whatever it was Timothy wanted, but he would never believe her.

Run!

She and Toby would have to get away.

She helped her son up and stood. They would have to leave right now, while Timothy thought she was looking for what he wanted. She retrieved the carpetbags from the wardrobe and plopped them onto the bed.

Why had she bothered to unpack last night? She had been restless and didn't know what else to do.

She grabbed her dresses hanging in the wardrobe then stuffed them into the larger carpetbag. She crossed to the bureau, scooped out Toby's clothes, and stuffed them into the smaller carpetbag.

When she returned for her underclothes, something outside caught her attention. She ducked to look out the window. Across the street, Timothy's cohort from last night and this morning stood, leaning against a tree, smoking. Keeping an eye on her no doubt.

If they slipped out the back, the man might not see them.

She crossed to the bed with her arms full of clothes, but instead of putting them in a carpetbag, she stared at the two bags.

It would be easier if she took only one carpetbag. But which one? The larger, she could fit more in. No, the smaller would be easier to carry. She needed to sort through what they would take and what they'd leave behind.

After throwing her underclothes on the bed, she picked up the larger bag and upended it, dumping the contents onto the bed. When she picked up the smaller bag to do the same, she froze, staring at it.

She breathed out his name. "Tobias."

Unknowingly, she *had* taken something of his. This was Tobias's traveling bag. Had there been something in there she'd never seen? She'd been in a hurry. But certainly, she would have noticed a ledger.

She pulled out Toby's clothes one article at a time.

Slowly pulling out the last garment, she held her breath, hoping something would be there.

Tears poked her eyes.

Nothing. Except the fabric covered bottom board.

She reached her hand in the small side pocket. Empty.

No! There had to be something.

She swung her arm and knocked the bag off the bed. Turning, she sat on the floor next to the bed again and struggled against her tears.

Toby sat in the corner. He'd apparently been frightened by her being upset and had made sure he was out of the way. Her poor boy.

She held out her arms to him.

He stood and came immediately but stopped at the fallen carpetbag. He righted it, tucked the bottom board back in place, and brought it to her.

She set the bag aside and pulled her baby onto her lap. "Thank you."

"Welcome."

What was she going to do? If she didn't give Timothy something, he would take Toby and hurt him. *Please, God, show me how to protect Toby. How do we get away from Timothy?*

Edric's words came to her mind. *Let me help you. I won't let him hurt you.*

Was Edric the answer? If she let him help her, he would feel betrayed when he found out what she had done. She couldn't do that to him. He deserved better than her. But what choice did she have? If Edric got between Timothy and what he wanted, Timothy would come after Toby or Edric's girls. Try to run again or ask Edric for help? She didn't know.

Toby held out his hand and slowly unfurled his fingers.

She blinked several times to clear her vision to see

what he had.

On his palm sat a small silver key.

She took it. "Where did you find this?"

Toby pointed to the brown carpetbag.

It must have been under the foundation board.

Tobias must have put it there. *Hidden* it there.

Maybe this would placate Timothy. If he thought it went to something important, it could garner her enough time to escape. She moved Toby off her lap and searched under the board in the bag. Nothing else lay hidden.

She kissed Toby's head. "I think you might have found our freedom."

Toby gave her a half smile. Not quite sure of the good he'd done but pleased to have made her happy.

She knelt and put her hands on Toby's shoulders. "I want you to stay right here in our room until I return. Do you understand?"

Toby pushed out his bottom lip. "Don't leave me."

"It will only be for a little bit." She held up the key between her fingers. "This key will make Uncle Timothy go away. I need to give it to him."

Toby nodded.

She combed her fingers through his too long hair. Then she pulled him close. "I'll be back as soon as I can." She hastened to the door and closed it behind her. Listening at the top of the stairs, she strained to hear voices. Was Edric still here? She'd heard him follow her home after her meeting with Timothy. But no voices filtered through the house. She walked down the opposite side of the staircase from the railing to avoid the three squeaky steps.

At the bottom, she reached for the closed front door. This door hadn't been closed all summer except at night. She twisted the knob.

"Don't go."

Lily gasped and spun around to face Aunt Henny in the hallway next to the stairs. After catching her breath, she said, "I have to. I won't be long."

The older woman leaned on her cane. "Who is this man who has you fit to be tied?"

She wanted to tell Aunt Henny, but Timothy's

warning weighed heavy on her. Timothy might hurt the older woman. And if she told Aunt Henny, Aunt Henny would tell Edric. "No one."

Aunt Henny hobbled forward. "Let Edric deal with this man."

"Is he here?" She looked around.

"No. He left. He's worried about you. Edric can make him leave town."

If merely getting Timothy out of town would solve all her problems, she would let Edric take care of things, but Timothy wouldn't give up easily. Even if forced out of town, he would return or send someone after her. "I have to do this. Then he'll leave." Then she and Toby would as well. "I have to go." Timothy wouldn't remain patient for long. She'd already taken too much time. She swiveled around and opened the door.

"Don't go. Edric will protect you and your son."

She couldn't face Aunt Henny. "He can't." She wished he could. She walked out, closing the door behind her and stopped on the porch.

She didn't want to go. She wanted to stay. Taking a deep breath, she trudged forward, down the walk and out the front gate.

Just passed Aunt Henny's yard, the man across the street pushed away from the tree. She froze in place as he crossed to her. What was he going to do?

He tipped his hat to her. "I'll escort you."

"I don't need to be escorted."

He seized her arm and moved her along. "He doesn't like to be kept waiting. He's an impatient man."

She twisted her arm to free herself, but his hold only tightened. Like Tobias's. She made small quick steps to keep up with him.

Then a menacing voice came from behind them. "Let her go!"

The man stopped and turned. Then cursed.

Edric glowered. He lowered his voice to a growl. "Didn't you hear me? Take your hand off her."

The man opened both hands and held them out to his sides. "I don't want any trouble."

"You courted trouble the moment you stepped into

my town." Edric took a stride toward the man. "I should throw you in my jail for manhandling the lady."

The man tossed Lily a worried look.

Timothy would be very angry with her if she allowed his associate to be put in jail.

"Let him go. Please."

Edric seemed immune to her pleas and didn't yield.

She gripped his arm. "Edric, please."

Her touch seemed to get through to him. He glanced at her hand on him then to the man again. He tossed his chin toward the stranger, who understood and strode backward several paces before turning and making a hasty departure.

Lily needed to go as well. Timothy would be furious, blaming her for his man being detained.

Edric took her hands in a tender gesture. "How do you know Mr. Bremmer?" His look became quizzical as he realized she had one of her hands in a fist. He turned that hand over in his.

She didn't want to open her hand, but at the same time, she wanted to show him she trusted him. Wanted to show the man she loved she trusted him. Even if a future with him was impossible.

She unfurled her fingers without him asking her to.

He took the key and held it between his thumb and finger. "What's this?"

The key stood between them just as her past would always stand between them. Keeping them apart.

"The reason he came." At least she hoped Timothy believed that and would leave.

"I'll take it to him and make sure he leaves. For good."

No! She couldn't let him do that. Timothy would come after her out of spite for not heeding his warning. She pinched the key, but he wouldn't release it. She cupped both her hands around his larger one. "*I* have to do it. It has to be me. There are things I have to tell him about it."

"What hold does Mr. Bremmer have over you?"

He knew what she had done. "I have to go." She pulled the key from Edric's loosened grip.

Now he cupped his hands around hers. "Don't. If I have meant anything at all to you, don't go to him."

He meant more to her than she could say. He'd given her hope. Hope in a tender kind of love. Hope in a God who loved. She didn't want him to let her go. But he must. "Edric, please."

Though his hold was gentle, barely a whisper, it again did more to keep her rooted in place than any tight-fisted grip Tobias ever put on her.

His eyes glistened as he released her hands, his look as though he was losing her.

She wanted to tell him that he would never lose her. But she couldn't. Her past was ripping them apart.

She didn't want Timothy to come after him for detaining his man and hurt Edric. The silence between them became unbearable. "I have to go." Lily's words lodged in her throat.

"Then go."

An ache grew in her chest as she slowly turned from him. Each step ripping her apart.

Even if her past didn't kill his love for her, walking away from him would.

Tears blurred her vision. She slapped them away. No time to pine over what never could have been. She took a deep breath and brought her emotions under control.

Twenty-Six

AT THE HOTEL'S ENTRANCE, LILY SQUARED her shoulders before marching inside. Timothy's associate stood inside by the window, no doubt watching her approach. He gripped her arm and yanked her toward the dining room. Taking quick steps to keep up, she tried to pull free, but he kept his hold. He brought her to the table where Timothy sat. Timothy flicked his wrist. The man released her and moved away.

"Hal says your sheriff caused a bit of a fuss."

"I handled it." She hoped Timothy didn't make an issue out of it. "I made it here."

He cocked an eyebrow. "Have a seat." A command.

"I won't be staying long enough."

He snatched her wrist. "I said sit."

She didn't want to. She wanted to get away from him as fast as she could.

Timothy tightened his grip to the point of pain.

She lowered herself onto the opposite chair. Best not to argue. Best not to anger him.

"Don't try to run out on me." When she nodded, he released her wrist. "It doesn't look as though you've brought me what I asked for. Or anything at all."

She set the key on the white tablecloth between them.

He picked it up. "What's this?"

"It was hidden in Tobias's traveling bag."

"This isn't a ledger or papers. What does it go to?"

She had hoped he wouldn't ask that question. She could tell him that she didn't know, but that would only serve to anger him. She could give him a number of possibilities concerning what it *could* open. Either way, he wouldn't leave town. Wouldn't leave her and Toby alone. "My father's safe." Better to sound sure.

He gripped her hand she had imprudently left lying on the table. Squeezing, he said, "Do you think me a gullible ninny?"

Wincing, she took a deep breath and ignored the pain.

"I've been in the family safe in the house. Worthless papers. Not even any jewelry or cash."

She knew that. She was the one who had taken what little of value had been in there. "My father had a second safe."

Her father's safe was one of the possibilities for the key.

"I don't believe you." He squeezed her hand harder. "Where is this safe?"

She needed to convince Timothy. "You're hurting my hand. Let go, and I'll tell you."

He glared at her a moment then slowly loosened his grip.

She pulled on her hand.

He tightened his grip. "Leave your hands on the table where I can see them."

"Why?"

"Who knows what you could have hidden in the folds of your skirt. I don't want to get shot in the gut."

He was as suspicious as his brother.

She gave him a curt nod.

He hesitated then released her hand.

Though she wanted to yank it back, she left it where it was and clasped it with her other.

He twirled the key between his finger and thumb. "Now, where's the safe you claim this goes to?"

"My father's office at home." Now that Tobias was gone, she wouldn't call it his.

Timothy narrowed his eyes at her. "I've been over every inch of that office. I pulled out every book on every shelf."

She pictured her father's office in complete disarray and it pained her.

"There isn't any safe in that room. The only safe in that house is in the bedroom."

Her father was a very cautious man and hadn't

trusted his papers and valuables to just one safe. If someone broke into one, he wouldn't get everything. And Timothy hadn't known where to look. Having found the one safe in the house, he probably hadn't searched real hard. "It's in the floor."

"I looked under the carpet."

"Then you looked in the wrong place."

Timothy glared.

"It's under the desk."

"I checked the floorboards there. No loose ones."

"Not under where one rests their feet. Under the desk itself."

"Now I know you are lying to me. Your father would have had to be a fool to put a safe under a heavy desk that he would have to move every time he needed to get into it."

Her father was no fool. He was clever and percipient. Astute. "As you are sitting at the desk, remove the bottom two drawers on the left. You'll need a candle. Push the floorboards at the back of the opening. The front will swing up on a hinge." She recalled when she'd showed Tobias this secret safe. Before she realized he was evil.

Timothy had the same awed expression that his brother'd had. "And the key goes in the door."

"It goes to the inner door. The outer door has a combination."

"What is it?"

"Fourteen, three, twenty-nine." At least that's what it was when her father had it.

"Did Tobias have it changed?"

She hoped not. She didn't want Timothy to come back. "I don't know."

"It can't be a very big safe under a desk. Is it big enough for a ledger?"

She nodded. "Not big, but deep." She hadn't seen that safe open since she showed it to Tobias. He forbade her to enter her father's den and kept it locked.

Timothy eyed the key with satisfaction. "Your father was a shrewd man."

That he was. The reason he had been so successful.

"You have what you want. May I take my leave?"

Pleased, Timothy covered her hands with his again but gentler this time. "I truly am sorry for all these unpleasantries."

By his charming expression, the same one Tobias would put on, anyone would think him sincere. She knew better. "Are we done? May I leave?" She wanted to pull her hands away, but wasn't sure he would allow it.

"You could come back with me. I'll treat you well."

Like Tobias had done? He had promised to treat her well in the beginning. Until they had married, and he had complete control over her. She yanked her hands away. "I would rather die."

His gaze flickered away and back, and his features hardened.

Had she pushed him to the point of violence like Tobias? She planted her feet, poised to jump out of her chair and flee.

"Your beau is becoming quite a nuisance." He pocketed the key.

Lily twisted around to see Edric filling the entrance to the dining room. A glare so stern it would have frightened her if it had been directed at her instead of Timothy. She looked back to Timothy. "You have what you came for. Leave town now."

"You took too long. No train out until tomorrow morning, love. You keep him away from me, or you'll be sorry. You and your mutt."

"Don't do anything to give him cause. And leave town."

"I plan to do just that."

Lily stood. "You won't come back?"

He patted his vest pocket. "If this is everything you claim, I'll have no need."

She hoped that was true. She didn't want to face Edric, but her desire to get away from Timothy was stronger.

Edric was torn between slamming Mr. Bremmer up against the wall or going with Lily. His heart won.

He opened the hotel's entrance door, and Lily seemed to be startled by his presence. He noticed her hands shaking. "Tell me what he's done to you, and I'll throw him in jail."

"No, Edric, don't. Just let him be. He'll leave now."

He wasn't as confident as she. Bremmer was not a man to be trusted. His word meant nothing.

Since Lily wouldn't tell him anything or allow him to help her in this situation, he walked in silence beside her all the way to the boarding house. He watched her proceed up the walk and enter the house.

When he turned from Aunt Henny's, Deputy Montana rode up on his horse. "This come for you." He held out a telegram.

Edric took and unfolded the paper. *Hal Jenson discredited Pinkerton. Tobias or Timothy Bremmer?*

A discredited Pinkerton detective? And a man who is the spitting image of Toby? That couldn't be good. What were they up to? Lily said Bremmer would leave now. He hoped so. But in case he didn't...

"Go back to the telegraph office. Send a return telegram that says, Both Bremmers."

"Is that it?"

"Yes, the man on the other end will understand it. Don't take your eyes off Jenson and Bremmer the rest of the day. If they go up to their rooms, I want you or Sammy outside their doors."

Montana nodded and rode off.

Edric didn't want either man getting close to Lily again.

Later after supper, Edric joined his deputy Cord at the saloon's long wooden bar. They each had an untouched sarsaparilla in front of them. Edric studied Bremmer in the mirror.

Cord waved a fly away from his glass. "He looks madder by the minute."

"Where's his friend?"

"Rode out of town this afternoon."

It was better to only have one to deal with. Simpler. "How much has he had?"

Cord shrugged. "Not much. Two, maybe three whiskeys."

"Not so much that he's drunk. But enough that he might be amiable to a chat."

"Unless he's one to get mean when he drinks. In that case, he might take a swing at you."

"Or shoot me if he has a gun."

Cord pulled a six-shooter from his coat pocket. "I had Roxy relieve him of this earlier before you arrived. I doubt he even knows it's missing."

Edric picked up his glass. "Then I think I'll go see if Mr. Bremmer has a mind to answer a few questions."

Cord left his glass and followed Edric, who pulled out a chair at Bremmer's table.

"You weren't invited, Sheriff." Bremmer held his glass cupped between his hands.

Edric sat anyway and placed his glass firmly on the table. "And I didn't ask."

Cord pulled out another chair and swung it around backwards before straddling it.

Bremmer shot Cord a glare then turned back to Edric. "I haven't had near enough to drink to converse with you."

He hoped the alcohol had lowered the man's resistance more than he realized. "How do you know Mrs. Lexington?" Start with something he might not be opposed to answering.

Bremmer furrowed his brows. "Mrs. Lexington?" Then he raised his eyebrows. "Oh, you mean the pretty blond with looks and a body to temp any man? Even you, Sheriff."

Edric fisted his hands at the man's insinuation. *Lord, keep me from hitting him. First.*

But if Bremmer took a swing at him, he'd have no

choice.

Bremmer shifted one hand away from his glass and rested it casually on the table. "Let's just say I knew her husband."

"Knew him how?"

Bremmer moved his hand to the edge of the table in front of him. "Business mostly." The scoundrel was trying not to be noticed as he went for his gun.

Edric glanced toward Cord and could tell by the slight up curve of one side of his mouth he too was tracking the slow progression of Bremmer's hand.

The slightest smile tugged at the corner of Bremmer's mouth when his hand slipped below the table. He was making his move.

Edric waited.

Bremmer's elbow cocked up slightly as he reached for the handle of his missing gun. His eyes widened. He glanced down and yanked open his coat.

Cord pulled out Bremmer's gun. "Looking for this?"

Bremmer cursed. "You stole my gun!"

"Just keeping an eye on it so as nobody gets hurt with it. Guns can be downright dangerous." Cord twirled the gun on his index finger.

His deputy's mocking tone fueled Bremmer's temper.

In a split second, Bremmer tossed his drink toward Edric. Most of the liquid missed, but splashed Edric's cheek. He threw the glass at Cord's face.

Cord ducked in time for it to only graze the side of his head.

Bremmer flipped the table out of the way and dove at Cord. The two tumbled to the floor. Bremmer cocked his fist to take a swing at Cord.

Edric yanked the man's hands behind him and pulled him off. Bremmer flailed, trying to get a piece or two of Cord.

He and his deputy wrestled Bremmer into submission and bound his hands behind him.

Cord rolled away and stood. "That was fun."

Edric shook his head and yanked Bremmer to his feet. "Let's go."

Bremmer jerked to free himself without success.

"You don't want to do this, Sheriff."

Oh, but Edric did.

Cord cocked a grin. "I'll do it."

Cord enjoyed his duties a little too much at times. But this was one prisoner Edric was going to take pleasure in locking up himself. "You're bleeding. Have someone take care of that."

Cord touched his head where the glass had hit him. His fingers showed a smear of blood. Cord cursed. "Let me *throw* him in the cell."

"I'll take care of him." Edric didn't need his deputy doing something stupid.

Roxy sidled up to Cord with a lace hanky in her hand that matched her blue satin and black lace dress. "Let me take a look at that for you." She dabbed at Cord's head.

Cord's anger visibly melted, and he smiled at the saloon girl.

Edric hauled Bremmer out the door, across the street, and into the sheriff's office. All the while, Bremmer kept telling him he better not put him in jail and he didn't want to do this.

Edric secured him in the back cell, and a serenity settled around him that he hadn't felt since before he knew Bremmer was in town.

Bremmer gripped the bars. "You best let me out of here, or you'll be sorry."

Edric glared at the man. "You aren't going anywhere. So, you might as well get comfortable."

Soon, Cord arrived with the gore cleaned off his forehead. No bandage, but Edric could see the small cut clotted over with dried blood.

Cord twirled his gun before laying it on the desk. "Time for you to head home, Rix. I'll keep an eye on our dandy."

Edric pulled Cord aside. "Don't open his cell for any reason."

"Why? You worried he'll get away from me?"

"I don't want you returning the favor for denting your hard head."

Cord shrugged. "He ain't worth the trouble." A little

attention from Roxy, and Cord seemed to have forgotten his anger.

"Good. I'll see you first thing in the morning." Edric opened the door but stopped when the prisoner spoke.

"Hey, Sheriff." Bremmer smirked. "Tell your sweetheart to come visit me."

He would not tell Lily about this. It was best if she didn't know. He didn't want Bremmer frightening her any more than she already was. Who was this man to her really? He seemed to be more than her husband's business associate.

Twenty-Seven

EDRIC HAD FOUGHT WITH HIS COVERS most of the night. He hadn't been able to stop thinking about Lily and the fear Bremmer struck in her. And why wouldn't she tell him who this man was or let him help? What was the threat Bremmer posed to her?

When dawn had finally arrived, he rose, hurried about his chores, and rode to the sheriff's office.

Outside, Cord sat in a chair tilted against the building with his hat over his eyes. "Ah, you brought me milk."

Edric looked at the milk still in his hand. He had obviously forgotten to stop by Aunt Henny's. Or maybe he had subconsciously put off confronting Lily about his prisoner. He dismounted. "You have some trouble?"

Cord let the chair thump flat as he shoved his hat away from his face. "That man has been yammering since dawn. Won't shut up. Demanding to be set free. Has a train to catch. Complaining that he has been unjustly incarcerated." Cord smiled then, his hat still low enough to cover the cut from last night. "I told him that I didn't know what incarcer-whatever was or unjustly. That made him mad. But he still wouldn't shut up."

Edric took a deep breath. He knew Cord's temper. "You didn't do anything to him, did you?"

Cord stood, twisting his back one direction then the other causing it to crack several times. "I was sorely tempted. I wanted to open his cell, grab him by his shirt, and *make* him shut up."

"Please tell me you didn't." As tempted as Edric had been to do the very same thing to the man, it was wrong.

"That's why I'm out here. To take myself out of temptation's way."

From inside, Bremmer yelled, "Is that you, Sheriff?"

Cord thumbed behind him. "He's all yours. Good luck." He stepped off the boardwalk and headed for home.

Conflicting emotions fought inside Edric. He wanted one of his deputies for moral support, and Montana wouldn't be here for a while yet. But if Bremmer decided to say something against Lily or say he had rights to her or Toby, Edric didn't want anyone else to hear.

He took a deep breath and pushed inside.

Bremmer stood with his forearms resting through the bars. "It's about time. Let me out."

Edric took his time in crossing to the desk, pinning on his star, then sitting on the corner of the desk. "Now why would I do that?"

"Because you want me to leave town as much as I want to leave town."

"Do I?"

Bremmer looked pointedly at him. "Lily does."

That rankled. How dare he use Lily's name as though he had intimate knowledge of her? Maybe he did.

Bremmer shook the bars to no avail. "Let me out. You have no right to keep me here."

Edric stretched out his legs and crossed his ankles to appear calmer than he was and to look as though he was in no hurry to comply with Bremmer's demand. And he wasn't. Bremmer could rot in there for all he cared. "I have every right. You assaulted me and my deputy."

"And I sat a night in jail. Let me out."

"You still seem a bit riled up. Maybe another night will cool you off. Or a week."

Bremmer shook the bars, making them rattle. "Let me out."

Edric folded his arms to show he wasn't impressed.

Bremmer glared then paced his cell. "Look. I just want to catch the morning train. You let me go, I'll be on that train, and you'll never see me again."

"You expect me to trust you?"

"I got no reason to lie."

"I doubt that. How about you tell me why you're in town?"

Bremmer thinned his lips.

"How do you know Mrs. Lexington?"

"That's not important."

"It is to me. Are you Toby's father?"

A smug grin stretched Bremmer's mouth. "Cute kid. Can't deny the resemblance." He draped his arms through the bars. "Let me go, and I'll tell you."

That was not going to happen any time soon. "Is Mrs. Lexington's husband dead?"

Bremmer appeared to think and studied the bars. "These bars sure do make a man's memories foggy."

He wasn't going to tell Edric anything. It was time to get some answers from Lily. As he pushed off the desk to leave, Bremmer spoke.

"Let's just say that Lily and I have a history, of sorts." Bremmer's mouth pulled up on one side, showing one of his dimples. "We're close. *Reeeal* close."

Edric took a quick step forward at Bremmer's insinuation. He understood all too well Cord's temptation to open the cell and make the man shut up. Instead, he turned for the door.

Bremmer chuckled. "You tell Lily I'm in here and see who she sides with. But make it fast, I have a train to catch."

Edric let the door slam behind him. It galled him that he'd let Bremmer get to him.

Lily stood next to the washtub in the backyard. She needed to bide her time until Timothy left town, then she and Toby could escape. She would make it appear as though all was well. All had returned to normal.

She put the feet of the washboard into the washtub and realized she'd forgotten the bar of lye soap. As she approached the screen door, she heard voices. It sounded as though Aunt Henny was talking to Edric.

"She's out doing the wash," Aunt Henny said.

They were talking about her. She motioned for Toby to stay put and opened the door quietly and slipped inside. She listened from the kitchen. Edric and Aunt Henny didn't know she was there.

Aunt Henny spoke. "Has she told you who he is?"

Lily could picture Edric shaking his head. She hadn't told him anything. She couldn't.

"He told me that he was a business associate of her late husband's. But I think he's a lot more than that."

Edric had talked to Timothy? She hoped Timothy knew she didn't have anything to do with that. He would likely blame her anyway. It didn't matter. Timothy was leaving on the next train out of town. And that should be soon.

"He can't hurt her," Edric said. "I've got him in one of the cells."

Lily covered her mouth with her hand. No! He was supposed to leave town this morning. Never to return. Her past would go with him. Never to haunt her again.

This was bad. Very, very bad.

She slipped out the back door and whispered to Toby, "Stay right here. Don't go anywhere."

Toby nodded.

She hurried off around the house and down the street.

By the time she reached the jail, she was out of breath. She took several deep breaths to calm herself. She would tell the deputy she needed to speak to the prisoner. Opening the door, she slipped inside the dim interior. No deputy greeted her.

A form moved on the cot in the farthest cell.

Timothy sat up. "You were smart to come."

Lily stayed by the door. "Why didn't you leave?"

"Two men at the saloon started throwing punches, and the good sheriff saw fit to put me in jail for disorderly. I was trying to break up the fight."

Did he really think to convince her he was simply a Good Samaritan? Being related to Tobias meant he wasn't likely a good anything. "You should have been more careful."

He pushed off the cot and came to the bars. "Your beau was following me around. I think he had it in for me. He was going to lock me up for anything he could.

Now get me out of here so I can catch my train."

"I can't do that."

"You better, or else I'll tell him all about how you killed my brother."

She held her breath. "Where is the man who was with you?" She hoped he wouldn't come in and grab her.

"Had business elsewhere. Rode out of town yesterday afternoon."

He pointed to the wall behind the sheriff's desk. "The keys are hanging right there. Just get them and unlock my cell."

"I can't." It wouldn't be right. Only Edric or one of his deputies could release him.

"Then hand me the keys, and I'll let myself out."

She stared at the keys.

He patted the front of his coat. "I got what I came for. I have no quarrel with you. I want nothing more than to get out of here and back to Philadelphia."

If he got on that train, all her problems would go with him. She walked over to the desk and reached for the keys. She stopped. If she did this, Edric would know she was the one to release him. He would never forgive her. She would lose him. If she didn't free Timothy, he would tell Edric about her killing Tobias, and she would still lose him. And could lose Toby.

She pulled her hand back.

Timothy cursed and shook the bars. "Toss me the keys!"

Confusion bounced around inside her. What should she do?

"He'll never know it was you. I'll be on that train and out of your life fast as a whip."

She stared at the keys. He would go. Toby would be safe. She reached for the keys.

"That a girl."

She lifted the ring off the nail.

"Now bring them over here."

Edric couldn't imagine where Lily had gotten off to. He strode down the street. Why would she leave Toby? She'd gotten more and more comfortable being separated from her son, but to leave without even telling Aunt Henny was strange. He stepped up onto the boardwalk in front of his office.

The door opened, Lily rushed out, closing the door behind her, then turned and ran into him.

He clamped his hands on her upper arms to steady them both. "What are you doing here?"

Her blue eyes were big and round. "I...um..."

"Aunt Henny and I were worried about you."

She stared at him.

He glanced to his office door then at her. "What were you doing in my office?"

"Nothing."

"You came to see your husband's associate, didn't you?"

"I only talked to him."

He wanted to ask her why this man frightened her so. What compelled her to come here? She'd said he was nothing more than her husband's business associate. But there was so much more neither would tell him. "Lily, I can help you. Tell me what it is about this man that scares you. Did he hurt you or Toby? Threaten you?"

She shook her head. "He only wants to catch a train and leave. If you'll release him, he will leave for good."

Why was she so eager for him to free this man?

"Please, just let him go."

"Give me a reason why."

She looked defeated. She didn't have a reason. At least not one she was willing to tell him.

Why wouldn't she trust him?

He studied her for a moment. "Is that what you really want? For him to go free?"

"Yes."

His gut told him not to, but he would... for her. "Then I'll do as you wish." Maybe when the man was gone, she would trust him to tell him why. He held the door open for her.

She hesitated then entered. She stood on the far side of the room from the cells.

Bremmer sat on the cot with his head in his hands but stood when he heard Edric and gripped the bars.

At least Lily hadn't done anything stupid.

"Mrs. Lexington assures me that you will leave town as promised."

Bremmer straightened. "Yes, sir. I will."

Edric crossed to the wall behind his desk and retrieved the keys. "Train leaves in ten minutes. You be on it." He slid the key into the lock.

"I will."

Edric swung the door open. "Your belongings are there." Edric pointed to the wall adjacent to the cells.

Bremmer gathered his suitcase and coat and headed for the door.

Edric clasped a hand on the man's shoulder. "I'll escort you. Wouldn't want you to *accidently* miss your train."

"Right kind of you, *Sheriff.*"

Edric turned to Lily as he left. "Wait here for me. I'll be right back."

He walked the man to the train station in silence, one step behind him, his hand on the hilt of his gun. He watched while the man bought an eastbound ticket. He waited on the platform with him.

The train pulled in and passengers disembarked.

"All aboard," the conductor called.

"Time for me to depart."

Edric pushed Bremmer against the wall of the station and pressed his forearm across the dandy's upper chest. "I have a couple of questions before you go."

Bremmer sneered. "What?"

"Is Lily's husband dead?"

"I am happy to report that he is." Bremmer pulled a smug grin.

So, she wasn't lying about being a widow. That eased his mind. "Are you Toby's father?"

"Gladly, no."

That too was a relief. He had one more question, and

it was important. "Is Lily Toby's true mother?"

"Last call! All aboard!"

Bremmer's mouth curled up on one side. "You've had your two questions. Time for me to go. You don't want me to miss my train, do you? Neither of us would like it if I was stuck in this pitiful town one minute longer."

Edric didn't think Bremmer would tell him even if they had all the time in the world. Bremmer knew the answer was important to him. He would hold on to it in case he needed it in the future. Just like he was using Edric's desire for him to be gone. Edric pushed off Bremmer's chest.

The man grunted from the increased pressure, straightened, and tipped his hat. "Much obliged, Sheriff."

Edric spoke in a low, threatening tone. "If you step foot in this town again, you'll sit in my jail until you rot."

The man had the gall to smile. "I have no need to return." He stepped aboard and disappeared inside.

Edric watched him through the window as he made his way down the aisle and took a seat.

As the train pulled out of the station, Bremmer had the cockiness to tip his hat to him. Edric watched until the train rolled out of sight. T. Bremmer was no more.

He turned and stalked back to his office. Lily was gone. He wasn't entirely surprised. At least he didn't have to worry about her husband showing up. Mr. Lexington really was dead.

He wanted to go after Lily and make her answer all his questions now that Mr. Bremmer was gone. But he wasn't confident she would cooperate even now. So, he headed to the telegraph office on his way.

Mort nodded to him. "I'm glad you're here, Sheriff. I was about to send someone for you." He handed Edric a folded piece of paper.

Edric read. *Tobias dead. Timothy missing. If you know the whereabouts of Timothy Bremmer, would like to know.*

He scratched his reply. *Timothy on the train to Philadelphia.* "See that this goes out right away." Edric smiled with satisfaction as he left the telegraph office. Mr. Bremmer may have escaped him, but it appeared the

Philadelphia police would be waiting for him at his destination.

Henny glanced out the front window in time to see Lily marching up the street toward the house. With the way her head was down, Henny knew the girl would head straight up to her room and lock the door again. She hobbled to the base of the stairs and planted herself in the girl's path.

Lily plowed through the doorway without looking up but stopped short of colliding with Henny and sucked in a breath. "Oh. I didn't see you." She stepped to the side to go around.

Henny poked out her cane to block the girl's escape.

Lily stared at the cane for a moment before slowly raising her gaze.

Neither spoke.

Finally, Henny spoke. "I would like a cup of tea."

The muscles in Lily's face twitched, but she mutely complied.

"Two cups." Henny headed for the settee but was slow moving. She'd lost so much strength lying around for weeks. Her injured leg still hurt when she put weight on it. Reaching her destination, she sat.

Giving the girl a task to focus on would get her mind off her immediate distress. Hopefully then, she would be amiable to talking.

Lily made little noise, bustling about the kitchen. The screen door in there tapped closed, and Toby's little voice filtered into the sitting room, but Henny couldn't tell what he said. Lily replied in a whisper.

Soon Lily entered with a tea tray, complete with teapot, cups, and a plate of sugar cookies. "Are you expecting company?"

"Only you, dear. Sit."

"I have a lot to do. I should get back to the wash."

Henny regarded Lily, hoping the girl would sit rather

than leave.

Lily shifted several times before yielding. She sat rigid though, on the edge of the chair.

"Would you pour?"

She took a slow breath then complied. She handed a cup to Henny but didn't pour a cup for herself.

Henny took a sip, studying the girl over the rim.

"If there is nothing else, I have laundry to do." The girl looked emotionally beaten.

"I want to help you."

"I'm capable of doing the wash."

That was not what Henny had meant and Lily knew it. "You can tell me anything."

"Thank you. I'll keep that in mind."

Why did Lily insist on being difficult? Though she did her part to keep up her end of the conversation, Henny could tell that Lily's mind resided elsewhere. Was it on worries because of that man? Or making plans? The girl seemed to trust no one but herself.

"If you can't tell me, you can tell your troubles to God. He will always listen and never judge."

"He already has. And rightfully so."

Henny wanted Lily to trust her but didn't know how to get through to the girl. "You are welcome here always." She saw Edric coming through her gate and stood.

Lily stood as well. "I'll get back to my work."

"Not yet." She turned toward the door before the knock. "Come in."

Edric walked into the parlor and was relieved to see Lily standing across the room even though her eyes were downcast.

Aunt Henny gave him a nod. "I'll leave you two alone for a bit." She limped out.

Edric spoke quickly before Lily tried to excuse herself as well. "Now will you tell me who Mr. Bremmer is to you?"

She didn't look up. "Is he gone?"

"Yes. I watched him get on the train and made sure he didn't get off. I watched until the train disappeared from sight."

"Then it doesn't matter anymore." She looked defeated.

He stepped closer and stood right in front of her. He tucked his finger under her chin and lifted her head. But still she wouldn't make eye contact. What hold did Bremmer have over her? Edric wanted to wipe the memory of this man from Lily's mind. "I will protect you and your son."

"I wish it was that simple."

"It is."

She shook her head.

He gripped her arms. She stiffened, and he knew she had reverted to that instinctual fear from her husband. He was tempted to release her but felt he was more likely to get her to see reason if she felt his touch. A gentle touch. He adjusted his grasp to a caress. "I won't let anything happen to you or Toby. I promise."

He studied her expression. He sensed her yielding. That she wanted to believe he could do as he said.

Her shoulders relaxed.

"Who is he? I *will* protect you."

The rest of her body seemed to relax, and she started to lean toward him.

"Don't hurt Mommy." Toby stared up at him but didn't pull his mother away as before.

Lily stiffened again.

The look on Toby's face broke Edric's will to make Lily comply. He let go of her and let his hands fall to his sides. He turned to the boy. "I would no more hurt your mama than I would you or my girls. Your mama would never hurt you or my girls, would she?" He glanced at Lily. The look on her face did not reassure him. "You wouldn't hurt my girls, would you?"

"I would never hurt them."

But he sensed she was going to. Maybe not physically, but their feelings were at risk.

And he didn't know how to stop it.

Twenty-Eight

ONCE AGAIN, LILY SLUNG THE CARPETBAG onto the bed and shoved in a dress, then her under clothes, and a petticoat. She had been tempted to pack last night but had been denying what she must do. She shoved in item after item. Filling the bag to the point it wouldn't close. The one smaller carpetbag didn't hold as much as she would like.

She unpacked and repacked it three times. Tears coursed down her cheeks as she worked. It had been difficult to not fall into Edric's arms and tell him everything. Difficult to remain unmoved while he pleaded with her. She had once been a master at schooling her emotions away where they couldn't hurt her. But with Edric—it hurt. It hurt more than she knew was possible. She had to leave. She had to get Toby out of here. As long as one person from her past knew where she was, Toby wasn't safe.

She slumped to the floor, covered her face with her hands, and cried.

She didn't want to leave. She liked it here. She felt at home here. Toby was happy and smiling. What would she tell him? He wouldn't understand their sudden departure. He'd come to trust Edric. He looked up to the man. How could she tear him away from that?

She could because he was her son, and his safety was her first concern. She would keep him safe no matter the cost to her. He was all that mattered.

Toby came into the room. "Aunt Henny says it's time for supper." He stared at her for a moment then sat down next to her. He put his hand in hers.

"We are going to have to leave, Toby."

He was silent for a moment. "Where will we go?"

He didn't question why. No matter what, he trusted

her. "I don't know. Maybe we'll go all the way to the ocean. Would you like that?"

"I never beed to the ocean before. Will I like it?"

Lily smiled. "I think you will."

He laid his head in her lap. "I like it here. No one hurts me. Could we stay?"

She stroked his hair. "No. We need to go."

"Oakey dokey." He popped his thumb into his mouth.

He was obviously scared about leaving and going to an unknown place. She was scared too. What if she couldn't find work that would allow Toby to be with her? What if she couldn't find work at all? What would they do then?

Before they went down to supper, she told Toby not to say anything about leaving to Aunt Henny or anyone. And Toby didn't tell their secret, in fact he didn't say a single word to anyone. When Aunt Henny asked if he was all right, Lily told her that he was tired.

Now, late into the night, as Toby lay sleeping on the bed in his traveling clothes, she sat at the small writing desk in her room to pen letters. She dipped the pen and dragged it across the rim of the well to remove the excess ink.

Dearest Aunt Henny,

You have been such a cherished friend. You welcomed us into your home and showered us with your love and generosity. You gave me work that allowed my son to be close. You put a roof over our heads. You have fed us. All of which I am extremely grateful for. You have given me far more than I have given you. The only thing of worth I can offer you in return is the truth. Now that my brother-in-law knows where I am, I cannot stay. I have done a terrible thing. I killed my husband, and I fear the authorities will come after me. I must keep Toby safe.

Thank you for everything. I can never repay your kindness.

God's Blessings Upon You!

Lily

Lily wiped away a tear before tucking the letter into an envelope, then she began one to Edric. This one would be harder to write. Aunt Henny had tried to tell her on more than one occasion that she would help Lily, and she believed she would now. If it were within the older woman's ability. But Edric's sworn duty would force him to put her in jail. And her love for him made that fact hurt all the more.

After she had folded the letter to Edric, she finished packing the one carpetbag. It would be easier to carry only one bag because she knew she would need to carry Toby at times as well. She had already proven to herself that she couldn't manage all three. She would take only one set of extra clothes for each of them. She tucked the toy train in last. Their other clothes, her mother's hand mirror set, and her father's Bible would be safe with Aunt Henny. Maybe one day she could return for them.

She lifted her sleeping son, draping his head onto her shoulder. It would be best if he remained asleep for this first part. She picked up the letters and the bag then tiptoed out of the room.

In the parlor, she dropped the letters onto the tea table and slipped out the back door. She woke Toby at the privy so he could use it, and she did as well. Then by the light of the moon, she set out on foot, heading west. She wasn't sure west was the wisest choice. Anyone Timothy sent after her would likely continue west, wouldn't they? Or would they assume she'd gone a different direction? She had told Toby they would head for the ocean, so the ocean would be their destination.

Go home was whispered in her soul. She thought of Aunt Henny's. It had seemed like home from the first time she laid eyes on it. She couldn't stay though. She had to take Toby where he'd be safe. He was no longer safe in Kamola. They had to find a new home.

Tears pricked her eyes as the town and its people lay farther and farther behind her.

A twinge twisted in her chest.

She walked for nearly an hour out of town. Toby became heavier with each step, and her chest felt tighter and tighter as she went. She had to keep going, but she didn't know how she could. What should she do? Keep going? Or stop and rest?

She wished Edric was here to help her. He would

know what to do. But he wasn't, and she had only herself to depend upon.

Keep going. The only thing that mattered was keeping Toby safe. And as long as Timothy could use Toby against her, he wasn't safe in Kamola.

Twenty-Nine

THE SUN HAD BARELY PEEKED OVER THE HORIZON, and already Estella and Nancy danced around Edric, chanting about the fancy tea party.

Nancy grabbed his hand. "Come see my dress." She pulled him into her bedroom. Lying on her bed was an old, wrinkled red velvet dress she had worn when she was three. Too fancy for a three-year-old in Kamola, but Enid had insisted the girls look better than any other children in town.

Edric knelt in front of his youngest. "Darling, this dress is too small. It won't fit you."

"But it's my favorite." Nancy put one hand on top of the other on her thigh and blinked several times.

Like batting her eyelashes was going to change the size of the dress.

He pulled her into a hug. "I know, but we have to find something else for you to wear." He hadn't even thought about the girls needing something nice for today.

He pulled a dress off the closet hook. "Wear this."

"No, Papa. That one's for church. I need a *tea*-party dress."

He didn't have time for this. He needed to get to work. Relieve his night deputy.

Estella brought over one of her old fancy dresses. Lavender with ruffles. "She can wear this one." It was one Estella had worn a couple of years ago when she was five, so it should fit Nancy.

Nancy hugged the dress in her arms. "It's prettiful."

That was one daughter taken care of. He turned to Estella. "What are you going to wear?"

Estella held up a pink dress with wads of lace. Another dress his late wife would have insisted was a must for their daughters. But Estella had also worn it two years ago. "Darling, I don't know if it will fit."

"It has to fit, Papa. It just has to." Estella had been chunky when she was younger and had grown taller since. If it did fit, it would be too short now.

Edric stepped into the hallway. "Pa!"

Soon Pa came into the room. "Where's the fire?"

"The girls need help with dresses for this afternoon. The purple dress should fit Nancy." He hoped. "But Estella's dress is too short. And I hope it still fits." His girls definitely needed a mama. He was sure Lily would have thought of dresses before the day of the event.

Pa held the pink lacey dress up to Estella. "I think it will fit." He pulled up the bottom of the dress. "The hem needs letting down."

"Can you take care of that?"

Pa gave him a look that said no. Pa was no better with a needle and thread than Edric. His poor girls.

Estella threw her arms around Pa's neck. "Pleeeeease, Granpapa."

That was all it would take for Pa to do all he could for one of their girls.

"I'll see what I can do."

"Thank you, Granpapa."

"Thanks, Pa." He hugged his daughters. "I'll come back and take the two of you and Mrs. Lexington to the party." He hoped Lily hadn't forgotten with her distractions of the last few days. But he was going over there now anyway to drop off the milk.

After saddling his horse, riding over, and tethering his horse to the post, he walked up to the door.

At his knock, Aunt Henny called for him to come in. She sat in her usually spot on the settee, but Edric sensed something was different. When Aunt Henny raised her gaze to his, he could see from her red-rimmed eyes that something was wrong.

"What happened? Did Mr. Bremmer come back?"

She shook her head and held out an envelope. "Lily's gone."

"What? Where did she go?"

"She didn't say."

"Where's Toby?" She wouldn't leave without her son.

"Gone too." She still held out the envelope.

He didn't want to take it, but he did, setting down the bottle of milk.

"I think you should read it here."

He pulled two folded sheets out, took a breath, and unfolded them.

My Dearest Edric,

From the moment I stepped off the train in Kamola, I felt as though I had finally come home. After six long years.

Please tell Estella and Nancy I am sorry to miss the special tea with them. I was very much looking forward to the event.

I never meant to hurt anyone. Especially you or your sweet daughters. I never meant to care. I tried not to care. But you were so good and kind, I found it difficult to resist my growing feelings for you. I never imagined I could feel so much for a man. I take full responsibility for every hurt of every person I have touched.

So, it pains me deeply to have to leave Kamola—

"No. She can't leave. She's supposed to take Estella and Nancy to the mother and daughter tea party. Pa is helping them with their dresses. She can't leave."

Aunt Henny's expression held compassion. "Finish reading."

"Why?"

"Because I assume she explains why in your letter as she did in mine." Aunt Henny touched the paper on her lap.

Edric didn't want to but continued to read.

—to leave you, and to leave your girls. I have come to love them as my own. But I cannot stay.

Yes, she could. Staying was easy. Just don't leave. Easy.

As long as Timothy knows where I am, Toby and I aren't safe.

I know you promised to protect me and my son, but this is something you cannot protect me from. You see, I have done a terrible thing. Something you would be forced to lock me up in jail for. I will not put you in that position. I have killed a man.

No! Lily was too kind and sweet to ever do such a thing.

I have killed my husband. I didn't mean to. But it is done, and I cannot undo it.

If Timothy returns, he could take me back and have me put in jail for murder. Or he could send someone after me. I must protect Toby.

Again, I am sorry for any heartache I have caused you and your family.

Love,

Lily

This couldn't be. Edric fisted his hand, crumpling the letter.

"Then she told you."

"Lily a murderer?" But it explained why she was evasive. Had he been made a fool of? "How could I have not known? I let her near my girls."

"Now, Edric. I'm sure there's a reasonable explanation."

"No. I don't want to hear any excuses. If she hadn't meant to do it, why not tell us about? Why keep it a secret?" Harboring the secret and not trusting him hurt the most. He tossed the letter to the floor and walked out.

It all made perfect sense now. Timothy Bremmer had come because he knew Lily had killed her husband. That was why she was so afraid of him. He was blackmailing her to keep him quiet.

Toby was the nickname for Tobias. So Toby was likely Tobias Bremmer's son. And why the boy looked so much like Timothy Bremmer. That made Timothy Bremmer Toby's uncle. Because mother and son didn't resemble each other, Toby was likely her husband's son from a previous marriage. She murdered her husband and stole his son. True, she loved the boy more than anyone. There was no doubting that. And she'd appeared to have been abused. So why couldn't she have told him? But people have been known to fake such things. He wouldn't have thought Lily capable of such duplicity.

How could he have allowed himself to be gullible? What kind of lawman did that make him? Not a very good one.

His heart ached for the woman he'd thought she was. The woman he longed to see. The women he could never see again. He wished she had never come to Kamola. He wished he'd never laid eyes on her. He wished... he wished... he could hold her.

He swung up into his saddle, but where to go? He had to think clearly.

Go after Lily? He didn't even know which direction she went. Or how she left. Train? Stagecoach? Wagon? Or even when she left. She could be anywhere and in any direction. She was right though. He was duty bound to arrest her. If he didn't look for her, he couldn't find her. If he couldn't find her, he didn't have to arrest her. He needed to forget all about her.

Should he go home and check on his girls? Then Pa would want to know what was wrong. He wasn't ready to admit his failings to Pa. And what would he tell his girls? He couldn't tell them what Lily had done. Then he had a terrible thought. She hadn't been planning to steal his girls from him, had she? That gave him a sour taste in his mouth.

Go to his office? And do what? He could at least relieve Cord.

He kicked his horse into motion. At his office, he tethered his horse and went inside. "Go home."

Cord swung his feet off the desk and sat up straight. "What's wrong? Did Bremmer return?"

"No. Nothing. Go home." He picked up his star.

Cord shook his head. "You can't fool me. You look about as well as a man with a noose around his neck sittin' atop a skittish horse."

Edric scowled at Cord and said through gritted teeth, "Go home."

Cord tucked his head into his hat. "All right then. But if you—"

"Go!"

His deputy finally left. He knew he could count on Cord for anything, but what would Cord think of him for falling in love with a murderer? He would lose his friend's respect.

Had Lily been manipulating him the whole time? He hoped not. But it wasn't the first time he'd believed a woman to be one sort when she was another. He couldn't trust his own judgment where women were concerned. Pa had tried to warn him.

He stared at the star on his palm, weighing it. He had liked his job... until now. Easy to tell the good from the bad. Easy decisions. Protect the innocent. Put the criminals in jail. Lily had seemed like an innocent. But was she truly a criminal?

He had a tough choice to make. Pretend he didn't know what Lily had done and let her fade into the distance? Or track her down and bring her to justice? He didn't like his choices.

He stared at the final telegram. *Timothy missing. Tobias dead.* At the time, it had meant little to him. Just that Timothy Bremmer wasn't missing. Now he knew the ramifications of the second part of the message.

Deputy Montana opened the door. "Howdy, Rix."

"Go," Edric growled.

Montana stared open mouthed, clearly not sure what to do. Come? Go? Speak? Or not?

Edric jammed on his badge. "Never mind." He stalked out, pushing past Montana still standing stunned in the doorway.

Lily knew she was dreaming, but she couldn't wake herself.

A bloody Tobias loomed over her. He pointed to Toby's corpse lying on the floor. "This is your fault."

She shook her head. She would never hurt her son. Her chest tightened in grief, and she struggled to breathe.

Tobias's hands were around her throat, punishing her for not giving him a worthy son.

Gasping for breath, she knew she had to wake up.

"Miss?"

Lily startled awake. The first thing she saw was a pair of man's boots. She clutched Toby tighter, waking him. Toby scrambled away from the man.

The man with a bushy brown beard held his hat to his chest. Though the man spoke, Lily couldn't understand him. At first, she thought he was speaking a different language but soon realized it was his heavy accent. He spoke more deliberate and slower with a Scottish brogue. "Are you all right, lass?"

"Yes, we're fine."

"I'm Shamus MacIan." He pointed behind him toward the road. "My missus insisted I check to see if you were all right. She feared you were dead."

Lily peered around him to a wagon on the road. "Yes, we're fine. Thank you."

"All right then, come along." He held out his hand to her.

She glanced from his hand to his face and back to his hand.

"Oh, lassy, you and the lad cannot stay out here by yourselves. My missus won't let me back in the wagon if I don't bring you along. You can ride with us."

A ride? That would be wonderful.

Don't go with them.

She looked at the wagon again. But were they headed the direction she wanted to go? She wasn't sure which direction was which. "Where are you headed?"

"Over the pass."

That didn't help her. "Is that west?"

"Aye."

She took his hand and stood then pulled Toby up. He hid behind her. "Thank you. We would appreciate a ride."

At the open wagon, he made introductions. "This is my missus, Eileen." He pointed to the woman on the seat then motioned to the back of the wagon to a boy of about ten. "This strapping lad is James. The bonny lass is Kathleen." He pointed to a girl of about eight then to a three-year-old girl. "The wee little one is Deborah."

"Pleased to meet you. I'm Lily. This is my son, Toby." Lily boosted Toby up then let Shamus help her into the back.

When she tried to inhale, her lungs fought her. She put her hand on her chest and took shallow breaths.

"Are you all right, lass?"

"I'm fine." It was probably just the cool night air affecting her. She would be better now that she didn't have to walk.

Shamus crinkled his brow but moved around to the front of the wagon and climbed aboard.

She would be better once they were moving. She was sure of it. She smiled at the three MacIan children, leaned her head back, and closed her eyes. The tightness in her chest would pass. She would will the discomfort away.

Return home.

She had no home. She never would again. She would have to move often to protect Toby.

Edric had put it off as long as possible. It was time to pick up Estella and Nancy for their tea party. He wasn't sure which was worse, wishing a deceiver and potential murderer was here to escort his girls to a party or disappointing his daughters?

In front of his house, he swung off his horse and tethered it. He started the walk up to the door, taking his time to notice a weed growing up in between the bricks of the walk. Enid never would have tolerated that. How could he have let that go? He leaned over and pulled it. Then another and another. Too soon he was at the foot of the porch steps. He couldn't delay any longer. Tossing the weeds aside, he hiked up onto the porch, took a deep breath, and stepped inside.

Pa stood, tying a ribbon in Nancy's long brown hair. He looked haggard with his own hair in disarray and his shirt partially untucked. Likely, his day had been a challenge with him getting the girls and their dresses ready. Edric shouldn't have put off coming home to let everyone know that Lily was gone. Pa had worked hard all day, and the girls had gotten their hopes up as they dressed and prepared.

His daughters in their finery turned to him, Estella in her pink lacy dress and Nancy in Estella's old purple one.

Estella curtsied. "Do I look pretty, Papa?"

"Do I look prettiful, Papa?" Nancy echoed.

He swallowed around a lump in his throat. "You both look beautiful." He sat on the edge of his cowhide chair

His girls stood in front of him.

He took a deep breath. "I'm going to take you girls to the party."

Nancy giggled. "Papa, you can't go. It's for girls."

Estella wore a more serious expression. "Why, Papa? Where's Toby's mama?"

"She can't make it. She had to leave town." And he hoped to never see her again and have to put her in jail. While at the same time, he wanted to hold her and pretend like the last few days had never happened.

Nancy stepped closer. "She has to, Papa. She has to."

"I'm sorry. She can't. She's gone."

"Go get her." Nancy planted her little fists on her hips.

He didn't know what else to say.

Through Nancy's bluster, tears welled in her eyes. Then she threw herself onto Edric's shoulder and cried louder than was real. He wrapped an arm around her.

A silent tear slid down Estella's cheek. Edric waved her over so he could hug her as well. But she turned and walked away, heading up to her room.

After a moment, Nancy pushed away from him and ran upstairs.

His poor girls. How dare Lily do this to them? Why hadn't she waited until after today? No. Now that he knew, he was glad she wasn't around his daughters.

"What happened?"

Pa's simple question broke through Edric's torment. Edric rubbed his face with his hands. "She left town."

"I gathered that from what you said to the girls. Did she tell you why? Or when she's returning?"

"She's not coming back, and I don't want her to."

Pa was silent for a moment then asked, "What did she do?"

Edric glared at Pa. "You were right. She had a secret. All along you said she was hiding something. And she was."

"That man that was in town? Is he her husband? Is that what it is?"

"No. I don't know. No." He couldn't be her husband if she really killed her husband.

Pa gripped his arm. "What is it? I have a right to know."

Edric yanked free. He didn't want to say it out loud. He gritted his teeth and said in a low voice, "She killed her husband." He turned and stalked upstairs. Let Pa chew on that a while.

He and Enid hadn't had the best marriage, and she could be quite demanding at times, but he'd never feared for his life or his daughters'.

Stepping into the girls' room, he saw Nancy sitting in the middle of the floor with her dress flounced out around her. She held Dolly in her lap, primping the yellow dress Lily had made. Estella lay face down on her bed in her petticoat and chemise. Her dress discarded in the corner.

He lifted Nancy off the floor and carried her over to Estella's bed. She clung to Dolly. He sat on the bed. The springs beneath the mattress creaked. He brushed the hair out of Estella's face.

"You can still go to the party. I'll take you."

Estella turned her face away. "I don't want to go."

Nancy gazed up at him with big brown eyes. She was struggling with what she wanted to do. "If Toby's mama isn't going, then Dolly doesn't want to go."

His heart ached for his daughters. How could he have been so foolish? He knew better than to bring another woman into their lives.

Women couldn't be trusted.

Not one of them.

Thirty

LATER, EDRIC TUCKED HIS DAUGHTERS IN bed and kissed them each good night. "I'm sorry about today."

Estella spoke in a soft voice. "When is Toby's mama coming back?"

He studied his girls' faces, one and then the other. He knew the answer they wanted. And he wanted to give it to them. But at the same time, he didn't want Lily back at all. "She's gone."

"Why?" Estella said.

"I don't know." But he did. She was running away as she had apparently been doing when she arrived in town.

"Make her come back," Nancy pleaded.

"I can't." He didn't want to.

Nancy sat up. "Yes, you can. You're the sheriff."

"Please, Papa." Estella sat up as well. "You have to go and bring her back. She was going to be our new mama."

"Pleeeease. I prayed it," Nancy chimed in. "Promise to bring her back."

He would not go after a murderer and have her around his little girls. Certainly not to be their mama. Their safety came first. His gaze shifted from one set of imploring eyes to the other. And he caved. Just a little. "I'll see what I can do." He couldn't disappoint them with the truth that they would never see her again, and he wouldn't go after her. He tucked them in and kissed them good night again. "Now, go to sleep."

Pa kissed them good night as well, and the two of them left the room.

Pa walked silently down the stairs, but Edric felt as though Pa was giving him a good scolding.

When Pa reached the sitting room, he turned on Edric. *"You'll see what you can do?"*

"What did you want me to say? That I'll go chasing

after a woman who could possibly be a murderer and bring her back for them, all the while putting our girls in danger?"

"I have never known you to lie to those girls."

"That wasn't a lie. I'll see what I can do."

"Which is exactly nothing."

"You want me to tell them that Mrs. Lexington killed her husband. That would break their hearts. I won't hurt them like that."

"Hurt is hurt one way or the other." Pa shook his head. "I guess you are in quite a pickle. Nancy prayed for you to bring Mrs. Lexington back. She's a powerful prayer. I believe God pays special attention to the prayers of children. You think you are strong enough to resist the Almighty?"

"Why are you suddenly on Lily's side? I would've thought you would be glad she was gone."

"I'm on our girls' side. The woman I met wasn't a cold-hearted murderer. If she hurt anyone, I can't see where she could have done so intentionally." Pa walked away.

Edric looked from the kitchen doorway where Pa disappeared through, to the stairs leading up to where the girls' bedroom was, then back and forth. What was he supposed to do? Though he hadn't out right lied to his daughters, it still didn't sit right. He knew they expected him to do everything in his power to find her. Retrieving a potential murderer was equally as displeasing. He would have to put her in jail. At least until it all got sorted out.

A right sour pickle indeed.

The MacIan's had been kind enough to let her travel with them as far as she wanted. It was nice to not be alone.

Shamus MacIan pulled two blankets out of the wagon. "James and I will sleep underneath. You ladies can be inside."

Lily shook her head. "I can't put you out. My son and I will be fine under the wagon." She and Toby had slept on the ground last night with nothing quite so grand as a wagon overhead to protect them or a blanket.

"Nay, lass. The boy and I will be quite fine on the ground." He leaned closer and lowered his voice. "We like the adventure."

The older girl, Kathleen, spoke up. "Da, I want to sleep under the wagon too."

Shamus clasped an arm around his daughter. "Then it's settled. The ladies and the two wee ones will sleep in the wagon, and us adventurers will sleep outside."

Eileen touched Lily's arm. "There is no sense arguing with that one. He's as stubborn as a three-legged mule."

Lily didn't know what made a three-legged mule more stubborn than a regular one, but she understood that no amount of arguing would change the arrangements. She climbed into the back of the wagon.

The tightness weighing in her chest eased after they had stopped traveling for the day. She hoped a good night's sleep would help even more. The strain of Timothy finding her, traveling during the night, and carrying Toby, had caught up to her. Her muscles, including the ones in her chest, were simply sore and giving her fits.

In the morning, she felt no better. The tightness hadn't ebbed. As she prepared with the others to pack up and leave after breakfast, she struggled to breathe around her tightening chest.

Eileen rested a reassuring hand on Lily's arm. "Are you all right?"

Lily put her fingers on her upper chest. "I'm fine."

"Nay, you aren't, lass. You nary slept a wink, tossing and gasping. Even now you draw air like a dying man."

Lily had thought she'd slept well. "I'm fine."

Eileen dropped it for the moment, but after they were under way. Lily could hear Shamus and Eileen talking from where they sat on the seat. Though pots rattled against the side of the wagon, the wheels creaked along, and the two older children chattered as they walked along outside, Lily could still hear their conversation.

"I cannot have her making my babies sick," Eileen said.

Shamus replied, "We cannot just leave her."

"I feel bad for her, but I have to think of my children before a stranger."

Lily understood exactly how Eileen felt. She too would protect Toby before a stranger. So, when they stopped at a stagecoach station to water the oxen, Lily thanked them and wished them well. And they her. She stayed behind with Toby and watched the MacIans travel on without her.

She turned to the station operator. "When's the next stage coming through?"

"It's due to arrive in a couple of hours." The man's white whiskers twitched as he spoke. "It could be later."

Having difficultly focusing her thoughts, it took Lily a moment to register what he'd said. "I would like a ticket for myself and one for my son."

"All righty."

The room seemed to move and shift, back and forth, and around. As though she were being jostled about in a wagon on a very rutted road.

"Miss?" The stationmaster stepped in front of her. Though his whiskers continued to wiggle, he didn't appear to be saying anything. Or was he?

Her knees lost their strength.

Then the man grew suddenly taller.

And the floor hit her.

She was looking up at him.

Toby's concerned face hovered over her. His lips moved, but she heard no words.

Thirty-One

EDRIC LEFT THE HOUSE IN THE morning before his girls got up. He didn't want to face them and tell them he was not going to look for Lily. He knocked softly on Aunt Henny's door in case she wasn't up yet.

Mr. Tunstall opened the door. "Have you found her?"

Edric bristled and shook his head. And he wasn't going to search for her. "Is Aunt Henny up?"

"In the kitchen."

The two boarders left.

Edric walked into the kitchen. When Aunt Henny raised her gaze to him in question, he held up a bottle of milk in answer.

Aunt Henny narrowed her eyes. "They aren't here."

He had brought the milk partly out of habit now and partly hoping life would return to the way it was before Lily's past had come to town. Before everything changed.

Aunt Henny sighed. "I was hoping you'd found them."

"I haven't looked." When Aunt Henny opened her mouth, he pressed on. "And I'm not going to."

"Why not? Who knows what kind of trouble they could be in?"

"She lied to us as to why she was here and possibly murdered her husband."

Aunt Henny raised the spatula she was wielding. "No. She said she killed her husband. There is a big difference."

"I don't see one. The man is dead. And by her own confession by her hands."

"You remember the bruises on those two. If she hurt anyone, it was only to protect her child."

"You don't know that."

"And neither do you."

"Why didn't she simply leave? Why'd she have to kill him?"

"Where would she have gone?"

"I don't know. But somewhere."

"There's nowhere for a wife to go that her husband can't drag her back from. He has total control over her life." Aunt Henny put down the spatula. "What did you say that first day she came to town? That God had put Lily in your path. Was that wrong?"

He had believed it at the time. He shook his head. Even after all her secrets and deceits, he still believed God had placed her in his life. But for what?

"Would God do that if you were not to help her?"

"Frankly, I don't know."

"What about Toby? The boy's come to trust you. And that's no small feat."

His mouth pulled slightly on one side. "I wouldn't say trust. Maybe less fearful." He missed the boy.

"And where did all that fear come from?"

Someone who had frightened him deeply. "His father?"

"I can't think of anyone else. If you won't go for Lily, go for the boy."

The boy Edric had hoped would become his son. He pictured Toby's round face sitting across from him at supper with Lily. He had pulled his mama's hand away from Edric's. Lily had said he was being brave to test Edric. Should he go after Lily for no other reason than to rescue the boy from her? A boy who probably wasn't even hers.

When Edric focused on Aunt Henny again, she was smiling. A smile that said she knew something. "What?"

"The trail's getting cold."

"I'm not..."

Aunt Henny stared at him in silence, waiting for him to finish. "Not what?"

Edric clenched his teeth. "I need to get to work. Relieve Cord." He turned and left before she could reply, but he sensed she was still smiling.

He wasn't chasing after Lily. He wasn't. If he found her, he would have to put her in jail. And *that* he would not do. Let someone else do it.

After sending Cord home and pinning on his badge, he went to the telegraph office. The closed sign hung in the door. Too early for it to be open. He leaned against the building and waited.

Edric hadn't realized he'd closed his eyes until Mort said his name. He opened them quickly.

"Howdy, Sheriff Rix. You need to send another telegram?"

"Yup."

Mort unlocked the door and left it open for Edric to follow him inside. "Must be important for you to be waiting for me so early."

He wrote his question on the pad. *How did Tobias Bremmer die?* "Send this right away and let me know as soon as you receive a reply."

Mort held up the paper. "Will do."

Edric left.

Less than an hour later, Mort's messenger boy, Johnny, found him. "Telegram just come for you."

He hustled to the telegraph office.

Mort handed him the one-word reply.

Shot.

She shot him? That couldn't be an accident. The poor sot probably didn't even see it coming.

He stalked out and to his office. Shot? She shot him? He couldn't picture Lily shooting anyone.

She wouldn't. He knew that deep inside. *Lord, Lily wouldn't shoot someone, would she?* A peace from above washed over him. He marched to the telegraph office again. He handed Mort his new question. *By whom?*

"I'll wait for the reply."

Mort nodded and sent the message. "I put that you're waiting."

"Thanks."

A half an hour later, came the reply. *His brother.*

What? Not the answer he'd expected. Lily said she had killed her husband. Maybe the officer in Philadelphia was referring to a different man. Edric had assumed that Tobias Bremmer was Lily's husband even with the different last names. It would explain a lot of things.

Even his brother Timothy shooting him. And Edric *could* picture Timothy Bremmer shooting someone.

He scratched out another question. *Did Tobias Bremmer have any family?*

The reply was swift in coming. *Brother. Wife and son missing.*

This still fit with Lily being Tobias Bremmer's wife. But not who killed him. *What is his wife's name?* He appreciated the officer at the other end staying in the telegraph office on his end.

Reply, *Lily Bremmer.*

He had expected that. Then why had she been going by another name? *Who is Mrs. Lexington?*

Again the reply was swift. *Mr. and Mrs. Lexington passed away over six years ago. Parents of Lily Lexington Bremmer.*

That was all he needed to be convinced. The Lily Lexington he knew was the same woman who was married to Tobias Bremmer whom his brother shot. But then whom did Lily kill? "Tell the officer thank you and that I have no further questions."

Mort nodded.

Edric left and returned to his office. He didn't know who Lily had killed, but he knew he had to help her. He inquired at the stagecoach company and the train station. Neither of them had sold tickets to Lily. That meant she left on foot, during the night. In her condition? He needed to go after her. He headed for home to pack. He doubted she would head back toward the east. That left three other directions she could have gone. *Lord, how do I find her?*

After he packed and told Pa his plan to search for Lily, he hugged his daughters. "I'll return as soon as I can."

Both girls jumped up and down, chanting, "Bring her home. Bring her home."

"I'll do my best." He knew this was the right thing. Regardless of how any of this turned out, he knew he needed to do this. He needed to find out whom she had killed—if not Tobias Bremmer—and why. Then, he needed to figure out a way to keep her out of jail. He didn't want her to have to be on the run with Toby the rest of her life. He wanted her to have peace. That surprised him.

He was ashamed of himself for believing the worst of her. Aunt Henny was right. There had to be a good reason for her to harm anyone. He believed that the only thing to cause her to bring harm to another was her son. She would protect him with her life. And for that, he could forgive her for hurting his girls. They would easily forgive her for disappointing them and leaving.

But the one thing he still wasn't sure of was Toby being her son and what he would do if he found out the boy belonged to someone else. And what of the child she carried inside her?

As he mounted his horse, the telegraph messenger boy ran up to him. "Another telegram come for you." Johnny panted.

Another telegram? He hadn't asked any more questions. Edric reached his hand down. "I'll give you a ride."

The boy gripped Edric's wrist and swung up behind.

At the telegraph office, Mort handed him a piece of paper. "He's waiting for your reply."

He read. *Do you know the whereabouts of Mrs. Tobias Bremmer?*

This telegram wasn't from the Philadelphia police. It was signed Perry Turner, Esq. Why would an attorney be contacting him about Lily? Had he asked too many questions and put Lily in danger?

He wrote his reply. *What is this in reference to?* "I'll wait."

Mort sent the telegram and quickly one came in response.

I am her father's attorney. A matter of utmost importance to her.

Utmost importance? Attorneys made Edric nervous. They were secretive and evasive. *What does this matter concern?*

Mr. Turner's reply, *As the family attorney, I'm not at liberty to divulge that information. It is imperative that I locate her.*

Secretive and evasive. But if he represented the family, he would be on Lily's side no matter what the case was, wouldn't he?

He wrote on the pad. *She lived in Kamola for two months but has left town.* He hesitated. Should he tell him more? Certainly her family attorney would be on her side. And if she needed defending in a murder trial, he could be quite helpful. He finished the message. *I am setting out to search for her to bring her home.* Would he receive a reply? He didn't have to wait long.

I hope your mission is successful. I will arrive by train within the week.

He was coming? And quickly. He waited for regret over divulging Lily's location—or soon to be location if he could find her—but none came.

He stopped by Aunt Henny's on his way out of town.

The older woman sat rocking in a chair on the porch. "It's about time."

Edric leapt up the steps without touching any. "For what? Were you expecting me?"

"For you to come to your senses and return Lily and Toby to where they belong."

"How did you know I was even going to look for them?"

"Because you can't resist championing those in need. You love her. *And,* you have your horse packed for some time away."

"But I could be going anywhere."

"But you're not. You're heading west."

"I am?" He glanced that direction. "What makes you think *she's* heading west?"

"Autumn is just around the corner, so she wouldn't want to go north into colder country."

"Maybe that is precisely the reason why she would. No one would be expecting it."

"She's fleeing, not thinking. A frightened animal will generally head in one direction unless something gets in its way and causes it to change course. She came nearly straight west from Philadelphia. It makes sense she will continue on that route."

That made sense.

"And I feel it inside." She thumped her fingers on her breastbone.

With no other reasoning to go on, he would aim west. Maybe stopping here was God's way of directing him.

Thirty-Two

LILY SAT UP WITH A START, sucking in stale, dusty air, and looked around. Where was she? Where was Toby? She sat on a small bed in a small, unfamiliar room. She swung her feet over the edge and stood on unsteady legs. Her and Toby's carpetbag sat by the wall, Toby's brown brogan boots sat under a chair. He was here. Someplace.

A voice filtered in from beyond the door. She opened it slowly.

Toby sat on a table with his bare feet dangling, his little toes wiggling. He took a bite of cookie he held in his hand. A white whiskered man stood in profile to Lily. He wasn't any taller than her and didn't see her. He appeared to be telling Toby a story.

As though connected, they turned to her in tandem.

Toby raised his arms. "Mommy!"

She scooped him off the table.

"I'm Charlie, the stationmaster," the man said. "Feeling better? You look better." He held up a plate. "Cookie?"

"Yes, much better." She took what appeared to be an oatmeal cookie. It was quite tasty. "Did we miss the stagecoach?"

"It came through yesterday."

"But you said two hours."

"That was yesterday."

Panic stirred around inside her. "How long have we been here?"

"Since yesterday."

She remembered feeling faint. She had slept all night. "When is the next stage due?"

Go home.

She ignored the impression.

"East bound one should be through late this

afternoon."

Not east. She would never go back that direction again. "What about one heading west?"

"Day after tomorrow."

"That long?" She didn't want to stay in one place so soon. Someone might find her. She needed to be far away from Kamola. "What about south?"

"You would need to take the east bound stage to Kamola. From there you could catch one heading south."

That was out of the question. She would have to wait. Or set out on foot again.

Edric had cut across the countryside to help make up the day and a half head start Lily had. Uneasy about the direction he was heading, he met up with the road and stopped at a stagecoach station near dusk.

The stationmaster was a muscular, bald man swinging a hammer at a forge. He saw Edric and stopped. "What can I do for you?"

Edric pulled back his coat to reveal his star.

"Sheriff." He acknowledged the badge with a nod. "You after an outlaw?"

He didn't like to think of Lily that way. "A woman and her son. She has blond hair. Her son has dark hair."

"She do something wrong?"

He couldn't bring himself to say yes. "She needs my help. It's important that I find her."

"Haven't seen her."

"She wasn't on the most recent stage that came through?"

"No, sir."

If she wasn't traveling by stage and she hadn't left Kamola by train, then by what means of transportation was she taking? "You have a bed I can use for the night?"

"Of course. And I have a pot of stew on the stove."

"I'd like that." He could head out fresh at first light.

At the end of the following day, he caught up with a

family in a wagon who had camped for the night. The father of the family held a shotgun across his arms. "May I help you?" He had a heavy Scottish accent, making him difficult to understand.

It took Edric a moment to decipher his question. He pulled back his coat to show his star then nodded toward the gun. "You run into any trouble?"

"A sheriff, are you?" The man lowered his gun. "Nay, but one can never be too careful where his family is concerned."

"So true. You mind if I dismount?"

"Of course. Come on down."

Edric swung down and tethered his horse. "I'm searching for a young woman and her son."

The man's wife glanced at her husband. They knew something.

His spirit came to life. "She's blond, her son has dark hair." He was sure they had seen her.

"She rode with us for a wee bit," the man said.

His wife stepped forward. "She wasn't looking all too well."

Lily was sick? Was it the baby? "Where is she?"

"She stayed at the station two days ago. She was inquiring about the next coach."

Two days ago? So, he was headed the right direction. "She caught a stage?"

"I do not know. I assume so."

"Was the stationmaster a bald man?"

"Ney. He was an older gent with white hair and whiskers all over his face. A wee bit of a man. The station before that one."

Since that stationmaster had no reason to lie about seeing her on the latest stage that went through his station, Lily likely took one in a different direction.

On the morning the west-bound stage was due to come through the station, Lily finished packing the carpetbag.

Not that there was much to do. It was one little bag, and they had few belongings.

Go home.

She was. A new home for her and Toby. One with salty sea air. The tightness in her chest, that had been absent for a day and a half, began with a gentle tug. She ignored it.

The stage was due soon, so she set their bag on the small porch, if it could be called that. More like a few planks of wood and a drooping awning.

Think of Toby.

She was. That was why she was leaving.

You can't keep running and hiding.

Yes, she could.

But could Toby?

He knelt a few feet away in the grass, coaxing a caterpillar onto a leaf. This was no kind of life for a child. Always moving. He deserved better. He deserved a permanent place to call home. She would find him that place. A good, friendly place. Her heart told her that she already had. But she couldn't go back. She would have to find a new home.

The stage clattered down the road and stopped in front of the station. There were only two passengers on the stage, so there would be plenty of room for her and her son. "Toby, time to go."

As their carpetbag was thrown up to the roof and strapped down, Lily's insides twisted, and the tightness increased. She grasped the support post.

Though she focused, it was difficult to breathe. All her organs felt as though they were trying to change places. Pains throughout her body. What was wrong with her? She struggled to draw in breath.

"What's wrong with her?" the driver asked the stationmaster.

She wanted to say that nothing was wrong, but she didn't have the air to speak.

The old stationmaster gripped her arm. "Here. Have a seat." He tried to guide her backward.

Toby gripped her hand. "Mommy?"

She shook her head and pointed to the stage. She

forced out the words "We have to go."

"I'm not taking a sick woman. Sorry, ma'am." He had her carpetbag tossed down. "I've a schedule to keep."

"No, wait." But she was too weak to resist Charlie guiding her to a stump. She sat.

"Sorry." The driver snapped the reins and set the stage in motion.

No. It couldn't leave without them. She whispered, "Wait."

The old man helped her inside and back to bed. "Don't you worry about your boy, I'll look after him."

She lay for a long while concentrating on her breathing. Aiming to have each breath deeper than the last. Sometimes she succeeded, but most of the time, not.

After a while the pains and tightness subsided enough for her to get up and join Toby and Charlie. Her son sat on the table while the old man peeled potatoes into a wooden bowl.

"Feeling better?" the old man asked.

"A bit." She didn't want him to know it was still difficult for her to breathe. And she really didn't want Toby to know anything was wrong. "When is the next stage heading west?"

Charlie studied her for a moment. "I think you don't really want to go west."

"Of course, I do."

"You're fine until you try to leave."

That did seem to be the case. "It's just bad timing. I'm sure I'll be fine now."

Charlie shook his head.

Not wanting to hear anymore of his nonsense, she went outside. She felt better already. She had only needed to rest.

But the ring of truth in the old man's words echoed inside her. She hadn't *wanted* to leave Kamola. She'd been forced to.

She realized she was facing toward Kamola and breathed in the fresh air. Her chest seemed to loosen. What did that mean? She turned west, and the tightness increased. Every time she tried to go west, her body rebelled. She willed her chest to relax, taking several deep breaths. The ache increased. She turned around and was able to breathe easier. This was absurd.

If she couldn't go west, where was she to go?

She wished her father were here to tell her what to do.

Trust in the Lord with all thine heart; and lean not unto thine own understanding.

It had been her father's favorite verse to quote. It seemed to fit any occasion for him. She didn't even know exactly where it was found in the Bible. Maybe in the Psalms or Proverbs.

"Lord," she whispered. "I don't know what to do. I can't seem to go forward. And I can't go back. I'll be put in jail and lose Toby. Am I supposed to stay here?"

Go home.

Home where?

The home that I gave you.

Images of Kamola flashed through her mind. Her first day stepping off the train. Or rather needing Edric's help to get off the train. Toby accepting a cookie with trepidation from Edric. The picnic with Edric and his girls, braiding their hair. Edric protecting them all from the stampede. Edric's kisses.

All the scenes had Edric in them.

She could breathe.

If she went back, what would become of Toby? Someone might use him to manipulate her. Or hurt him. She wouldn't let that happen.

Then it was clear. Toby was only in danger because of her. If she turned herself in, Toby couldn't be used against her. The only way to keep him safe was to give him up.

Thirty-Three

LILY SURVEYED AUNT HENNY'S FROM THE safety of the side of the chicken coop. No buggies or wagons yet. The quilting circle would arrive soon though. She needed to be gone before they did. She entered through the back door with Toby at her side and stood in the doorway between the kitchen and dining room.

Beyond the dining room in the parlor, Aunt Henny faced away from her. The older woman was moving the dining table chairs into the parlor for the quilting circle ladies. When she turned to retrieve another, she gasped then smiled. "Lily! You're back." Aunt Henny limped over without her cane and hugged her then Toby.

Lily needed to speak to Aunt Henny alone. "Toby, why don't you go find Miss Tibbins?"

Toby swiveled his head back and forth. "Where is she?"

"I think she's curled up on my bed. Why don't you go see?"

Toby ran off.

Lily dared not move. "Are we welcome here?"

"Of course. Always."

Lily swallowed hard. "You read my letter."

"Yes, child." She took the carpetbag and set it on the floor. "The ladies will be so happy to see you."

But she didn't want to face the ladies. She thought she heard footsteps and listened for Toby returning but heard nothing more. It was safe to speak freely. "I can't stay."

"Of course, you can. I will not hear of you leaving again."

"I can't stay. You have been so gracious and kind to us. I hate to ask anything more from you."

Aunt Henny took Lily's hand and patted it. "Ask. I'll

be happy to do anything for you and your son. Anything."

"I need you to look after Toby for me."

Aunt Henny eyed her suspiciously. "How long?"

Lily's eyes filled with tears. "I don't know. I'm turning myself in. I could be in jail for years."

"You're not going to jail. Edric will sort this all out."

"I killed my husband. I can't keep running. I have to turn myself in. I can't go on living this way. Toby can't live this way. I need to know my son will be well cared for. He likes it here and knows you. Please."

"Of course. But it will be only for a short bit. I'm sure you'll be back by supper."

Lily knew she wouldn't. She hugged Aunt Henny.

Aunt Henny held on to her and whispered in her ear, "You are like a daughter to me."

The tears Lily had held at bay escaped down her cheeks. "Thank you. I have to go before he comes out of your room."

"You aren't saying good-bye to your son?"

"It will be easier if I don't. Thank you for everything. Tell him I love him very much." Lily hurried for the door and pushed through the screen.

Five of the quilting ladies stood on the porch, Franny, Agnes, Marguerite and her daughters, Isabelle and Adelaide. They parted for her to pass. Not one of them said a thing to her nor looked at her. The floorboards captivated their attention.

Lily had heard footsteps after all, just not Toby's. She trotted to the gate and left.

A few minutes later, she opened the door to the sheriff's office. Coming had been the right thing. She'd had no trouble breathing or tightness in her chest since deciding to return.

A man stood behind the desk with his back to the door.

She cleared her throat. "Excuse me."

The man turned around. He wasn't Edric. She wasn't sure if she was relieved or not.

He smiled and swooped off his hat to reveal a shock of blond hair. "Howdy, Mrs. Lexington. I'm Deputy

Montana. What can I do for you?"

He knew her name? Had she met this man before? It didn't matter. "Is the sheriff around?"

"Sheriff Rix is out of town. Is there something I can help you with?"

She supposed it didn't matter who did it. "I'm turning myself in."

His smile drooped. "Pardon, ma'am?"

"I killed my husband back in Philadelphia and need to be put in jail." The Lord hadn't let her rest as long as she was running. Maybe she would be like the Apostle Paul in jail and help others.

Deputy Montana swallowed hard, sending his Adam's apple to bobbing. "I can't do that."

"Why not? You're a deputy, and I've confessed to a crime."

"But-but... You're Sheriff Rix's sweetheart."

"That doesn't put me above the law." And she wasn't Edric's anything anymore. Except his prisoner. Obviously, Edric hadn't told his deputies about her.

The deputy stared at her for a long moment, then he skirted the desk and arced wide around her as though she had the plague. At the open door, he put two fingers between his lips and let out a loud, shrill whistle.

After a moment, a young boy of eight or nine ran up onto the boardwalk. "Yes um, sir."

"Go fetch Deputy Cord. He should be at home. Tell him it's urgent. There'll be a nickel in it for you."

Kicking up dust, the boy ran off like a chicken being chased by a fox.

Deputy Montana took a deep breath before turning back to her. His forced smile made him look suddenly ill. He pulled a chair away from the wall. "Please, have a seat."

"Shouldn't I be put in one of those?" She pointed toward the two cells.

Deputy Montana scuttled across the room, positioning himself between her and the cells. "Not just yet. We'll wait on Cord. He's senior deputy."

What difference did it make who closed the door?

The deputy motioned toward the chair. "I'd feel much

more at ease if you'd take a seat."

She obliged.

He exhaled as though he'd been holding his breath then moved around behind the desk and sat.

"Shall I tell you how it happened?"

"Happened?"

"When I killed my husband."

"Nope. We'll wait for Cord on that too."

The deputy seemed nervous and did look quite young. Maybe he thought she would try to hurt him.

"When do you expect the sheriff to return?"

"Few days. If we're *real* lucky, today. He went out looking for you."

That made sense. He was the sheriff after all. It was his duty to put criminals like her in jail.

Though the silence stretched long and awkward, she waited. This deputy didn't seem inclined to take any actions or put down her statement until the other deputy showed up. He sat stiffly in his chair and stared at the open door. He appeared to be willing the other deputy to arrive faster.

Soon, booted footsteps clomped up onto the boardwalk and inside.

"Montana! What's so urgent—?" He stopped. "Excuse me, ma'am."

Lily stood and turned.

Deputy Cord's face broke into a wide smile. A smile she suspected had disarmed many ladies. "Sheriff Rix will be mighty glad you're back."

She bet he would. To lock her up. He'd probably be upset at wasting his time and being out of town away from his family. Away from his precious girls.

Deputy Montana motioned Deputy Cord over near the far cell and whispered, "She wants to be put in jail."

"What! What for?"

"Says she killed her husband."

Cord rubbed his hand across his stubbly jaw. "We can't do that. I'd sooner face an angry mama bear than Rix when he found out we did that."

"I know. What should we do?"

Though they whispered, she could hear every word.

The room wasn't that big, and neither were adept at speaking softly.

Deputy Cord glanced at her then back at the other deputy. "Well, if she confessed to a crime, go ahead and put her in a cell."

"I'm not gonna do it. You do it. You're senior."

"That's right, so I give the orders."

Deputy Montana vigorously shook his head. "I like breathing way too much."

Certainly Edric wouldn't hurt them for doing their duty? But she was sure that neither of these men would lock her up, so she walked over and into the nearest cell. The only thing in there was a metal cot with a dingy, stained mattress.

A strange peace washed over her. She was doing the right thing.

"What are you doin'?"

She startled at the sharp voice and turned. "Clearly, the two of you are having difficulty putting me in a cell, so I have done it for you."

Deputy Cord's eyes widened in horror. "You can't be in there."

"Why not?"

"You just can't. Now come on out of there." He motioned with his hand to her.

Cringing on the inside, she lowered herself to sit on the cot, but only very lightly and on the edge, where it was cleaner. "You may close the door and lock it."

Cord sucked in a deep breath and heaved it out again. "Ma'am, we trust you not to leave town. Why don't you go back to Aunt Henny's, and when Rix returns, we'll let him know where you are?"

She couldn't look into Toby's sad face and then leave him again. "I'm staying put until the sheriff returns."

"Please, Mrs. Lexington. I beg you to go back to the boarding house. Rix won't be happy if we keep you here."

She was sure Edric would be quite satisfied with her being right where she was. "I can't return to Aunt Henny's. My son won't understand." A clean break was best. He was already going to be confused.

"This isn't a proper place for a lady."

"I'm staying put."

Deputy Cord gave a heavy sigh and shook his head, seemingly resigning himself to her staying. "Let me know if you need anything."

Henny stood on her strong leg, using her weaker one to balance. "I think it's time for us all to join in to quilt one of our members' pieced tops."

The women all chattered that it was about time to do some quilting, how the piecing had gotten tiresome.

Henny shook out Lily's sunshine and shadow quilt that mirrored the young mother's life. Lily had done a wonderful job on the piecing. Henny expected the women to grab the edges of the work and start discussing the pattern to quilt it in. A feather pattern? Shadowing the seams? Leaves and flowers?

But all the edges of the quilt save hers fluttered to the floor in the middle of the circle. Like a dead bird falling to the ground.

Each woman hushed, sitting straight as boards, lips pursed, looking at their laps. Not one of them would even glance at Henny or the quilt.

Since no one would speak, Henny did. "I think we should stitch shadow lines in the dark portions of the blocks and little suns in the light portions."

Still no one spoke.

Henny shook the pieced top so that it fluttered. "Ladies?"

The uneasy silence grew to an awkward nervousness.

Isabelle, Marguerite's adult stepdaughter, opened her mouth to speak. Marguerite put her hand on the young woman's arm, and she closed her mouth.

Henny couldn't believe these women. "What's wrong?" She looked from lady to lady. "Franny? Trudy? Neva?" No one would meet her gaze. "Agnes?"

Agnes cleared her throat. "Henny, I think I can speak for the whole group. We aren't comfortable working on that woman's quilt."

All the ladies nodded.

That woman? "This is Lily's quilt top. You all like her."

"She murdered her husband."

"And abandoned her child."

"What decent mother would do that?"

Henny was appalled. "Where did you hear those things?"

"From the porch, it was hard not to overhear her talking."

"You were eavesdropping?" Henny looked from woman to woman.

"She didn't sound at all remorseful."

Henny's anger boiled. "What she said was she killed her husband. There is a big difference."

"Dead is dead and at her hands."

"You don't know the circumstances. You know Lily. You know how sweet and kind she is. You can't possibly think she would harm someone intentionally? You're condemning her without all the information?"

No one replied.

"He *or she* who has sinned not, ye cast the first stone."

Several women shifted in their chairs.

Henny didn't want to drag out dirty laundry, but these women were being foolish and needed to see reason. "Trudy, shall we condemn you for losing the man you loved over a petty squabble. A man you still pine for?"

She didn't wait for a reply but went to the next person in the circle. "Franny, don't you and your father charge the Mexicans more for items in his store?"

"Adelaide, do your parents know that you sneak off to the kissing tree with young men?"

Marguerite jerked around to glare at her daughter.

"Marguerite, does your husband know about your background?"

Marguerite's cheeks flamed.

"Dorthea, shall we discuss your son? Your oldest son."

Someone in the circle whispered, "Oldest son? I thought she only had one son."

Henny went on. "Not one of us is perfect. We have all made our share of mistakes." She certainly didn't want to air her own faults and faux pas from her youth. "When Lily and her son arrived, they were both covered in bruises. Agnes, you know what that's like from your first husband."

Now, the women had a reason to be silent.

Isabelle lifted the corner of the quilt top. "I have some yellow thread. I think we should do the suns in yellow."

Betsy grabbed the edge of the quilt. "And gray for the shadow lines."

"I have some muslin for the back."

"And I have cotton batting. I was going to put it in my quilt but I can get more."

The approving murmurs went around the circle as each woman took hold of the edge of the quilt.

Now these were the women Henny knew and loved.

Late in the afternoon, Lily couldn't believe her eyes and stood from her cot. Aunt Henny, followed by Trudy, Franny, and Agnes, entered the sheriff's office.

"We brought supper." Aunt Henny limped over to Lily and enveloped her in her arms. "Mercy. This is worse than I imagined."

"It's not so bad. Deputy Cord has been keeping me company."

Aunt Henny turned to him.

The deputy stood from behind the desk. "I'll leave you ladies to your visit. And iffen you can talk her into going back to your place, Aunt Henny, I'd be much obliged." He strode out.

Aunt Henny faced her again.

Lily shook her head. "I can't leave. Toby has been through too much these past days. I can't put him through anymore."

"He misses you dearly. I can't leave you here. It just isn't right."

Agnes put a hand on Aunt Henny's shoulder. "She's right, Henny. It will be easier on the child this way. She won't be in here long. The sheriff will sort this all out when he returns."

Lily was surprised that Agnes would agree with her and even more surprised at her soft tone and the gentleness in her eyes when she looked at her. But she could see that Aunt Henny wasn't ready to give up the fight.

Franny stepped forward with a quilt in her arms. The quilt was folded with the top side in so Lily couldn't see what it looked like. It was kind of them to bring it for her. It would be much better than the scratchy wool blanket that lay on the end of the cot.

"All the ladies worked extra hard at circle today to finish this for you." Franny held the quit out to Trudy who grabbed a corner. The two shook it out between them.

Lily sucked in a breath. "My sunshine and shadow quilt."

"We finished it for you."

Lily was surprised they would do this for her after the way they avoided her this morning. And since they didn't ask why she was in jail, they likely already knew, so this was doubly surprising. Tears stung her eyes. "Thank you. I don't deserve this."

Thirty-Four

AFTER A WEEK IN THE SADDLE, Edric hurt all over. Hadn't done that in a few years. And he hadn't found Lily. A couple of people had remembered seeing a blond woman with a dark-haired boy, but the pair seemed to have vanished. He would rest at home for a day and head out again.

He reined in his horse in front of Aunt Henny's and tethered him to the fence. He needed to tell the older woman he hadn't succeeded yet and to see if she had heard from Lily. If fortune was with him, Lily would be here, waiting for him. But he couldn't figure out any logical reason why she would come back.

He plodded up the walk and onto the porch.

"Come in, Edric," Aunt Henny called even before he knocked. He swore that woman could sense him coming.

Aunt Henny sat sipping a cup of tea. Agnes Martin came from the kitchen with another cup and poured him some.

He accepted the offered cup and took a swig. He had to be careful with his words. He didn't need Mrs. Martin and the whole town finding out what Lily had done. Or might have done. Or might not have done. "I only stopped by to tell you I wasn't successful yet."

"I know." Aunt Henny pointed toward the dining room area.

He shifted his gaze. It took him a moment to see what she was after him to see.

Toby lay curled up under the table, one arm hooked around the cat, the other around his train engine, his big brown eyes staring at him, his thumb in his mouth. Misery etched on his young face and in the wilted appearance of his body.

Even so, Edric's heart leapt for joy at the sight of the

boy. "Howdy, Toby."

Toby didn't respond with words but sat up, dragging the cat onto his lap.

"Where's your mama?" Edric looked toward the kitchen. He didn't hear any noise from in there, so he went and peered in. No Lily.

He came back out.

Toby stood next to the table now. The cat was gone, and the engine abandoned under the table.

He looked hopefully from the boy to Aunt Henny. The older woman appeared despondent as well. He wanted to speak to her alone, without Agnes Martin.

Toby crossed over to him and barely leaned against his leg.

Edric's insides tightened, and his breath caught. Toby looked so sad. *And* he'd come up to Edric without anyone coaxing him to *and* was leaning on him. Something was terribly wrong. Edric didn't know what to do, so he gently placed his hand on the boy's head as a way to return the child's unexpected affection without scaring him.

Toby mumbled something.

Edric crouched. "What was that?"

"Will you bring my mommy home?"

If not with her son, then where was Lily? The sudden clench of his insides knocked the wind out of him. He shot his gaze to Aunt Henny. He needed to speak to her.

Aunt Henny must have sensed it. "Toby, would you go out in the garden and pull ten carrots for me. You know how many ten is?"

Toby flopped his head about.

Agnes stood and held out her hand. "Is it all right if I help you?"

As Toby took her hand and went with her, Edric stood. When the boy reached the kitchen doorway, he returned and tilted his head to look up. "You won't go nowhere?"

"I'll stay right here."

Toby took Agnes's hand again and left.

As soon as Edric heard the screen door close, he asked in a low voice, "Where is Lily? She wouldn't leave

Toby."

"And yet that's exactly what she's done."

Couldn't be. Lily would never— "Where is she?"

Was that a hint of a smile on her lips she was trying to hide?

"She's sitting in one of your jail cells."

"What? That can't be."

"It's true."

Which one of his fool deputies saw fit to incarcerate her? He would release her immediately. Edric moved toward the front door.

Aunt Henny spoke in a sharp tone that stopped him in his tracks. "You can't leave."

"I have to let her out."

"You promised the boy you wouldn't leave before he came back inside."

He held his hands out from his sides then dropped them. Held them out again and dropped them. He looked toward the kitchen listening for the door. Then he paced.

Aunt Henny sighed, and he swung his gaze to her. He couldn't help it if he was impatient to see that Lily was all right.

"You can go outside and tell the boy you need to go."

He lifted his head a little higher. "Right. I'll return with Lily."

"I know."

He went through the kitchen and outside.

Toby had both hands around a carrot top and was pulling with all his weight. When the root came free of the ground, Toby toppled backward.

Mrs. Martin praised him and helped him up.

"Toby," Edric said.

Toby's eyes widened, and he dropped the carrot. He came over and stood in front of Edric, titling his head back as far as it would go to look up at him.

Edric crouched, resting his forearms on his thighs. "I have to go."

Toby shook his head.

"I'm going to get your mama."

Toby's expression brightened, and he nodded.

Edric put a hand on Toby's shoulder. "I'll return

soon."

Then Toby did a most unexpected thing. He raised his little hand, looked at it a moment, then placed it on Edric's arm.

The boy was trusting him. Not only not to hurt him but to bring his mama home.

Edric patted Toby's hand. "Everything is going to be all right."

Toby leaned into Edric's shoulder. He didn't hug him, but it was obvious the boy trusted him enough to be this close and this vulnerable.

Edric rested his hand on Toby's back to reassure him. Surprisingly, Toby didn't flinch or pull away. It was time to go get his mama. "I won't be long." He left.

As he rode up to his office, he saw one of his deputies leaning against the front, with a rifle cradled in his arms. Was he expecting trouble? Edric's insides twisted.

Montana pushed away from the building, gripping the rifle and alert, but then relaxed. "Sheriff Rix. I can't tell how glad we are you've returned."

Edric pointed to the rifle. "You have any trouble?"

Montana stepped off the boardwalk and grabbed the horse's halter. "No, sir. This was to keep trouble from happening."

Edric swung down. It was good to know everything had been quiet. "I hear you have a prisoner."

His deputy paled. "Yes, sir. Well, sort of. I can explain. It wasn't our fault."

"Did you accidently lock her up?"

"No—No, we didn't. I mean we didn't lock her up—accidently or otherwise. She insisted. She turned herself in and wouldn't leave."

"Is she safe?"

"Of course. That's why I'm out here. Cord's inside. We made sure nothing happened to her."

It was good to know his deputies were seeing to her safety. He wrapped the reins around the hitching rail and stepped up onto the boardwalk. Before turning the knob, he prepared himself for what he was about to see, Lily sitting in a dreadful cell. But he wasn't prepared for what he actually saw.

The first cell looked more like a home than a jail cell. A wood and lace room divider blocked most of the view of the cot, but he could still see a quilt or two draped over it and another one on the end. A washstand stood by the near bars with a ceramic bowl and pitcher. A decorated towel hung from the side. A rug covered the floor. A quilt was strung up on the bars separating the two cells.

How long had she been here?

Lily sat in one of Aunt Henny's wingback chairs. Her head back and eyes closed, a Bible on her lap.

And lace curtains on the small window. But none of that was the strangest thing. The strangest thing was that the cell door, also with a long section of lace, hung wide open. Never in his life had a prisoner been held with the door open.

Around the quilt separating the two cells, he could see Cord's booted feet on the cot in the other cell. He likely was on duty all night and caught his sleep here during the day with Montana stationed outside.

Edric knelt on the rug in front of Lily and touched her hand as a way to wake her.

As she opened her eyes, she sucked in a startled breath and made a small noise. When she appeared to realize he wasn't a threat, she calmed. "You're home."

He heard the gun cock one second and release the next.

Cord let out a mild curse. "You nearly scared me half to death." He holstered his gun.

Edric swung his gaze to his deputy. "You locked her in a cell?"

"No. No, I didn't—well, one time we locked it—but that was to make sure no one came while we were out. Wouldn't've had to if she'd just've gone to Aunt Henny's."

Edric stood.

Cord took a step back. "She's a stubborn one. And it was all her idea to be in that cell in the first place."

It was fun watching his nothing-got-him-flustered deputy flustered.

Edric held his hand out to Lily. "Let's get you out of here. Toby is anxious to see you."

Lily remained seated. "I can't. Didn't you read my letter?"

He nodded. "You didn't kill your husband."

"But I did."

"Your husband was Tobias Bremmer whose brother, Timothy Bremmer, came to town?"

"Yes."

He made his voice firm so she would believe him. "*You* didn't kill him."

She stared at him a moment while that information settled in, then her face paled. "Oh, no. He'll come after us."

"No, he won't. You're safe."

She stood and gripped his arm. "You don't understand. Toby! You have to make sure Toby is safe."

He was about to explain to her that *she* hadn't been the one to kill him, that Timothy had, when he heard several sets of footsteps behind him, coming in the door. He turned to see his third deputy, Sammy, escorting an older man no taller than Lily with cherry-red cheeks, a thick middle, and spectacles perched on his bulbous nose.

"Mr. Turner?" Lily said.

"Lily." The attorney edged past Edric and enveloped Lily in his arms. He faced Edric. "I demand you release Mrs. Bremmer immediately."

"I'm not holding her."

Lily spoke up. "I can't leave."

Mr. Turner turned from her to him.

Edric shrugged. "Maybe you can talk sense into her."

Mr. Turner faced Lily. "What's going on, Lily?"

"I killed Tobias. The only way to protect Toby was to turn myself in. Edric said he's not dead, so he'll come after us. We have to make sure Toby's safe."

"Now calm down." Mr. Turner patted her arm. "Tobias is dead, but you didn't kill him."

Edric could see Lily's confusion plainly on her furrowed face.

"But I hit him. He fell. If he's dead, then I'm to blame. I ran away so no one would know."

"Here. Sit down." Mr. Turner guided her to the chair.

She sat, rigidly. "Yes, you hit him. And he was madder than a swarm of hornets and a riled-up nest of rattlesnakes all in one when he came to. But you only knocked him out. When he woke, he must have figured you were hiding at his brother's. He went looking for you there with a gun. He didn't believe Timothy when he told him he hadn't seen you. They struggled over the weapon, and it didn't end well for Tobias."

"So, he's really dead?" Lily asked, clearly having difficulty accepting it.

"Yes, child."

"And I'm not the one who killed him."

"No, child."

Lily relaxed into the chair.

Mr. Turner swung his gaze to Edric. "May I use your office here to confer with my client in private?"

"Of course." Edric looked from one deputy to another. "If we are all here, who's minding the town?"

Montana and Sammy scuttled out. Cord tipped his hat to Lily. "Mrs. Lexington, I, for one, am pleased to see you leave this establishment. Have a good day." He left as well.

"Mr. Turner, I've had a better thought. I promised a little boy to bring his mama home." Before he could finish his idea, Lily jumped in.

"Toby. Yes, let's go to Aunt Henny's."

Mr. Turner raised one white eyebrow. "Aunt? You don't have any aunts."

Edric spoke up. "Aunt Henny is aunt to everyone. I'm not sure if she's *actually* aunt to anyone in town. She runs a boardinghouse. You'll need a place to stay anyway."

"Splendid idea." Mr. Turner picked up his carpetbag.

"Let me get that for you." Edric took the bag.

"Much obliged." But Mr. Turner held onto his satchel.

Edric hooked the carpetbag over his saddle horn and led his horse by the reins. "I'm sorry I don't have a buggy to take you both to Aunt Henny's."

"After sitting on that train for days," Mr. Turner said, "I welcome the walk." He looped Lily's hand around his arm. "How is your son doing?"

"He's doing well."

"And you?"

"I'm doing well."

Lily probably thought that Edric was angry at her for leaving and disappointing his girls and not telling him about her husband, but he wasn't. He was so happy she was back, he was as giddy as a schoolboy. He should be upset at her for disappointing his girls. But he was too happy to be angry. And his little girls were going to be so happy as well. They had been more upset she was gone rather than missing their fancy tea. He couldn't wait to tell them she was home.

He could say nothing to quell any fears Lily might have about him possibly being upset with her. At the moment, Mr. Turner prevented him from speaking his mind. No, from speaking his heart. He had to wait. But he could do this. He wrapped his hand around hers.

Her hand stiffened in panic, then it relaxed, then she curled her fingers in an embrace. All while not missing a beat in her conversation with Mr. Turner.

Edric's heart warmed at this small intimacy.

When they reached the boardinghouse, Lily hurried up the walk and in through the front door.

Edric got inside in time to see Toby run into his mama's arms. He removed his hat and watched mother and son smiling at each other.

Toby turned in Lily's arms and stretched out a hand to Edric. He stepped over to the boy and knelt. Toby put his little hand on Edric's shoulder. "You bringed her back."

Edric couldn't help but smile too. "As promised." He gazed into Lily's appreciative eyes.

After greetings and introductions were made, Agnes Martin excused herself and left.

Mr. Turner asked, "Is there some place I might confer with Lily in private?"

Lily spoke up first. "That's not necessary. I don't want to have any more secrets." She gazed right at Edric, and it warmed his heart.

"I must protest," Mr. Turner said. "It is a matter of

lawyer-client confidentiality."

"But if I'm the client...?"

"The client I'm referring to is your father."

Edric didn't have a problem with giving the pair privacy.

But before he could speak, Aunt Henny spoke. "Edric and I will visit on the porch while the two of you talk. Would you like me to take Toby with me?"

Toby squeezed Lily tighter.

"He's fine with me."

Edric didn't think Toby was going to release his mama any time soon. He walked outside with Aunt Henny and sat in the rocking chair adjacent to her. "She didn't kill her husband or anyone else."

"But she thought she did?"

"She hit him and only knocked him out." He didn't know why she'd hit her husband, but he could guess. "Apparently, in his anger when he woke, he went to his brother's—the man who came here looking for her. They struggled. Her husband was shot and killed."

"That's a relief. The guilt of that must be what was weighing on her." Aunt Henny pushed her chair into motion. "Why don't you head home? I'm sure your family is anxious to know you've returned safely."

Edric was torn. He wanted to go home, but at the same time he wanted to stay and have a chance to talk to Lily.

Aunt Henny patted his arm. "You go home and get the trail dust washed off you. Then you bring your whole family for supper."

"My girls would like that." He stood. "Thank you."

Thirty-Five

LILY SQUEEZED HER SON TIGHTER AGAIN. She was so happy to be with him. She had thought she might not see him for years. And now she had him in her arms again for good.

"Let's sit at the table." Perry Turner, her father's lifelong friend, set his satchel on the table.

She sat and adjusted Toby on her lap. She felt freer than before her parents died. Her parents. "Mr. Turner."

"Call me Perry. I am your attorney now."

That would be strange after growing up knowing him as Mr. Turner. "When Timothy came, he insinuated that Tobias had something to do with Father's and Mother's deaths."

"Yes, we finally found the evidence we needed after Tobias's death. Both brothers were co-conspirators. Thanks to your sheriff, Timothy was apprehended as he stepped off the train. I'm sorry for you and the boy. I have failed my longtime friend. Had I realized how bad it was for the two of you, I would have done more to help."

No one knew. Tobias wouldn't let them. And Lily had been too ashamed to say anything, not that Tobias gave her much of a chance. "They planned it so they could get all of my father's money."

"Not all." Mr. Turner pulled a stack of papers out of his satchel. "Your father was a shrewd businessman. He took many precautions."

"Tobias took everything he could get his hands on. He transferred everything to his name, including the house and Father's business."

"And as his widow, everything reverts to you."

"Timothy is on the papers as well."

"He's going to jail."

"Well, I'm afraid the only thing Tobias might have left

me are his debts." She hugged Toby. "And my son."

He handed over a few sheaves of paper with writing. "Your parents set up a trust for you, to be activated at my discretion. I am choosing to activate it now."

"What? I never knew."

"And that's a good thing, or Tobias, as your husband, might have petitioned to the courts to have that money released to him." He handed her another set of papers. "Your parents set up a trust fund for Toby as well."

"How could they? I wasn't even married or pregnant when they died."

"It was for any future children you might have. Tobias couldn't touch it and didn't even know about it."

She was glad to know Toby would be taken care of.

"I'm sure I'll have to use both of those to pay off Tobias's debts. But if it means they will all be taken care of, I don't care."

"I can sell your father's business for you and use those moneys to pay off the debts."

"Do you think it will be enough?" She would love to have money left over to get her and Toby a little house here in Kamola.

"I will need to assess how much damage Tobias did, but you still have the house and its contents."

"He sold off most of the items of worth, so it would just be the house itself. And I know he mortgaged that as well."

"As I said, your father took precautions. Unlike most people, he didn't stop at one safe."

"I know. Tobias cleaned out the bedroom safe as well as the one in my father's den."

"Is that all?"

"And the one at work."

Mr. Turner smiled. "That is only three. Your father had five safes. He didn't believe in keeping all his money, important documents, and other valuables in one place. So, Tobias never found the vault?"

"What vault?"

Mr. Turner's smile stretched, then he went over the last list he had of what was in the vault at the time of her parents' deaths. A wealth of items.

After Mr. Turner had laid out for her all her assets, he said, "Would you like to keep the house in Philadelphia? I believe you will have the money to do so."

Go back to Philadelphia? She'd never considered it. Did she want to? It had been her home for most of her life.

Lily stayed in the kitchen when Edric and his family arrived for supper. She wasn't sure how Edric felt about her. She had withheld the truth from him, not trusted him, and disappointed his daughters. He had been nice and polite to her at the jail and walked her and Mr. Turner to Aunt Henny's, but she imagined he would rather be anywhere than where she was. After all, he'd spent a week trying to track her down after she'd confessed to being a criminal.

Then he'd done the strangest thing. He'd taken her hand. At first, she'd been terrified with images of Tobias trapping her and squeezing her hand to the point of intense pain. Edric had held her hand gently, and she could have easily pulled free.

But what did it mean?

Edric and his father carried the wingback chair inside Aunt Henny's house and put it in the parlor where it had come from.

Estella and Nancy each carried a quilt. All the things that the quilting circle ladies had brought to make her more comfortable at the jail. They were precious ladies.

"Miss Lily!" Estella and Nancy called together and ran for her.

She knelt and caught them up in her arms. "I missed you both."

"I missed you," Estella said.

"I missed you more than I do," Nancy said.

Lily wasn't sure exactly what that meant, but she knew the girl had missed her. "I'm so sorry for not being here to take you to the tea party."

Nancy put one of her little hands on each of Lily's cheeks. "That's fine. Granpapa said when you comed home, we could have our own fancy tea."

Lily glanced up at Saul Hammond who gave her a nod of consent. How surprising. The elder Mr. Hammond was the last person she would expect to be on her side. He'd always seemed suspicious of her. But now, he looked encouraging. She faced the girls. "That would be lovely."

Lily was grateful that Estella and Nancy, and even Toby, occupied her so much throughout supper and after. Edric didn't even try to get her attention. He was probably biding his time until he could graciously leave without losing face. Propriety dictated he should stay for a while after supper to show his hostess proper decorum. Aunt Henny was his hostess, and he could leave without any disrespect.

After supper, once all three children were occupied with the elder Mr. Hammond, Edric took Lily's hand and led her out through the kitchen door.

"I don't know how much time I'll have to say what I need to say."

She didn't want him to say he didn't want to court her anymore, but she was sure that was what was coming.

"First, I need to know about Toby. Is he truly your son?"

She hadn't expected that question, but she knew it crossed most people's minds when they saw the two of them. "It is truly amazing how little we look alike, but I gave birth to him. He is all mine."

Edric smiled. "Second, I am so sorry for doubting you."

She hadn't expected that either. "Doubting me? About what? Toby?"

He shook his head. "Killing your husband."

"But I thought I had and told you as much. There was nothing to doubt."

"For a while, I believed you were capable of murder. I let the words cloud what I already knew about you. I knew in my heart that you would never hurt anyone on purpose. You had to have a reason. So, I'm sorry for ever doubting that."

"Thank you. Tobias was choking the life out of Toby. I had to do something, or he would have killed him."

"I would have hit him too. Probably more. He *wouldn't* have gotten up."

She was relieved that she hadn't been the one to kill Tobias, and she felt guilty for being relieved that he really was dead. But she was so thrilled and relieved Toby was finally safe. Once and for all.

"That day I asked to court you…" Edric said.

Lily had expected this. She didn't blame him for regretting that. "Toby and I can return to Philadelphia so you can save face."

"Save face? Is that what you want to do?"

"If we don't stay in Kamola, I don't know where else we would go." She didn't want to leave, Kamola had felt like home since she stepped off the train, but she didn't know if she could stay here with the love she had for Edric. The ache of seeing him in town regularly and knowing she had ruined what they'd had. Or worse, watching him fall in love with someone else.

He took her hands in his. "What I wished I had asked was, will you marry me? I will raise Toby and the baby as my own."

She stared at him a moment. "You want to marry me?"

"Almost since the first moment I saw you on the train, cradling your son. I love you. Please say you'll stay and be my wife."

She was about to say yes when one of his words came back to her. "Baby?"

"Aunt Henny and I suspected that's why you weren't feeling well."

"I'm not with child."

"Are you sure?"

"Very sure."

Edric's whole demeanor relaxed.

"Is that why you proposed?" She hoped not.

"No. Not at all. I didn't want that to prevent you from

saying yes. I love you and want to marry you very much."

"Then yes! I love you too. I meant to tell you that day you first said it, but then everything got complicated."

His smile stretched wide, and he stepped closer. "I—"

Lily couldn't wait for him to warn her. She threw her arms around his neck and kissed him.

He held her close, and it didn't scare her.

He pulled away. "Let's tell the children. Wait. I want to ask Toby first. But one more kiss."

She sighed into his kiss. She wasn't sure how Toby would respond to the news of her marrying Edric.

When she and Edric turned toward the house to go inside, Toby stood on the top step of the porch. How long had he been there? Since Edric had just been kissing her, she was sure Toby had seen them. He hadn't said anything or tried to come between them.

Edric took a deep breath then knelt on the step below Toby. "Toby, I love your mama very much. And I love you too. I have two little girls, but you know what I don't have?"

Toby shook his head.

"A son. And my girls don't have a mama. I would very much like to marry your mama so my girls will have a mama and then you would be my son. Would you like that?"

Toby stared at him then glanced at Lily.

She wasn't sure Toby fully understood what Edric's question meant. She nodded to her son and held her breath. She hoped Toby was ready for a new father, a kind father, and a whole new family.

He blinked several times at Edric. "You won't hurt me?"

"No. I won't."

Toby's mouth pulled slowly into a smile that kept stretching until his dimples shone. He put one hand on Edric's shoulder. "You won't hurt Mommy?"

"Never." Edric reached out a hand for Lily.

She joined them.

Toby put a hand on her shoulder as well and nodded.

Edric wrapped one arm around her and the other

around Toby. And Toby hooked his arms around their necks.

Edric said, "Shall we tell Estella and Nancy?"

As Toby nodded, Estella said, "Tell us what?"

The girls stood in the doorway.

Edric said, "Do you want to tell them, Toby?"

Toby straightened. "I'm going to be your son."

Lily laughed at her boy's misunderstanding. Edric laughed as well.

Nancy planted her hands on her hips. "You can't be our son."

Lily said, "What he means is that he's going to be your brother."

Both girls' eyes widened.

Edric said, "And you girls are going to have a new mama."

The girls cheered and ran for the trio. Lily braced herself, expecting to be knocked over, but Edric caught them and held all five of them upright in his strong arms.

Edric stretched his head over the children and kissed her.

Finally, all the shadows of her past were gone, and sunny days stood in her future.

Author Note

Ahhhh, romance! I love romance. If there is a specific gene connected to romance, I must have it.

Several years ago, a publishing house had started a quilting romance series with both historical and contemporary stories. My agent asked if I'd like to come up with an idea to submit. Since I've been quilting since I was eleven, I jumped at the chance. Romance and quilting together? It doesn't get much better than that.

The problem is, when my brain starts storming, it won't stop until it's exhausted multiple possibilities. The ideas tumble out one on top of the other. (Waving at you, Kathy. My friend Kathy Kovach has experienced these brain explosions of mine first hand. She just shakes her head and laughs.) So, I sent my agent not one, not two, but *six* ideas, three historical and three contemporary. My agent had to rein me in. I think we submitted two of them.

Then, due to changes at my literary agency, I had a new agent. She told me that I had enough quilting romance ideas to think about creating my own quilting series. I loved the idea. I decided my various ideas might not mash together too smoothly. They were all over the map. But, I thought that one idea, *The Widow's Plight* with the quilting circle, would work great as a series. Once again, additional ideas for this series tumbled out, making a mess all over my workspace.

For *The Widow's Plight*, I pictured this young mother on the run who falls in love with the wrong man in town, the sheriff. Of all the people, he is the one person she needs to stay far away from to protect her son. But, the heart does what the heart wants to do.

Then I needed to figure out where this widow's story should take place. I love it when I can set a story in my home state. Washington State has a wide diversity of climates from semi-arid to rainforest, so it can host a great variety of stories.

Next, I needed a town. Towns can be tricky because

it's nearly impossible to get every detail right in a real town, and someone out there will know if one little thing is wrong. Even in a historical. Someone's grandma had the house on that particular corner and never ever would have painted it the color that's in the book. Or a street you have referred to by the correct name wasn't called by that name because of some feud between this person and that. So, depending on what side of the feud you were on would determine what you call the street. Then there's the problem of a real town not having all the elements you need for your story.

So, in the end, it's easier to make up a town and base it on a real town. I fashioned Kamola after Ellensburg, the town where I went to college. Go Wildcats! I chose the name Kamola because that was my dorm. There are a couple of other names I've used from my alma mater.

I hope you enjoyed Lily and Edric's story, the first in the Quilting Circle series.

Happy Reading!

Mary
☺

DISCUSSION QUESTIONS

1. What was your favorite quote/passage? Why did this stand out and how could you use it in your own life?

2. How well does the book's cover convey what the book is about? Do you think the back-cover copy did a good job of indicating what this book is about? If the book were being adapted into a movie, who would you want to see play Lily? Edric? Aunt Henny? The children? Timothy Bremmer?

3. Which character did you relate to the most, and what was it about them that you connected with? Can you relate to Lily's predicament? To Edric's? Are their actions justified? To what extent do they remind you of yourself or someone you know? Do you empathize with the characters?

4. Describe the dynamics between Lily and her son, Lily and Aunt Henny, Edric and his daughters, Edric and his father, Lily and Edric, Edric and Lily's son. How has the past shaped each of their lives? How do the characters change, grow, or evolve throughout the course of the story? Have you ever been in a situation where the past shaped something in your present life? How did you deal with that?

5. Today, we have laws that protect a person who kills someone else due to defending one's self or another person. But back in the 1800s, Lily didn't have this same benefit of the doubt. She would have been presumed guilty and gone to prison. What would you have done if you were her? If Lily hadn't returned and faced up to what she thought she had done, what might her life had been like in the next town she tried to settle down in? Would she have ever stopped running? Did God have a hand in Lily's life even when she thought He didn't? Looking back, where can you see God's hand in your life

when you thought He wasn't there at a time you were going through something difficult?

6. Do you think Edric and his father were doing a good job at raising Edric's two daughters by themselves? Edric was able to forgive Lily because he'd gotten to know her and knew her heart. Do you find it easier to forgive someone you've known for a long time or someone you've just met? Why do you think that's so?

7. What are the major conflicts in the story? What events in the story stand out for you as memorable? What main ideas—themes—does the author explore? Are they relevant in your life?

8. Discuss Lily's choice of a quilt pattern, Sunshine & Shadows. How did this reflect her life? What were the various "shadows" in her life, both past and present? Did "sunshine" get cast on all these areas? Do you have anything that reflects your life? Why is it important to you?

9. Did any parts of the book make you uncomfortable? If so, why did you feel that way? Did this lead to a new understanding or awareness of some aspect of your life you might not have thought about before? Has this novel changed you or broadened your perspective?

10. What do you think will be your lasting impression of the book and why? Did the issues that were raised touch or impact you in any way? Would you recommend it to a friend, and if so, why? Can you see yourself reading it again?

NOW—A SNEAK PEEK AT BOOK TWO

THE DAUGHTER'S PREDICAMENT

RELEASING MAY 1, 2019

One

Central Washington State 1893

ISABELLE ATWOOD RODE HER BICYCLE ALONG the main street of Kamola, pumping with one foot then the other. The bicycle had emancipated women like nothing else. She no longer had to wait for a man to hitch up a buggy or saddle a horse. Her Bloomer bicycle dress, with the blousy trousers under the mid-calf length skirt, made riding so much easier. No more bunching up her skirt and petticoats to keep the hems from getting caught. She steered around a chuckhole in the road and wobbled but kept her vehicle and herself upright.

Ahead, the White Hotel came into view, and, not to disappoint, Grant sat on the bench out front. He worked as a desk clerk there.

She squeezed the brake lever with her right hand and slowed to almost a stop before putting her feet out as the bicycle tilted to one side.

Shaking his head, Grant stood. "Izzy, you're twenty-two. Why do you ride that thing?"

Grant was the only one who called her Izzy. "Because it's gives me freedom and it's fun." She leaned it against the boardwalk railing.

"You're going to get hurt on that."

Grant, like her father and step-mother, worried too much. He lived in a small room at the back of the hotel. He had the early shift at the desk and sometimes got called to help during the night if a problem arose. He could afford to rent something bigger, but he was saving every penny to buy a house someday. Such a practical man.

She unstrapped the food basket from the back of her bicycle. "I brought lunch."

He relieved her of the basket and held out his hand to assist her.

She clasped it, stepped up onto the boardwalk, and sat on the bench. She unpacked the food and held out the bowl of cold fried chicken.

He chose a drumstick and took a bite. "Mmm."

She bit into a piece of her own.

After polishing off the drumstick, he wiped his hands and mouth on a cloth napkin. "I've been fortified. I'm ready now."

"For what?"

"Bringing me lunch usually means you're trying to soften me up for the next young lady you plan to set me up with."

Isabelle had nearly exhausted the supply of suitable ladies in town. "No one this time." No one was quite right for her childhood friend, but she hadn't given up. The right lady was out there, and she would find her.

She dropped her half-eaten chicken into the bowl and licked her fingers while she pulled a folded piece of paper out of her skirt pocket. "Yesterday, I found this wound between the spokes of my bicycle."

"What is it?" He picked up the bowl of chicken, gazing into it lovingly, and licked his lips.

Men. More interested in food than anything.

She unfolded the paper. "This is a love poem."

Grant held up one hand. "Oh, no. I'm not sending a *love poem* to a lady I haven't even met."

"No, silly. It was left for me by a secret admirer. Let me know what you think."

He groaned. "I'll need more nourishment to endure

oversentimental musings written by some confused, lovelorn sap." Grant took another piece of chicken.

"It wouldn't hurt you to write a few sweet lines to a lady. Maybe then you would find one who doesn't think you completely emotionless."

"I'm not going to be someone I'm not. A lady's gotta take me as I am, or what's the point?" He ripped off a big bite and motioned for her to proceed.

He made her job more challenging than it need be. Isabelle cleared her throat. "'The rose is red, the violet's blue, the honey's sweet, and so are you.'"

Grant made a retching sound.

She slapped his arm with the paper. "Don't be like that."

"Ow." He clutched his arm, pretending to be injured. "That isn't even original." He put his chicken-free hand over his heart. "*The man is boring, not a brain in his head, you'd be better off, filling him with lead.* See I can do it too." He ripped off another bite of chicken.

"Stop it. That's not nice."

He laughed.

She shook her head. "You're impossible."

He stopped laughing and made an effort to not smile. "Do you seriously like this kind of mushy sentimentality? It's not even a very good poem."

"Shows what you know. It's not about the poem or even if it's any good. It's that it was thoughtful. Someone I don't know thought enough to secret this onto my bicycle. There's something romantic and enticing about that. And I'm going to find out who. Your problem is you're too practical. You could learn a thing or two from him." She held the poem a little higher.

"What about that cowboy you've been talking about?"

"Rancher. He's a cattle rancher. Shane Keegan." Just saying his name made her a little giddy. "He has quite a spread outside of town."

"He's still a cowboy. I can't see you with a *cowboy* stuck out on a ranch all winter. You would be bored inside of a month. Tedious before the honeymoon was over. He'll be gone for weeks at a time, and you'll have nothing to do. And when he will be at home, what will you talk about? You have nothing in common with his type."

"I could find many things to occupy my time. I can sew and bake and read and crochet doilies."

He sputtered out a laugh. "I don't think ranchers have doilies."

"A rancher with a wife does."

"If you say so." He chucked his second chicken bone into the trash bin outside the hotel and licked his fingers. "So, in all the ladies you've tried to set me up with, why never Adelaide?"

"My half-sister? Oh, no. She is *all* wrong for you."

"How so? She's mighty pretty with that blond hair and round face."

"I love my sister, but she's a bit selfish and about as deep as a saucer. You would literally have nothing to talk about with her. *You* would die of boredom."

"But she's pretty. That has to count for something."

Her sister *was* the picture of beauty with ringlets around her face and rosy lips. Isabelle couldn't blame Grant and other men for falling for her, but Isabelle wouldn't subject her good friend to life with Adelaide. "Is that all men care about? How a lady looks?"

Grant held up a cookie he'd fished out of the food basket. "And cooking."

"Impossible." She threw her hands up. "Well, maybe I *will* arrange something between you and my sister. You're both shallow and self-centered. You deserve each other."

"Because 'the rose is red' has so much depth and is so profound."

"If you bothered to think about it for even a minute, you would know that it's not about the color of the rose. It's about the truth of the statement. Not one. Not two. But three true statements to validate and give extra weight to the fourth. The important one."

He squinted at her. "You got all that out of those four little lines?"

"I did. And, it's not the words themselves, but that he thought to write them down and deliver them is what makes them special."

He shrugged and glanced away then pointed down the street. "Speaking of boredom, isn't that your cowboy coming out of the telegraph office?"

She cast her gaze that direction. "That's him." She sighed. Shane Keegan a rancher who stood well over six feet tall, with a saunter that said he was comfortable with who he was, and his smile crooked up on one side that could fairly make a lady swoon. And when he tipped his hat and said *good-day, ma'am...* all sense and reason left her.

"Maybe he's your secret admirer."

A rush of anticipation swooped through her at the thought. She'd run into him a few times, saw him at church once or twice, but not regularly. She'd never had a lengthy conversation with him though she'd like to. "Do you think so?" She would very much like it if he were the one.

Grant shrugged. "As good of a guess as any. You should go talk to him."

"You think so?"

"Sure. Ask him what he thinks of dull, sappy poetry. Unless you're scared."

She knew a playful taunt when she heard one. "Maybe I will."

Grant folded his arms. "Bet you don't."

"Why do you say that?"

"I've known you a looong time. I've never known you to be daring, except to ride that fool bicycle. You talk about doing exciting things, but you seem content to read about others doing them."

He was right. Her head told her to be careful, but her heart told her to be bold. If she took a risk, she might get hurt, either physically or emotionally.

She squared her shoulders. "I'll do it. What should I say?"

He spoke in a voice a few octaves higher than his normal voice. "Tell him what a big strong man he is, then bat your eyelashes at him." He clasped his hands together under his chin and batted his own lashes. "'The rose is red, the violet's blue, the honey's sweet, and so are you.'"

She swatted his arm. "You're no help."

"You could drop your handkerchief and wait for him to pick it up."

"Seriously? Would you fall for that? Because I don't think a man like him would. Why do I even bother asking you anything?"

"Because you know you'll get an honest answer." He pointed down the street. "He's getting away. You lost your chance."

Shane Keegan stopped near the livery and talked to the sheriff.

"He's been waylaid. Now or never." Grant elbowed her.

Dare she go? Stuffing the paper back into her pocket, she gulped in a deep breath, grabbed her bicycle, and peddled down the street, wobbling at first until she got going. She would head over and say hello to the sheriff and pretend not to see Mr. Keegan.

Right as she drew near and was about to squeeze the brake lever, a horse spooked and stepped backward into her path.

She swerved to avoid running into the horse's hindquarter but put herself on a collision course for Shane Keegan.

Shane Keegan stood outside the livery, talking to Sheriff Rix when a shriek cut through the air.

"Oh, no! Look out!"

Shane jerked around at the panicky words.

A woman on a bicycle careened straight toward him.

He jumped back, and as she swooshed past, Shane reacted without thinking and plucked the frantic woman off her bicycle. Her vehicle went on without her and crashed into the side of a wagon.

Uh oh. Had he ruined this lady's transportation by plucking its driver off? He had neither meant to grab her nor wreck her bicycle. "Are you all right?"

She turned toward him, her pretty face inches from his. He held her in his arms. He'd just had the misfortune of harassing Miss Isabelle Atwood. She was in a different class from Shane altogether, and she smelled of flowers. A polite *how do you do?* was the most he ever expected from someone like her toward someone like him.

"Are you all right, Isabelle?" Sheriff Rix asked from somewhere beside him.

She stared up at Shane. Probably in shock from him grabbing her. "Um, I think so."

His heart pounded in his chest. All he could do was stare. Wisps of brown hair framed her heart-shaped face. Clear blue eyes. Lips the color of ripe strawberries. And a fetching blush to her cheeks. Of course, a lady was more than her appearance.

He shouldn't be holding her, so he set her down but kept her in his arms. "I want to make sure you're steady on your feet before I turn you loose." She was likely fine. He was the unsteady one, using her shakiness as an excuse to be close to her.

Strangely, she didn't pull away from him in disgust. "I'm quite well. Fit as a fiddle, in fact." She almost seemed pleased to be near him.

Couldn't be.

The sheriff cleared his throat. "Good thing Shane caught you."

Oh, that was right. Shane wasn't alone with this alluring, young filly.

She looked from the sheriff to Shane. "Did you snatch me off my bicycle?"

He offered her a lopsided grin. "I guess I did." He had not so much caught her as acted out of self-preservation. When someone was heading straight for him, he either needed to duck out of the way, stop them, or punch them. Well, he had known enough not to punch the lady, and he had been too caught off guard to duck. So, he'd done the only thing he could. Wrapped his arms around her. She did fit nicely there.

She gifted him with a smile that could make a man do almost anything for her. "Thank you for rescuing me."

Rescue? Is that what she had thought he'd done? "I didn't want to see you get hurt. I can't rightly stand the sight of blood." Now she was going to think he needed mollycoddling.

"Not a scratch on me thanks to you."

Was she flirting with him?

Sheriff Rix tapped him on the shoulder. "You can let go of her now."

Shane released Miss Atwood and glanced toward her bicycle. "Let me get that for you." He walked over to the corpse of her contraption and wheeled it back, the front tire wobbling. "It appears to be damaged." *Great going, Shane. You sure know how to impress a lady, destroy her property and tell her you're a milksop.* "I'm afraid that's my fault. I can't help but feel if I hadn't been so hasty, you probably had everything well in hand."

"I can assure you, I did not have it well in hand. That horse spooked, and I swerved. If not for you, I would've been in a heap right along with my bicycle."

Nice of her to spare his feelings by being polite.

"If you say so. These things can be dangerous. You should be more careful." He should not have criticized her. He wasn't handling this situation well at all. He found her riding a bicycle endearing. It showed an adventurous side to the fair Miss Atwood.

She gripped the handlebars. "I will. Thank you very much for retrieving my bicycle and for rescuing me."

"Mighty welcome, ma'am—I mean miss." He touched the brim of his hat. "I'm new in town. I don't believe we've been properly introduced." Though he'd asked around and knew much about Miss Isabelle Atwood. "I'm Shane Keegan."

"I know—I mean I've heard your name mentioned before. Town folks talk."

The sheriff suppressed a soft chuckle. "Shane, this is Miss Atwood."

Shane tipped his hat. "Pleased to meet you, Miss Atwood." So very pleased.

"Do call me Isabelle."

Bold move to offer him the use of her first name. But he preferred ladies who didn't put on pretentious airs. He felt the right side of his mouth automatically hitch up. "A beautiful name for a beautiful lady. *Very* pleased to meet you, Miss Isabelle." But his delight was short lived when he glanced up the street. He motioned. "Your fella's waiting for you." He had seen her with the hotel clerk often.

Isabelle turned toward where he'd indicated. "Grant? He's not my... fella. He's only a friend. We've been palling around since we were children."

Not her beau? That was good news. "Very pleased to hear that." Her smile emboldened him. "Would the lady think it too brazen of me to inquire if she has a beau?"

Her widening smile encouraged him. She wasn't as unapproachable as he'd imagined.

"The lady *would* think it quite brazen."

He'd stepped in it now.

"*And*, no, she does not have a beau." Though she'd made a point to let him know she was unattached, she glanced away shyly.

"Would the lady consider eating with a brazen rancher? Say Monday, noon, White Hotel dining room?" He should have waited for her to answer the question before giving a time and place.

"Lunch Monday?" She paused as though thinking. "I'll let you know Sunday after church."

Was that a delayed no? Or that game ladies played where they feigned disinterest or pretended to be neutral to string a fella along? Make him wait in anticipation of her answer. Drive him mad with wonder. He folded his arms. How could he get out of the rendezvous and save face for both of them? "I'm not going to be able to make it into town on Sunday."

Her expression shifted from playful to disappointment.

He hurried on. "I usually do some sort of Bible reading and such for my men—who would never cross the threshold of a church. So, I'll tell you what. I'll be at the White Hotel's dining room at noon on Monday. If you show up to eat with me, I'll consider it as the good Lord smiling down on me." A graceful way for her to back out.

"And if I don't show up?"

What he expected would happen but still disappointing. "I'll be eating alone. A man's still gotta eat." He was not up for her inevitable rejection in person and so turned to the sheriff. "I'll talk to you later." He tipped his hat to Miss At—Miss Isabelle and strode away, resisting the urge to run. Why was talking to ladies so nerve wracking? She was just a person, just like him. No, she was nothing like him. She was refined. He was a dusty cowboy.

Come Monday, he'd be eating alone.

Isabelle watched Shane Keegan saunter away. She'd received several smiles, two cowboy saunters, two hat tips, and a lunch invitation. Quite a productive interaction. She'd wanted to accept his invitation right away, but it was considered poor etiquette for a lady to answer too quickly. Could make a man think she was desperate. Didn't a lady needed to seem elusive to keep a man's interest? Yet, he'd been the elusive one and had piqued *her* interest.

She nodded at the sheriff. "Good day, Sheriff Rix." She walked her wobbly bicycle back up the street to the hotel, her insides as unsteady as the wheel.

Grant frowned. "You made quite an impression on that scoundrel."

"Scoundrel? He was very chivalrous." Like a perfectly set romance novel.

"Chivalrous? I saw the way he grabbed you. Opportunist, if you ask me. You have to watch out for his kind."

"Well, I *didn't* ask you." She didn't want to talk about Mr. Keegan anymore and rocked her bicycle forward. "The front tire is bent. Will you help me fix it?"

"You mean will *I* fix it?"

"Please?"

He shook his head. "If you are going to insist on riding this thing, then you need to learn to repair it. We can work on it together."

She smiled. "Thank you."

"Sure. Park it around back by Hurley's workshop."

That's what she liked about Grant. He didn't treat her like a helpless female. He'd taught her how to do many things, like fish, balance the hotel ledgers, ride a horse—*astride* no less—and even shoot a gun. She'd only done that once. The sound had hurt her ears, but she'd hit the target he'd set before her.

After parking her bicycle, Isabelle walked home and headed into the two-story house by way of the kitchen entrance. She snatched a small handful of raisins from a ceramic canister on the worktable.

Molly, the cook, tsked her. "You'll spoil your supper."

Isabelle chewed and swallowed. "No, I won't. Nothing could spoil today." She had a social engagement with Shane Keegan.

Marguerite stalked in from the front hall. "Finally, you're home. Where have you been?"

Even her step-mother couldn't spoil her mood. "My bicycle got banged up. I had to take it to be repaired."

"That thing is a menace. You're a young lady, not a hooligan. Not to worry. You won't be riding that anymore."

"Why not? It's mine." Isabelle's bicycle gave her freedom. That it irritated Marguerite was a bonus.

"Because it's unladylike. Come into the parlor." Her step-mother strode back the way she'd come. "Your father and I need to talk to you."

Isabelle tagged along in her wake. She didn't like the superior tone in Marguerite's voice. It always meant trouble for Isabelle. "About what?" She stopped short over the parlor's threshold.

Her father stood by the fireplace with a worried expression. Her half-sister sat on the settee, picking at the threads of her embroidered hankie.

Something was terribly wrong. "What's this all about?"

Her step-mother eased herself onto a wingback chair. "Your life is about to change. *All* our lives are about to change."

"Change? How?"

"We've arranged a marriage for you."

Isabelle sucked in a breath and choked on the air. She coughed several times before she could speak. "What? To whom? I don't want to marry someone I'm not in love with." Right now, she wasn't in love with anyone.

"Oliver Mallory."

"The banker? He's so old."

"Watch your tone," Marguerite snapped. "He's only thirty-six. That's not so old."

Isabelle shook her head. "Why would I agree to marry *him*?"

Her step-mother, sitting on the edge of her seat, didn't blink. "It's for the good of the family."

Marry a banker? For the good of the family? Isabelle shifted her gaze to her father. "Are we in financial trouble?"

He gave a snort of dismissive laughter. "Don't be silly."

"Then why would you want me to marry a banker I don't love *'for the good of the family'*?" When her father remained silent, Isabelle turned to Marguerite. This had to be her doing. "Why?"

"It seems Adelaide has gotten herself into a little bit of trouble." Her step-mother's voice wavered slightly on the last word. She never got rattled.

"What kind of trouble?"

Marguerite's jaw worked back and forth, and her lips parted as if to speak but then didn't.

Isabelle shifted her gaze to her sister. "What kind of trouble are you in?"

Adelaide chewed furiously on her bottom lip as she spoke. "I... sort of... I'm kind of..."

Her father finally blurted out the words. "Your sister has gotten herself in the family way."

"What?" Isabelle sat on the settee next to her sister. "How did this happen?"

Adelaide didn't have a beau. Did she? She was barely eighteen, old enough to get married, but still young. "He said he loved me."

"Who?"

An odd animal-like sound came from her sister.

Marguerite narrowed her eyes. "She won't tell us, but that really doesn't matter. You will marry Oliver Mallory and pretend to get pregnant right away. Adelaide will remain in seclusion for the duration of her time. When the child is born, you'll say it's yours, and my dear sweet Adelaide will be free of this burden."

While saddling Isabelle with it. Unbelievable. "Has Mr. Mallory agreed to this?"

"He owes your father a favor."

Probably not one this big that will last the rest of his life. "Why me? Why doesn't Adelaide marry him?"

"You're the oldest. You must marry first. Adelaide is too young."

Obviously not.

Isabelle turned an imploring gaze on her father. "Say I don't have to do this."

"I think your mother knows what's best." He looked resigned.

Isabelle wasn't. This couldn't be her fate.

First of all, Marguerite wasn't Isabelle's mother, but Isabelle wasn't allowed to voice that fact. Hers died when she was very young, and Marguerite never truly treated Isabelle as a daughter.

Second, her step-mother *didn't* know what was best for Isabelle, and third, her father didn't argue with his wife. Marguerite wouldn't let him. He always gave in to her because it was easier.

"I won't do it. You can't make me."

Her step-mother raised one pale eyebrow. "Can't we?"

That look sent a cold shiver down Isabelle's back. "Why must I pay for Adelaide's mistake?"

"Because she has a bright future. I've been in correspondence with Lord Blaine in Boston. He's very interested in meeting your sister. He will be a wonderful match for her. He has a title. You wouldn't want to deny your sister this opportunity, would you? You aren't going to be selfish, are you? Think of your sister's future."

Marguerite was trying to arrange a marriage for Adelaide with a lord, so Isabelle was to be the sacrificial lamb to sweep Adelaide's transgression under the rug?

Adelaide sat next to her on the settee with her shoulders hunched and arms crossed over her stomach.

"All things work together for the good. And this marriage is for the good of the whole family. Don't be selfish and think of only yourself."

Isabelle hated it when Marguerite spouted Scripture for her own benefit. She understood her step-mother's need to protect her daughter, but to sacrifice Isabelle to do it wasn't fair. She didn't have much choice when Father sided with his wife. Was there any way for her to get out of this?

33239479R00181

Printed in Great Britain
by Amazon